Centauresses of the Silver Dragon

by Lynn Marron

To contact Lynn or view more of the author's works please visit: **www.lynnmarron.com**

First Publication of Centauresses of the Silver Dragon
March 6, 2015
Rev. 1 9/18
Copyright © Lynn Marron Bloom

This saga is a work of fiction with all names, characters, events, and places created in the mind of the author. I hope you enjoy it.
My best, Lynn

By Kear Press, Stratford, CT

Library of Congress Number: 2015936998

Paperback Book edition ISBN: 978-1-942888-01-7
Nook E Book edition ISBN: 978-1-942888-00-0
Kindle E Book edition ISBN: 978-1-942888-02-4

For his support in getting this book published
it is dedicated to Michael Intemann,

who is almost always right (at least about my writing!)

(In spite of what Gabriella and Michaela says)

Chapter One

Our warriors won all the battles,

Diplomats and peacemakers lost us the war...

Jace of Thunderhoof Regiment

War of the Yellow Hide Dominion

Scrub wood and sharp salt-grass flattened under their hoofs. A curve of the low hill–no sand dune--ahead. Massive brown and white Two Spot, yellow hided Deadrick, and some of the younger warrior centaurs lunged heedlessly over the top. Jace shook his tail in disgust. Discipline breaking down. Axel and Garrison paced with him, with the less than fifty others behind.

Jace silently cursed the pain in his rear leg, as he trod hard up the dune. Normally the heavy battle harness, that stretched from his withers to his flanks, went unnoticed. Now, that his back hind leg gave him constant pain, the carry harness with his weapons, pouches and few possessions dug into his flanks.

Stopping to rest, Jace lifted his head, breathing in the tang of salt water. Ahead, was a sea of turquoise, with white tipped waves, lapping on a green sea weeded beach; down by the waves, firm white sand would be easy trotting. But which way?

While he decided, a strong sea breeze rippled his curling black hair and thick tail. Cool wind blew rough against his tanned chest and dusty, chestnut-furred hide. The breeze even picked up his white feather-hairs over his massive hooves. Others reaching the top registered relief and excitement by prancing and half rearing. Jace remained with all four hooves planted down. It still hurt. He stroked his disheveled beard. Usually, it was neatly trimmed off his cheeks, growing just under his nose and down his chin. Now he was fully bearded. It had been a long time since his troop of centaurs could groom in a proper rest camp. The outlawed had to keep moving.

Others were looking to him—waiting for him to pick a marching direction. He was tempted to just call a rest halt so that they all could drop harnesses, wade into the foaming waves, roll down in the sand and kick their hooves high.

Deadrick yelled, "Smell it–shes!"

The excitement caused Jace to rear up on his hind legs. The shooting pain reminded him of troubles not past, but he now smelled hes as well as shes. The wind came along the beach, from the Yellow. A big tribe? A gathering ahead? Friendly? Or ready to fight?

He started leading the others down to that flat white beach. Nay other hoofprints. It looked like the tide was half out. If they camped here, there was seaweed they could eat. He could see mussels and scuttling crabs, which would take the edge off some of the hunger. Jace also smelled fresh water, tantalizingly at a distance. But his warriors were looking toward the scent of females. Nay doubt, those shes would have males to guard them. The aroma too strong to be a small group moving through.

To sword arm, was this a camp that would trade food? Or would they fight anyone who stepped a hoof on their territory? To the sinister side–what? Anyone downwind would smell them, long before they were seen. An ambush?

Jace saw his second in command, Garrison, raise his gray-bearded head. He looked with concern towards the beach before them. Jace turned his nose and took a deeper breath. Another smell. Faint. Repelling. Well remembered from his years on the battlefields. The stink of death.

Square-faced Deadrick reared and kicked his white stocking legs high. "Old one, why do we stand? I smell shes and cooking fires!" He jumped forward as if expecting the others to follow. When they did not, he trotted in a tight circle, coming back. The others were looking at Jace, who was not that much older than Deadrick. In fact, he was younger than many in the Regiment he commanded. Yet the decision was his.

The sea was ahead, with nothing in sight to swim to. Sword arm they would gallop to a group of unknown centaurs. Retreat back, where they were outcast? Or take the sinister path along the beach, to what?

Jace trotted down the dune. "We will go sword-arm. Cautiously. Let us see whose scent we are getting."

Garrison nodded, "We will make better time trotting on the wet sand."

Deadrick taunted above the gull calls, "Easier on Jace's sore hooves?" Deadrick liked not the others filing out at Jace's commands. Black and white hided Axel was only second in size to Two Spot. He moved to the side, forcing Deadrick to clear a path for Jace.

Deep sand on the dune had been a problem with his sore leg, but now Jace could trot freely on the hard packed beach near the waves. It felt good.

Incoming waves of foaming, cooling water wet the white feather hairs covering Jace's hooves, that brought some relief from the deep pain. Habitually the others spread a fighting front across the beach. Jace shook his head, using hand commands to "Break ranks. We seek no fight. Form a non-threatening group."

Some of the others nodded their heads. They had won all their battles, but lost the peace, when weaker centaurs bargained their gains away. Their patron allowed them to be outlawed. Now–they were mercenaries without cause. Lost were their war carts loaded high with weapons and plunder. They had to find something to fight for or scramble for varmint food.

No one commissioned Jace now, but in habit, the others followed his lead they broke into straggling groups. Carefully spaced out groups that could reform with a brief gallop. Warriors needed discipline and leaders and an objective. With none, they turned to Jace for guidance.

He looked over the remnants of the command, a little over fifty. New, first-blooded Axel, second biggest in the group, a white and black hided stud. Big, raw-boned, strong muscled, but raised from herds that peacefully lived off their fields of seeds and fruits. Grizzled headed, short curled, Garrison, with his roan hide lightened with white hairs of age, was long a warrior before Jace was first-blooded. A centaur, with his knowledge of the world, could have found himself an easier life than that of a mercenary–perhaps a trainer to some prince.

Deadrick had the flash of yellow hide and white hair and tail. He had courage and boldness, but not the brains required for him to be the supreme leader he felt he should be. The biggest, brown and white Two Spot, tramped alongside red-haired and hided Rufus. Ardon, Snake, and Nighthawk were smaller breeds, but still three heads taller over the average male centaur, 1,500 pounds to their 900 pounds.

The shes were also formidable fighters. Reet, mated to Per Ben. Willow mated to her poleaxe, with her two young foals trotting at her hooves. The Regimental trainer, Sandi, had two nearly grown colts, Ross and Kent. They would soon go onto the field as warriors in their own right. If the Regiment broke up, where would they go? Mercenaries were better on the field fighting than hunting boars.

But the Sultan hated Jace's Regiment that had trampled his lines and routed his troops. The boneheaded prince who had commissioned the Regiment leaped for a peace offering. He willingly sacrificed the Regiment's freedom, for a treaty with his new "brother." His peace would not survive the grain ripening, but Jace was glad they were not supporting the varlet any longer.

That dead stink was getting closer. Jace's eyes scanned the mounds of seaweed and scrabbling crabs. Then a larger mound, in a depression of sand. Under the seaweed, a darker mound of sodden hide.

Axel was the first to reach the body. It lay close in the incoming waves, in a scooped out area. A dug area with boulders. "A male–dead!" Axel reached down, using his sword to push back the head, to see his face. With a clanking of the chain, the head rolled back.

Startled, Axel reared his forelegs. "He's chained at the neck!"

Garrison nodded, "Aye. Chains on his legs too."

Axel looked at them in shock. "They chained him here to be drowned when the tide came in?"

Jace killed many a centaur in the fire of battle; never liked looking at the bloated bodies the next day.   Grim-faced, he nodded, "Looks like we have found civilization. Trot on, lads."

With downcast looks, the others filed past. White sand beach curved to the rocky headlands. Just above a dune, something moved. Animal on the salt grasses, or the top of some sentries head?

Warriors long legs made quick work of the beach. They reached the headland and would have been rounding the point, but Jace hand signaled a halt. The smell of shes, fresh water, and roasting beast was growing. But so was that of the hes. Favoring his sore hoof, Jace headed out of the water, on to the deeper, dry sand. Above the high water line, he unbuckled his battle harness and dropped it to with a clanking thud. It had his long sword, round shield, trade metal, bow and quiver, a sack of dried berries, his small pouches--all he had left of a lifetime of fighting.

Bending down low, he retrieved two long strapped flank pouches, with all the coin he had in the world. Over a shoulder, he slung scabbard with a short sword, over other with his long, carved drinking horn. After the full harness, they were light. Jace turned to Garrison, raising his voice above the waves, "Short rest here. Eat what you can. Just three or four of us will scout the lay of the land."

"I'm going!" Deadrick proclaimed.

"Fine." Jace.

"And Two Spot too. And Rufus and..."

Jace finished for him, "And myself. It's not a war foray. Garrison, set sentries. Axel, you and the others can gather some of that black seaweed. It will be tasty. Ardon, see if you can smell out some fresh water over that dune, to rinse the salt out. Since we are downwind, you can set a fire for shellfish. But keep harnesses on and be ready to bolt if we come galloping back."

Axel looked concerned, "If you do not come back?"

Garrison shot a knowing look to Jace. The colt barely grown to stallion was learning.

Jace nodded to Axel. "Then follow Garrison, as he moves back White along the beach. Other fields may they be sweeter."

"Nay!" pronounced Axel. "We must go for you!"

"If I cannot talk our way out or fight our way out, you will not be able to help us."

Axel gave a dismissive sweep of his long black tail.

" Do you take my orders?" Jace's question was a command.

Axel raised his head to argue, then briefly bowed it. "Aye, sir."

Jace pivoted on his back legs, sending shooting pains up his hindquarters. Deadrick truly wanted to lead, and Jace had no desire to be the first on someone's spear. "Leadoff, Deadrick, Just take it easy."

"Your leg hurts more?"

" We look less threatening if we trot in slowly."

Deadrick was off, proud to lead, but Two Spot and Rufus ceded Jace second place. As they rounded the head point, Jace noted more blue boulders.

"This was where they got the slabs to build their drowning pit," Rufus yelled over the surf.

Jace nodded. "Probably laid it as a warning to those that would come their way."

After they rounded the headland, Jace could see another, smaller crescent of beach, curving inward to high marsh reeds. After that rose a distant mound, with pennants flying from tall sticks. Their hooves drummed on the sand, as they drew closer to the reeds and a mud-brown river that emptied into the long, smooth sea-flats. On the other side, just two lopes across, that higher mound rose, planted with colorful, wind flapping banners and sun skims above what looked to be dealer's stalls.

Jace tightened his lope, as he looked closer. The standards were brightly colored, wind flattened cloths, emblazoned with designs of wine amphoras, shields, fruits. Nothing looked like war identification. Just like merchants trying to catch the eyes of some fat pouched patrons.

Deadrick twisted back to yell over the seagulls screeching, "It appears to be a gathering." Jace scanned the distant hill-lock. The banners were faded reds, blues, yellows–looked as if they had been in the sun a long time. Must be twenty, thirty stalls on this side, with cloth shade screens. Not a transient gathering. "Mayhaps a stationary bazaar?" At the base and in rows higher up Jace noted fetlock high stone walls, loosely set in a semi-circular fashion around the hill. Not much of a defense but it would break a charge.

In spite of himself, Deadrick had halted and habitually looked back for Jace's go ahead.

The shortest distance would be to trot over the seaweed, mud flats and the shallow river. But Jace noted that higher up on the beach, before trees, was some sort of a gate. Two tall pillars of dry-laid stone matched on the other side of the river by two more pillars. Totally defenseless.

Jace hand signaled. They would go into this bazaar properly, through the pillar gates. Deadrick bounded up on to the deeper, drier sand. Harder going for Jace's burning hoof. They reached the grass, then a beaten hoof marked trail leads them between the pillars to the embankment above the river. Jace took the lead down the mossy river bank. The water looked muddy but was cool and shallow. Midway, the water at its deepest was only up to his fetlocks.

Nearly across, Jace yelled to Deadrick, "Hold." With him, the others stopped, hands slipping to the hilts of their swords. Jace causally untied his carved drinking horn and dropped it into the river. The gesture of a harmless, thirsty traveler, in no great hurry. The others followed his lead, talking a bit, laughing and dragging their drinking horns down into the murky flow. It tasted brackish, from mixing with sea-water–but drinkable.

Ahead they could see lesser centaurs gathering, coming out of their stalls and moving down to the river. Signing to others. Looking in their direction.

Deadrick whipped his body around. "They have seen us."

Jace smiled widely and nodded to him. "Well, they should. Just refresh yourself. There is no need to hurry. They seem to be merchants. Merchants are always in want of patrons with coins."

Rufus took a sip and spit it in the river. "We have little coin."

"They do not know that."

"Yet," Rufus replied.

Jace flashed him a sardonic smile and dipped another deep draught. "See any weapons?"

Two Spot appeared to be just looking around, but his experienced gaze had fully covered the centaurs crowding the shore. "Yon black hide has a blood dripping, wide-bladed sword in his hands, probably was gutting a fish."

"Aye."

"Two young fellows to his sinister, with two colored tails. They have a solid warrior stance." Rufus added.

Jace just nodded. "No one seems to be looking for a leader." By one and twos, hes and some shes were coming out to the embankment across the river.

"Just a welcoming committee?" Rufus queried.

Two Spot craned his high head. "Not really armored, but more are coming. Most fat and old. Those bays are young enough for battle."

Jace swished his tail, throwing off water droplets. "They are just curious." He made an elaborate show of finishing his drink and slowly re-tying the horn to his pouch sling.

Deadrick shifted with impatience. "We lose surprise."

"We need no surprise. We want only peaceful relations here." Pushing past Deadrick, Jace felt his knees clearing the water, as the riverbed rose towards the other shore. His sore back hoof struck an awkward, sharp rock, and he grimaced, then covered quickly.

On the embankment, the others parted for a short, very stiff-backed centaur with dun-colored hide. He was coming down at a fast trot. The dun was bald at the top of his black-haired head, with a short, black tail. Instead of entering the river, the solemn-faced one trotted out to a rocky over-crop. There he planted four hoofs flat and waited. Standing there proudly with some sort of heavy squared chain about his neck. A badge of office?

Jace stayed in the river, but stepped to a deep spot, just under the dun's rock. This allowed him to look up to a centaur, whose head would have barely reached his upper stomach. Up to his flanks in the water now, Jace just lazily swished his tail to clear it of water drops and smiled warmly. With him still in the water, the dun should feel secure--for most small ones, unfamiliar with his big breed, had no idea how fast a warrior could scramble up a bank.

His courtesy brought a proud smile to the little dun, who recognized proper manners and lowed his head just a bit, as he stepped closer. "I be Sandor. Mayor of this Bazaar."

"Jace of Thunderhoof."

"You fine fellows by yourselves?" It was an innocent question, but Jace saw the Mayor's eyes narrow and ears prick just a little. The others also seemed to be anxiously listening.

"Are we not enough for you?" Deadrick began.

Jace finished. "Actually, there are more of us beyond the headway. But we wished to see if the land is friendly before we accidentally blundered into some local battlefield."

The Mayor seemed to relaxed a bit. It was a truthful answer that he wanted. Again Jace suspected they had been spied upon from the dunes. "Aye. These be perilous times, but we are peaceful here. Our bazaar is Trade Truce." He stopped and looked hard at them. "Not everyone respects this..."

"We will," replied Jace firmly.

The Mayor nodded. "Then you and your companions are welcome."

Jace looked about. "In the Purple lands, we have heard of a great bazaar they once called *Caravan Headland*?"

The Mayor's face saddened. "This was it. Once we spread on both sides of the river. Up past the dunes, down to the caravan trail. But there has been unrest in the land. We have been spared, but many of our merchants have moved on."

"It is a bit foolish to kill trade," Rufus commented.

Jace looked at the tents rippling in the breeze. "I have read that the Headlands can provide goods from every direction."

The Mayor stiffened with pride. "Our merchants still have much to offer you." But then again concern in his eyes, "But what brings you to our shore?"

"We are soldiers for hire."

"Whose hire?"

"At the moment, no one. "

"We have nay call for soldiers here."

"Excellent. Having finished our last commission, we would appreciate a time of peace. We only rest and pass through. And replenish some of our arms."

"Then here you will find armorers, wine mongers, and food roasters. Weavers and such. You are welcome to come in, but be warned–we do not allow thieves or fighting."

Only years of discipline kept Jace from smiling. "Understood." His troop could subdue these few merchants before mid-sun, but then what?

Again the Mayor dared to trespass on the bounds of

courtesy. "Where do you go after this?" He asked.

Jace turned a bit away from him, "Those trees across the river from where we came. Would anyone object to us camping there?"

Wisely the Mayor would trespass politeness no more. "That would be a good place. Beyond the trees, there is a good sized meadow, with a sweet spring. There is food to be had in the Bazaar," he looked directly at Jace. "And for those who would hunt their own, there is game up the river. Send for your friends." There were loud murmurings behind him, Sandor stopped, seemed to listen, then turned back to Jace as he continued, "but perhaps, only a few of you should come...at first, to let us know the smell of you."

Jace nodded. "Much better. Some of our kind are raw, open range folk. We will learn your ways and counsel them." To speak to Rufus, Jace turned broadside against the river's current, the cooling water caught his flanks as he waded back to the others. "Rufus, go scout yon meadow for a camp. Mayhaps we dig a fire pit before gloaming."

Rufus commented in an undertone. "Heat up the mush, make it taste a little better?"

As an order, Jace tossed his tail then looked to Two Spot. "Canter back to Garrison and bring up the rest to the meadow. We will enter the bazaar, but slowly. Maybe three or four of us at a time. Let the Bazaar dealers get used to us before we blunder in something. I will go the Bazaar now."

Deadrick looked annoyed. "Just you go into the Bazaar? Nay!"

Arguing in front of strangers reflected poorly on them. Jace thinned his lips. "You and I shall go in now. After we settle, the Regiment will go into the bazaar four a time." Jace looked back to Two Spot. "Draw lots for a list." Two Spot sometimes took orders and sometimes did not. This time he nodded and turned tail, without even looking for confirmation from Deadrick.

Jace waded back to the Mayor on the buff, "Could you show us about, good sir?"

Before the Mayor could nod, Deadrick started to scramble up the bank, expecting the little Mayor to back out of his way. Sandor did not, forcing Deadrick to halt and then sidestep. A little dance that put a brief smile on Jace's lips. This Mayor Sandor was small, but a scrapper.

Sandor did respectfully give ground when Jace climbed up the bank. Up top, Jace looked down and asked him, "And you could tell us of your ways so we will not offend."

The Mayor nodded. "We try to keep our dealers honest, but some do drive a hard bargain. If one is unwary, one may get a poor deal."

Jace nodded with his tail. "As everywhere."

"We do business when the sun rises. The freshest fish, fruit, and meat comes in then. We have several plankers serving morning tastes. At sunsinking, those who do not have a stall must leave."

What did they consider their camp perimeters? "Is across the river far enough?"

The Mayor nodded. "Across the river will be fine."

At three arms length, Jace followed the little Mayor, who paraded between his dealers as if he had captured the whole Imperial army. Deadrick followed, taking it all in. Imagining how to breach their pathetic fortifications no doubt.

A well-worn trail wound around the mound, past stalls of leather harnesses and leg tied hunting birds. Jace smelled apples and clove, as he trod up to the next level. Except for the armorer's displays, Jace saw almost no weapons, but he guessed there might be some in the chests under the dealer's planks.

Massive rock slabs were showing through the sand and dirt of the hill lock. This whole mound was probably a centaur built hill. Paving rocks lead through stalls of goods. Baskets of fruit plucked fowls, and dried fish made his stomach rumble. Oh, the tempting smells of orange spice, vanilla, savory mincemeat, even the stink of tanners. Once Jace could have been commissioning a finely tooled harness to replace his old. Now? Now his troop desperately needed to replace weapons, wagons, shields, but first, they must find a fat pouched patron to pay for it all.

This bazaar really had no fortifications. There was undoubted coin here and food and fine cloth, but where do you enjoy such things, if you destroy your gathering grounds? Yet some of his troop might not see it that way. If the more foolish of his comrades took over an unarmed settlement, they would truly be outcasts, even worse than now.

The three rounded another loop, climbing higher on the mound, again Jace could see the blue water. More stalls of cloth bolts and weavers, wood-wrights and potters. Under a red-striped awning, two bosomy public groomers brightened up and stepped boldly towards Jace.

"Fine, sir, let us comb your dark hair–so thick and wavy." The golden-haired she, with the biggest breasts, ran her fingers down his furred jaw and tanned chest. Her nipples brightly pointed up, as she huskily spoke, "I be Honey. This is my sister, Laurel."

At her name, Laurel swished her pale golden tail and blushed prettily, coming close on Jace's other side, pressing her rough coated flanks up against his. Smilingly, she ran firm fingers down Jace's hindquarters, "Such handsome red-brown hide."

Jace ruefully smiled. The sweetly-smiling she would

do a lovely job with large combs on his dusty hide, while her friend could trim the wavy head hair that had grown down his back, but it would take coin. Coins he had need for more pressing wants. "Not this sun, ladies. Be graced for asking."

Undeterred, Honey turned to Deadrick with soft giggles and softer words. "And you sir, such a tall centaur, with moon-white hair and stockings. See, sister, his flanks are the color of warm sunlight." Now it was Deadrick's turn for his tanned chest to flush deeply.

Laurel's hand was soon stroking low on his flanks. "Oh, your color, fine sir, I have never seen such golden hide. And with those white stockings. Oh, you must let me burnish your hooves until they glow!"

As Laurel rubbed her back thigh up against Deadrick hindquarters, Honey continued, "Sister, you must comb that fine whitetail while I trim his beard. You do wish to be clean shaven?"

Deadrick pranced proudly. He could not turn down any centauress' attention, even if he knew it must be paid for.

Jace and Mayor Sandor left him there as they continued up circling the rising mound with its Stalls of purple silk cloth, cooking pots and sweets. A full tent ahead, in it, must be items that could not be rained on. Jace stopped treading to peer inside. As he suspected it was piled high with rolls of parchment and thin copper. The Mayor followed him asking curiously. "You read, sir? That is uncommon in these lands."

"I know some marks, in a few languages."

Sandor twisted his torso looking about them, "Maxima, you have an interested party." As a gray-flecked centaur hurried back from a cheese stall, the Mayor continued, "A learned centaur is much appreciated here."

When the elderly centaur looked up at Jace's height,

Maxima appeared intimated. "Uh sir,...ye wish..." He began confusedly.

"Mayhaps he wishes to purchase a scroll." The Mayor turned back to Jace. "I must return to my plank. It is at the top of the mound. I sell fine and raw meads. Your patronage would be appreciated."

Jace nodded with his tail. "Something for me to investigate. Graced are you."

At Sandor's acceptance of Jace, Maxima settled down. Now he clasped his hands and tilted his head, "Please enter and look at my fine scrolls. Many bright paintings await your pleasure."

From the sea, a strong breeze ruffled the stiff shade skims. Jace had to drop his head low to even just look into Maxima's tent. The dark, hot, closeness of the interior closed in on him. Inside, Maxima had devised shelves of planks, raised above each other on flat rocks. Each plank was stuffed high with scrolls. Pushing past Jace, the elderly dealer stepped in and unrolled a skin scroll, garishly painted with the antics of gamboling, lusty centaurs, and centauresses. When Jace showed no interest, he unrolled another of long-tailed beauties, stretching most elegantly.

Jace nodded "Very handsome, but I wish..."

Maxima was already pulling out a long, green beaten metal sheet, "I have poetry from the court of Emperor Rediacofsky. Plays penned by the great Running Hoof. *A Centauresses Dilemma* or the *Wicked Cloven Hoof*."

Jace smiled appreciatively but did not reach out for the offering. "*The Centauresses' Dilemma*, I have seen it performed."

Maxima looked up eagerly. "You have heard his words before?"

"Aye. To the Purple, in the court of the Emperor

himself."

"Running Hoof read his plays?"

"Nay. They were performed."

"Performed? That means?"

"Enacted by his troop of centauress players. Each centauress memorized his scrolls and repeated them as if they were just happening. The centauress who portrayed Golden Hoof was of milk-white skin and hide. Her eyes were bright red, and her voice resounded with the high, sweeping sound of a silver bell. A rare beauty." Jace's voice softened appreciatively with the memory.

"When did you see this wonder?"

"When I was given charge of Emperor Rediacofsky's household guard, Running Hoof arrived at the court with his troop of female players."

"All centauresses? But what of the male speeches?"

"The shes took the male parts as well. The female centauresses who played males donned masks and strapped on massive..." Jace indicated under his hindquarters, and Maxima laughed appreciatively. "On a full moon, the court marched out to a level plain, where a buff of rocks rose. The troop performed in front of the rock bluff by torchlight, one play a night."

Maxima's eyes shined. "Such a sight to see."

"When they finished all Running Hoof's scrolls, they cantered away to the next great gathering to perform for others."

Maxima's sadly shook his tail. "They shall never come here. Once perhaps, but now with the unrest...."

Jace's tail stiffened slightly but tried to appear not uninterested. Still, played correctly, this might be a commission in the offering. "What is the nature of your 'unrest'?"

Maxima looked down. "Marauders."

"Marauders?" Jace's eyes narrowed in interest.

"Robbers and killers. The wilder desert tribes, the Scarlur. They used to come here to trade, to beg." Maxima's tail rose in nervousness.

"This changed?"

"They found a leader, Red Tooth. He gathered them together to start raiding."

Jace was shocked. "They raid here? A Truce of Trade?"

"Nay. But the caravans that were our life-blood...only a trickle comes now..."

"Mayhaps you should fight them?"

Maxima shook his head. "We are not fighters."

"Pay others to fight for you. The Regiment I march for could fight for you."

"Nay." Maxima looked away, reaching for more scrolls. "Mayhaps they will go away."

"You study the scrolls so you must know the past. When others attack, a weak response just emboldens them." Jace looked about the tent with its shelves of parchment and green copper scrolls. "Quite a collection but I require charts of the local territories."

"Charts?"

"Maps?"

"Oh. Drawings of the trails?"

"Aye."

Maxima registered disappointment. "Not with me but further up the mound, you will pass by another tent. A centaur even older than myself by the name of Var-tee. He might have some." Jace politely swished his tail in acknowledgment, then headed up the sandy trail. He smelled the sea breeze and grapes fermenting as he trod past a plank set with sinew thread and iron rings to mend his travel harness. He should purchase them before someone else did, but Jace wanted to see what was ahead.

Further on the climbing, spiral trail, a deep blue-green skim ruffled in the wind over the small, ornate caskets of a jeweler. Jace had some pieces of captured jewelry in his travel pouches, maybe he could trade them here later. A tall pole frame threaded with onion ropes, peppers and gourds reminded him how hungry he was.

At the top of the flattening mound, the trail looped around to a view of the turquoise sea and Jace could see Mayor Sandor tapping one of his clay jars. Sandor had a triple sized stall, with stout kegs and amphoras stuck into the sand. Seeing him, the Mayor moved to his brew plank, looking up at Jace with pride in his eyes. "This be my stall. Honey mead? Berry brew? Sweetgrass mash? Been readying for your warriors."

"What have you raw and grainy?" Jace did not add cheap as he untied his drinking horn. "My friends will seek strong and harsh."

The Mayor looked to his larger kegs. Finally, he pulled a huge one up on top of the plank. "Seed and fruit based. Called hereabouts as 'Plains Rain.' Very refreshing and modestly priced." Sandor carefully eyed Jace's huge drinking horn to estimate its volume. "Quarter copper for a fill."

Holding out his drinking horn Jace nodded. The Mayor easily hefted the large keg, swiftly pouring a sample taste of the sudsy, brown brew. "If you like it, tell your mates."

Jace held it under his nose inhaling deeply. It had a strong stout smell, like sweat foam on a she's hide. He took a sip. It was warming, tart like green apples, and had a robust flavor that was still not bitter. Good stuff for a fair charge. Jace nodded to Sandor, who poured the horn generously. Drinking fast and deeply, Jace downed the whole hornful. "Make it half copper. Two horns are needed to wash away the trail dust."

Nodding in agreement, Mayor Sandor poured again. The second pour was even more generous than the first, its foam overflowing his horn.

Finishing most of the horn, Jace nodded. " I will tell the rest." He handed Sandor the half copper and moved on.

As he glanced around the top of the bazaar mound, Jace noted smithies with their spear points and swords gleaming in the sun. His warriors needed to replace lost weaponry, but the ones he saw were scaled for smaller centaurs. His large breeds would require custom forged and that would be costly. The prices would be higher once the merchants realized they had a flood of new buyers.

Looking Orange -ward he saw another full tent, with a plank of scrolls before it. Jace trod over. The proprietor, an old, gray hided centaur started to rise stiffly to his feet.

"Fair sun to you." Jace nodded in a friendly fashion.

"I be Var-tee." The voice surprising strong and deep, for one so frail looking.

"Jace of Thunderhoof. Sir, have you treaties on this area? Charts or maps of these lands?"

"Aye. Somewhere." With a long, scrawny arm, he dug into the tent and dragged out several scrolls of parchment and a folded, leather skin.

Jace studied the first. Fine line work, painted with earth colors. It had a bazaar as its center, probably this one, but twice the size of this one. A long line of coastline to the sinister, populated by a huge sea monster. Some sort of scaled worm to the Blue; a flying beastie to the Red. Colorful, but not enlightening. The next scroll was a passable map, but of what terra? A third purported to be the fields of his youth, with two lost lakes instead of one. The others Jace did not even recognize as maps. He carefully returned them to their owner. "Finely drawn, but I was looking for more detailed paths from here."

The old centaur nodded with his tail, "The Caravan trails. I have more buried off side. In another sinking?"

Jace nodded his tail. "I will trod this way again." He started to walk away, his leg hurting badly. "And the flies bite my hide so, do you have an herbalist that sells potions? "

"Merdi. Very skilled in the healing herbs. Go down to the beach. He is to the Yellow. Look for a full enclosure and two snake skins streaming from a pole."

"Graced you be."

The novelty of the bazaar had taken his mind off the pain in his hindquarters, but as ever, it returned as he started the harder work of going downhill. Nearly at the bottom, he saw Deadrick still being groomed by the two giggling centauresses. Saucy Laurel was cutting his blond hair to shoulder length, which would tangle in his helm, but Deadrick liked flash. Honey pressed her breasts against his chest as she reared high to shave Deadrick's square jaw.

She was leaving a mustache with a beard only on his chin, a style that Jace usually fancied. So Deadrick wanted to be a leader. Was he trying to outdo Jace? Deadrick's polished hooves already shone. His brushed golden hide rippled. That would put him in better humor until it was time to pay up. It would feel good to have these two ladies rubbing his hide, but Jace would save the coin and trade grooming with Garrison or Axel.

On the other side of the bazaar, he came back to the beach and trotted to the Yellow. There on the fringes was a large wooden pole structure curtained all around; before it hung a green banner sewn with centaur bones and two forearm-thick snake skins intertwining. This had been what Jace was looking for, yet he hesitated. The world of a bazaar was one of foolish, constant prattle. When a warrior searched for a commission, one should not be heralding weakness. Yet anyone who watched could see he limped when tired.

He had put up with the pain for so long. Still, this was one calling that depended on keeping their patron's secrets. At the pole, Jace called out. "May I enter?"

The curtains did not part, but a male voice answered, "Advance."

Jace lifted a heavy cloth flap and stepped into the square enclosure, fighting down that tightness in his throat at being confined. Fortunately, the enclosure was open to the sky. That helped. Paying no attention to him, a thin, red-haired centaur stared down as he intently ground gray herbs on a scooped stone. Jace looked around. From the pole frame hundreds of vials hung from twisted vine ropes; vials of glass and wood and clay, twelve to twenty-four a roping. Even with the sea breeze above them, this stall smelled strongly of lavender and other drying herbs.

Yet the hated, trapping walls pushing in on him as Jace tried to focus on the far wall. There stretched a parchment, detailed with the painted skeleton of a centaur. Finally, Merdi finished scraping up the ground herbs with his hands and fed them into an amber-glass oil flask. When he finally looked up, Merdi seemed shocked by Jace's height. "Sir?" The centaur asked sharply, then quieted his tone. "I be Mardi, healer, and herbalist."

"Jace of Thunderhoof Regiment. You deal in pain remedies?" Asked Jace carefully.

"Aye." The herbalist wiped his hands on a soft-furred

skin. "What be your complaint?"

"A pain. Long in my sinister hind leg."

"Come to me, sir." His tight stall was not built for one of Jace's massive size, but the herbalist moved adroitly and was running his large hands down Jace's left hind leg. "You have heat within." Involuntarily Jace flinched from the pressure of Merdi's probing fingers. "That is not good."

Jace said nothing, allowing Merdi to lift his leg and examine the frog of his hoof. "I see a new scar?"

"At least one moon ago, I stepped on a spear in battle while killing its owner."

The healer frowned. He ran his hand up the injured leg, along Jace's withers and up to his upper chest. Merdi took a wooden goblet and handed it to Jace. Jace expected a potion to drink, but inside the dry goblet was only several small snake vertebrae. What did he do with this–chew it?

Merdi enlightened him. "Cover the cup with your hand, think of your pain, shake the cup, then drop the bones on this plank."

Jace looked to his side where withers high Mardi had raised a flat slab of wood on stick legs. Looking closely Jace saw the plank was carved in an octagonal pattern with numerals and sky symbols scattered about. Concentrating, Jace thought of the endless pain, then he scattered the bones. Yellow vertebrates touched a carved coiled snake, a sun symbol, a woman's head.

The healer pushed him back to better study the bones' lay. "Your wound healed, but the spirit of the dead man has entered your leg."

"Spirit?"

"Aye. He wishes vengeance." Said Merdi gravely.

"What can you do? The pain is growing. " Cynically, Jace expected that his purse might heal the spirit, but the healer only ran his hand on Jace's back fetlock again.

"I could cut the lower leg off and strap a wood stick to it?" The herbalist appeared too eager.

"Nay." Said Jace, although if it would end the pain...

Shrugging his shoulders, Merdi stepped to his ropes of vials. "For the pain, I have some small cakes." He seemed to search long, fingering one vial then another. Finally, he turned to a large jar, scooping out a yellow pressed cake the size of an almond. "What have you in trade? Metal?"

Jace reached into his carry pouch and fished around. He had gold, but he guessed the Merdi would take less. He pulled out half a copper disk.

The healer brightened. "Aye." He looked his vines, and from a hanging basket pulled out a thumb thick sized wooden box with a sliding lid. In to this, he loaded twelve cakes as Jace silently counted. "You chew two when the pain comes but if you take it in at sunrise, do not take more until mid-sun and sun-sink. They are very strong. Eight, maybe seven taken at once will kill you. "

"Will this cure me?"

The healer looked rather sad and shook his tail. "The cakes will take the pain away. Mayhaps your leg will get better. Mayhaps worse. Give offerings to the Twisting Snake Twins."

Jace started to chew the first cake. It tasted bitter like his life had become. With a thankful toss of his tail to Merdi he stepped out. If the spirits of all the centaurs he had killed could claim vengeance from the old earth, he was truly doomed.

Chapter Two

Unfamiliar waters,

Go in one hoof at a time...

Old Centauress' Wisdom

Jace chewed on the second bitter cake as he trod on back through the bazaar. A ring around the hillock allowed one to bypass the upward coiled trail. He stayed on that circular path until he reached the river gate. At the ford, he saw stubby legged dark-gray hided Per Ben and his lady Reet. Both were square and solidly built with short hide hair and no feather wisps above their hooves. They were smaller than Jace's breed but still a good deal larger than those here in the bazaar. Jace noted that even with this lean rout Reet had been putting on weight. Her flanks and square face had filled out a great deal.

Behind them coming out of the river was the black skinned and hided Nighthawk with all pale-gray Snake, both eager to see what awaited them in this bazaar. They lifted tails in a friendly salute. Jace nodded back. "Three armor sellers. Maybe more with fat deals..."

Full faced Reet added with a knowing look. "At fat prices."

Jace smiled as they moved past him. "High in the bazaar, a small dun called Mayor Sandor has a plank under the white flag with a storm cloud. Drank his Plain's Rain. Smooth on the throat."

"Been wishing for a wet throat," said Per Ben longingly.

"Quarter copper for my full horn."

As Reet nodded a 'gratitude' with her tail, Jace still

found himself turning to caution. "Look at all before you bargain." Nodding tails they moved on.

He stepped into the now colder river. What was the matter with him? Warning seasoned bargainers like Per Ben and Reet? Shrewd Per Ben could skin a running cat, and his Reet could stretch a full cape out of it. Anyone who cheated the short-fused Snake or the shrewd-eyed Nighthawk would be stomped by gloaming. Why should Jace always be worrying about them? Mayhaps they could all find their next meal without him.

Getting deeper into the water, Jace lengthened his strides. He was halfway across the river when he realized something was different. Something felt strange. His pain had receded like the tides. In amazement, he stopped and planted all four hooves solidly–no pain. It had been so many moons since he could put his full weight on that back, sinister hoof without shooting stabs. Jace tightened his hindquarters and then in a spray of water, he bolted forward with joy. The herbalist's tiny cakes were working. He was cured!

The river grew more shallow as he reached the other shore. He threw his two carry pouches up on to the bank, then waded back in. In deeper water, he gave in to the luxury of rolling over in the water on his long back. Water up to his neck washed his dusty hide and chest hairs. Twisting in the river, he kicked all four legs high above him. Reluctantly he righted himself and arose with water streaming from his long hair curls and thick tail. It felt so good! With his full weight on all four hooves, Jace splashed suddenly back toward the shore reeds.

Raising his head high, he deeply inhaled familiar troop smells and the tantalizing aroma of roasting meat. With his stomachs rumbling, he came out of the water in a half lope, grabbing up his pouches, following a freshly trodden trail of broken river reeds up through low bushes. As he climbed up the weedy bank, he could see one of the Regimental sentries standing motionless, just within the saplings ahead. Good. A watch had been set again. They had grown far too lax on this rout.

Nodding to Clay who was on guard, Jace trotted briskly as he followed a path through ferns and taller trees. It was a nice screen for a camp. He emerged into a large meadow circled with saplings, probably used as a camping ground for bazaar outsiders, but by the height of the grass, it had not been used recently.

At the entrance, one of his had planted a spear mounted with the red and black streamer of the Regiment. Their last streamer. Once Jace proudly trotted between two lines of an honor guard of eighty Centaurs, each standing with his red and black flags flying from their spears. Now not even one full marching flag was left. Just a long, snake tongue streamer, hanging despondently without wind.

Jace did a fast count. Nearly thirty centaurs were drinking, rolling in sand pits, dropping their battle harnesses, and laughing as they pawed their bedding areas. Jace walked in slowly, doing a round of the camp. Working on his latest project, old Urzi rapidly limped from a small pond, moving over to strap something to Abel's lean back.

Bald headed, slight bodied Urzi had a broken front leg that mended crookedly, but he still marched–or limped to the battle calls. Always clever with his hands, Urzi was bending wet wood in a circle, measuring it against Abel's battle harness.

Seeing Jace, Abel nodded in respect, "Have they work for us?" He started to take a step forward.

Urzi shook his head. "Steady!"

Jace lowered his shoulders to get a look at the

contraption strapped to Abel's gray-brown barrel. "That is?"

"Beginning of a battle drum set to replace what we lost," Urzi answered, stretching the wet hide to measure it against the drum frames.

"Good." Jace nodded. "We need Abel pounding out the calls. Keeps the charge line solid."

To avoid answering the original question, Jace moved on. Kear, a just blooded recruit looked up. "These bazaar dealers need our hire?" Kear was dark hided, light skinned. A lot smaller than Jace's breed but very feisty and fast in battle.

Jace forced a confident smile. "Mayhaps. But we must let them realize it slowly."

Long blooded warrior Lerestra smiled back. "You will work us a deal."

Others also looked to Jace for answers he did not have. He just gave a confident nod, the green recruits looked relieved, but those with a bit of scarring looked to him with worried eyes, asking not.

That mouthwatering aroma of meat roasting grew. Ahead a fire pit had been hastily dug, and a raw stag skewered over a blue smoke fire. From the woods, a flash of light tan hide and skin, as Sandi's youngest colt, Kent, came trotting up with an arm full of dry sticks. As Kent fed the flames, Jace admired the fat buck. "A fine catch. Whose?"

Scarlet hided, rough-voiced Rufus yelled out. "Kent, the mighty hunter!"

Kent colored with the acknowledgment. "He was so fat, he could not outrun my spear. I can get lots more." He finished proudly.

"We hunt again at twilight," Rufus called out. "We have many hungry mouths here."

Good. They were sharing food again, acting like a fighting brotherhood. He could keep the Regiment going if he could just get them a commission!

Others were coming over asking questions of him. Where did one find the best amour? Where did the groomers look the comeliest? Jace only smiled, cutting himself a piece of still half red meat. "Give me time to eat."

As he ate, he could see Sandi trotting near the pond. Like her two sons, her skin, hair, and hide were a light tan. In the sand or dry dirt fields she could almost disappear, a trait she used for her advantage when fighting. Sandi used everything to her advantage when fighting. Not one to stand endless grooming, she cropped her unruly curls and tail short. On the march, she covered her head with an undyed linen scarf to protect it from the sun's heat. As her only concession to she vanity Sandi always wore three polished, cloudy jade beads on a leather thong about her neck

A worker skilled with leather, a wood wright, and metalsmith, Sandi was still a fast and deadly fighter. Although short for even normal centaur size, she was a deceptively strong and tough centauress. Barely a filly herself, she had come to the Regiment with two huge warriors, Mica and Smokey. They fought as a unit for years, and when Sandi gave birth first to Ross, then later to the playful Kent, both Mica and Smokey swelled with pride over "his" progeny. All the Regiment eagerly anticipated a blood challenge between these two giants. But strangely those two deadly centaurs never fought each other, probably because that pair of fierce fighters were totally dominated by their fast moving little she.

Mica died by sword at Yellowland and Smokey was lost at the Battle for the Tin Mines. With two youngsters to run after, Sandi spurned the life of root digger and stayed with the Regiment, first as a cook, later as trainer and fighter. It made Jace feel old to think it, but in not too many seasons both Sandi's young colts would be full Regimental material themselves.

Still eating, he walked to her. When Jace got closer, he could see she had the bent a sapling down over a small pool of water. Sandi had tied a bucket to the sapling and was using the tree to bring up full buckets.

"How is it?" He asked.

"Drinkable. Almost sweet." She cocked her head to the side. "It is cold and running, that means spring water flowing off in that small stream. Should be pure enough if those fiddle foots do not dung all over the hillside."

"Mark around it with the water streamers. Do we have any left?"

Sandi smiled wryly. "Gone with my pull cart." With narrowed eyes, she looked about, then smiled wickedly. "I can steal some blue silk ribbons from Willow's hair braids. I will say it was your orders."

"Thanks." He said dryly.

As they both watched, two young warriors speared a stump. Finally, a serious-faced Sandi looked up at him. "The bazaar dealers smell money, so I am sure they will want us here..."

"Til we run out of coin."

"Any royalty that needs propping up?"

"They seem not that civilized here."

"Jace, if we do not get a commission...."

"If you go in the bazaar early there might be work for a she as clever as yourself."

She smiled sourly. "An aging she with two huge hoofed colts following her tail?"

"A she who can sew harness, forge iron and carve wood. I would think there must be coin for such as you." As much as he wanted her around, she deserved to have things a little easier.

Sandi looked back up at him, her mouth set. "Get us a war, Jace. One where I can cleave some varlet's head in."

Jace swung his tail as he prepared to walk off. "I will try my best."

"You have never let us down before," Sandi called after him. "Kent got that juicy one roasting. You bivouac with us. Ross! Fetch me the kettle boiling there." Sandi's older colt had been ignoring orders lately, but this time Ross came trotting with the heated pot. His mare poured some in her goblet, then poured some into Jace's drinking horn. A simmering brew of dried leaves and sweetening berries that was strong and wakening. Sandi truly had a way with herbs, might be good as someones' cook.

This time even Jace had to raise his eyes to meet those of the tall white and black splashed he joining them. Axel was looking hungrily at the roasting beast. With a wry smile, Sandi nodded her tail. "We can spare a bit for you. Ross, pour him some of the soakings too."

Holding out his black drinking horn, Axel bent his head to smell it. "Cherries, sweet grass...." He tasted it with the tip of his tongue. "Humm. What else?"

"Mayhaps yellow-toad skin poison?" Sandi tartly commented.

Axel took a brief sip which he sloshed about his mouth. "Nay. Not that numbing."

"You have tasted yellow toad?"

"Clay showed me a glass vial in his pack–he makes a paste to put on his arrow points. It will kill..."

Sandi shook her head. "A youngling. A full warrior in battle will only be numbed. May cause them to amble dizzily, but you tasted it?"

"Just a tiny drop on a pine needle."

Sandi now shook her tail as well. "Fool."

Axel slowly drank more of her leaf brew. "Lemon leaf?"

"And?"

He tasted again and then shook his head. "Tart fruit. What is it?"

"Chokeberry."

"Choke?"

"It is that small blackberry that grows yon, through the trees. Kent picked it for me."

Axel's eyes followed her gesture "Will you show me?"

"When the sun rises enough to see it."

Axel blazed a smile. "Sunrise, Jace takes me to the bazaar."

"Those poor innocent souls, having your great hooves trampling them."

"If I find a stick for a torch, will you show me the berries tonight?"

"You want me to go into the wood with you? Of course." Flashing a triumphant smile to Jace, Sandi bounded off leading Axel away.

Many times Jace had heard Sandi proclaiming she wished not another colt, but a mating between her and Axel would produce some warrior–he or she. After finishing a drink and meal that warmed his belly, Jace loped over to Garrison.

The grizzled haired old warrior looked him up and down. "Leg looks better?"

Jace nodded, trying to change the subject. "What do you think our count is?"

"Nearly forty. Losing some every sun. Half would leave if they had any place to go."

Jace nodded agreement. "Equipment?"

"Dead loss. Everything not on our backs was in those baggage carts that got overrun. We picked up nothing on the field, because of the blasted negotiations."

"Run a tally on what we need to get battle ready."

Garrison perked up. "Anything smell interesting?"

"There are rumors these bazaar dealers have a problem with outlying tribes, but they are sitting tight."

Garrison's tail lowered. "Jace, face the wall head-on. We lost the whole cart caravan. My shield cracked in battle, some lost helms, it would take months of smithing just to get the minimum chest shields and weapons that fit our sizes..."

"We will buy what we can here. Forge what we need later." He finished confidently.

"My old friend, your warriors are walking off daily. This bazaar does not seem to want a regiment. Mayhaps if we continue trotting Green. I hear the Imperial is growing."

"We have both served them. If you are not of their blood, they would put you at the front to be cut down first. Your portion is always collected last."

"What else is there?"

"Get me a count. Tell them all to rearm if they can."

As Jace trod off, he looked about the meadow in terms of some attack. Trees might break a charge. He thought of the bazaar's total lack of defenses. Perhaps they could be persuaded that a wall of great blocks could be erected, like those circles of blue stones on the wide plains. His warriors were strong and could easily build it. It would keep them active and fed. Mayhaps he should talk to Mayor Sandor about this?

Sunsinking, then gloaming, as the fires about camp flared up. Small groups of his centaurs were bedding down, getting the first quiet sleep in a long time. Had Garrison set night sentries? Jace did not even have to ask. As he trod down on his sinister hoof, pain shot up his leg. That familiar ache was coming back as Merdi's magic herb cakes wore off. No cure then. He might be without pain as long as he could afford the herbalist's medicine, but how long would that be?

Group headed his way. Jace braced himself. The bright yellow blaze that was Deadrick, huge Two Spot, golden Ardon and blue-roan hided Lerestra, some of the Regiment's best. Probably coming to ask for their final portions.

Only Lerestra briefly bowed his head respectfully when they reached him, "Sir."

Jace returned the nod formally.

Anger flashed in Deadrick's eyes. "We are not a regiment. Not even a troop. We have nay 'Sirs,'" A throw of his head indicated the meadow. "This is where your leadership has gotten us."

"We are alive," Lerestra spoke calmly, showing he was unafraid of Deadrick. "We have done well in the past."

Two Spot ignored them. "We need to start again. Jace, ye have a plan?"

Deadrick stomped his front hoof. "This is the plan. We take this bazaar. We will have food, coin, armor, shes..."

"Shes who will cut your throat, when you fall off to sleep?" Jace shook his tail. "Armor too small for our size, but then you will have slain the metalsmith, so he can not fix it. Coin, we will have lots. But where do we spend it? We are outlawed in the Orange and Empire. If we wash our tails in merchants blood if we dishonor a Trade Truce, who will deal with us? We do not attack this Bazaar."

A mutinous Deadrick looked from Two Spot to Lerestra who would not meet his eyes.

Two Spot shifted his huge hooves uneasily. "We are down to what? Old Urzi with his limping leg? A wild wing of fighting females? Sandi, Willow, Reet...."

"They can fight, especially Sandi." Lerestra pointed out.

Two Spot spat to the earth. "We are not the Regiment–we are a tribe, wandering with younglings and elders, with nay portions in sight."

"Is that it?" Jace calmly ask, even with his anger seething inside. He continued firmly. "We will nay be robbers. We will re-arm. We will find a commission either here or when I say we move on."

"To the Imperial?" Asked Two Spot.

"It is being considered."

"How long do we stay at a dry hole?" Deadrick asked angrily.

"That I will decide or your next leader if you chose another."

They stood not speaking, unwilling to be openly defiant. As usual, Jace preferred to take the hurdle straight ahead. "Deadrick, we need strength. You will recruit for us from the bazaar." Deadrick glared at him. Jace continued. "Whoever leads will need more sword arms."

"And what about old Urzi?" Two Spot queried. "What will ye do about him? Short of strength, we can not carry a limping oldster."

Jace coolly stared up at Two Spot's eyes. Would he dare to bring up Jace's own injury? Deadrick seemed to be silently urging Two Spot forward, but the huge centaur dropped his eyes first. "Ye say we must be strong."

Lerestra glanced at Jace. "It is a decision that does not have to be made this night." Then Lerestra turned tail and trod off, and Two Spot followed. Deadrick finding himself alone, moved away.

Jace took another deep drink of Sandi's comforting

leaf brew. It had cooled and tasted uncomfortably sharp. If he searched for a commission too long, perhaps it would be just him and Urzi. Feeling tired, he stamped down a grass circle for a badly needed night's sleep. Jace had just folded his great legs under him and rolled on to the earth when to his surprise Sandi was cantering over to him. "My lady, me thought you would be in the bushes standing much, much longer?"

"Axel said he wished me to go into the woods and show him berries."

"And?"

She lowered herself to the ground near Jace. "He is still there, studying the berries."

Laughing deeply, Jace rolled himself closer to her. Putting his arms around her shoulders. She looked so hurt, he leaned forward and kissed the nape of her neck. At that Sandi started to laugh too, as she rolled her warm flanks against him. Jace had mounted Sandi a time or two himself and well knew Axel definitely missed a wild opportunity to learn about life. He would have to speak to that youngling.

Chapter Three

Fine Wares,

Fine Price

Dealer of the Headlands Bazaar

With sun almost over the trees, Jace hauled himself up on stiff legs. That deep, cursed pain was back. Trying not to limp too openly in front of the others, he reached down to pull on his travel harness. It seemed so heavy this morn. With effort, he started slinging it up on his back as Sandi loped up.

"I stuck Willow's face pan under that plump bird yesterday. I will render out some of the fat and this morn the colts, and I will be greasing our harnesses. I will do yours and mend that cut strap."

Undecided Jace looked at her. That harness held pretty much all he had left, long sword, grooming brushes, bow, drinking horn, personal pouches–the few items he had managed to hang on to all these ages.

She knew what was on his mind. "If we have to cut and run, your harness will be on my back."

Jace looked down at the worn leather straps with their stained iron rings and bulky pouches. Not much to show for a lifetime of tramping, but all he had. He dropped it to the ground with a clanking of loose metal. "If you have to cut, just run bareback out of here. That is an order! We will find better harnesses elsewhere." From the pile of leather, Jace untied his two long strap pouches. The short sword one went over the sword arm shoulder, as uncommonly he wielded his sword with his sinister arm. The personal pouch with drinking horn he slung over his withers.

"Here." Sandi handed him a bulging leather coin bag, four times the weight of his own. "The others volunteered."

"Volunteered?" At the end of her sword no doubt.

"Saw the wisdom of pooling our metal to give our representative something to parley with. You can treat the locals to brew until their tongues loosen or buy more of your endless maps."

"I am trying to get some charts." He untied his pouch and put her heavy sack in. "The others, do they want to fight on? Break up?"

"There are some, like Deadrick's tail mates, that talk of great prizes and ventures."

"Taking the bazaar by force?"

"Hungry centaurs will listen when there is nothing else."

"Aye."

"Is there someone in the bazaar who can help your leg?"

Most would not have dared say that to him. He felt his face flushing in anger but Sandi just calmly stared up at him.

He hesitated before answering. "An herbalist has pain cakes. He says I am beset by the spirit of the last fool I killed."

"That herbalist is the fool."

"Still his yellow cakes take the pain away."

A huge black and white hide loomed over Sandi. "Jace and I are going to the Bazaar–it is my first!"

She smiled at his unabashed eagerness. "Axel, you will not fit your huge flanks on their narrow pathways."

"Then I will kick them bigger!" Resting on his front legs, Axel kicked out playfully with his hindquarters.

"Jace," Sandi shook her head ruefully, "teach this rough meadow muffin the ways of the civilized."

"Impossible task, my lady," said Jace with a smile.

Axel only smiled wider at their teasing, showing even white teeth. "Are you coming with us, Sandi?"

"And who will scrub the cooking pots?" She glanced at Axel's ill-fitting harness, picked up in his first battle from its late, much smaller owner. "If we have some time here, and you can get me some decent tanned leather for strapping, mayhaps I can make that harness almost fit you."

"Jace hunts us a fat commission. We will soon have riches, and I will have a truly great harness made! I will pay your son Kent to tool it with fine designs."

Sandi gave Jace a wry look, but he noted her tail lifted proudly. "Hunt well for us, Jace."

At the gateway to camp Garrison joined Jace and Axel.

"Going cross the river?" Jace asked.

"Aye."

"How stand we?"

"Almost everybody has at least one sword or knife. A lot had their carry harnesses on in battle, but a third do not have shields. Half have nay helmets. The loss of our cook cart cost us our stew pots, kettles, and water kegs. Not many arrows, but this is fine because not many have bows..."

"And not much coin to buy more. Mayhaps we can trade hauling boulders, building a defense for the bazaar?"

Garrison shook his grizzled head as they started down the hill to the river. "They will not realize the danger until their throats are being cut."

Jace ordered, "Search for weapons we can buy. All need a long sword and a shield. If we get a commission, it will have to have an advance...."

As they headed out of the river, Garrison was looking to Axel who was staring at each stall and colorful banner. "Is this your first bazaar?"

"Is it like a harvest fair? Where one trades an excess of wheat for an overage of apples?"

Jace nodded. "More like a gathering, where you would make up shields and try to trade them for arrows. Only gatherings are just held on the five seasons. This, I suspect, is here all the time."

"How do they find their food?"

"Others fish or hunt and bring it here to trade," Garrison explained.

Axel looked down the beach at the line of stalls. "They have no defenses."

Garrison nodded. "A bazaar is protected by Truce of Trade. All who would steal or attack a bazaar must be resisted by everyone."

"This works?"

"Most times," Jace replied.

Axel could only stare in amazement. "Look at the bright red banners and the blue-green. What crushed leaves gives these colors?"

"They also make dyes from shellfish or crushed rocks." Explained Jace.

Frowning, Garrison pointed out. "This is a permanent gathering and obviously an old one, one that is well known in the area. Yet look to the Orange and the mountains. Nay tracks."

Jace nodded. "There is a well-worn trail to the foothills from Black with no fresh droppings. And on the other side to the Green, I see nay tracks."

Garrison nodded his tail and still looking back the way they had come. "It is strange that there seems to be so little traffic. I asked about in the bazaar. All I got were averted eyes."

"We are strangers to them."

" We tramped on an ancient trail from the Purple. It was also overgrown. Unusual for such a large bazaar."

Jace looked over his shoulder at the undisturbed sand drifts. That was uncommon. A problem that his warriors could correct? Without being impolite, he must find out more from the merchants.

The trail split here. Merchants to the side around the beach, and the other merchants on either side of the curving trail that led up the mound. Garrison halted before an armorer. "Good sir, that helm in the back. The large one. Might I heft it?"

If Garrison was beginning negotiating, that could take until sunsink. Sometimes Jace thought that merchants would just hand an item to Garrison just to stop the endless haggling. Jace nodded his tail toward Axel. "We will go on without you."

Absorbed in his bargaining, Garrison only absently nodded his tail, as Jace and Axel took the upper trail. Here the pathways were narrower. Some of the careless merchants had allowed their baskets to encroach on the path. Looking up at Jace and Axel's huge size, they hastily began pulling those baskets back from possible damage.

Axel stopped before a plank set with trays of baked fruits, covered with tents of white gauze. Before he could move forward, Jace held up a hand and spoke lowly. "All here is for a price. Even the attention of the ladies."

Axel looked shocked. "Shes wish coin to...?"

"Aye. Some of them do." Jace smiled grimly. "Ask first."

"There is a fine sword."

"And the dealer will only have a few, but look about first. Question the price. Offer less than you want to pay. Pace yourself–there is more to come."

They passed the first few planks smelling kegs of a beer seller, smells of baked pastry sweets and stinks of sweaty hides. The trail split again and started to climb again.

Axel trod toward a dealer with baskets of arrows. As he did, he carelessly raised his tail and dropped huge plops of dung on the trail. Jace winced. He should have warned Axel and the other rawer recruits not to go messing the bazaar trails. An older centauress behind Axel radiated outrage, but the arrowsmith ahead only saw a potential customer and hauled his larger arrows forward.

Jace pulled closer to Axel, saying in an undertone. "Nay dunging on their trails."

Axel had stiffened, his nose high to the air. Jace raised his head and smelled it too, as a pretty, giggling, full-bodied she hurried down the trail. She was ready, they could smell it.

She looked long in Axel's eyes as she brushed past. Chestnut hair and tail, neat white stockings and a come-hither look over her pale shoulder.

Axel looked at Jace. "Do they charge for just smelling?"

"Nay."

"For walking after her and watching her haunches rise?"

"Nay."

Axel smiled. "Mayhaps I shall see you later."

It was a mistake, but even the biggest colt must learn. Jace trod upwards alone, studying the various banners and pennants over the stalls. Picture of fruit, outsized leather pouches, thrust spears trumped their wares. As Jace headed up he was passing another armorer, here with a yellow standard, he noted Per Ben's pale gray, barrel stomach and stout legs and Reet, his she and his match, ever beside him. Her full face shrewdly studied the merchandise. Trust them to be the first out of camp to hunt bargains. Jace had to side step to get around Reet. He addressed the dealer, who sat with his legs bent beneath him. "Sir, may I heft yon shield?"

The sour-faced armorer looked up from the sword he was sharpening and smiled thinly at three possible patrons. "Fine price for fine work."

Jace nodded. The shield of oak wood had an iron capped center with a solid leather arm hold. A good, solid thickness, crafted for a smaller centaur then his size, but better than a bare arm.

He passed it to Per Ben who slipped his arm in the leather strap behind it, hefting it as he asked, "Do you smith to order?"

"Aye. But the best work takes time. That is twenty pieces silver." Seeing Per Ben not too receptive to that, the merchant rose and rummaged through his stacks, pulling out a brass-studded wood rectangle painted with a faded red border. "Here, look at this. More to your girth."

The armorer handed him the larger rectangle, paint scraped and sword scarred, but still solid. The dealer nodded. Seeing interest in Jace's stance, he was encouraged. "Better price, even if it not just birthed and shiny."

Per Ben bargained briefly and bought it. Jace nodded, the low price showed that the lightness of their money bags must be showing. Later as they walked away, Per Ben pointed out in an undertone, "Mayhaps, we should trim our beards, before they offer us alms?"

Later, camp at sunsink seemed as before: warriors sharpening their swords, joking, settling into bedding areas. Willow's young colt grabbed a wooden toy from his sister and galloped before her screams of rage. As ever, peacemaker Urzi limped between him and the screaming little she. He quieted things by offering a scrap of cloth for her to run with. As a dozen campfires crackled under turning meat, Jace signaled for Ardon to join him. When the deep amber hided centaur trotted up, Jace said, "We need to call a drum."

Ardon smiled crookedly. "Our drums are smoke now."

"Have you your ram's horn to blow?"

"Lost in battle, sir–but I can herald quite loudly."

Jace nodded his tail. Ardon loped off to holler out before each group. Soon an inner ring of the females and shorter warriors formed, with the others striding into a large ring beyond it. Jace waited patiently for the drum to form. Finally, he spoke, "Most of you have been to the Bazaar." Jace smiled. "Fine drink. Pretty shes."

"Some nicely flanked hes." Piped up Sandi. The others laughed appreciatively.

Jace nodded. "But soon we must move out. In the past we could commission armor to be hammered out for all us. Now we must replace what we can from this bazaar stocks..."

"Should we?" Wheat hollered from the back. "Or is the Regiment finished?"

Silence from the group. Jace would have hoped for a few 'Nays' from the back, but they all seemed to be waiting to hear from him. "Not if we wish it."

Two Spot resounded deeply, from the back. "Have you a patron for us?"

"Not yet."

"But there is a chance?"

"Aye. I am looking at several opportunities. We may get a hire here, we may provision and move on."

"What of our shares from the last battles?" Someone called from the back. Another cried out, "We have no weapons. No patron. There is nothing!"

Jace looked down, then straightened his shoulders.

"Your shares were lost with the carts. We start from the grass. You have what you carry on your harnesses—it is the same for all of us."

"No metal was saved?"

"A bit, but the Regiment will need that for food and carts..."

"That should be paid for by the patron." Wheat objected.

Deadrick had trod into the ring. "Mayhaps if we had another leader?"

Chapter Four

Will He Attack?

Watch The Narrowing of His Eyes

The Lift of his Tail

Orson of Danbar

There was silence. In the twilight, Deadrick's eyes were shadows. Would he fight? Jace asked outright. "Do you challenge?"

Deadrick stopped. His golden hide and white stocking legs gleaming in the firelight. "You have no patron! We have no trail to follow! Mayhaps others will wish another leader, one who has lost us less."

No murmuring among the others. They were waiting for Jace to say something. Before he could, Ardon weighed in. "We are barely armed, let us not fight among ourselves."

"Aye." Garrison pronounced. "Give Jace time to feel the firmness of the land. He has led well for us in the past. He will find a rich trail again."

Seeing his triumph lost, Deadrick called out. "This bazaar is rich. It is defenseless !"

Silence. The audacity of breaking a Truce of Trade shocked them. Not many wanted to be thought of as a total outlaw.

If Deadrick imagined the others would demand his leadership, he was mistaken. Nervously he pranced in place, his hooves giving hollow thuds on the grass.

Jace nodded with his tail. "I will seek a patron for us. Ardon, the Regimental funds will pay for a ram's horn to summon us to battle. Urzi, how are the battle drums coming?"

The old warrior nodded. " I have bought some better-tanned skin from the bazaar."

"The rest of you, we must hoard our metal carefully, until we once again are commissioned. Prepare as best you can spend what you have on shields, spears, swords. Some carry harness repairs can be done in camp. Grooming can be done in camp. We hunt our meat and eat it here. Soon the Regiment will march again." Jace nodded and moved off, only to stumble slightly as his back hoof painfully hit a sharp rock. Silently he cursed the fact that the rest saw.

At the grayness of sunrise, Jace's pained hindquarters made further rest impossible. He opened Merdi's small box. Only a few pain cakes left. He chewed one and some of the cold meat from the night before. It would leave pain but stretch out his cakes. Leaving his harness behind, he left camp and trod down to the river, dropped his carry pouches and rolling in the water, washed off the dust and cooling his back leg.

When the Bazaar came alive, he trod up the trail to Var-tee's plank. The old merchant smiled to see him. "I have some scrolls that might please ye."

"Good."

Var-tee again had three scrolls. The first, an old rendering of a huge bazaar. "This was what we once looked like. Hundreds of stalls. Caravans from all the directions."

Jace studied it. "What happened?"

"The tide comes up fully, then it recedes..." He was unrolling another scroll. This one caught Jace's interest. "This is of the caravan trail, the one that goes Yellow over desert and mountain."

It was a fanciful piece. Elaborately painted with sea monsters to the sinister and strange two-headed beasties, mingling with local game that Jace had observed. A line of blue dots indicated the river that separated his camp from the bazaar. Further along the trail, Jace could see other ovals, painted in blue dots. "Are these watering holes?"

Var-tee held the scroll farther from his eyes. "I think so." He squinted at it. "Aye. That one closest to us is Inda's pond. Sweetwater. The others, I can not vouch for. I was foaled in the high grasses by the sea, and I have never roamed farther."

The third scroll may have been a detailed map of something, but Jace could not figure out what or where. He and Var-tee settled in for some haggling over the second scroll. Jace had the impression that Var-tee more enjoyed the haggling ritual, then he did the actual sale.

Jace looked down at his newly purchased chart. "You call this bazaar the...?"

"Bazaar at the Headlands."

Jace looked about the stalls around him. "Do you have a burnt stick?"

"Burned...oh, to place your marks on the scroll?"

Jace nodded.

"I have much better." Var-tee rummaged in a basket near his shelves. "You mark with charcoal stick and ink?"

"Aye."

"The black-burn stick blows away, the ink pots eventually spill in your pouches."

"Aye."

"Try this, good sir." Var-tee took out a thin, dark, straight twig shape and handed it to Jace. "Tis dug near here in the Black mountains and pressed into sticks. Rub it on the scroll."

Jace did. A dark line appeared.

Var-tee took his finger forward. "You can rub some of

it off, but it stays much longer than charcoal."

And it was much easier than trying to spit on an ink stick and pull out a brush, Jace had to admit. If he had known about this stick, he would have tried to get it included in the scroll negotiations. As it was, he had to start bargaining with Var-tee again. "This piece is dusty, and it blackens my fingers. You can not wish much for such a worthless ..."

After Var-tee, Jace loped up to Mayor Sandor's plank. This sun he ordered only one horn full. A cheap, sweetly-sour drink that drowned the dust nicely.

"What think ye of our bazaar?"

"Very fine indeed."

"Aye."

Jace took a deep sip. Sandor was busy with many customers, many of them Jace's warriors. Still, Jace waited patiently for his chance. Finally, the others moved on, and Sandor seemed mellowed. "What is this talk of raiders?"

Sandor lowered his eyes to the empty rundlet he was cleaning with sand. "There are always robbers, but they are beyond the Bazaar."

"Still, it saps your patronage..."

When the Sandor did not answer Jace continued. "You are 'Mayor.' Is there a council that runs this Bazaar?"

"Aye, a few of us keep order."

"My Regiment could roust out your troublemakers..." said Jace casually.

Sandor looked up at him. "I will speak with them about yer offer." He looked to two locals coming up to his plank. "Red-tail and Lucan, what have ye today?"

Jace could not stand and drink all sun, he started back down the mound. Ardon's light hide approached.

"Did you find a ram's horn for the Regimental calls?"

Ardon held up a white, brown-speckled oval, larger

than two hands, with a twisted pink lip on its side.

"What is it?"

"A seashell here they use it for horns." Ardon raised it to his mouth and blew, a strong, musical blast.

Not as powerful as a curling ram's horn, but Jace nodded his tail. "It will do for a while. See if it lasts tied to your bouncing carry harness."

Leaving Ardon behind, Jace stepped to the herbalist's enclosure. It was empty, Merdi was somewhere else. He needed more pain cakes, but not this sun.

The cooling river water helped the heat of his pained hoof. Still, the pain was increasing. Back in camp, he half limped back to his carry harness. It was newly oiled, and two of straps had been repaired by Sandi. Pulling out his pouch, he dug out the wooden box of yellow cakes. He swallowed one whole. Then chewed another bitter one. And waited. For a time that pain stayed, briefly seemed to increase, then to his relief, it receded like a slow tide.

Before the cakes, he felt tired and defeated, but once the pain was gone, Jace brightened up. Aye, his Regiment was beaten down, but it would rise again. He would find them a patron. Head held proudly Jace moved to put back the potion packet, then stopped and carefully counted. Only four bitter cakes left. He had to get more. Aye, soon he would be spending his last coin to get relief.

Wheat trotted towards him. "Sir. Dust to the Blue, headed this way. Many hooves or carts."

Frowning Jace pivoted and followed Wheat back to the trees. Was this the marauders the locals spoke of? He asked Wheat. "Could it be dust from a herd stampede?"

"Seems too narrow to be a ranging herd. Mayhaps a column coming in?"

Jace and Wheat galloped through the tree line to the

highest ridge, joining Garrison where they could see the river below with the colored tents of the bazaar to the White of them. Across the river to the Yellow, was a beaten trail leading over low foothills. Beyond that must be sand and scrub growth rocks, that was where the column of dust came closer, something big coming in steadily, in a narrow formation. They stood watching as it drew closer.

"Those robbers they fear?" Asked Garrison.

"You would think as they got closer to Bazaar they would pick up the pace to a charge." Wheat noted.

Jace gave a long look across the river. "Nobody is setting up battle lines in front of the Bazaar."

Garrison swatted horse flies with his tail. "I have noticed some extra activity. The merchants coming down and seem to be watching." Garrison shifted his haunches uneasily. "Should I order harnesses on?"

"Aye. Right now, our dusty friends are upwind of us. Probably will not even know we are here if you can keep the camp quiet." Jace looked to his other centaurs, now drifting out of the bushes. He commanded Blue Horn, "Return to Camp! Spread it on!" On tight hindquarters, he rotated to Garrison and Wheat. "Keep them quiet. Set sentries. Keep them armed but behind the bushes." He looked about quickly. Kear, there was barely larger than a normal centaur. Just the two of them would not stand out too much. "Kear, come with me. We need a better place to spy."

Garrison turned and was off in a bound. Kear followed down as Jace cantered through reeds into the chilling river.

It was narrower here and deeper with a bit of a current to push at their flanks, but nothing Jace could not handle, even with his weakened hindquarters. On the muddy bank, they slowed and loped to the edge of the Bazaar, where a flatten trail indifferently marked with small boulders headed

Blue into the short hills. Beyond those hills, they could see that faint column of dust drawing ever closer.

Jace scanned the locals. Some of the upper trail merchants had come out to the outer ring and were just pacing back and forth. The edge merchants were straightening their goods as they glanced to the inland road expectantly. Again Jace wondered if the Bazaar set watchers about. No one was doing anything outwardly different, but all seemed alert with noses pointed to the rocky ridges.

Jace saw a plank vendor placing out his drink drums. A good view of the trail was what they needed. To Kear, he muttered, "Make your drinks last."

Kear answered with a bare swing of his tail as Jace led him to the beer merchant's weathered plank. Taking out metal from the Regimental pouch of Sandi's Jace said, "Good sir, we wish a raw ale for myself and my friend. What is your best priced?"

"Bitter berry? Honeyed brew?" Asked the merchant looking to the distant dust.

"Bitter stout."

"You might wish to try this Orange Rain." Jace nodded, and the beer merchant poured a stingy sip for him to taste. Nothing for Kear.

The pouring color was dark amber that foamed high. It tasted fruity and bitter and quickly numbed the tongue. "What for a full horn?"

"Quarter of a copper. It is kettle brewed." The merchant said, while still looking to the hills.

Jace nodded and placed a full copper on the plank as he held out his horn. Kear also held out his to be filled. The plank merchant poured Jace to two thumb's worth below the rim, but his attention seemed focused on the deeply worn trail between the short hills. Kear looked to Jace who waited a bit before speaking. "My comrade's too."

The merchant looked back at them and shook his head. "Pardons, sirs." He poured more generously into Kear's drinking horn, but still, his attention seemed totally consumed by the empty trail.

As Jace and Kear idly discussed the charms of various ladies, Jace studied the merchants out of the corner of his eye. He and Kear might as well not be speaking, for all the attention the plank merchant paid them. This worthy had a tail raised excitedly as he moved his stock about, first setting one keg on the plank, then replacing it with another. Yet the eagerness for new metal seemed to be balanced by the worried lines deepening in his face. He had fished out a heavy looking leather pouch, deeply hidden, and was tying it around his waist. Preparations to run? What was coming over those hills?

The sun slipped over the high hurdle and Jace ordered another round as the dust column grew closer. The other merchants slowly gathering down here also seemed to be a strange mixture of anticipation and anxiety. As Jace paid for two more sudsy refills, he raised his foaming drinking horn. "To the Regiment!" Kear followed suit with his.

Jace had been making a show of drinking, but to stretch it out, he only sipped the dark, bitter brew. Not that even the beer merchant seemed to notice and his throat had quickly tired of the bitter brew. This was not at all like the superior stuff of Sandor's. He followed the brew seller's eyes as the dust column drew closer. Mayhaps he could get this worthy talking? "We be of Thunderhoof Regiment. I be Jace. This is my comrade, Kear."

The brew seller seemed embarrassed by his lack of hospitality. "Coalman is my name."

Kear innocently asked. "Good, sir. What comes over

yon hill?"

"Could be the caravan from the plains of Laurel. They were expected foal-moon. It might be them." Coleman looked away. Jace noted a slight trembling in the brew sellers flanks. He seemed to be too nervous for just a caravan coming in.

The dust column beyond the ridge was now a dirty brown cloud, growing bigger as it drew closer. More merchants had come to the outer edge, and Jace looked up then inwardly groaned. Massive Two Spot, the biggest centaur in the Regiment, was coming down the bazaar trail. He stopped and brightened to see his comrades. "Jace. Kear."

Curse it. Brown and white Two Spot would stand out like a woolly mammoth, but it would better to keep him with them then have him lead the way to their camp. "Merchant, I buy my friend a drink."

Two Spot grinned widely and fished for his equally huge drinking horn. "Did ye see that pretty groomer Laurel? To be chasing her tail across the meadow."

Jace and Kear laughed appreciatively.

They could have dropped the old friends show for the beer merchant's sake, his whole attention was now focused tightly on that notch in the short hills as that dust column drew closer.

As Jace ordered a fifth round, and a fifth and sixth for Two Spot, over the ridge came two dark, high stepping centaurs. They marched alongside each other. They had gravy-brown skin and hide with black hair and tails. Smaller than average for male centaurs, but build strong, with solid muscular legs and arms. Short, powerful hindquarters marched in unison.

The first pair were followed by two other centaurs, harnessed to a two-wheel cart piled high with bundles. The cart's wheels were high for rolling over rough trails. The cart's contents--something covered with fur–nay–oiled cloth, were tightly tied down. In unity each pair of centaurs stepped, each sword-hoof falling to the same beat. Even the pairs' distance from the two pullers before remained the same.

As the first cart wheeled down the trail, a second pair of centaurs were high steeping over the crest pulling another high piled cart. They were followed by cart after cart. Jace had to admire the martial discipline, as each pair maintained the same set distance as the first. All at a steady, strong trot. From the approach of that dust cloud, they must have been doing this since sunrise, yet there was not a bit of stain foam on their withers. What a disciplined march line.

All had long dark hair and tails and walked with the same tight movements.

Kear raised his drinking horn, covering his mouth as he spoke. "Want me to trot over and greet them?"

"They might not like that." Jace scanned the identical hooked swords they carried on both sides of their withers. He looked back at the merchants at the edge. "I do not see any of these others scurrying over." Taking a drink, Jace returned to studying the high stepping cart pullers. All smelled as males.

"All of them are armed," Kear noted.

"Short swords and spears."

"How many carts?"

"Eleven, twelve...thirteen...more kept coming." Two guards ranging free at the rear like those in front.

Even with their destination in sight, these disciplined ones kept a steady, measured pace. He noticed the leader raise a hand and they all seem to halt as one. Probably at the sight of his big breeds standing ahead of them caused some concern. The leader paced forward and back. Trying to smell out any danger?

After a long haul, Jace expected them to come right up

to the bazaar's edge and get a drink, greet friends, offer goods. Instead, the seeming leader loped in a large oval over a flat piece of ground, while the second, front centaur stood on stiffly spread legs, staring at the bazaar probably directly at Two Spot and Jace.

When the leader rejoined his second, they both stared briefly in Jace's direction, then apparently decided all was well. The leader did a silent lift, then sideswipe of his tail. Still, in march line, the cart pullers seemed set on following his footprints, as they circled their carts in an oval. They were obviously setting up a tight, defensible camp. Again, as a unit, they stopped, Waited and only dropped their cart pull harnesses together. At once the heavily loaded two-wheeled carts listed forward, landing on their pull tongue.

An excited buzz came from the bazaar. More dealers were coming down, obviously eager to be first to the goods but holding back. These new caravaners were unharnessing, digging several fire pits, generally setting up camp. Two or four at a time, found a dirt spot and rolled on their backs, legs kicking high. Obviously relaxing stiff pulling muscles, drying wet hides and getting off the bugs took precedence to the dealers waiting.

Any of those sun-browned centaurs would have been welcomed in Jace's Regiment. They were short but tough and disciplined. Ones with carts piled so high obviously had need of guarding but looked like they were used to handling protection themselves.

The lead Centaur was cantered up to where Jace stood drinking. His black hair and tail were worn long but tightly bound with black beaded cords. He had a slight slant to his yellow eyes. Halting two lopes away, he called out loudly to all. "We break our fast, then open to buyers or sellers!"

Nodding and low talk from the merchants waiting.

This was expected. They knew it looked like a long wait, but none wanted to leave and give an advantage to his rivals.

Still studying Two Spot and Jace, the lead caravaner trotted over to the plank. The beer merchant looked faintly surprised when the head caravaner stopped before him.

Dark skin politely nodded. "Coalman, a pour, if you please."

Obviously, it was not a regular request, Coalman querying. "What wish you?"

The headman had not taken his eyes off Jace and Two Spot. "What do these fine sirs have?"

Jace smiled. "Oak brew, dark and tart. He calls it "Orange Rain." Washes the dust from the throat." Jace chanced he might step on some local taboo, but he held out his drinking horn. "Taste mine before you chose."

A hesitation, then the yellow-eyed, dark-skinned caravaner reached a solid, muscular arm for Jace's drinking horn. He took a sip and then he returned it smiling.

"They have not taken the stinger out. Yes. I would like some of that pour."

The merchant poured, without waiting for coin. The caravaner obviously had credit. Mayhaps an expected order the caravan was bringing?

The caravaner took a deep drink, then looked up at Jace. "I be Tar-bel. We run a caravan from the Plains of Laurel. I do not think I have seen ye here before. Are ye dealers?"

"Nay." Jace doubted that the local politeness code would authorize such bald questioning, but you do not get commissions unless they know who you are. "I be Jace of Thunderhoof Regiment." He did not incline his head to give the location of the others.

The caravaner crinkled his forehead, glancing from

Two Spot to Kear. "Regiment?" It seemed a word he knew not.

Jace enlightened him. "We are a traveling troop of mercenaries that offer our swords and protections to our lieges."

Tar-bel's face hardened. "What if one does not wish to purchase your services?"

"Then we find someone else, elsewhere. There is always those who want a well-trained force."

"Have you taken over this Bazaar?"

"Nay. None ask for our services here, yet. We will rest and look over the wares, then if we find nothing, we will move on."

Not even pretending to drink, Tar-bel studied Jace, evidently not quite believing what he was hearing. Then, curse it, the wind changed, blowing from trees across the river. Jace indicated Tar-bel's band. "Those carts look well loaded. Have you traveled far?"

"From the Plains of Laurel, two full-faced moon's march from here."

"Do you sell charts or maps?"

"Nay." A fast, frosted answer. Tar-bel did not want anyone knowing his routes.

With the wind came the smell of a large body of centaurs and their camp cooking. It must be hitting Tar-bel. He was already letting his gaze wander to the river and trees beyond.

One of Tar-bels own trotted up, probably his second in command. He was almost identical to Tar-bel, but with an upper arm bound in cloth wrappings. A nasty gash oozed as it healed on his flank. The second caravaner kept his face and tone flat as he spoke in an unhurried fashion to his leader. "*Strong scent. Across River. Many in the woods. Do we arm?*"

Even while obviously listening, Tar-bel had turned his eyes to continue to study Jace.

These caravaners were speaking a dialect of Hami that Jace was familiar with, that probably no one else in the Bazaar knew. Coleman certainly looked on with puzzled curiosity. Jace could keep quiet and have the advantage of secretly knowing their tongue, but he decided it would be better to take the hurdle straight on. He answered back in Hami, *"No need. The scents are of my companions. We are not robbers."* Then he lifted his drinking horn to take a sip.

The second caravaner started to instinctively reach for his sword. His leader raised a staying hand. Shifting position of his forelegs, Tar-bel's eyebrows and tail lifted. "You speak Hamish, Jace of Thunderhoof?"

Jace finished his sip first. "Poorly."

"What did ye say?" Two Spot demanded of Jace.

"They catch our prodigious aroma and are concerned. I explained we are not robbers and we are not hiding. We camp in the meadow beyond the river."

"Aye." Tar-bel squinted towards the trees across the river. "That is a good place to camp. We prefer open lands, where we see all who come close."

"Your friend..?"

"Eli?"

"Eli, you have some grievous wounds. I have heard the lands about are dangerous..."

Eil evidently understood Jace's words, but he only looked to Tar-bel, who cut off further comment by dryly saying, "The desert has many stingers and serpents."

Jace nodded.

When Tar-bel spoke again, he spoke very carefully. "Pardon if I offend, but in these lands, there are robbers who prey on the caravans. If they wish to hire ye?"

"We chose who we fight for. It has never been for rabble."

Tar Bel still stared, then made his judgment and spoke to his second in Hamish, *"Accept them as peaceful. Continue.".* Eli promptly trotted away. To Jace, Tar-bel politely nodded speaking in trade. "May your trail be high." then he briskly trotted off to rejoin his encampment.

Kear spoke lowly. "I see bandaging on some of the others. Jace, ye should have pressed more about those wounds."

Two Spot spat on the earth. "That might be a discourtesy they would not pardon."

Jace moved away from the brew plank. Kear and Two Spot followed his lead. A purple parley standard was being planted in the caravan camp. Dealers from the Bazaar trotted, then loped as a mass to be the first to see the contents of the baskets being unloaded from the carts. "Two Spot, go back to camp. Tell Garrison the caravaners seem no threat, but post at least one guard watching in their direction."

"Aye."

"Kear." Jace fished out some small coins from the Regimental pouch and slipped them into his hand. "Trot over to that camp. See how they are dealing. What weapons they might trade. Mayhaps treat one of the caravaners to a few drinks. See what you can learn."

Kear nodded as he managed to join four dealers hurrying over to the camp.

The pain in his hindquarters growing greater, Jace took a lope over to the Yellow side of the Bazaar. Merdi was scraping snake skins outside his tent. He looked up to Jace with a sad smile, then turned and opened his tent flap. Jace moved inside, again chaffing at the confinement of Merdi's tiny stall.

"Good trails, sir. Did the cakes aid you?" Asked Merdi hopefully.

"Aye. They stopped the pain...for a time."

Merdi was running probing fingers down Jace's hind leg. "Warm. Still swelling."

"The pain grows."

Merdi did not meet his eyes. "You do not wish the leg removed?"

"Nay. The pain cakes, will they heal?"

"Mayhaps."

Jace reached into his pouch for a small gold nugget and held it out. "For this, how many cakes?"

"Sir, too many of these doses will kill you, you understand this?"

"Aye." He was dead if he could not walk, he would be dead if he took the pills. Jace held the gold over Merdi's plank

But the herbalist was continuing in a low voice. "The pulp of the sleeping red flower is very powerful, for is coiled with a strong spirit. This spirit grows as you chew more potions. First, this spirit will take over your dreams, then it may take over you."

Jace placed the gold down.

Outside, Jace breathed in the salt spray and shook off the confinement of Merdi's tent. As he strode back to the lanes climbing the bazaar, baskets of peppers and onions spilled out onto the narrow path blocking his way. This whole bazaar was too cramping for one of his size but where else would his warriors go? No commissions were forthcoming here. Follow Tar-bel? Caravaners always wound up in some sort of a gathering or bazaar. They needed buyers for their goods, but Jace suspected having his hungry looking troopers following his tail was the last thing Tar-bel would wish.

The groomers Laurel and Honey were doing a great business trimming the beards and tails of Abel and Snake. With the she's slender, strong fingers caressing their flanks both hardened warriors were smiling quite contentedly. Yes, it was too long from a decent rest, but his were running through their metal much too fast. Where would they go to get another commission? Could he cut a decent deal with the Imperial? Doubtful. They would all be next to slaves.

Raised voices reached his ears, and Jace straightened his back. Screams of rage, anger. The Dealer nearest him grabbed her hair ornaments, and jeweled hoof picks to hide them. Others topped their baskets as two wild-eyed centauresses raced past Jace.

That deep, distant, outraged bellowing sounded familiar.

Jace trotted to it.

It was not far. Curious others clogged the lanes. Jace had to push past them, and his size won out. In the group just watching were Nighthawk, Wheat, and Ardon while some locals and his troopers were placing bets. Jace used his great weight to shove the hocks of the final hes in front of him, pushing further through.

In the center was a great flash of red hair and red hide. Rufus! Four dealer stalls were already trampled with their merchants just cowered against the crowd. Huge Rufus held on to a struggling, screaming she by her thick hair braid, while with his other massive hand he had a stranglehold on the throat of a purple-faced male he was forcing down on all four knees.

Jace yelled, "Report!"

"Sir." Rufus looked to him, drawing both his victims lower to the ground like straw stuffed pells. "She steals from me! She and her villainous he took me gold nuggets!"

"Release her." Using her hair as a handle, Rufus thrust the she toward Jace. The red-faced centauress was thrown down on her knees before Jace.

Instead of appreciating how close to death she was, the centauress rose in high indignation, loudly bewailing her mistreatment. "I be Amber. This is my...mate, Slate." she indicated the terrified, white-eyed small male pinned at Rufus' other side. Amber pointed to Rufus. "He gave me the necklace! He gave it willingly!"

"The necklet? That string of gold nuggets as thick as my knuckles that Rufus wears on his chest?" Jace asked unbelievingly. Rufus was known for his tightness with metal. "He offered you that as a gift?"

The she looked fast to the crowd for support, but she found none. Never the less, Amber stuck her shoulders high and pronounced. "Nay. Payment. Payment for my services!" She stood her full height, coming not up to Rufus' chest. "He wished to mount me, and I said the necklace he wore about his neck would look pretty about mine. He agreed. We had a deal!

"Liar!" Yelled the outraged Rufus.

Jace studied her. "Rufus has a big neck, a bigger chest. That thong of gold nuggets would be worth the ransom of hundred truly comely public groomers."

"He promised and mounted." She pouted.

Jace nodded. "What say you, Rufus?"

"I nay pay for a skinny, short-tailed wench like her!"

"Beast!" She screamed. "You had your way with me, and now you will not pay!"

Rufus reached out and grabbed Amber's hair braid, viciously yanking her up by the hair, forcing her forefeet off the ground. "Thief!"

"Let her down," Jace spoke quietly but in a commanding tone. Rufus lowered his arm letting Amber touch the ground with her front hoofs, but he did not release her hair. Amber foolishly tried to run, only to be painfully jerked back by Rufus' hold.

Crying in pain and rage, the she sobbed. "Tis the law of the Headlands! Honest coin for an honest deal! Tis the rule!"

The local crowd was murmuring angrily, turning ugly in favor of one of theirs. Jace's Hardies were egging Rufus on. Soon there would be open bloodshed.

Jace continued to focus on Rufus. "What did happen?"

"She got me to buy a horn of drink from this varlet." He contemptuously indicated Slate. "She sprinkled herbs to 'flavor' it for me and walked me down by the river. I drank. Felt sleepy," Realization dawned on his face. "Twas those herbs! They closed me eyes! She drugged me!"

Jace looked to the bold Amber who was shaking her head in disbelief. Some of the locals murmured in support. He turned back to Rufus. "Just tell me what happened."

Rufus stomped his huge hoof. "She rubbed my hide, and I fell asleep...woke up when she be pulling the gold off me neck! Bounded off with a toss of her tail. Kinda groggy, I followed her hoofprints, caught her with this one!" He indicated the thoroughly terrified centaur at his feet.

From the back, some foolhardy dealer yelled. "A deal is a deal!"

"Nay." Snake of the Regiment cried out. "Ye traded me solid coin for rotted cloth. Tis a thieves bazaar here!"

A few more of Jace's Hardies were joining the crowd from the other side. One of them was Abel, with his shrewd eyes and long, stubbled cheeks. Jace silently signaled with his fingers to Abel who quietly forced his way up behind Slate.

Mayor Sandor was also elbowing his way through the crowd. The short dun looked truly worried. Some of his dealers were muttering, backing the locals, others were looking about white-eyed, realizing the danger. If Jace's breed decided to trample this hill they were gone. Sandor looked straight to Jace.

From the back, a local yelled. "Aye. They pulled the same herbed wine trick with me. Got me short knife." Several others started to yell on Amber's side.

Jace held up an arm for silence. It was respected. He had better come up with something good and fast. He looked to several of Amber's defenders. "Sirs! We are strangers in these lands, what is the price of an honorable lady's short mount?"

A roaring laughter from one of the locals. "Amber an *honorable* lady?" Laughter from more of the crowd. Good, some of the tension was breaking. That was the trail they should trod.

Jace asked again. "The price for a mount perhaps in ones' sleep?"

More laughter. Then a yell from the back. "For a comely wench, a short mount would be half a sliver...for a she with worn hooves, well, maybe fifth-cut copper!"

Amber's fists pressed at her withers, her cheeks burned in helpless rage. "Like you could get it up to mount anything, Barley! It took me a half a sun to rub up your limpness!"

Both the locals and Jace's warriors roared with laughter at Barley's discomfiture.

One of the locals, who seemed to be enjoying this called out. "Mayhaps Amber should have paid yon tall warrior. His sword must be prodigious." Again both sides laughing. Good.

If Amber would just have sense enough to walk away, but she did not. Her struggling male looked terrified but his female defiantly reared to bite into Rufus muscular arm. Bad move. Letting Slate go, Rufus raised his fist high for a crushing blow.

"**Hold**!" Jace bellowed. Rufus's arm froze in mid-air. Taking advantage of the distraction, Slate half rose to his feet, keeping low and scudding backward. His desperate hindquarters scrambling escape might have worked if he had not found himself trapped against the solidly planted forelegs of Abel. With a warrior aside Slate, one behind him and Jace in front of him the hapless Slate should have realized himself doomed. Instead, he looked to the other side. Abel just stretched his lean trunk forward and reached down, imprisoning Slate's tailbone in his hand. As a hold, it was probably was less painful than Rufus', but it was certainly just as unyielding.

To give himself time, Jace idly mused. "Where is the gold necklet?"

Amber briefly flashed her eyes toward Slate, but he did not meet hers. She faced Jace defiantly. "Your warrior has lost *my* necklace!"

"Humm. I thought after his mount you took it?"

Amber hesitated. "He slept. I should not have wanted to appear a thief. And..." She held her arms up high and pranced about. "I have nothing on me! This you can all see." Her attempts to prove innocence pulled her amble breasts higher with it truly obvious that no harness, no collar, no vest or no pouch concealed anything on Amber.

"You took not the necklet." Jace mused loudly. "How considerate. You walked off, planning to claim the necklace later and then some other centaur came and stole it."

She whipped her tail vigorously. "But he still owes

me!" She pointed at Rufus.

Jace turned his attention to the imprisoned Slate, who seemed to realize what deep trouble he was in but was infected by Amber's bottomless greed. "Good, sir." Jace politely asked, "Do you know where Rufus' necklet is?"

Down on his fore-knees, Slate wet his lips. "Nay. I know not."

The locals were muttering again. Two of their own were being harassed, and even if Amber and Slate did not appear to be model citizens, the locals would side with them.

Amber did not have the necklet on her, mayhaps her herbed wine did not knock out the big sized Rufus as long as she expected. She could have buried the necklace but had little time. She was too greedy to have thrown it in the river. Jace looked to Slate who had a newly oiled pouch slung over his shoulder with a pouch strap that cut deeply into that shoulder. Jace pulled his own worn carry pouch from its rest on his hip. "My bag is so worn. Slate, mayhaps we can work a deal. Yours looks so fine. Truly beautiful is it not, Abel?"

Still maintaining his hold on Slate's tailbone, Abel reached his other hand toward the bag whose strap was slung tightly across Slate's chest. Looking at it, Abel smiled widely. "So pretty too. Leather stamped with blue painted flowers and that blue matches your eyes. Oh, Jace, you would look ever so handsome wearing in this."

Slate yelled out, trying to hold the pouch close. "I do not wish to trade!" He looked for support from Sandor and the other dealers. They stared back with cold eyes. This bazaar did not take kindly to thieves.

"I have nay bid a price yet. I may offer so high you will gladly take it." Jace stepped his solid feathered hooves closer to Slate. "I must see it closer. Abel?"

The lanky, but tough muscled Abel was lifting Slate

off the ground by his pouch's neck strap. Finally, Abel yanked the pouch from Slate's sweating hands.

As he pulled the pouch free, Abel grinned wickedly to Jace. "Oh, the yellow butterflies are truly you, Jace." The crowd roared. Then he shook the pouch. It clanked. Abel appeared puzzled. "But it may be too heavy for you."

He tossed it to Jace who caught it with both hands. He let them sink a little to make a show of being surprised by its weight. "It weighs more than my broadsword! Those delicate, painted flowers are heavier than I thought." With the crowd again snickering, Jace deftly untied the clasp and with dramatic flourish let the contents fall to the earth. Gold coins. Rings. A long thong strung of gleaming gold nuggets. "Well, we have found Rufus' neckpiece," Jace smiled benignly at Slate. "But it is not yours. You have said this. Some person wishing you evil must have placed it in there without your knowledge. Am I correct?"

With Abel giving his tail a jerk, Slate rose to his feet, eyes white-edged in terror. "Aye. It--It is not mine."

Jace nodded. "Good."

Amber was truly a fool. "It is mine!"

"What my lady? What is yours?" Jace innocently asked. "The pouch? The coins? The jewelry on the dirt? Certainly not Rufus' necklace. If a he sleeps through a mounting, it really is not worth a half a silver, much less a prince's ransom." Jace scooped down and picked up a bent copper from the dirt and tossed it to Amber. "This should be payment for your herbs in the wine." She caught it, her lips drawn tightly over her yellowed teeth.

Rufus let her go and stepped forward, grabbed for his thong of gold nuggets and tossed its heaviness across his chest.

Cursing under her breath, Amber grabbed the pouch

from Jace. Then bent down to the dirt to gather up the rest of her jewelry. Mayor Sandor reared a little with his front feet to be heard as he proclaimed loudly, "**This matter is over!**"

Jace looked to the dealers who still stood there. "Nay!" He held up a staying hand as he grimly looked from Rufus to Amber to Slate. "This scuffle has destroyed four dealer stalls. Rufus, you will pay for one third the damages."

Rufus opened his mouth to object, then discipline overrode. "Aye, sir."

"Return to camp." Jace looked to Mayor Sandor. "Find an honest price for me. Rufus will pay you a third of it." Abel still held a beaten Slate in position by his tail. Even Amber appeared to quail before the Mayor and the crowd's anger. So Jace continued. "Do you need help collecting the rest from these two?"

Sandor glared at Amber, then reached down to the dirt and picked up an exquisite set of jeweled hoof picks. "This should pay for *all*. I am sure it too was placed in the pouch by a thief. That is correct is it not, Slate?"

Slate wet his lips, he looked from Amber's furious face, then back at Sandor. "Aye." He tried to move away, but Abel still had hold of his tail. Abel looked to Jace.

"Release him."

"Sir." Abel released Slate who grabbed Amber's arm and pulled her away. Jace looked about. An old centauress struggled to right her baskets of fruit. "Abel, you and Snake help reset this lady's plank and banners. Help them all set up their stalls again. Thunderhoof Regiment leaves in honor."

"Aye." Stooping low, with a face that had frightened a thousand enemies, Abel smiled gently at the old centauress as he righted the barrels holding up her dealer's plank. Snake picked up broken pots across the aisle.

Jace looked about. These dealers seemed to have no

defenses if they had problems. Yet who had staked that centaur out to drown on the beach? The only authority Jace had seen was Mayor Sandor. Undoubtedly a brave centaur, but a small one, alone. Sandor was already gone, back to his plank no doubt. Jace paced up the trail, returning friendly nods of dealers grateful the battle had not spread.

Sandor was at his plank. Seeing Jace, he hauled a large amphora from the ground. "Jace of Thunderhoof Regiment, just the centaur I wished to see. Sip this for me. See if it is to your breeds' taste." With a short bladed knife, Sandor cut a red wax seal from a jug and twisted out the stopper. Jace held out his horn. The pour was blood-red, clear and generous. Then Sandor poured a goblet for himself. Jace took a moment to inhale and savor, before tasting the fine brew. Not the stuff of his thin pouch. "Rich taste."

"Aged long. Carried on carts from the Blue." Sandor tried to appear casual, but the stiffness in his shoulders and hindquarters betrayed a gambit that must be played out. "We appreciate you stopping that fight."

" They were thieves."

"Aye." Sandor reached to pour again as Jace put metal on the plank and held out his drinking horn. "It used not to be tolerated. Once we had a marshal, a fine stalwart centaur called Cinnabar. Not as big as your kin, but big boned and very strong. He believed in honesty and honor. Cinnabar kept the peace. He would not have allowed Amber and Slate to remain in the Bazaar after this sun."

"Where is Cinnabar?"

Sandor looked out to the sea. "A young dun colt grabbed a necklace off the neck of an elderly she. The thief ran off over to the foothills. Cinnabar raced after him. I yelled for Cinnabar not to go alone."

"No others would help him?" Asked Jace angrily.

"I would have, but he just took off. When I finally gathered enough, we followed his big hoofprints. We found him, dead. Teeth and tail chopped off..."

There was silence between them for a time, then Jace spoke. "Mayhaps your Trade Truce is failing?"

"Try to tell the others that." Sandor drank deeply as if filling up with courage. Finally, he spoke again. "Your hind leg, sir, sometimes it seems to give you a bit of pain."

The rudeness of that remark shocked Jace. He glared down at Sandor.

Sandor only raised his hand slightly. "Please. Do not take offense. Others have noticed that you sometimes limp. You visit Merdi. His potions help sometimes, but sir, on three legs, you still would be tall and commanding. Your warriors naturally obey you. You are respected here." He stopped for a breath, then continued. " I nay speak to insult you, I offer a commission. Here at the Headlands, we do not need, well, we will not hire a force of warriors. Yet, someone, such as yourself could be paid to settle disputes, keep order. Some drink too much, some steal. I have spoken to the other dealers. We could provide you with wine, food, metal and you, in turn, would keep the peace for us. Marshaling here in the Bazaar would not require you to lope for days. Here the sun shines, the fields are fresh, there are shes worth several silvers coins that you would not have to pay."

Jace found his cheeks coloring.

"Please. I talked with the others, even before you so handily settled that dispute with your Rufus. This is a offer in good faith. To the advantage of all, think well of it before ye answer."

Jace nodded politely. "But your problem with the outland robbers. Have you spoken to your dealers about hiring my Regiment to clean them out?"

Sadly, Sandor shook his head. "They wish to stay safe."

"When the caravans are gone, you will be their next prey."

"Aye." Sandor looked at neighboring dealers. They did not meet his eyes. "Aye. I have told them that. They will not hire your Regiment."

Jace nodded. "Then we move on shortly. Although, I will consider your offer. I think a peacekeeper would be very good for this bazaar."

Mayor Sandor stood watching him. "There is that offer," he hesitated a moment before continuing, "and another."

Jace looked down at his new found benefactor. "More?"

"A commission for your troop."

"All of us?"

"Aye. But one ye may not wish."

Chapter Five

A tail temptingly to the side

half-lidded eyes and a cloying smile

a call to action louder than any battle drum

Plank merchant while pouring

"There is a party who wishes a force of centaurs." Sandor continued carefully.

"In the Bazaar?"

"Nay. Have ye heard of the Silver Centaurs of the Black Mountains?"

Jace shook his head.

"They are metal smiths of great artistry. Their finest sword blades have a wavy look, like water-rippled sand."

He had seen such river-metal swords with subtle, black wavy lines attesting to their strength and endurance. Jace had even lusted after those blades. Their allure was almost enough to make him go renegade and kill one of his own. "They are light, strong and incredibly sharp."

"Wrought by Silver Black Star and his kin."

At the Battle of Yellow Dominion, Jace had seen Orlong clove an enemy's iron helmet with such a sword. Yet that night, a tiny centauress loped a dance around their camp. She cast her scarlet silk veil to the wind, which blew it towards the fire pit. Orlong swung with his sword to save it, but the sharp blade sliced through the dancer's veil as it dropped through the air. "Truly swords of wonder, none cut sharper."

"They hold their edge." Sandor must have had a

hidden hole cut in the back of the plank as now he reached under and pulled out a long, thin blade. This he reversed, presenting the ridged bone haft to Jace. "They are hard to come by."

Jace hefted it. Light. Incredibly balanced. A sloping blade with thin, faint wavy black lines, like the mud ripples in a river. "These Silvers wish a mercenary?"

"They wish all your lads. And more."

Praise the War God of Lightning Hoof! "For what?"

"They did not say."

Probably to take over some land. "Can they pay?"

"Silver centaurs are known as protectors of vast wealth."

"Fire platform tales?" Jace kept his voice neutral as his excitement grew.

"They were always a hard-working, frugal kin. Not ones to pay for fine grooming or out land delicacies, but old Silver Bolt relished the aged brews. Many a fat purse was dropped in to my hand for a keg that most would not have dared dream of sipping. Silver Bolt commissioned my first caravan from the Green's legendary vinelands. He was dead long before the caravan came in. I well knew his sons Silver Beard and Silver Sword never had bought a mellowed wine, so I thought myself burdened with amphoras no one would ever claim."

"Could you not sell them to someone else?"

"The brews were excellent but very, very costly. Too much for most of this Headland's folk. Still, when next I saw his sons, I offered to keep the brews myself. Instead, they honored their sire's deal without a blink. "

"Why does this Silver Sword and Silver Beard wish the service of mercenaries?"

"Silver Sword passed long years ago. Silver Beard has

not trotted to this gathering in more moons than I can count nor his sons. We have not smelled the hides of any of the Silvers for ages, then this group of shes comes."

"Where are their hes?"

"The fair ones do not invite confidences. They just wish a fighting force. Silver Star speaks for them."

"It is usual for the females to hire?"

"Nay."

"You know the Lady?"

"I have seen her with her grandsire and uncles. Usually only the males parlay."

"While their females smile at the lads?"

"Nay." Sandor shook his head regretfully. "The Silvers keep to their own. Every male in this bazaar would have wished to run after those long, black stocking legs, but the Lady Star be too proud for us. Now her sister, Silver Crescent, ye might try your luck with her. That high stepping she promises a lot with that whipping tail of hers." Sandor smiled wistfully, then got back to business.

"Many times our mercenaries have been hired by parties that want our services but had no purses to pay."

"I do not weight her coin pouch, but if they need nuggets they just dig them."

"But no hes come to deal, mayhaps the males still guard their mines?"

"Or they are dead." Sandor finished his goblet. "The shes want to hire not just fighters but diggers."

"You have no males in your lands?"

"Silver Star first sought help from our lads."

"I have seen many here who could be fighters."

Sandor shook his head. "Nay, they all wish to huddle on this knob of rock and be safe."

"That will not work forever."

"Well I know, but the fools listen not."

Jace placed more metal on the plank. "I wish another pour of that fine brew, and I request that you share one with me."

Mayor Sandor hesitated. Accepting the hospitality of a drink obligated him to the boundaries of friendship but squaring his shoulders Sandor poured a round for Jace and set his own goblet on the plank. "My throat does go dry." His tail nodded gratitude. "The Silvers have always bargained with honor." They drank and then he continued. "Your lads grow restless and some of my dealers are worried that ye just wait to overwhelm us."

"Not while I lead."

Sandor nodded gravely. He well understood what was implied by 'not while.' They drank quietly for a time then he stated, "The Silvers offer to treat you and mayhaps two or three others to a fine banquet. You can both observe each other."

Jace nodded consent. "We will talk."

Mayor Sandor nodded back, looking very relieved at the chance to have Jace and his Regiment deployed away from his bazaar. " I sense haste with the Silvers. You will meet with Silver Star and her sisters at Sorrel's dining terrace when the sun canters to the top of its run."

"Do you trust her?"

Jace noticed a slight avoidance in the Mayor's eyes. A shifting of his back hooves. "In these times it is hard to trust any." But sharing another's drink commanded a certain loyalty, so at last Sandor continued. "No one promises great riches for riskless duties."

"Understood." The dull ache in Jace's leg was coming back. He shifted his great weight to his other hind leg.

Sandor gave a wry smile. "At least you will all have

a fine meal. Sorrels serves the best of my brews. I will have him serve ye Old Harlot."

"These Silvers wish to pry us with wine then drive a tight contract?"

"An experienced fellow like yer self would drink lightly in any dealing."

"This dining terrace is in the bazaar?"

"No, a furlong from here along the shoreline. Sorrel and his Rosey run as fine a dining terrace as ye will ever trod. Gallop from the bazaar due Blue-Green along the beach, ye will see smoke rising from the hill, and there will be a black boulder lined path leading to the top of the dunes. Ye will smell rich meat long before you reach it. I will arrange it for when the sun reaches the highest hill. The meal alone will be worth your time."

"It seems we owe you..." Would be coin for a keg? Or half the venture? Jace left it to the Mayor to name his price.

Sandor stiffened to his tail. "I just help two parties who seem to need each other. I cannot vouch for either of ye. I will not."

Jace well understood. "I will bring three others to parlay. As for your needs, you will have a bazaar, Marshall. We will talk of this on the morrow. "

With pain growing in his hindquarters again, Jace started down the bazaar. He made yet another stop at Merdi's. This time Merdi did not warn him of the danger of eternal sleep, he just looked sadly on as Jace produced gold for more yellow pain cakes.

Jace chewed slowly as he headed back through the bazaar. An angry Abel was arguing with the sour-faced armorer, something about a deal not honored but old Urzi stood by, he would calm the waters. Jace's centaurs needed action, disciplined duty or soon these petty bazaar merchants would feel their confined fury.

Jace trotted back to camp, the offer of employment for all them lightened his hoofbeats. Not much of a military camp with some drowning in brew, others milling about, rather lost. His officers would have to organize training again. Jace signaled Garrison and Axel to stand beside him. "We form a drum!"

To Kear and Blue-Horn, he ordered. "When we form the ring, you two trot patrol on the other edges. See that we have no listeners." They moved out into the trees in different directions, quietly loping a circling path around the area. Garrison half reared, giving a high summoning call. Abel gave several beats to a small drum on his harness that Urzi had completed. The others walked smartly forming two circles of a talking ring. What was left of their ranks? Only twenty-three? Those that were absent from camp, would they be coming back?

Females, Sandi, Willow, and Reet, battle-hardened but shorter than the hes, stepped into the inner circle. As the shes spoke, many of the males would follow. Jace waited as the inner circle formed then another behind it. Deadrick and Two Spot took the position exactly opposite of Jace. Signaling trouble to come?

Some pawing at the grass others nervous rustled their battle harnesses. All knew Jace would speak of important tidings. He waited until all hoofs quieted with just the muted sounds of waves breaking on the beach beyond the trees. "This bazaar has sweet drink."

"Sweeter shes," called the red-haired Lancer.

Jace smiled appreciatively as the others laughed. "But our coin-sacks are not endless."

Some of the others nodded sadly.

Jace continued. "Thus we need to find a patron."

Urzi asked, "Could we defend the Bazaar?"

"From who?" Asked a deep voice.

"Ourselves?" Came an answer further back. Several laughed.

Jace let the quiet return. "The Bazaar thinks its Trade Truce is holding. They feel themselves safe, even as their caravans are attacked." Jace let his eyes rest on all of them. "And they claim they have little coin."

Deadrick's voice was harsh. "If we took them, mayhaps they could find more?"

Jace ignored him as Garrison pointed out. "If supply caravans are in jeopardy if their customers do not come..."

Jace shook his tail regretfully. "Sometimes a short-sighted centaur cannot be led to the water, even as he dies of thirst."

Two Spot shifted impatiently. "The caravaners and their carts show signs of attack."

"I have spoken with the caravaners. Aye, they need protection, but they will not pay for it. They feel they can handle the problem themselves."

Another voice from the side. "Will they join us?"

Actually, Jace had been thinking along those lines. "First we must get a patron."

When some looked hopefully at Jace, Deadrick called out loudly. "This Bazaar is rich. Coin. Food. Silk and amour. We could take all!"

Urzi shook his bald head. "And trade where? Merchants do not take kindly to encouraging thieves."

"Aye," Willow responded.

Per Ben pointed out. "They are on their ground and would not give up willingly."

Having taken a stand behind Deadrick and Two Spot, Thunder would not meet Jace's eyes. Deadrick, Thunder, Two

Spot, Rings--who else would vote against him? To stay leader Jace would have to sway those who had not chosen a trail. "In the past we were honorable mercenaries, fighting for a cause. Always a cause we stayed true to. Are we now to be just robbers?" He scanned his brothers at war. None looked proud at the thought of being a thieves herd, but all knew they must do something and soon.

Deadrick reared for attention. "Just take this Bazaar!"

"We could very easily," Jace replied. "However, the locals who trade here might surprise us. Under those planks and baskets, they have weapons. I have seen swords and bows. If we overcome them and do not kill them, they could ally with the robber clans..."

"We have peace now..." started Urzi.

Jace finished. "But our welcome will run out with our coin. There are alternatives. We could disband. For a very few, there might be chores in the Bazaar. To the Green, is the Imperial..."

Lancer shook his head. "Two of my shield brothers served with the Imperial. If you lay down with dogs, you get a hideful of fleas. They do not want comrades or mercenaries, they want slaves to be cut down before their own troops enter the fray."

"Aye. They are not known to be honorable," Jace continued. " To the Red, along the beach is open land. We might be able live off it. Hunt and get fatter."

"Talk some shes into joining us?" called out Rufus from the back.

"Mayhaps but there are rumors of hostile tribes. Those that journey there never come back. Maybe even centaurs who eat their own kind."

Two Spot spoke. "As a Regiment, we could wipe them out."

"Probably. But we know not how many we face." Jace let that sink in, then continued. "There may be an alternative. A possible commission." Even the distant ocean waves breaking on the sand seemed quieter as all listened.

Ardon looked to him. "For how many of us?"

"From the word, they wish a fine army. As many as they can get. For what, I do not yet know."

Garrison queried. "Can they pay?"

Jace shrugged. "Tonight I go to parlay with them. I take two, maybe three others of us with me. Who is interested so far?"

Most of them had followed Jace for years. None backed out of the circle. They eagerly waited for Jace to announce the three going. He looked across the lines. Garrison was good for wisdom. Axel had yet to dine upon a fine terrace, a polishing he badly needed. Deadrick pulled many of the comrades. "I take Garrison, Axel and Deadrick."

Deadrick was not losing his ground, "Old one, what is this deal?"

"I do not know, but I think it is worth our while to find out. Axel and Garrison have stomped their front hooves. They come with me. Will you?"

Deadrick wanted to lead. A new leader must push the others in a different direction, but Jace guessed Deadrick had no real trail to follow. Finally, he spoke. "I will parlay for us with Garrison, Two Spot, and Thunder as well as you and Axel."

Jace's turn to evaluate it. Two Spot, Axel, and Thunder were the biggest, most muscled centaurs of the Regiment. They would impress the most jaded of prospective employers, but six...

Before he could decide, Garrison shook his tail. "We are allowed four and should not appear as a disorganized rabble. Jace, you, Deadrick, Axel and Two Spot will go. When you return, we will all hear." Thunder nodded in agreement to Deadrick.

Deadrick looked torn. He wanted to be the leader of this proposed deal, but coin hunger trumped. "When do we go?"

"When the sun climbs toward midday, we will canter to the others side the Bazaar and be there before it rises to its highest point. Battle harnesses with only light weapons showing. Leave the cooking pots and drums in camp." He raised his voice to the outer circle. "In the meantime, these Bazaar ones are set in their ways and will execute those that break them, so let us try to keep peace..."

"Until we take them over!" Deadrick yelled.

Raising his front legs in a slight rear, Jace signaled an end to the ring. And pained his hindquarters. The others quickly broke ranks as the hope of future employment added colt-like bucks to most steps.

Garrison withdrew his long shears from a carry pouch as he walked to Jace. "Get out your brushes. I will try to get you and Axel looking respectable before these generous patrons see you. Sandi, can you sharpen these blades?"

Sandi unsheathed a sharpening stone and leather strop. As she began sharpening, she commanded. "Ross, start currying Jace's tail. Kent, brush down Axel, he is nearly brown." She glared at Axel. "Must you always roll in every dust hollow?"

Jace lined up parallel alongside Axel, nose to tail. As Kent and Ross began grooming their hides, Axel leaned over and brushed Jace's broad back. Jace stood tall, with his back legs outstretched behind him as Garrison stirred a brush in shaving lather. When Sandi had honed his first blade, Garrison moved to shave Jace's cheeks. "How do you want it?"

Jace instructed, "Trim the cheek sides, leave the mustache and chin beard. Cut my long hair too. Leave it helmet length."

Sandi had begun combing Axel's tail. "Cut those feather hairs over Jace's hoofs, too."

"Nay." An Jace objected. "I like those."

Sandi looked down at his four massive, white stocking hooves. "It makes you stand out in battle. If your long hairs were cut short, you would only have a bit of white stockings flashing against your dark chestnut hide."

"Those long hairs make his hooves look bigger and more formidable," Axel teased.

Jace nodded, stamping a front hoof. "That is right. Formidable!"

Garrison was mixing more soapy lather to spread on Jace's face. "I will leave the feather hairs over the hooves. There is just enough sun to clean your jaws and untangle your tail. At least we will not have to polish your massive hooves."

As Garrison trimmed his long beard, Jace murmured. "I am sorry about you missing the meal. We could have used your wisdom."

"Stop talking!" Garrison admonished as he stripped lather from the blade. "I will live with a missed meal. You will bargain well for us." They finished with the sun nearly one finger below the sun's highest canter. Stepping off by himself, Jace took another two of the yellow cakes to end that growing ache in his coupe. He needed to trot strongly in front of prospective patrons.

The potions gradually dulled then numbed his pain. As the sun rose higher above the turquoise sea, Jace leads an eager canter past the bazaar. He even joined Axel jumping his hooves into the cold, foaming waves.

As they trotted, Axel looked about, always eager to learn. "We trot to a 'dining terrace'? What is a terrace?"

"In the Purple, the powerful emperors had splendidly paved corrals where they held court and ate their feasts on them. Their terraces never muddied in the rain. They were smooth without tallied-burro holes to trip on. Soon some of the nobles insisted on dining with their hooves on polished slabs of their own. At a good dining terrace, the best cooks prepare game and vegetables over raised fire platforms." Jace cast him a sharp look. " And one never lifts his tail and puts dropping on their precious flooring!"

"No droppings? Ever?" Axel looked horrified. "What if one must go?"

"You gallop to the tall piles outside the terrace. They have marker poles to guide you and have long cleaning sticks. Some even have lads to shovel away..."

"The shes must love it." Laughed Axel.

"The mound for males is on the opposite side of the screened mound for shes."

Axel looked in askance. "If they take away her urine, how does one smell ripeness of a she?"

Two Spot laughed deeply. "Shes will find opportunities to enlighten you."

The wind shifted slightly, and Jace could smell roasting beast and another quite intriguing aroma.

Axel bounded back into formation. "She smell! There is a she in heat."

Two Spot stopped, then reared on his hind legs, to smell deeply, pawing the air with his huge front hooves. "More than one!"

Jace was not that impressed. "Tempt us with a come hither. Mayhaps these are most accomplished ladies."

Axel shook his tail. "They can not fake that!"

Jace laughed as he joined in the trot going to a gallop. "Oh, there are shes they say that can call up scent and wetness on command."

Deadrick tossed his long white hair and tail as he laughed too. " No! They have seen what a handsome troop we are and can not keep quiet their excitement!" He took off as their lazy lope became a gallop.

"Warriors!" Jace yelled above the pounding surf and their growing excitement. "We are disciplined warriors!"

The white sands stretched out from the sudsy foam and rolled up to a flat-topped bluff. Off sword side, Jace could see a black-rock trimmed path curving upward where he could see several curling plumes of white smoke. The lined path they took loped around and behind the flat bluff, lined with green sea grass. They came up and out on to a paved plateau seemingly encircled by cerulean sea. Jace saw six or seven raised stone platforms curling smoke as polished white, Green-veined marble slabs resounded under their hooves.

Relentlessly drilled, Deadrick dropped back. Jace took a middle position as the other two peeled off, spreading into defensive wings alongside them. In the center of the terrace, the largest stone raised platform's fire pit roasted meat. It's slate edges were piled high with platters of raw cut fruits and greens. Standing in holes in the pavement were amphoras of wine alongside barrels of ale. Placed all around the terrace were smaller stone platforms, each with its own small smoking fire in the center and a slate topping surround to eat off of. Of all the public dining terraces Jace had been privileged to use, this was the finest looking.

At one end, a red-hided male offered fruit platters to a couple. As Jace's comrades entered, a short, red centauress pranced quickly to them. "Jace of the warriors?" He nodded his tail. "I be Rosey. That is my he, Sorrel. We serve you this night." She stepped neatly beside him turning his attention toward the platforms overlooking the sea. "You are expected by those fine ladies over there."

Jace turned and saw three of the most magnificent females he had ever beheld. Tall shes, not fully the height of his solid sisters but long of slender legs and high of proudly lifted heads. Each she had identical, long flowing seafoam hair and pale gray skin and hide with dabbles of creamy white on their smooth, black flanks. They also had long black stockings past their knees. As Jace walked forward, he marveled at their shining hair and luxurious tails, sparkling in the sunlight. Three perfect snow storms of beauty, walking poems on opalescent hooves.

Feeling massive, Jace bounded toward the shes with his thick hooves clanking on the smooth marble. That fast move cost him searing pain, and inwardly he cursed. The central she seemed to follow the path of his pain with concerned green eyes. He ignored it and landed hard and strong before the ladies. "I be Jace of Thunderhoof Regiment."

The central she raised her head higher. On her pale, pinkish gray forehead she was marked with a darker gray, four-pointed star. Her lips and breast points were a rose pink. She wore an elaborately wrought vest of decorative silver chain mail, that clung to her full breasts, leaving tantalizing viewing holes. Now she boldly stepped toward him Jace was surprised to note cloven hooves and a slight point to her ears.

He was also surprised and embarrassed to note a growing excitement of his own. Jace wanted less to talk of business than to mount her. Dung! He was acting like a colt. Yet, he glanced sideways to see that none of the others got too close to the lead she.

"Good warriors, we bid you join us," said the central

she in a soft but strong voice.

"My lady?" Asked Jace respectfully.

"Star. Silver Star of the Black Mountains."

"Jace of Thunderhoof Regiment." He repeated, then like a young fool, he just stared at her, not knowing what to say. A deep throat cleared. Jace looked back at the knowing eyes of Two Spot. He could feel his ears flushing. Hopefully, it wouldn't show much in his curls of hair. Jace had to gain control. "We are here to parlay. My companions are," he pointed. "Two Spot, Deadrick, and Axel."

Star introduced her kin. A sweet smiling gray named Silver Sunny had a circle marking on her forehead. She reached for Axel's hand, quickly drawing him to another stone raised serving platform. Two Spot was also led away by Silver Crescent, a confident, bold-eyed high stepper. She had the strongest invitation smell but looked as if she could control her aroused passions.

Deadrick, curse him, stayed rooted near this fascinating creature. Jace threw him an '*I will parley look,*' but Deadrick ignored it. Jace knew Deadrick's coin pouch was even emptier than his, the yellow hided warrior wanted this commission desperately. And there was a hint of laughter in Deadrick's eyes, he had seen a man drowning in she aroma before.

Star kept her eyes on Jace. "Join me please." They walked in a stately fashion to one of the rock piers. Rosey carried over a large wooden leaf-shaped platter which she set before them and from her servers' harness she set out horn goblets, that stood on their own silver stands. Deadrick reached for the first in front of Star, thinking they were sharing.

"They bring two for each of us. Brew and water," Jace quietly corrected. Looking abashed Deadrick withdrew his hand. Soon the male carried over three jugs of honey wine, strong oat beer, and water. Ignoring Jace's look of warning, Deadrick constantly held out his brew horn to be refilled. The servers continued pouring the smooth honey brew, more dangerous for the mellowness that masked its strength.

Rosey next carried over a serving platter of berries, roasted seeds, and cut vegetables. Deadrick filled his platter and bit in. Jace wished he had warned Axel to eat sparingly of the first dishes as there would be many more. He glanced to the main platform. What was cooking on that hearth would have fed his entire troop. He settled in for a long interlude of eating well. Seemingly nervous, Star took little on her platter and touched less.

As the sun started its canter to the sea, Sorrel carried over a large spine spiked fish marinated in some citrus sauce and prepared with head, bones, and fins showing. Alongside it, Rosey delivered root vegetables, nuts, and stewed green shoots. Sorrel cut slices from a roast beast skewered on an iron rod that he had carried over to their platform. It had a fine, dark crust, pink-fleshed with bloody juices running, and Rosey placed a bowl of purple currant sauce before them. Jace lifted a bone and bit into juicy, tender meat.

Worriedly Star ran her eyes over him and looked quickly to the others. "There are only four of you? Are more coming?"

"There are many more of us in camp," Jace answered. "Just we have come to parlay for them."

"Oh." She prettily colored from her cheeks to her breasts. "Yes. Mayor Sandor said that. I...I have not done this before."

Deadrick interrupted his sloppy eating to look at the half cooked haunch that Sorrel was turning above the fat popping flames. "There are more of us to pay. What do you pay?"

Jace glared at him briefly then stepped forward with his body blocking Deadrick from Star. "We can wait to discuss your commission until this fine feast before us is done."

Star turned back to the high stone platform that came up to her lower shoulder. Jace shot a look to Deadrick that said *'Else the lady would think us too hungry.'*

Between removes, Rosey trotted back with a copper basin of warm water. Well aware Jace had guarded and even dined with emperors, Deadrick tried following Jace's lead in meal manners, rinsing his hands off before the next course.

Sorrel brought baked tubers in a sour sauce, a honey sweet, milk-curd dish and briny shellfish in butter. Remove after remove of fish, roasted beast, glazed fruit, stewed greens. Oh, Jace had attended Imperial victory feasts, and this one was right up there with them. Star still ate little and just seemed to watch him and the others with a bit of worry in her eyes. She clearly was in charge, but she did occasionally exchange glances with Sunny and Crescent at the other platforms, as if wanting their agreement.

When even Jace felt too full, Star moved gracefully to the servers, thanking them politely and passing Sorrel a heavy looking leather bag. It seemed strange to have a she pay for him, strange but not such a bad feeling. Maybe they could extend negotiations out this whole night, to a sunrise meal that he would pay coin for?

Star apparently did not want her business talked before everyone on the terrace. They followed her and her sisters for a short trot down to the beach. Two Spot and Axel seemed to be kept back by Crescent and Sunny as Deadrick followed Star closely. Jace found he had to increase his strides just to keep up with her. Lords, with those slender legs, she could move so gracefully. With that high streaming tail running ahead of him they galloped down to the firmer sand at the waves edge.

"It should be safe here to parley, my lady," Jace called out above the waves crashing.

Star wheeled to face him. Deadrick edged against Jace, to push him aside. Jace planted all hooves solidly in the sand and moved not.

Star saw but ignored the male play. "How many are you?"

"Thirty–thirty-five..." At her questioning look, Jace explained. "I will propose our venture, and we will see who signs on."

She bit her lower lip. "That will not be enough."

"Our full Regiment is about seventy-two, but we are not talking badly trained conscripted fighters. We are a warrior breed. Forty-eight fighters of Thunderhoof Regiment prevailed over a thousand troops at the battle of Glendell." He finished with justifiable pride.

"How could you do that?"

"My lady, in battle a fighter can deflect the enemy's shield, making an opening, but if he has not a comrade trained to follow up on that opening, it is lost. Our Regimental troops are drilled to fight as a unit making them very effective in battle."

"Can you get more? More warriors?" She demanded.

"Mayhaps." Jace saw concern in those emerald eyes. "We could recruit locally–send for others of our training, but it would take three moons, longer..."

"Nay!" She shook her long tail vigorously. "There is not time."

"What do you wish warriors for?" Deadrick

demanded.

Star hesitated, then wet her lips. "An escort back to the Black Mountains."

"An escort only?" Jace studied her eyes before she adverted them.

"There may be robbers along the way," She said softly.

"Can you give me an estimate of their force?"

Star looked helpless. "I do not know. We will take the back trails. We may not see them at all, but we need strong fighters to free our mines."

"Why did you not go with the caravan?"

"I have spoken to Tar-bel." She looked disappointed. "He is sorry, but he says he cannot help. We need more hes..."

"For just an escort?" Jace asked carefully. There was something more to her quest he was sure. She looked from him to Deadrick and saw Deadrick seemed to be studying her elaborately wrought silver chain vest. Probably scheming how much coin that jewelry would bring in the bazaar. How could the fool ignore those beautiful pointed breasts?

"You specify strong hes. For what purpose, my lady?" Jace repeated.

Deadrick's eyes wandered from Star's shining vest to her jeweled hair ornaments. The fool would take her metal and force her companionship. Such a foolish one might try, but he would wake with a knife in his throat. Jace did not see such a proud lady ever being forced to be a trail follower.

Clearly upset, Star finally spoke. "We wish no gossip in the bazaar. We will make our full needs clear as you come with us."

This did not bode well. Jace trod a fore hoof down solidly. "Milady, we do not gallop into the dark."

Deadrick ignored Jace's misgivings. "We work for

metal, and I do not see this with you?"

Jace glared at him again. Star raised her head even higher, meeting Deadrick's eyes firmly. "We have much metal. You will see it all when the dragon is slain."

"The dragon?" Jace queried.

"A dragon?" Echoed Deadrick.

She looked back at Jace with those wide, clear eyes almost pleading. "My people are metalsmiths. Our forges are in the valley of our mines where we dig. My uncles were digging a new tunnel into the deep when this creature attacked us. Its poisonous breath destroyed the mine supports, bringing down a rock slide that has cut us off from tunnels."

"A dragon has done this?" Asked Jace.

"A huge creature, seven times the size of your Two Spot. With opaline scales, webbed wings, and massive fangs that drip poison. It caused a rock fall that closed off the mines." There was genuine terror in her voice.

"Not fire?" Deadrick asked sarcastically.

She kept looking in Jace's eyes. "You must get us to our mountain, dig out the rock fall and slay the dragon. You will be rewarded with much metal and jewels." She looked to Jace's eyes only. "Will you do it?"

Mines. Confinement. Buried Alive. Jace felt if he had been wounded again. Digging in the dark, confining mines... the commission she offered was not one he could ever do, but he had others to bargain for. "My lady, my comrades have killed all who oppose us. Not yet a dragon, but my warriors are disciplined fighters and strong. We could move rocks, and a rich booty would be welcomed, but an army, even a small one, does not canter on promises only. We will need metal for supplies and weapons."

She looked confused. "You are warriors. Have you not weapons?"

"Well, some..." But Jace did not choose to say the rest lay on the fields of the Dominion. "But there are expenses and good faith requires some payment in advance."

She looked to Deadrick and seemed to recoil from the naked greed in his eyes. Then she looked back to Jace, her eyes were filled with fear and mistrust, but she studied his face for a long time. Star must have seen something comforting in it, for she relaxed. "There is gold we could advance. Can you march on sunrise?"

Sunrise? So fast? "The price my lady is two silver coins each sun for maybe thirty to thirty-five warriors. Four silver coins a sun each for seven officers, all enemy plunder, and a bonus when your mines are free."

"That-that is high." She looked to her sisters but seeing no answer, turned back to him. He expected her to haggle. Instead, she set jaw. "A craftsman is worthy of his hire. But with forty warriors, only the first moon may be paid until our mines are secured again."

How lovely that seafoam colored hair curled around her face and tumbled down her shoulders. How glossy her flanks. He wanted to follow her tail. But he knew what confinement in a horror pit felt like. A mine was just a deep, long, dark confining pit. "My Lady, I must speak with the others."

"But they must march at sunrise." she said with determination.

"Should we march, my lady, we must first provision and plan. Perhaps this dragon of yours will just go away?"

"No." She lowered eyes. In despair? In guilt? "It will not leave." She looked back up, pleading, "Please hasten with your centaurs. There is little time. My sisters and I camp in a meadow behind Sorrel's terrace. Let me know of your decision."

With a polite nod to them both, she was off, back to her sisters who were now escorting an enraptured Axel and Two Spot towards them. Jace felt a peace come over him, just watching her gracefully pace away.

Deadrick had only one thing on his mind. "She has metal. She is not in the bazaar. Not under the Truce of Trade. We follow her and take all!"

Jace wheeled his body perpendicular to Deadrick. "Mark me! We will not be robbers!"

"You think this 'dragon' exists?" Deadrick's voice dripped with scorn. "Have you ever seen a dragon?"

Two Spot was listening with a doubtful expression. "Dragons?" He asked.

Jace spoke slowly. "In many lands, I have seen strange beasts I never would have believed existed."

Deadrick exclaimed. "Dragon's are tales for colts! She is luring us into a trap!"

It was Jace's turn for scorn. "We are such rich, defenseless prizes."

"She and her friends do not know that. They have sent tempting centauresses to lead us down a false path. And you, nostrils flaring. '*My lady this, my lady that,*' you will follow like a milk-gambol to slaughter!"

"We will hold the drum this night, and all will decide." Angered Jace turned his back to Deadrick and started trotting away.

"Does she know she commissions a cripple? The leg of yours, old one, it is giving way. Three moons and it does not heal. Will the surgeons cut it off? Will you hop on three legs? A warrior does not slow his comrades. Will you abandon us? Or should we all slay you, as in olden custom?"

Jace tried to ignore him but deep within his leg, the pain was returning. Leading Axel and Two Spot, he started back toward camp. Behind them, Deadrick raised his voice, over the surf and taunted, "Perhaps you can hope her dragon will be merciful and kill you!"

Chapter Six

To make progress

All four feet have to go in one direction

   Grandmare's Proverb

Camp had little peace to give, and he returned to the shouts and dust of warfare. Jace lengthened his strides to a canter. Ahead were loose rings of his warriors, shouting, so that is where the trouble would be. Two fools fighting as always. Jace pushed his way through broad rumps. In the center, gray hided and pale-eyed Ghost reared against yellow-hided Wheat. Both now bloodied as they smashed staffs from raised hind legs. Deadly front hooves kicked out at the withers while arms were swinging wooden staffs, that could break bones and crack skulls.

   Blood ran from Ghost's nose and Wheat's shoulder. They broke from the foreleg hold, twisting down. Both kicking out at the other one. Ghost bend low for a bite. Wheat raised his staff. They were fighting to the death over who knew what. A centauress? Gold? Just too long with little to do? A loose circle of onlookers ranged from disinterest to enthusiastically placing bets. Sandi was maneuvering to call a halt, but side arguments were starting. This was how a full camp melee irrupted.

   Jace charged the field, yelling. **"Halt!"** Both combatants parted, breathing heavily and no doubt grateful for a momentary respite. Even with Jace roaring at them. "The Regiment is shamed! You fight so poorly! You can not hit! Can not faint! You need trainers!" He scanned about the ring of watchers. "Sandi, trot center! These varlets need proper drilling."

Sandi immediately responded. Her short curled head barely coming up to their chests, but her voice was sharp and commanding. "Your blows were worthless! Your stance is terrible! Ghost, you shovel food into your mouth with your sinister hand, why is your sword in your other hand? Wheat, you saw him charge wildly, why did you step into his staff?" Sandi looked about then ordered. "We start with spears against that rotten log over there. Kent! Fetch six or seven spears." Sandi's son instantly bolted off for spears as she turned back to the shame tailed combatants. "You will stand two strides from that log."

Wheat protested. "We have staffs."

"You are not focused enough for staffs! First, you must learn not to drop your spear." Sandi trotted ahead, then pawed at a rough line parallel to the log with her hoof. "Axel, Ross, you need this too. Stand up to the line."

Kent had grabbed someone's spears. He galloped to Ghost and handed three to him and then three more to Wheat. Then he turned tail and grabbed some of his own hand-carved shafts. These he passed to his brother Ross and Axel. The pain had cooled the blood and anger of Wheat, who just stepped to the line. Willow had moved up with large leaves to wipe the blood off Ghost's face. He too seemed relieved to have his battle to the death turned into a fighter practice.

Jace raised his voice. "No more fighting in camp or the bazaar! We will need our strength for a commission. There will be a drum held on the beach at full darkness. We will discuss our next marching. Pass the call."

It was a very minor skirmish, but more bloodletting would be coming soon. Ardon trotted up with Deadrick following. "Ardon, mark a course about the perimeter of the camp. We will be setting up other training exercises." Ardon nodded and bounded off. Soon most of the camp were trotting a rambling course, ducking poles or banishing stick swords. It gave them importance, discipline and soaked up destructive energy.

Even Deadrick could see the need but had to press Jace. "Will you try to solve all our ills, old one? This night others shall speak!"

If Deadrick had the answer, Jace was perfectly willing to march behind his tail. But the likelihood was that Deadrick's fat purses would turn to useless bloodshed and make them further outcasts.

After the others ate, Jace and Axel headed Red, away from the camp, down to a sandy crescent beach. Picking up driftwood logs, he and Axel kindled two large bonfires on the sand at a distance of two lopes, the flames' yellow lights reflected on the rolling waves slapping the shore. Seeing no one looking, Jace dipped two of the pain cakes out of his pouch. Tonight he would have to walk like a strong leader if the others were to follow in his hoofprints. In the distance, he heard Ardon's summoning drum beats. As the blue gloaming clouds darkened into black night, Garrison trotted the camp down to the white sand away from listening ears in the bazaar. Ardon and Wheat were sent to lope guard as the others gathered in a two long ovals surrounding the fires.

When all quieted, Jace looked about and started to talk as he walked in front of his warriors. "You have served well. Other troops shiver at our hoof-falls..."

Deadrick interrupted. "And for this, our harnesses are empty of coin!"

Jace ignored him. "Times are hard. We can disband and trot our separate trails..."

From the back came a saddened. "Aye."

But Jace continued. "Or we can stay together and fight

as the Regiment."

Deadrick pushed into the firelight. It gleamed on his yellow hide and white stockings. "We fight as one! Take this bazaar's riches! Shes! Weapons!"

Jace ignored Deadrick's intrusion into the leader's circle. He only dryly commented, "Mayhaps on your list of robbings, the weapons should be first?"

"You do not want the bazaar taken, old one? Is your wounded leg making you afraid?" Deadrick turned on his hindquarters, taking an attack stance before Jace.

Jace spoke quietly but firmly to the others. "Do we want to be greater outlaws than we are now? When we steal the coin and wine and food from the bazaar, who will then trade with us? We will have violated a Truce of Trade. Who knowingly deals with rabble and thieves?"

The others were ominously silent. Heads were kept stiff and unnodding. Not even one tail swung in acceptance or rejection. With most of their faces in shadow, Jace did not know how this drum would go.

Deadrick did not care. "Ten of us–no five of us could run over these fat merchants!"

Abel stepped forward slightly. "These dealers have survived on the edge of a warring land. As freeborn, they will not be subjected easily. Unless you kill them all, they may be cutting our throats at night. Or galloping for reinforcements with the robber tribes."

Several tails swished in agreement.

Jace decided it was time. "I have parlayed with a possible patron, a Lady Silver Star."

"A fair she Jace seemed to be endlessly smelling," Deadrick sneered.

Again Jace ignored him. "This lady offers two silver coins per warrior, per sun, to be paid to the Regimental fund until her quest is completed. Each of you marching will receive one silver coin for each sun marched with the Regiment at settling up. Twenty-nine suns of this will be paid up front to the Regimental pouch, the rest to be given only when we secure her mines and settle out."

"How many warriors does she want?" Came from the darkness.

"All she can get."

"What is this quest? She pays for just an escort?" asked Rufus.

Deadrick pranced before them all, saying mockingly. "Nay–she has a 'dragon' to slay."

There was silence and then a background of mutterings, snorts, and pawing. From the back a plaintive demand. "Dragon? What is a Dragon?"

Deadrick's voice dripped poisonous sarcasm. "Old shes put their grand-colts to sleep with tales of mighty beasts, huge of body with boney protective plates, giant claws, and breath of flames."

Sandi's colt Ross yelled out. "Deadrick is right! The bazaar is ours for the taking!"

Jace decided to ignore Ross' impertinence, and he let the head-shakings and mutterings die down before he spoke. "Like many of our patrons, the Lady Star must trust us before she speaks all. It is well known her kin mine the mountains for riches and that the land between here and her mountain is lined with ambushing robbers. When we reach her lands, there has been a rock fall. To open her mines and earn our reward those will have to be dug out."

"And her dragon slain?" Mocked Deadrick.

Rufus was asking. "But a dragon, Jace, have you seen such a thing?"

"Nay." Jace felt his own tail lowering. "But in my

travels, I have discovered stranger tales to be true." He loped slowly around the inner circle. "We know what we came from with petty dictators, changing allegiance with the wind. To the Yellow is the Imperial, who would treat us as interlopers. To the Red, we have only tales of hostile centaurs who eat their own kind."

"What about the bazaar?" Ghost asked. "Will, they not pay to be free of robbers?"

"Nay. Neither will the caravaners. This lady offers us the only chance to stay together and fight as a regiment."

Some voice called out from the darkness. "You lead?"

Jace hesitated. "I have been offered another position. But I advise you to march with the Regiment under Garrison or whoever you decide to choose as your leader." He stopped speaking, and there were only the sounds of the fire embers popping and the rolling surf for a long time. "I know that together, you are warriors to be reckoned with. Otherwise, you are just a huge troop of stomachs to feed. Think this night. On the morn, Ardon will keep a scroll of those who sign on."

Jace turned and walked into the darkness. He could hear Deadrick haranguing. "Look, he limps away from you! He would lead you away from a fat prize of merchants to march to some prancing she's mirage."

Jace just lengthened his strides, this endless arguing sickened him. Drumming of hoofs from behind as three or four shadowy forms galloped passed him. Then Sandi, Kent, and Axel cantered alongside Jace.

Axel shouted to Sandi. "Sign me on to the dragon quest!" Sandi nodded, but Axel continued to her. "Your son Ross is following Deadrick hoofprints?"

Kent laughed. "My brother just wants to anger my mare."

Looking down, Jace shortened his lope to be next to Sandi. "Will Ross march off with Deadrick?"

He could not see her face in the moonlight, but she tightened her voice to a command level. "He will follow where I trot!"

She cantered ahead to the seagrass, followed by Axel and Kent. Jace slowed, wishing to be by himself. He was until he heard hoof beats behind him causing him to turn and stop. Even in the moonlight, he could make out the gray hairs on Garrison's grizzled head. "Jace, I am to be in charge?"

"I should have told you before."

"Why not ye?"

"I have been offered a commission."

"Doing what?" asked a surprised Garrison.

"Peacekeeper to the Bazaar."

Garrison stared at him in disbelief. "That is not ye."

"My leg weakens."

"It has seemed better lately."

"Only when Merdi's cakes kill the pain, then it grows worse," said Jace flatly, hating his words.

Garrison hand signaled for Jace to wait as several other of the Regiment galloped past, hooting and shouting. "They are excited again. Riches ahead. Battle."

"Aye."

In the moonlight, Garrison lifted his head, his eyes brightened as those of a young he as a small smile played on his face. Finally, he spoke, "Jace, we both have cheated the vultures many times. To die in battle is better than taking handouts from a bunch merchants."

Jace shifted his weight not wishing to speak, but knowing Garrison was owed the truth. "This quest–we must dig into a mountain to slay her dragon."

"Oh." Garrison was silent for a time, then spoke

softly. "Ye were imprisoned in the pits. That was before we met. Ye have never wished to talk about it. How did that happen?"

"There was a battle at the Salt Plains. It went badly. We fought well but were outnumbered. At sunsink, we were pushed back to the foothills. There was a valley cut that offered escape." Just remembering it brought much pain. "It was decided that the main body would break out and disappear into the mountains."

"A good strategy."

"To cover for the rest, a few of us were to keep campfires going, make noises. Just before sunrise, we were to cut and run. But they attacked early-- their forces came on and on. Finally, I faced the mighty Sultan Iron Tooth. My sword shattered against his, or he would be dead. His minions threw rope nets over me–ropes of leather. "

"Why did they not kill you?"

"It was more amusing to listen to us cry out as we died."

Garrison left the silence stand, and finally, Jace spoke again. " They dug huge pits. One for each. We could not move our flanks or lay down. There was no food, no water. The hot sun and freezing night. I smelled the others die, one by one."

"How did you survive?"

"The troops we helped escape regrouped and returned with reinforcements. It must have been five suns before they could retake the position. I was the only one of us left alive."

"It is over Jace."

"Nay. Many nights, I am back in that pit. I will not–I could not dig myself into some mine."

They loped in quiet for a while, then Garrison asked, "Do you believe in her dragon?"

"She is a poor liar. There is no dragon, but from the set of her shoulders, the mine part rings true. She wants us to dig to something in that mountain of hers."

"Has she gold to pay?"

"Some to advance."

"You have seen it?"

Jace stopped for a moment. "Nay."

"We must see the color of her metal before I lead."

Jace nodded. "Let me speak with the Lady."

"Solid coin for a moon's march?"

"The rest to be paid when you free up her mines."

"From a dragon?" Garrison shook his head. "And I am leader–I will be challenged."

"You could back down. Let whoever else lead."

Garrison shook his head. "Nay. Jace, there are no old warriors. Perhaps it is better to die fighting, even if it is only a challenge."

Jace would not face a challenge. He would be peacekeeping in a bazaar. Not the way he planned to end things, but with his hindquarters shivering in pain, peace seemed a good thing to keep. Back at camp, he stepped over to Kent. With Sandi's smile, her son handed him a steaming horn of raw brew that warmed his throat. As he turned to look about the camp, Sandi was trotting up to him.

"How many have signed on?" Jace asked, not expecting to like the answer.

"Only ten so far. More will sign on when their prospects are bare in the sunlight. But Jace, they ask that you lead?"

"It must be Garrison."

"Garrison will die in challenge to Deadrick." Sandi shook her head. " Two Spot perhaps could take him."

"Deadrick is valiant in battle."

She shook her tail. "He is a bold fighter, he would make a great second. He is not a leader. Deadrick only sees the sword he is going for, not the troops he must command."

Jace had no answer to that.

"Two Spot? Strong, steady, but no grand plans..." Sandi continued. "Jace, we are not a troop without you. Why will you not march?"

He owed Sandi the truth too. "This patron wishes us to go into her mines and dig. Confining dark tunnels..."

"So?" When he did not answer, she bends her head to the side, looking up at him. "Those times you cry out at night. The pit prison at the Salt Plains?"

He chose not to answer.

Sandi's face was dark in the moon shadows. "Long have I followed you, Jace. I fought beside you. You will not quit, you will lead us down to eternal coldness if you must."

As the sky grayed lighter, Jace stiffly rolled off the ground, painfully hauling himself up on all four legs. Nay, he could not lead a troop of fighters, not when he could barely stand. Yet he owed it to his successor to see that his warriors marched as smartly as he could arrange. If the Regiment would march at tomorrow's sun, they must provision. His sub-leaders were lining up. "Ardon." He called over. "What is the count?"

"Nineteen. More still thinking it over."

"Hopefully we will have two hands full, or three hands."

"Thirty-six? We will see," said Ardon not too hopefully.

"Deadrick, recruit from the locals. We will train on the trail. Garrison, we need at least six carts and water barrels."

"Six? And we pay with what?" asked Garrison.

"Then get four–get what you can." Jace unhooked Sandi's coin pouch and passed it to Garrison. "Pass the word. Each of the warriors should try to replace their weaponry as best they can." He turned as Sandi trotted up. "Find what leather, sinew we need. Sewing needles? Tools to repair."

"Medicine?" She asked.

"We have nothing now?"

"Two Spot stripped our surgeon's kit off of Whitlock's body," said Ardon.

"Good. Who will be our surgeon?"

Sandi spoke up. "Willow."

"Nay." Deadrick objected. "We need not a she, with two barely weaned foals struggling after our steps."

Sandi glared at him. "She has no choice."

"She can stay here," said Deadrick.

"As what? A public groomer? We have no portion to give her." Sandi looked desperately at Jace. "You need bodies to impress your patron! Willow is tall and strong looking. She is a fighter!"

Deadrick shook his tail. "Not with two foals at her fetlocks."

"We will hide the foals behind the carts." Sandi pleaded.

She looked desperately at Garrison, who also shook his head. "Nay."

Sandi looked back at Jace. He looked over the field. Willow was there, staring at them, so was Urzi, waiting for him to decide their lives. Suddenly Jace felt very weary. He would make no decisions this sun. "Let us get a force together before we decide who to exclude. Ardon, we need dried fruit, fish and meat. Hopefully, we can bring down enough game on the march."

Deadrick's comment was dry. "Old one, how do we pay?"

Jace looked to Ardon who held out a wax tablet with figures for him to study. Over half the troop might be coming for their ending shares. There was not coin, metal or recovered weapons enough to cover that. "You and Snake grabbed two looting sacks. Take the plate, goblets and jeweled picks to the bazaar to see what you can trade for. The dealers will soon realize we are provisioning and raise their asking."

"For those coming to claim their final Regimental share?" Ardon asked.

Jace looked at the figures. "Pay five silver per trooper."

Deadrick was appalled. "Only five?"

"The first ones coming in will get it all. The rest have re-sign."

Ardon nodded and swung away. The others headed out. His pain growing, Jace almost limped but hauled on his full harness. He noted the others moved as if they had wings on their hooves. The Regiment lived!

Later in the bazaar, Jace ran his hand down a spear shaft of ironwood that was straight and polished. Could have a better hammering on the metal spear point but a decent fighting piece. He looked up to query the owner but the spotted centaur was looking away from him, his gaze down the trail was hard and a little afraid. Jace straightened up and looked over his shoulder. The other sellers were also looking apprehensively down hill. Jace took a deep breath unpleasantly inhaling the stink of dead meat.

The she dealer across the way was hastily pulling her gold rings and silver beaded hair nets back from her smooth plank. The centaur beside Jace was removing his short hanging blades from reach. Down the trail, Jace could see a group of duns–short-legged, black stockings, black haired. Males leading with females and colts in the center.

Whoever these coming centaurs were, one did not leave expensive wares in their path. Jace studied the tight group, led by a young male of dun hide and tanned skin. As he goes closer, Jace could see blood red patches on his flanks. All the males were the same dusty color, as were some of the shes. As the proud headed male strode closer, Jace could see the red marks on his hide were not marking but dried paint or blood on matted hide.

These duns all had wide black stripes from their long, dark head hair, down their broad backs, to their short black tails. The males wore a leather loop around their waists, with long, wide bladed swords and shields. Their round shields were marked with a yellow moon and two blue stars. There were at least six adults marching up, followed by a swarm of youngsters. All colts–no fillies.

Bold black eyes swept stalls. They knew they were disliked and reveled in it. Several of their colts ran to a meat seller. She braced herself but seemed unable to stop them. An older dun centauress ambled up and scanned the raw haunches hanging from the framework. She slightly nodded at one, and the youngsters were all over it with greasy, dirty hands. Jace noted the proprietress said nothing. Her mouth set in a tight, thin line, as her two previous customers quickly drifted off.

The older dun she gave a toothless grin and began haggling with the meat vendoress. While the two centauresses argued, two young dun colts continued marking the meat with their dirty fingers. The leading males were coming closer to Jace, rudely coming three abreast, blocking the trail.

Jace put down the spear and stepped out into the

pathway. He noted the male duns wore something on their arms. Some sort of clan badge of dark rags, strapped just below their shoulders, hanging down their arms, swinging to their knees. Two, no three males and four females with five youngster colts. From their painfully overstuffed double basket harnesses the females did the heavy carrying. Two more short-legged males followed behind them.

The arrogant young lead drew closer to Jace. With sudden revulsion, Jace realized what was hanging from his arm. Not rags--hair. Tail hair. They must be wearing the tails of their vanquished enemies.

In battle, he had seen much savagery. Furious, bitter fighters who after the battle cut off ears, fingers, even tails. Only the most monstrous primitives would hang centaur tails as their battle standards. These duns wore them for socializing.

The brown-skinned, wrinkled centauress bought her finger marked meat and hefted it on to the harness of one of the younger shes. She must have gotten a reduced price, but neither she or the proprietress looked happy about it. As they drew closer, Jace could see the first female had a disfiguring rectangular scar on her cheek. She and the other dun centauresses wore long necklaces yellow beads, from a few strands on the youngest, to the mass of necklaces cascading down the wrinkled chest of the oldest she.

The lead dun seemed to be hesitating. He had not expected Jace to step so boldly into his path. For all his proud strutting, the lead dun was young and obviously unsure of himself. When Jace did not clear a path for him, he did not know what to do. Jace just stood his ground. The dun could challenge or step aside and brush past him.

Instead, he halted, as if surprised Jace did not clear the way, his hand moving near his knife hilt as Jace just calmly followed him with his eyes. Even if the dun pulled, Jace knew he could clear his weapon equally fast. Still, his shield was back in camp, and these bazaar tenders would not help him, and the dun had his friends. But one war cry from Jace would bring half a troop of his warriors down on this petty rabble. Of course, he might be skewered by then.

The oldest dun Centauresses, with the most ropes of yellow beads, had pushed up behind the leader and seemed to be egging him on. But he was glancing back down the winding path. The dun must have passed Garrison. Maybe Two Spot and some others on the way up. He looked back at Jace, biting his lip.

Jace did not want a battle here and now. But if he would be hiring out as a mercenary, he could not be seen backing down from the local bully boys.

This young dun did not want to back down. He started off with a nervous skip on his front legs, Jace expected a verbal challenge. Instead, the lead dun just dropped his eyes, moved to the side and brushed past Jace.

The other males and females followed. The centauresses ranged from a middle-aged she, who glared at him angrily as she pushed past, to a young, red-haired she that gave him a long, coquettish glance as the male behind her slapped at her flanks to hasten her past. The redhead, too, had a deep rectangle scar on her cheek. All these shes did.

Eyes angry, the oldest dun female still glared at him–she seemed to have more sand than her leader. Her black hair was graying, and she too had the wide black stripe down her back, with a mixture of gray hairs in it. Her cubby, stocking feet were black, and now she froze and glared. He did not move. Finally, she brushed past him walking stiffly, but she carried her head like ruler of all.

With his lips involuntarily curling, Jace realized that

the scar on her cheek was branded. Were these shes slaves? Or mates? Or both? As the old, rough-coated she brushed past him, Jace saw that the multiple strings of yellow beads that hung from her neck were not beads, but teeth. They looked like centaur teeth. When the tribe left, Jace stayed in the pathway. Even after they were out of sight, the dealers kept their best merchandise covered, since these disliked duns could soon be returning down the hill.

Tired of the game, Jace headed down the hill himself. He noted the dealer's armor stock was going down. His warriors must be girding up.

He walked further down the hillside, stopping before a booth of brightly woven banners. Green and blue, orange and brown. A saucy she with a flower painted on her cheek sat on folded legs as she wove a green banner on her loom. Near her a small he wound thread on a spindle. The lady smiled enticingly. "My lord, does thou wish a fine banner for your warriors to stride under?"

"What have you?"

"Black and brown sheep shearings. White fluff from the plants. Worm's smooth thread that could be dyed. I have it all." Her smile was ever so tempting so Jace found himself smiling back. Her male sourly glared at Jace as he stepped to his loom.

The Regiment always marched under yellow and black banners or did until they lost them. He saw several skeins of soft, black yarn. "Do you have bright yellow?"

From a basket, she pulled out several white skeins. "These could be dyed."

"How long will that take?"

"The herbalist, Merdi, has given me a butternut dye. I will have to heat up a pot, and the thread will have to sundry between multiple dyeings if you wish a rich color."

That would not be done in time for this dragon hunt. "Mayhaps the next time we come through it could be done. What would be the price?"

She eyed at his solid muscles and smiled boldly. "For ye a special deal could be worked." On the larger loom the male centaur, obviously, her he slammed his shuttle. Jace smiled wickedly at her and moved on.

Voices raised. Distant accusations. Weary of it all, Jace still headed down the bazaar hill. Ahead of him he saw the broad, black striped back of Mayor Sandor and a handful of others, including some of his crew. Jace used his massive strength to push his way past the locals. In the center Snake and Blue Horn were fighting. That big breasted groomer, Honey, stood to the side, obviously quite proud of this battle over her charms.

Kear, Urzi, and Ardon watched from the sides in the midst of the bazaar folk, betting on the outcome no doubt. And another head, held proudly high above the yelling mass, Lady Star. She stood behind the lines, anxiously watching the brawl. As Jace moved to the center, he saw Star pick up a long mash stick from a cook's plank. In defense of him?

With a chuckle, Jace turned his full attention to the brawl ahead. Those two fools were squaring off, but he noted with relief that Urzi was maneuvering his solid body between them.

In a cajoling voice full of humor, Urzi urged them, "Come on, lads, save it for the field of battle. Why we can have a contest for these fine folks. One we can all wager on."

"Aye! A fair contest!" A local yelled out. That seemed to gain interest with both his worthies and the locals. Jace took it up, "A tournament for the fair centauress' honor." With his arm bent before his chest, Jace folded a front leg and did a gallant courtier's bow to Honey. "Mayhaps my lady will attend?" She immediately thrust her chest out with pride.

Urzi lead the cheer. "We will hold it away from these stalls where we have fighting range down on the beach."

Jace closed. "Mayhaps my Lady Honey will judge the winner?"

Obviously flattered, she nodded.

Urzi quickly picked it up. "Excellent. We have a contest! At high sun. Aye, lads? I will go and lay out a field course."

The crowd moved off as relieved merchants stepped back to their unmolested planks. The Mayor nodded approval to Jace as he hurried past. Another donnybrook avoided.

A sweet scent drew near, one already familiar. Jace looked about to see Star had stepped beside him. By the Lords, she trod those cloven hoofs of hers so quietly.

"Your warriors obey well," she said.

"They had no wish to trample this gathering–not yet at least." He noted with amusement that she still held the long stick. "The danger is over, my lady, you can safely disarm."

Hearing the amusement in his voice, her smooth, silvery skin pinked with embarrassment. "These gatherings–they do not deal kindly with outlanders."

The memory of the neck chained, drowned centaur chilled Jace. Star was a centauress of uncommon courage, perhaps her kind bred warriors? The males mined, the shes fought? Is that why they had sent females to raise an army? He had seen breeds with aggressive females before, compact, fast and smart they could be formidable foes, especially if fighting for their young.

"You fight for us?" Star asked a bit anxiously.

"We have held a drum. The Regiment will march for you." He said, wishing that he would be marching too.

"What is this drum?"

"Before a battle or an important announcement the sub-leaders give a pattern of rapid beats on the drum heads. It means all are to draw near as the plans are announced."

"You will tell them what they are to do?"

"The Regiment is not under my command anymore. Those that accept your commission will choose officers." He said regretfully, but firmly.

She looked distressed. "But I trust you. It must be you that leads!"

"Nay." Not into the bowels of some stinking mountain. "Nay my lady. There are others who will lead."

Chapter Seven

If ye closely follow her tail

Hope she trots nay off a cliff

Lost Lover's Musings

Star shook her long, silky tail. "Nay, that is part of the commission! You shall lead."

Into what? A torture pit of darkness? Even beauty such as Star's could never banish the dying pits from his memory. "My lady, we are not an army anymore. We are mercenaries looking for our next brush feud. As the Regiment gathers all will talk and then each will choose his own trail. I have had another offer that I have already accepted."

"Oh." She appeared to want to say more but looked about at the vendors. "May I walk with you?"

"Aye."

"Do you wish to see your warriors tournament?" She asked.

"Nay. I have seen the contests many times. I have not seen the outer tents to the Yellow side."

Star nodded and followed Jace to a narrow trail that leads to another outer ring. He allowed her to proceed him slightly. Going slowly rewarded him with a fine view of her long, glossy back, her tight dabbled flanks. Such a proudly held head, so slender of leg, this one must run like the wind. To pace alongside her, drop behind her tail...he had better keep his mind on business.

Down the other side of the mound, they passed stalls stacked with fruits and racks of dried fishes as Jace smelled cheap brew. Two bold, but rather worn public groomers were patrolling. They looked eagerly at Jace but then saw Star brushing protectively against his flank

To Star, most of the dealers turned a welcoming smile, but Jace sensed she had nay interest in their bangles or them. Her mind must range on battles to be fought elsewhere.

Ahead wide patches of white on black betrayed Axel as Jace's mouth tightened in disapproval. The fool was using his few coins to buy gaudy beads for a most appreciative looking Laurel, who eagerly reared to kiss his cheek. Cheeks and chest reddening, Axel shifted, then reached down to pick up the matching bracelet that would finish his purse. Jace stepped forward hoping to catch Axel's eye.

The bearded dealer crouching like a spider in his web saw a second couple with another foolish male who would pay dearly to impress his fancy stepping she. "My lady, I am surprised you do not stop to study my fine silver work?"

Star glanced contemptuously at the dealer's wares commenting loudly to Jace. "His workmanship is crude and poorly soldered."

The merchant protested. "It is the best in the gathering!"

"Is it?" Star reached with her fingers, slightly lifting the necklace on Laurel's thick throat. "It flatters you not. It draws attention to the heaviness of your neck." Laurel flinched and took it off.

Jace noted that Axel closed his coin pouch, probably more by seeing Jace's disapproval then by Star's contempt of his probable purchase.

Seeing his trades slip away the merchant protested. "Its silver value alone is worth twice my price!"

Star took the necklace from Laurel, seemingly to weight it with her fingers. Then she held the string of beads high to where the sunlight shafted between the banners and muslin cloth skims. The gray beads showned yellow-orange dully. "Tis tumbaga! It is nothing but tin and lead with grease polish! Even the faking of value is done artlessly!" she said with disgust.

The beaten merchant snatched back his necklace bitterly excusing himself. "These beads were purchased from another."

Star stared hard at the merchant. "Then he cheated you royally!"

Sobered now Axel moved off, looking a little warier of Laurel but still following her tail.

Star and Jace stepped to several more booths, but he could see her attention was furlongs away. They both heard a call from the distance. With a neat turn, Star was brushing past Jace, her smooth, short-haired rump rubbing against his hip-withers. Jace could see that past the tent of hanging dried herbs that one of her sisters was on the beach, waving her hand.

"Crescent wishes me." Those emerald eyes searched his. "You will rethink leading your regiment?"

He swung his tail politely, and Star must have taken that for a possibility that she would win out. She smiled again. That bright, happy smile. Then she turned and raced away as Jace found himself warming to just watch her. Anyone built with such fine legs must always want to run.

He headed back up to bazaar, passing his warriors buying shields as he stepped by one of those strange duns with the red painted handprints on his flank. The dun held a leather tool in his hand as if he was considering trading for it, but he seemed more interested in Jace's passage. Jace briskly half trotted up the higher pathway around a blind curve. There he stopped to study the inside of a stall of vegetable bins. From the corner of his eye, he saw his dun follower trot around and break stride. The dun hesitated, then moved forward, determinedly not meeting Jace's eyes as he walked past him. So someone was interested in Jace's movements? These duns did not look like they would pay to hire a warrior. Were they foolhardy enough to try and rob one?

Only the growing pain in his hindleg returned him to his situation as Jace passed that nervous smelling dun, as he headed up to the path to Sandor's plank. Again he had the sweaty feeling of being watched. Targeted. Climbing higher he scented the aroma of a fine, grape wine. It would taste good, but his purse decreed rawer brew.

Some of his troopers were at Sandor's plank. Clay, Abel, and Kear were already downing some of the Mayor's best. Abruptly finishing Clay nodded a tight smile to Jace, then hurried away, showing he would be in Deadrick's camp. So be it. Jace watched him leave then put down half a copper on the plank. "Cheap and raw."

Sandor pushed his coin back. "No trouble in the bazaar, that is worth a toast to the peacemaker. Are ye our new peacemaker?" He asked as he poured.

"The Regiment must be settled first."

"Aye." Watching the other big centaurs move off, Sandor frowned. "Your troopers grow restless..."

"Most will be marching soon."

"They take the centauresses' commission?"

"Many of us will."

Sandor still looked concerned. "Do ye march with them?"

Jace evaded answering by taking a long sip from his drinking horn. Even the raw berry had a satisfyingly warming taste, Jace nursed it long, and the drink pushed back his leg pain. Several more of his troopers and some locals joined them at the plank to be served. After pouring for them, Sandor seemed to want to talk more, and finally, he beckoned Jace to the back of his stall. "Good, sir. You have a taste for the berry. Mayhaps you can rank this brew I think of buying?"

An offer to serve as a taster would bring another free drink. Jace nodded and followed Sandor back to his stacks of clay pots and barrels. With Sandor ahead of him Jace noted his distinctive dun coloring was even more noticeable, especially that black fur line down the Mayor's back over his long spine. Sandor hefted a leather bag and poured a generous taste into Jace's drinking horn. Smelled like sour berries and tasted strong and good. "Will be well-liked."

Sandor nodded. "Then try this." Sandor reached for another pour.

As he waited, Jace asked. "In the bazaar, I have seen several centaurs that appeared to have coloring such as yours, with red-brown smearing their hides. Are you of their kin?"

"Scarlur." Sandor spat the name out. "They are not of mine!" He flushed angrily, even to his front stomach as his short black tail swished high with indignation. "My mare was taken and held by them until her kin could pay the ransom. Their leader, Red Knife, took a liking to her and gave her the *'honor'* of becoming one of them. Of being tied down and ritually branded. She bit him every time he came near! I am the result of her imprisonment, but none save fools hold it against me!"

"These duns..."

"They call themselves the Scarlur–we call them marauders."

"They paint themselves with blood?"

"Stinks like it–but no, they use a paint-pot rock they find on the beach. When you wet it, it rubs dark red on your fingers."

"They wear chopped centaurs' tails?"

Sandor looked sickened. "Aye. And necklaces of centaur teeth." He busied himself pouring more ale in his own drinking horn. "In my grandsires time, the Scarlurs were just scrabbling clans that lived off the scrublands. Not smart enough to be dealers, nor trustworthy enough for caravan work. Then they got war leaders, Red Knife, and Red Sun. Small bands came together, so they gave up hunting and turned to raiding. When Red Knife was killed his sons, Nine-Kill and Bloody-Ax, took command."

"No one stops them?"

"There is usually no one left to complain." Sandor lowered his eyes and tail in shame. "We are merchants, not fighters."

"If you hired us?"

"I have spoken of this, but the others say the Scarlur leave us alone. They do their killing away from the Headlands Bazaar. To the others, this is something we just must live with or leave."

"But if the Regiment stopped the caravan raiding your trade would increase."

"Or if the Bazaar allied with ye and ye failed, we would all be killed." Sandor looked around him. The nearest vendors averted their eyes. "Long and loudly I have spoken with the rest. Ye will get nay hiring here, more is the shame on our heads. Bloody-Ax and Nine-Kill are killing off the trade routes that keep us alive." Sandor looked up, "I have patrons." Jace followed Sandor out and stood while he poured several rounds. When it was quiet again, Sandor turned to him. "If your warriors stay here they may kill us before the Scarlur do?"

Jace ignored the implied question. "A commission would be good for all.
But these comely silver ladies—do you think we get a straight

run from them?"

Sandor's lips thinned. Ferment merchant or not, this centaur did not wish to pass on gossip, but Jace must press. "Are you sure they be the shes of those fabulous silver mines?"

"Aye, they are old Silver Beard's get. Why did Star say she needed you?"

It was a prying, impertinent question. One a mercenary might draw sword before answering, but Jace desperately needed to know what trail they would trot. "She spoke about a dragon infesting their mines."

"Dragon?" Sandor frowned.

"Have you ever seen a dragon?

Sandor reached under the plank and pulled out another jug. "Grape wine from the Yellow lands." He poured another for himself and gestured to Jace. "On the plank." Jace had more than had his thirst quenched but allowed a short pour. A merchant who poured his wares without pay did not last in merchanting long, but Jace had the feeling that Sandor ordinarily did not treat his customers. That the Mayor was digging for something.

"Dragons. Heard of them." Sandor said as they both drank. "In high tales around the fire platform."

Jace sipped the burning brew. "Pepper based? Interesting." It gave a warming numbing to his body. "Dragons are tales to tell youngsters?"

"I have heard the tale singers chant that the Silver centaurs had mined into the mountains and come upon an immortal dragon. One of their wise ones learned the creature's weaknesses. He was fascinated by their polished mirrors, so they made an unholy alliance with him. Some say their smiths even controlled the dragon's burn, forcing him to breathe on the molten metal as they forged their unbreakable swords."

"Well trained this fierce beastie." Commented Jace dryly.

"Never believed in fire mound yarns that I have not seen myself."

"Then you do not believe in dragons?"

Sandor took a deep sip before answering. "When I was bare past a colt, one of the Silver centaurs came to the Headlands. He had tight, scar-white skin over his chest, stomach, front legs, down to his hooves. As an impertinent youngling, I asked what caused this. He laughed and said he had been scalded by a dragon's breath."

"Sounds like a smith who had been careless with his forge fire."

Sandor again lowered his eyes. "With great wealth, there are always those others that wish it for themselves. In the past, I had heard of parties that sought the wealth of the Silver centaurs. Those who hunted their hoards never came back."

"What killed them? Dragons or Scarlurs?"

"Or the Silver centaurs themselves. Hard muscles grow out of digging those mountains, and deadly swords are hammered from their fires."

"Scarlurs--why does your gathering sell to outlaws?"

Sandor's smile turned ironic. "They seldom buy. They wait until the unwary are out of our sight, and then they harvest pouches, teeth and tails."

Jace shook his tale in anger. "Mayhaps after the Regiment defeats the Silvers' dragon, we will return here and solve other problems."

"Then ye are not our marshal?" Sandor's drinks were not watered. Their potent haze was driving out Jace's leg pain and buoying his hopes up as Sandor continued, "Ye did well with the fighting ones. If you stay as our peacekeeper, mayhaps if we had a leader such as yourself..."

It was a rich offer, for a limping, battered warrior, one he should take while it held. Jace looked up, over the white tipped blue sea, the sky darkened with orange-tinged clouds. "We will talk again."

Jace started down the hill, expecting to pick up a comrade or two but the others must have hurried to have first cuts at the fire pits. If he were late, Jace would have only the tougher leg meat, unless Sandi guarded a platter for him. Jace's hind leg was hurting again. He thought of the yellow cakes in his pouch, but his coin was thinning. He would be wiser to save them, and he was already taking more than Merdi said safe. The beach sand gave way to dirt and river grass. He stopped to take the weight off his leg, smelling the fresh water ahead.

He stood in the trees, on a well-trodden trail along the river. Sounds behind him of banners and skins were being furled in the bazaar. Across the river, some sounds of chopping wood but he saw nay sign of any of his guards. Were they hidden by the trees or were they all hacking at the spitted meat? Garrison should be handling that.

Another sound. Closer. Off to his side flank. Jace pretended to be looking into his coin pouch, as he listened intently, trying to fix its source. In the shadows of the trees, he could make out the leg and chest line of a centaur. Male. Waiting. Following him? Ambush?

Jace casually reached down, with his fingers he deftly slipped off the holding cords on his sword and knife. Back on his harness was a blowing horn for summoning reinforcements in battle. He could blow the ox's horn and have half a dozen warriors charging out of the wood across the river. Then what? They might rout out some poor soul taking a shit in the tree screens?

Another slight movement. Could have been taken as a breath of air blowing the leaves but Jace was sure there were at least two. Following him. Why? Bad place for an ambush. Foolish, desperate thieves or just two lovers trying not to be seen?

By Thunder's Horn if only the wind would shift and he could get a whiff of who was there. Should he move, plunge into the river and start wading to camp? That would force them to show themselves or abandon pursuit. It would put Jace closer to reinforcements, but with his leg so bad, fighting in mud would be a definite disadvantage. Especially against two or more opponents that could surround and cut him down.

Jace carefully started to swing his hindquarters around, planting all four hooves on solid ground, facing the woods and his stalkers. The wind was turning, starting to come from the trees before him. Good.

Ahead a vision of beauty walked out of the shadows. Star, with her soft halo of snowy hair, her slender black legs. She was moving towards him. For a second that thrill of joy at seeing her...

But something was wrong. The smell was not Star's sweet seaweed, nay, it was of desert sand and dry thorne weed. The movements were smooth but had not the fluidity of her graceful walk.

The she ahead had Star's pale gray skin, soft cream colored dabbles on her hindquarters and tall, proud head. But the full breasts were too full, the long legs too muscular, the heavy body was almost a parody of Star's. This she was covered in jeweled necklaces, with pounds of gold chains cascaded from her throat to her belly. The lips that had Star's fullness were a bit too wide. The darker green eyes and the lips were thickly painted by black lining.

And on her sinister cheek, this centauress had a white, rectangular brand burned into her face. Now he knew who followed him. Had they trapped him? Nay. If necessary, he would run down this traitoress, with her treacherous false smile.

"Good, sir." She said softly as she walked to him in a stately fashion. As she stepped, her many gold chains chinked softly against each other.

He cocked his head to one side, hoping to keep her string pullers in sight. "My lady." He said coolly returned her greeting.

They stood at an arm's length from each other. She had apparently expected her beauty to bedazzle him, but it did not.

She tried again with an even more winsome smile. "I believe you have met with my sisters."

He just returned her gaze. "And you are?"

"Silver Belle, sister of Silver Star, Silver Crescent, and Silver Sunny."

"Your sisters did not name you."

She did not protest that. "I understand you deal with Star?"

"Does your sister tell you this?"

"Are your warriors in her hire?"

"Mayhaps you should ask your sister, my lady."

Her smile hardened. "Did she tell you why she hired you?"

That Jace felt he might now learn if he could keep her talking. "Our contract is clear."

"Your duties?"

"To obey, my lady."

Belle waited, then decided he would speak no more.

"I speak with love for my sisters. They do not need fighters. If they come to me, my clan will protect them."

"Your clan is?"

She drew herself up with great pride. "The Scarlur!"

"Then the Scarlur will protect your sisters from who-- the Scarlur?" He asked sarcastically.

Her lips thinned, and her eyes glared. "Do not enter into something you do not understand!"

"Explain it to me," He calmly replied.

She looked briefly to the side as if waiting for her hidden comrades to burst out of the trees. When they did not, she turned and defiantly braced her legs. "Understand this, Star's coin is covered in blood. It buys only death for you!"

Before him, someone's misplaced hoof struck on rock. With his left hand slipping over the hilt of his long sword, Jace leaned his other arm across to his hindquarters and grabbed the ties to his ox horn. With it in his hand, he brought it up to his chest, wetting his lips. "My lady, it is fair dangerous for you to be out here. I fear that some varlets lurk in the shrubbery, obliviously intend on robbery. Shall I summoned my warriors to our aid?"

She glared at the shadows behind her, then seeing no movement, turned back at him. Her voice lowered in anger, "What has Star offered you?" She waited, and when he said nothing. "I can offer more."

Jace looked at her hard eyes, thickened ankles and mass of jewelry hiding her bosomy chest as he smiled sadly. "Nay. You can not."

Chapter Eight

When in doubt

Charge!

Jachom of Iron Shield

Silver Belle tensed for the attack that did not come. Obviously, her two bush mates decided that Jace's size evened the odds. Her frustration with their gutlessness further harshened her features. "My sister is a liar! She has no gold! You will be paid nothing for your valiant fighting!"

"You wear much gold around your neck. Will, you not sacrifice that for your beloved sister?" He said in mocking tone.

With angry eyes and a tight lined mouth, she twisted her torso to stare back into the trees, but there was only silence. Turning back, she glared at Jace. "You tell Star if you march with her, she will watch you die!"

Tail high in anger, Silver Belle, turned and bounded off into the marsh grass toward the trees. By the rustling in the bushes, her two comrades were rapidly fleeing before her anger. Concerned, Jace retied his blow horn to the back of his harness. Why had Star not mentioned this sister and her Scarlur comrades? It boded ill that his patroness be concealing obstacles. He plunged all four legs into the river's coldness. It would feel much warmer to be among his troop of warriors.

On the other shore, he took the hillside at a trot. Up the trail, Garrison had set a guard concealed within the trees. When Jace surveyed the meadow, Ghost and Wheat turned their heads, rather than look him in the eye, so they probably were dropping out. Golden tanned Brandy looked at him and smiled brightly. Out of long habit Jace hungrily ran his eyes down her breasts, stomach, and withers, but although Brandy was as lush as ever, he found himself comparing her to Star's slender perfection. Dung!

He walked to the water spring and as he hauled up the community dipper to sip he got that "targeted" feeling. Antsy Jace looked up and around to see four figures were headed his way, with shoulders squared: red-haired, white-hided Arnfinn and Arjuna, behind them their younger brother, Aneurin, who still had mostly black hairs on his whitening hide and their sister, Ana. She at last grown to full age, had long, light scarlet hair hanging down her pure white skin and hide.

Usually, flirtatious Ana always returned his glance with a come-hither smile. Now her sapphire eyes were cast down. Jace braced himself. Big Arnfinn spoke first. "Sir..." Then dropped in to uncomfortable silence.

"You wanted?" Jace prompted.

Spearing was Arnfinn's talent, not speech making. He looked helplessly to Arjuna who then looked to the youngest, Aneurin, who stepped up. "Sir. We have served under ye for many long trots."

"And you have prospered." Jace formally answered.

Aneurin looked to Arjuna and Arnfinn, they all nodded tails in unison, "Aye."

Ana sounded rebellious. "I told ye that!"

Aneurin continued. "We wish to move on." He stopped and looked at his brothers as if lost.

Jace decided to help them. "Where will you go?"

"To the Yellow. Arnfinn hears the Imperial be on the move again. They will take outlanders."

"And put them in the front lines to be scythed down." Jace pronounced.

"That be as it may." Arnfinn looked to both his brothers. "But we will be warriors fighting."

Jace turned to Ana. With her sweet welcoming smile, she spread unspoken promise. Still she seemed unaware that her brothers made it clear that no one dares touch her. "Ana, you know that the Imperial does not take she fighters?"

With wide eyes, she turned on her brothers. "They do not?"

Arnfinn shifted his hooves uncomfortably."They take cooks and those who clean up."

Ana excelled at spear, was fast in charge and Jace had been schooling her in archery, but now she would be relegated to just roasting meat. The Imperial would not make a public groomer out of her–at least not while her brothers lived.

Arjuna eyes were downcast. "We had signed on to the Regiment, but now we wish to leave..."

Jace finished. "With honor. Go to Ardon. There will not be much of a portion, but tell him I have ordered yours." Jace nodded, stretching his arm out. "May all your canters be successful."

Arnfinn put out his sword arm out in the air, Jace stepped forward and clasped his elbow holding it firmly. "Arnfinn, may many die under your hooves."

After his brother walked away, Arjuna came to Jace seemingly too choked up to talk and just held his arm. He was followed by Aneurin, who quietly stated. "Much food have we gained from you." Jace nodded his tail in acknowledgment.

As her stiff-backed brothers trotted away, a tear rolled down Ana's cheek. She stamped her dainty front hoof. "They will not listen to me!"

"Aye." Jace reached out with two fingers and brushed the tear off her cheek. "But they love you, and they do what they think is best. Go lightly, lovely Ana. Mayhaps our trails will cross again."

Her lips pursed, she seemed about to speak, but shameful tears were filling her eyes. Ana abruptly turned tail and loped away.

Sandi and Garrison trotted up beside Jace. Sandi glared angrily at Ana and her brothers' departing flanks. "They bugging out?"

"They are released by me. What is the count?" Jace said, trying not to sound concerned.

Garrison habitually straightened his shoulders and took a respectful stance as he reported. "It was twenty-six. Four less now, that those white hides are gone."

"Only twenty-two?" Lady Star would not be happy with that.

Sandi looked mutinous. "Where do the white dungs go?"

"Imperial."

"Fools." She trotted off her tail raised in anger.

Garrison looked thoughtfully across the field to the four white centaurs trotting away. "Ana always pinked whenever ye came near. Mayhaps if ye talked sweetly with her..."

"Arnfinn sets his sister's trail."

Garrison narrowed his eyes, "Perhaps if ye..."

"Seduce her? Fine. Then I have her three brothers to fight."

Garrison sadly shook his tail in agreement. He looked out over the camp. "Not all are counted yet, some are still deciding. Mayhaps I can push a bit more to our side."

"Deadrick getting anyone from the locals?"

Garrison still looked away. "He is trying, but they are a short-legged lot."

"You signed on?"

A surprised Garrison turned his head back to look at Jace. "Aye. What else would an old warrior do?"

"Training? Merchanting? Run a herd of seducing shes for metal?"

Garrison chuckled. "Nay. I will die in a weapons' harness." His face became a frown. "And ye, my old friend, how does the leg do?"

Anyone else Jace would lie to but, "It stays the same." Garrison's eyes sharpened, forcing Jace to amend. "Nay. It gets worse."

Garrison spoke softly."Then mayhaps this dragon quest will be mercy for the both us."

"We might win gold amour..."

"And emerald dragon scales..." Garrison whipped his tail in a gesture of dismissal and started to move off when Jace held up his hand.

"Weapons procurement?"

Garrison, twisted his torso back. "All have at least one sword, some arrows, and bows. We could craft more spears if we have time."

"Nay. Armor?"

"Poor. What is in the bazaar is generally too small for our breeds. We have gotten shields, some chest padding." Garrison reached back into his harness for a round of iron with a nose guard. "This helm fits for me. They had not even sanded off the ear blood from its last owner."

"Goodly sized warrior."

"At least his head."

"The others?"

"Only eight helms to the whole Regiment. The dealers promise more–we will see."

"Have Sandi trade for tanned leather. She and Urzi

can craft some basic head protection for us on the march. Have her set Ross and Kent to piercing sewing holes."

"Urzi is working on drums and chest protection. Does Urzi march with us?" Asked Garrison carefully.

Jace ignored the question. "Anyone working on armor does no rotations of camp chores or cart pulling. This sunset Rufus and Snake to cutting down some of those long, straight trees that can be trimmed to fighting poles."

Garrison nodded. "We should start practicing pole ax fighting again."

Jace moved alongside Garrison's flank so he could speak softer. "There are some new hes in the bazaar. Short. Bullying. Dun-colored, with dark hair and wide black stripes running down their backs to their tails. They brand their she's cheeks and decorate themselves with centaur tails and teeth."

Garrison nodded. "The amour merchant spoke of ones they call '*marauders.*'"

"Scarlur is the tribal name."

"Sounds as if they have been killing the caravan route. Anyone interested in hiring us to take them on? Be a lot easier on both of us if we could forget the hard march and just hang around on the beach waiting for them to attack."

"Bazaar merchants think they can have peace by turning a blind eye."

"Fools. So we do not get to seek out the Scarlurs."

"Actually they seem to be seeking us. Or at least me."

Garrison shifted his hind legs again. He must be getting some hindquarter pain too.

Jace continued. "I stood in the way of some young stud, one with more pride than sand. He backed down, but he may have sent his brothers to hunt me. Over by the river, a she who looked kin to Lady Star tried to talk me out of our dragon hunt. When she could not, she expected help from her two comrades in the bushes."

"They attacked you?"

"Too shy to show their faces."

"Or building courage to get another one of us alone? I will pass the word."

"It concerns me that Lady Star told me nothing of this Silver Belle."

"Nice of the Silvers not to mention this to us. They babble of dragons and talk nothing of these desert tribes?" Garrison stomped a front hoof in frustration.

Jace shook his tail. "Star proclaims she needs more warriors. We need more recruits–Get Deadrick to work harder."

Garrison looked away. "What about Urzi? He is older than us and hops on three legs."

"He taught us both how to fight."

"Aye."

"Where would he go?"

"Jace, he can not keep up."

"We need bodies."

"Ye need warriors who can gallop into battle. Urzi's time has gone!"

Garrison wanted to argue, but Jace cut him off. "Urzi has limped long. In battle, he throws a spear through sinew and bone."

Garrison finished. "And when his spears are gone, he hops in to kill all with his sword, but Jace on a forced march he cannot keep up."

"Mayhaps he will not sign on."

"He already has. That is how we made twenty-two–but it is wrong! Ye have to tell him he is out!"

Feeling the pain deep in his leg again Jace looked over the camp. He limped, Garrison walked with stiffness and

Willow played with her sireless youngsters. As Reet walked away from them on her stocky legs, Jace noted again she had put on a lot of weight this forced march. Jace suddenly realized just how far she swelled out. "Reet's flanks seem to grow."

Garrison looked over at her, stroking his graying black beard. "She is of a stocky, solid breed."

"Look at her from the rear. She is way out."

Garrison followed his eyes and answered regretfully. "Aye. I will get Sandi to ask her if she is with foal but she and Per Ben have signed on."

"Dung! We need her. We need him even more."

"If she is carrying and we have a battle, she will drop it. They always start labor during the battles."

"Reet can guard the provision carts," said Jace thoughtfully.

"Jace, ye do not need a pregnant she on a dragon hunt!"

"If we leave her behind, we lose Per Ben. They camp with Arnfinn, Arjuna and Aneurin. I am surprised they are not also marching to the Imperial."

"Per Ben is loyal to the Regiment. Maybe he will leave her here and march with us?"

"We need all the bodies we can show, pregnant or not. Dung!"

Garrison shook his tail. "Bodies is what we may all be." With a twist of his lips, Garrison moved stiffly off. "I will try talking with Arnfinn."

Jace should have told Garrison that he would not be marching and that he was staying behind as peacekeeper to the Bazaar. But the others? What was Garrison marching them all off to? A dragon hunt? A Scarlur massacre?

In battle, Reet could stay with the baggage carts but if

she was with foal and Per Ben died on this dragon hunt they would probably all die, while Jace was back at the bazaar as a peacekeeper. Yet peacekeeper was an honorable post with steady food and drink, not much work and friends to talk with. It was time he did not have an entire Regiment dependent on him with its endless worries. Aye. The Regiment should march without him! But somehow that reasoning did not comfort him.

Finally, the rich smell of roasting meat overrode his worries. Jace trotted over to Sandi's fire pit. She waited, guarding long sticks skewered with strips of dripping pink meat.

"Ah, Sandi, your enticing aroma irresistibly drew me..."

"Gravy and boiled roots. You be such a romantic suitor. Here we saved the best for our leader."

At least Sandi knew the path he would take. Jace bit into burn crusted meat. "Kent is a good hunter." Jace waited until Sandi s selected a second cut from the stick, then he cut off another for himself. "On the second sunrise the Regiment moves out."

"Four sunrises would be better. There be a grove of straight, tall trunked trees a short lope from here. I could have Ross and Kent cutting them for spear shafts. Our weapons run low."

"Our patron says haste is necessary."

"Her dragon will fly off?" Sandi raised a quizzical eyebrow.

"We have a commission that pays in gold."

"So we must unfurl the black and yellow banners from every spear when we parade out. Only we have lost all our banners and spears with the baggage carts."

Jace lowered his tail, sadly, he had forgotten that. He

looked to the Bazaar. "Mayhaps we could trade for cloth?"

"They want too much metal for black cloth. I bought yarn, Brandy can weave some in time but not by sunrise." Sandi pointed to the sinister side of the field. "Per Ben just traded for that bright green capelet for Reet."

"That is nice." Jace concentrated on cutting another piece of meat from the third stick. Juicy.

Sandi was scanning the entire field. "And Willow managed to hold on to her lovely blue flank cloak. She wore it into our last battle."

Jace finally realized where she was going. "It will be hard to wrest a new cape from Per Ben. He keeps a tight purse, it must have taken all of Reet's wiles to have him to gift her with such luxury."

"Reet is loyal to the Regiment. She will cut and sew the banners. The fighting one will be Willow, she has long embroidered on that blue cloak." Sandy braced her four legs for battle. "Sir! Permission to change the Regimental colors from black and yellow to green and blue."

"Go for it." She was already trotting off as Jace yelled behind her. "But do not expect me to guard your hindquarters when the battle begins! You females fight too deadly!"

Sandi's laugh danced over the field. So now the Regiment would march under blue and green. As his sire, Jachom, would say, '*When the trail turns, it is easier to turn with it than tramp a new one.*'

A flash of bright yellow and white as Deadrick high tailed it in to the center of camp, followed awkwardly by three, no four youngish centaurs. As Deadrick raised a hand, they halted clumsily, milling nervously about. Deadrick's hand signaled an order for them to stay, then he turned and trotted toward Jace. One local started to follow Deadrick, who just halted, turned and herded the offender back into place.

When he cantered up to Jace, Deadrick spoke in an undertone. "Keep your face looking grim and shake your head a lot. I want them to think I am trying to talk you into accepting new recruits."

Setting his mouth to look grim was easy as Jace surveyed the four yokels. Only one over 16 hands at the hip-shoulder but that one looked muscular. The others, probably dealers' colts expecting adventure, were but average size. For show, Jace shook his head no again. "Any fighting experience between them?"

"None." Deadrick kept his face serious as he gestured broadly with his hands as if he was pleading their case before Jace. With a wide sweep back towards them, he smiled and lowly said. "Nay training and not much in the way of aptitude among them. One of them, Jerrick, tells me we will be facing some rough lads in that desert to the Blue there."

Playing along, Jace stared at the candidates from head to hoof then shook his tail 'no,' but spoke quiet words. "The Scarlur. They have already warned us off their lands."

Deadrick raised his head, his eyes widening with anticipation. A fight was coming, and he would gallop full out to meet it. "There are still some I could approach if we could offer gold?"

"Only if they are fools enough to march on promises. What have we got?" Jace quietly studied the recruits. "That short legged gray, with dark hair and light tail?"

"His name is Horn. He is a hunter and butcher."

"The chestnut hided?"

"Jerrick. His dam has a plank in the bazaar. That brown skinned, white hide splashed with brown, the one with half a head of white hair and half of brown and with the matching tail, that is Barley." Deadrick explained. "He claims he is a champion fighter."

Jace smiled grimly. "And the big roan hide?"

Deadrick smiled. "Skull. A gift from your friend Mayor Sandor. Seems the bazaar folk would be happier if he marched with us. Might actually have some fighting ability."

"Do they have weapons?"

"Eating knives. A bow or two. One has a cooking pot he could use as a helm."

"In the Yellow Dominion, I turned down any under 17 hands tall. The ones we accepted all had to have a full battle harnesses, helms, and swords."

"The Regiment marches when?" Deadrick reminded.

"Aye." Jace forced a tight smile. "Let me greet our new troops. Sandi!" He signaled her over. He would have Sandi start instructing these green stalwarts in basic hand signal commands. With the march coming up, they would have to learn fast.

She trotted over to him to him and Deadrick.

"Those are our new recruits." Pronounced Jace.

A tight, bitter smile on her face she asked, "Deadrick, you could not find any that also hopped on three legs?"

Deadrick glared at her and said lowly. "How many have you recruited?"

"Silence," Jace growled. The waiting recruits shifted nervously under his withering gaze.

Deadrick trotted up to them. "I present to you Jace of Thunderhoof Regiment, renowned warrior of a thousand battles!"

Skipping the exaggeration, Jace lowered his head. "Good evening, sirs. This sun you join a regiment of great distinction. In time you will be trained to fight among the best. Before sunsink, finish your dealings with kin and creditors. This dark you will sleep within the Regiment's camp for soon we march. Sandi here will introduce you to your officers."

"Officers?" asked Skull.

"Officers. Members of the Regiment you must obey. Deadrick. Myself. Sandi, here. Others you will meet." He looked to Sandi and continued. "These recruits must be instructed in basic hand commands this gloaming–we march next sunrise."

He walked off, but Sandi followed, finally getting his attention. Her eyebrows raised slightly she spoke softly. "Jace, they are too short to be considered. They do not even know how to form a line."

Jace forbore pointing out that Sandi herself was smaller. "If they need training, train them."

"My sons Kent and Ross would make good trainers."

She was angling for two more shares. One, even two younglings were not worth a full share, but they had been taking on greater responsibilities for the Regiment, especially Kent. "They start as trainers at a quarter share each. Have them begin with these recruits."

Sandi wheeled toward the new recruits, short tail high as she trotting smartly before them. "All right, you varlets, let see if you can pick up a spear!"

Jace went off to chew his pain cakes. As he ate, he had that feeling of hair rising on his tail again. In battle, he would know he had been targeted so now he looked around. Dung! The roan-hided Lerestra was trotting his way. Why do you always lose the good ones? Knowing what was coming, Jace just wanted to lope away but did not.

Lerestra planted four hooves in front of him. "Jace, I have marched with ye from Knife Grass plains to the Yellow Hided Dominion."

"Aye. Fine battles we have had."

"But we grow older."

"That is not bad since there is only one other choice."

Lerestra could not meet his eyes. "I do not march this time."

"Why?"

"Jace, I have followed your tail through mud and blood, but ..."

"You do not believe in dragons?"

"If we find a live dragon, we kill it. If it is a myth, we keep the lady happy and collect her gold."

"Then what disturbs you?"

"I always follow a strong leader, one who knows how to fight. One who knows when to fight. One who keeps me alive." Lerestra spoke earnestly.

This made Jace looked away. "Not always."

"Not everyone can come back from battle." Leresta was a fighter who did not falter. "I have followed you long. If the Regiment marches without you, I too leave."

"Leadership is still being decided."

Lerestra hesitated, but he was fearless in battle and never stopped from jumping a high hurdle. "Jace, even if you did take command, your leg does not heal. Can you do a hard march? I think not."

Neither continued. In his heart, Jace knew Lerestra was right.

Lerestra finally looked at him straight in the eye. "If this dragon breathes fire and kills you, there will be no leader for me."

"Garrison."

"Is a good warrior. He could lead, but he will not be allowed to. Deadrick or Two Spot will challenge. If he chooses to fight, he will be killed. Two Spot is too slow to lead, he comes up with no strategy."

"Deadrick leads charges..."

"And can fight as a warrior, not as leader. He will proudly charge when we should flank. He will listen not to those who are wiser."

"You go to the Imperial?"

"Nay." Lerestra swung his tail aimlessly. "I do not know. I will trot bare for a while."

Jace put out his arm. "We fought as comrades, we part as comrades. Go to Ardon. See if there is a share left, but I doubt it."

Tail lowered, Leresta pivoted on his hind legs and loped off. Willow had been listening as with a stiff back Lerestra trotted off. Now she called after him. "Coward!" She spun on Jace. "Why did you not order him to stay?! He signed on after the drum call!"

"Marching with forced comrades is a fool's crusade."

"He deserves not a share."

Jace amusement lightening his load. "Are you ready to challenge Garrison for lead?"

Willow twisted her lips in a wry smile. "At least you should have asked Lerestra to stay for the review of our new patron. After we marched past her and started on the tramp, he could have dropped behind and gone his way."

Actually, Jace had considered just that, but Star's sharp eyes did not seem to miss much.

"What about Urzi?" Willow asked.

Jace turned to look, and he spotted Urzi's graying hair and tan hide over by the fire. By the Gods, Urzi was old when Jace started Thunder Hoof Regiment. Urzi was still strong but after a battle fall his front leg had never really healed. He strided with a small hop on that front stiff leg. Jace had gotten used to it, but now with his own leg aching, he fully appreciated the toll Urzi faced. But a lame warrior could slow the march. Or others endlessly trying to shield a weakened comrade in battle would exhaust the line. As much as he needed warriors, Urzi's time with the Regiment was over.

Willow still stared at him. "He can not march!

"Aye." With pain shooting up his own hind leg, Jace strode slowly over to Urzi.

The old centaur saw him coming, and he cast down his eyes, busily finding something that needs fixing on his travel harness. Jace stopped before him and waited for Urzi to finish tying the loosened thong.

"This harness is wearing out faster than I am." Said Urzi finally looking straight into Jace's eyes.

"Still a lot of life in it," Jace replied.

"I signed up for your dragon hunt."

"I know." Now it was Jace who lowered his eyes. "You have marched with the Regiment for many campaigns."

"Now I do not march, I hop."

Jace looked down at the ground, pawing a bit of grass. Urzi spoke first. "The others do not want me?"

"It will be a hard tramp."

Uzi looked away from Jace. "I understand. Time I....mayhaps go see more of the world."

"There is still a little to apportion." Jace reached for the remnants of his own pouch.

"Not necessary, Jace. The Regiment has been good to me. Had my full pouch with me in the last battle. I should be paying you coin..." He looked about. "But there is still much for me to finish. I am trying to replace our–your war drums. You will need chest protection."

"Urzi..." Jace was trying to speak without emotion.

"I will complete as much as I can before you march. Then I will stand at attention as you march out. The Regiment has been good to me."

"You have been good to it."

"Nay. It is time I leave."

Memories flooded back. "You taught me strategy–you were the first to sign when I formed the Regiment." Jace stopped and looked at the trees, as more memories flooded. Urzi patiently sparring cross staff with him. Teaching him a better way to feather arrows. Jace looked back at his old mentor. "As long as I lead, if you want to march or hop with us, you will."

"You lead?" He sounded surprised.

When Urzi had spoken about watching the Regiment march away, Jace had envisioned Star's proud head and beautiful pumping haunches loping away from him. He could not let her march away. Nor could he lose his Regiment. "Aye. I lead."

A grateful, relieved smile spread across Urzi's face. "I did not know what I would do without the Regiment..."

In that moment, Jace had finally made up his mind. "You can march with us, but I have another path for you to consider. There was an offer made to me but think I can get them to take you. This Headlands Bazaar needs someone to keep order. Someone who thinks before he acts. Who stops trouble before it roots."

Surprised, Urzi looked to the bazaar's direction. "As a peacemaker?"

"No long marches. No galloping into battle. Comrades to talk to every sun. The bazaar dealers will provide you with a largess of food and drink."

"What would I do?"

"It would be just like the training of the green recruits you do now. They respect your size. You will lay appropriate rules. The bazaar, to a limited extent only, will back you. In time you will cultivate comrades who fight beside you."

"Not many in that crowd." Commented Urzi

disparagingly.

"Aye. But some. Mayor Sandor would probably fight with you if need be. He has said there are others. They are not all craven fools, but they do face those raiding tribes."

His brow wrinkled. Urzi must have been thinking of this before. "I have never been in a gathering long-term, but as a peacemaker..."

"You will do as well as anyone."

Urzi pressed his lips together. If the Regiment marched, it would be his whole life marching away. Jace knew it as well as he did. Jace waited a few silent moments, then said, "I must give them an answer on the morn. There are others that I could recommend, but you are the best. Give it some thought."

"Aye." Urzi was looking about the camp. For a moment Jace thought both their throats were too tight to speak but then his old comrade said, "If I decide to march with the Regiment?"

"As long as I am leader, you will come," Jace said firmly. He would fight to the death for that.

Brow furled, Urzi nodded. "I will think."

Jace nodded his head and moved away to tell Garrison he was no longer leader.

Pain. Endless pain in his hindquarters. Sweating Jace woke to it. He should sleep standing up as he would on a forced march. Keep the weight on his three good legs, but that would only tire him more. What would he do on this dragon hunt? Urzi might be out hopping him? Jace looked about the field. The notion of Urzi had come probably by a slight, familiar aroma as he approached. Strange that on a field full of comrades' smells you could pick just one out.

"Jace, good sun." Urzi faced every sunrise with optimism.

"Aye." Jace shifted his weight off the hindquarter that hurt so much. How could Urzi hop for so long?

"I have thought much on my choices..." Urzi stopped speaking and looked longingly about the camp. "Mayhaps it might be a challenge to be the Bazaar Marshall."

Jace nodded. They both knew what Urzi was given up and now with Jace's deepening pain that Marshall job sounded very, very good. Yet Jace replied. "It will be best. In time it may be something you will be pleased with. At quarter-sun, you will join me at the Bazaar's river gate. I will guide you to Mayor Sandor and parlay for you."

Urzi nodded his tail in agreement. "That will give me time to complete a set of battle drums that Abel can wear on his withers. Not the best quality but they will work until I..." He paused, then quickly corrected himself. "until Sandi can craft better."

Jace nodded and walked away.

The box of yellow cakes was now empty. Jace knew it. Still he still fumbled with it. He had to get more. He would, but first, he would have to see Star again. The thought of her glossy hide and bright green eyes lengthened his strides.

Past the Bazaar. A long, beaten trail he cantered until Jace could see one of the Silvers in the woods by the river. This one had a shadowy circle on her forehead, so it was Silver Sunny. He slowed to a trot. Sunny's chest glittered in the sun and Jace could see she was wearing a necklace of elaborately wrought blue gems and silver chains. Now she looked up and smiled at him, then looked to the trees by the water.

"Sisters, we have a guest." She had a sweet, happy voice.

Crescent came out of the trees, followed by Star. They both must have been bathing in the river as water rivulets ran down their white blonde hair and pale pearl skin. Crescent shook her tail free of droplets as she and Sunny moved to the side to let Star step up to Jace. It was a rare female that Jace could look straight in the eyes without lowering his head. This proud she smiled directly at him as if joyful to see him.

"Good, sir, does your Regiment march for us?"

"It provisions prepares and I lead it..."

Her face brightened, and a smile spread. "We have asked the Goddess for this..."

"My lady, you understand we must have some advance payment before we march."

Sunny and Crescent were listening. When Star looked to them, Crescent nodded her head in assent and Star bounded away into the trees.

Surprised Jace just stood there. In a moment, Star returned carrying two bulging leather sacks that seemed almost too heavy for her to carry. She held them out to Jace. "You must be paid. This is the beginning, you will get more when you secure our mountain."

He was surprised at the heft the sacks he took from her. They weighed even his muscled arms down. To carry both, Star was a tremendously strong, fully equal to any she in the Regiment. He set one sack to the ground and untied the other. Gold and silver nuggets and jewels were jumbled in the bag. She had just handed over a fair fortune–what if he just ran with it?

Star seemed unaware of her lack of basic centaur sense. "Can you march now?"

"In two sun rises." He replied.

"There is haste." She protested.

"Aye, but we must provision."

"How many have you?"

"Thirty," Jace lied.

She bit her lip, but her disappointment showed on her face. "That is not enough..."

"How big is your dragon?"

"There are other dangers..." She started, then stopped. He knew she would not go farther.

"Thirty trained fighters are an army of great power. We will defeat your dragon and secure your mountain. This I vow."

Star stared into his eyes, questioning, then trust seemed to flood her own. "If that is what we have, we will march."

"The Regiment will fight well for you."

"You are leading?" Those wide green eyes looked so trusting into his. Two cool, green pools he could drown in. All thoughts of dank, dark pits and suffocating traps left him.

"Aye, I will lead it." He felt himself warming just to be breathing in her honeyed scent.

"Jace, I have spoken with Crescent, and she thinks we should host a feast for your warriors. Is that right to do?"

"It would be appreciated." Jace deeply inhaled her alluring aroma. "My warriors would be grateful for their patronesses' largess."

"Good. Sorrel and Rosie will prepare it. There are too many of you for the terrace..."

"On the beach near our camp. We can dig fire pits for them."

She looked embarrassed. "It will not be as elaborate as we served before, just ale, roast meat, and a vegetable pot."

"That will be most appreciated, my lady."

"Would they like mead?" She seemed anxious.

"Aye. Even more, appreciated."

"I will speak to Mayor Sandor. Silver Beard always said his brews were the best."

She smiled as he hefted the two huge sacks of gold. An experienced patron would not have handed all over to some traveling warrior, and she still had to pay for the Regiment's feast. Did his patron have more bags of gold? Perhaps he should set a guard on her camp.

Star was already moving off toward Sorrel's dining terrace. Bright light danced on her glossy black, white-dabbled flanks. When she shook that lush plume of a tail, he could see sunlight through her silky hairs and white bone tail. By the Gods, before he faced her dragon, he would mount her!

Chapter Nine

Every tramp over the high mountains

Begins with a single hoof fall

Ancient proverb

With her gold weighing down his carry harness pouches on both sides, Jace trotted back towards the bazaar. At the herbalist's, Jace spent the last of his metal on pain cakes. "We march at sunrise."

"All I have left until we get a caravan from the Purple if we ever do. In the meantime, try to rest and soak the leg as much as you can. And burn incense to the Twisted Snakes."

Jace thanked him, but Merdi still warned. "Eight of those will give eternal sleep so use them sparingly."

Jace nodded and was on his way. He met Urzi at the gate but told him to follow at a distance. Alone, Jace stopped at the instrument crafters and studied a cleverly carved flute, then two of two yellow cakes before stepped up the trail towards Mayor Sandor's plank. On the vendor's trail upwards, Jace swallowed two of the pain potions.

He nodded at new friends as he stepped up past their planks. Jace loved the smells and the sights of a bazaar, yet he would not miss the feeling of being penned in by these smaller centaurs and their stalls. It would be good to be on open plains again, feeling the wind whipping his chest. A hard rock resounded against his aching hoof and Jace slowed his stride. How could he take on this dragon hunt, knowing it must end in some stinking, confining cave?

Ahead a centauress was hanging out translucent silk scarfs–they were streaming in the wind from her booth. Blue-green with a grass pattern, bright orange with red butterflies...all the colors and creatures shes love to decorate themselves with. If he had any coin left, Jace would have bought the green willow pattern for Star and he would have wrapped it across her shoulders, just to see happiness shining in her eyes. This vision flooded his mind. Aye. He would follow her cloven hoofs, fool that he was.

Jace looked behind to see Urzi examining a finely crafted harp. Good. Jace trotted on to Sandor's plank where several locals were being served. He just waited patiently, until Sandor looked up expectantly, saying. "Your warriors say the Regiment marches for the Silver Centauresses next sunrise?"

Locked in his stall, Sandor still seemed to be everywhere, hearing everything. Jace nodded. "Aye. The Regiment marches and I will lead them."

The Mayor tightened his lips in disappointment. The welfare of his bazaar obviously meant as much to him as the Regiment did to Jace. Sandor shook his head. "It would have been good to have your stewardship."

"I am not leaving you unguarded. In fact, I have a warrior in mind for your peacekeeper. Our own peacemaker, Urzi." said Jace carefully.

"He is?"

"You have seen him. Tall, tan hided." Take the biggest hurdles first. "The one who limps."

Sandor had a puzzled look on his face then remembrance came into his eyes. "Urzi. Aye, the one who broke the fight up between your warriors by turning it into a game?"

"Tournament."

Sandor laughed. "Won metal on that tournament! Hauled an ale barrel down to the beach and sold dipper fulls, too."

"A tournament runs off the fighting spirits."

Sandor seemed to be giving Jace's proposal heavy thought. "That limp is bad as he seems to hop..."

"He has marched over mountains with it. Hopped into more battles then you have ever seen. He is a good fighter, but better yet a warrior who can prevent a battle."

"Aye." Sandor seemed to be agreeing. "Ye be right. A he who can misdirect trouble is what we need."

"The Regiment marches at sunrise. Uzri will march with us unless you offer him a position." Jace waited as Sandor poured a horn of cherry smelling wine for a patron.

When Sandor turned back to him, the Mayor spoke carefully. "I will speak with others, but I think we will be proud to have him."

"Then prepare to pour a toast for us three. Urzi!" Jace called out, briefly forgetting his pouch was empty. But as Urzi smartly hopped up, Sandor poured on the plank, saving Jace's warrior from having to pay for his own toast.

They drank then Sandor said, "At sunsink, I bring kegs to the feast the Silvers hold for your warriors. I think I will be permitted to make an offer to your comrade then."

"He will serve you well."

With the pain cakes working, Jace could trot back camp where he called in his officers. "We march at sunrise. Prepare! After this sunsink, we will form a march line. I will lead us to our patroness on the beach, who will provide a feast where we will pledge our allegiance. Pass these orders. All must attend!"

Three of his warriors took off with whoops of joy. Jace slowed and headed to Ardon. "You will be in charge of our funds from the Silvers." He took the two bags from his pouches.

Ardon reached and smiled crookedly at the weight of the bags. "Fine issue."

"Do not count it in front of the others." Jace loped off to Garrison.

Garrison was showing Barley how to wrap a spear point as Jace trotted up. Garrison looked to him. " Lerestra is back on the rolls now that ye lead."

Good. "Urzi will take the peace maker's position. You have found carts?"

"Well, there is a cartwright in the bazaar. For extra coin and brew, says he can fashion us one in a moon."

"No time. Our patron wants us to march. You were able to buy nothing else?"

"There is something back of those trees." Garrison's unenthusiastic tone worried Jace, who lengthened his strides as he followed. It was worse than he expected.

The first carts two high wheels slightly tilted outwards.

"Worn hubs."

Garrison nodded. "Sandi is sure she can straighten this along the trail, but for now it will haul the amour, drums, and weapons." Garrison moved to the next cart. " This will take the water barrels."

Jace staring in horror at the second cart. It was long and had four wheels, with pulls for four centaurs. "By the Gods?!" The cart was painted bright red and yellow, with blue flowers and orange eggs, green snakes and purple birds...

Garrison sighed. "It is some sort of festival cart. They pull it for the awakening ceremony to the Goddess and God of New Growth."

"Paint it!"

"What? Barter for pigment, oil. Mix it? Jace, we march on sunrise! It will be a moon before it dries!"

"Every enemy for miles will see that monstrosity!"

Garrison shrugged his tail. "Let them know we are coming."

"Was there nothing else?" Jace tried not to sound desperate.

"Only one other. There was a sound six-wheel cart in dark wood."

"Can we get that?"

"Some varlet with a dead nose uses it to haul and store dead fish. Jace, I will not march with a cart that smells worse than sweaty troopers!"

Jace looked at the two wretched wagons. "We must have that one too for the water barrels."

Garrison shook his head. "Do we take brew?"

"Nay. Spare the coin this marching. We will commission two more carts later,"

"Who pays for that build?" A relentlessly practical Garrison asked.

"After our successful dragon quest."

Garrison pointedly studied first the dilapidated two wheel then the garish festival wagon before turning back to Jace. "Actually, sir, methinks we are finely provisioned for a dragon hunt."

As his troopers prepared, Jace went down his own list. When they marched, his own harness must be in order. What else could he get before they left? A new bow? Arrows? His coin was gone, he would have to barter one of the few things in his harness. The pain in his leg radiated out his whole flank again. It was a pity Merdi had nay more pain cakes to sell.

Bending to the ground, Jace worked to free one of his underbelly harness buckles as he reviewed the Regiment's marching needs in his mind. Willow would stay as Regimental Surgeon. He would assign Axel to head a detail to prepare the beach for tonight's banquet fires. A feast was always welcome, but the sooner his warriors were out of brew and sobered up the better. Still, as the sun sank, he trotted to Garrison. "Give the order to round up our troops to follow after me. We go to our banquet."

A dour Garrison pointed out. "Which may be our last."

"Better reason to eat and drink deeply." Jace trotted to the front of the line, where his troopers marched by twos as into the darkening gloaming they trotted down to the sandy beach. Axel and several other warriors had helped Sorel setup four great, driftwood bonfires, arranged in a rough square. Jace watched as their high flames reflecting on the incoming waves.

Sandor carried two huge, wooden casks under his arms and set them down on the sand beside the eight others already there. Sorrel and two of his locals were roasting whole animals on the beach, while his she speared vegetables from a bubbling pot. Rosey was proudly sporting the elaborate jeweled chain necklace that Silver Sunny had once worn. Silver Star no longer wore her jeweled vest. That was probably how this feast was paid for. Jace hoped the Silvers had gotten more than just mutton and yams for their jewelry and he wondered what paid for Sandor's brew–Crescent's gemmed cap?

Jace ignored the first pits with roasting meats. The wide moon rose over the waves and with it, the wind briefly changed and Jace caught a scent like sweet seaweed–Star. He could see her and her gray sisters cantering along the white beach. Her blackened stockings and smooth gate made her appear to almost float over the pale, packed sand. She came to him opened eyed, smelling of passion and Jace knew he could have her this darkness. He was sure. He started to reach for her waist, but she was thrusting something into his hand. "More metal."

"What?"

"We traded my rings, Crescent's hair ornaments, and Sunny's jeweled anklets. Now we have more coin left over for your hire."

He wanted to pay her just for the privilege of standing beside her. Instead, he just took the sack and transferred to one of his pouches. "Graced be you."

She looked anxiously about. "Have you more fighters? I heard you were recruiting in the bazaar?"

"Yes." He nodded. They were recruiting, all the while they were losing more warriors through desertion. "We have taken some new ones into training. The Regiment always does that, but we have more than enough. Now, my lady, please stand here. The Regiment will parade."

And parade they did in one line before her. Each warrior throwing down a spear or a knife in the sand before her feet, a vowing of loyalty.

When it was done, Star nodded and called out to all. "Please feast with us."

And swam of disciplined warriors became a hungry herd, reaching for chunks of meat and untying drinking horns. Sandor galloped for more brew and the roasted beasts soon disappeared. The bright white moon rose and ran a wide trail across the waves. With stomachs filled, his warriors dragged more wood to the fires as high shooting sparks reflected on the dark waves hitting the beach.

At Jace's signal, Abel unhooked his flank drums. Then Deadrick led two lines of six centaurs out into the center sand. The others gathered eagerly made way to watch the military tattoo, where the most accomplished centaurs high trotted in precession figures.

Abel started a slow pounding beat. At Deadrick signal, his line and the other began high stepping parallel lines that loped away from each other then circled towards the center, each line crossing in an x formation in perfect timing. Each warrior passing just finger lengths from the one crossing before him. In the fire and moonlight, they circled, reared and crossed sides, all at equal distance. Crossing, reforming, then charging forward only for each line to meld past the other in perfect symmetry.

Jace watched Star's fascination with the precisely stepping warriors. Wishing so that his leg would allow that fancy stepping. Wishing that it was he who she stared at with such open admiration. Star looked up at him with shining eyes. "It this what they call a formal step dance?"

"The military version."

"May we join them?"

That startled him. His soldiers drilled long and sore-hoofed to make each careful movement look so effortless, but a misstep could result in a pile of injured dancers and perhaps shattered bones. "My Lady, false timing could crush a leg."

"We will be careful."

Jace was shaking his head 'nay,' when Deadrick whirled up. "My pleasure, my lady." Deadrick bowed with his front leg and held out his hand. Silver Star proudly took it, as they stepped forward in unison. Ardon took Sunny's hand, and Garrison reached for the hand of Crescent, who politely bowed, before joining him in line.

Abel slowed the drum beat as three troopers dropped from Star's line. Again there were two lines of six facing. Deadrick and Star facing each other. At first, they just stepped slowly in simple movements then they performed more and more elaborate figures as Abel increased the drum beat. Hooves beat sand faster and faster. Each line pair seemingly in perfect unison.

Axel stomped next to Jace. "Ardon may hurt Sunny. They should not risk it."

"But they are." As Jace watched Star gracefully swirl alongside Deadrick, he felt a flash of anger. Unreasonable but ...

Axel was not as experienced. "Ardon trots too close to Sunny."

What angered Jace seemed rather amusing reflected in Axel's eyes. "You should have led her out yourself."

Axel shook his head. "Most likely I would have trod on her tail. We are warriors, not court jesters."

The firelight gleamed on the dancers shining hides as their hoofs seemed to fly. It was as if the Silver shes had gracefully leaped the circles, squares and precision lines all their lives. While envious of Deadrick, Jace could still enjoy the incomparable beauty that was Star trotting into the close crosses.

Finally, they finished to the appreciative snorting and hoof stomping of the others. With a slight sheen from exertion that reflected the moonlight, Star pranced over to Jace. "That was uncommonly joyous."

"Much more a sweet to observe." Again he thought of joining the other couples, pushing her toward the dark dunes, kissing her back, biting her shoulder, mounting her, but duty required tasks that must be done. He maneuvered Star over to one of the bonfires, so he could see her reactions better.

She frowned. "Your warriors still drink of the mead. Will they be fit to march on sunrise?"

"Aye." But may not feel like it. "We will march for you. Now about our route. Do you have a chart?"

She looked puzzled. "Chart?"

"Some call it a map. Here..." He reached in and pulled

out Maximus' two wooden spindles with their roll of parchment, and he unrolled the first spindle. All along the edges, it was decorated with fanciful creatures, fierce dragons, burning birds, horned monsters. "This is a chart."

She shrugged her shoulders. "It is a roll of thinly scraped skins sewn together."

"Aye. The markings stand for the route we will travel. The caravan trail." His one hand rolled up the second spindle, as his other unrolled the first spindle. "Here. See. That says 'Black Mountains' that is your mines?"

"The caravan route does not go to our mountain. You must leave it at the valley below the mountains."

"This map is the caravan trail...."

"That is an ancient map. My Grandmare and Grandsire wished to keep the thieves and varlets away from us. Silver Beard closed the pass, so the caravan goes some other way. I know not it."

Frustrated Jace rolled the scroll back to the beginning and pointed to the chart, then to the waves on the beach. "See there is the sea." He traced his finger on the chart. "Here is the river that runs by the bazaar." He pointed again. "We are on the beach over here."

As she wrinkled her forehead in concentration, Jace realized he was more interested in touching her soft hair than marking his charts.

Star looked up at him with those wide eyes. "There is a sea serpent there."

"Merely a decoration to make it pretty. Now, my lady, study this. Here we are, across the river, see this is the Headlands Bazaar."

"That painting has more tents than the Bazaar has. It shows tents on both sides of the river."

"As you said, it is an old map."

"Oh."

He tried again. "Now, at sunrise, we follow this trail that is marked as the caravan route with a red line that leads from the Bazaar."

"Nay."

"Nay?" Jace had a sinking feeling.

He could tell by her eyes she was trying so hard to please him. "We go a different route. The caravan goes on that red line. We will start on that, then at the foothills, we will go another way."

"Another way?" Jace nodded. "Do you have a chart of this other way?"

"Nay."

"My lady, on this chart there are blue blotches that could be water holes. And these blue dashes are rivers?"

She gave his map a dismissive look. "It is poorly drawn."

"I suspect so, but you do recognize these water holes ...are they correct?"

"We will not go that way."

"We do not?" He looked from her to his pricey, worthless chart. "Which way do we go?"

She traced her fingers in the trees, along the river and pointed to the Blue -Black.

"That is the way my sisters and I have come."

Jace fished into his pouch, for a small cotton bag. From it, he extracted Maxima's marking stick. "Get Crescent and Sunny to come over here. You must show me where we will march and where we will find water."

In the darkness, others merrily drank, mounted, sang and bet on races run on the wet sand while by firelight, Jace struggled to pull a decent marching route out of the Silver sisters' misty memories.

Chapter Ten

With some centaurs

The only peace they will give you is death!

Garrison of Thunderhoof Regiment

Head proudly erect, Jace stepped forward to join Star and her sisters, standing before the bazaar's lower trail, as in columns of two Thunderhoof Regiment prepared to march before its patrons. Hoofs stomped, and harnesses jingled as warriors lined up. Jace scanned the ranks of bazaar dealers who lined the trail and had come to watch. Would they be impressed enough to hire the Regiment when this dragon hunt was over?

Off to the side, stood old Urzi. He waved and smile bravely as his only friends marched off without him. It put a lump in Jace's throat. In the distance, Ardon blew an "assemble" blast from the seashell. Sounds of solid hoofs striking the dirt. Mayor Sandor had come down, to stand beside Urzi. Jace silently asked the Gods to give them both long and uneventful lives.

As the double column reached them, Garrison peeled off lead position and trod to Jace, tail held high. "Regiment marching, sir."

So many times they had done this. So many times they had been proud of their formidable force. Now their depleted ranks were filled with shes, untrained locals and younglings and down the line, Jace could hear that damnable cart's wheels squealing. Still, above it all, two of Reet's blue and green two flags ruffled in the wind as Thunderhoof Regiment marched proudly.

Still Garrison, obviously struggling not to laugh

looked away from the line to Jace. Jace looked away from his Second and tried to focus what they could do with what they had: they would have to grease those squealing carts on the march; craft more weapons; train the green troops and start sketching a map of the land they trod.

Stiff-backed Deadrick and Wheat marched past with the new Regimental colored banners atop their spear shafts. Massive Axel and Two Spot followed, then Lancer and Nighthawk, Snake and Ghost. The jingling of battle harnesses and weapons melded with the dusty, drum of hoof beats.

Per Ben and Reet followed, with Domino and Clay. In matched twos, they marched. The fighting shes were placed center forward of the carts, tall Willow and Cloud, shorter Sandi and Brandy. Pulled by Lerestra and Orson the brightly painted fool's cart squealed past, mounded with weapons, leather, and tools. The second loaded with dried meat and fruit wobbled along behind, followed by the stinking long cart with its water barrels lashed high.

Green recruits followed the carts lead proudly by Kent and Ross. Finally, a solid rearguard was brought up by tall Rufus and Abel. They were just about past, when wild yells and a trample of hooves heralded four red-haired centaurs, Arnfinn, Arjuna, Aneurin and Ana were racing up. With a scramble of hooves, Arnfinn halted in front of Jace.

"Pardon, sir." saluted Arnfinn. "Late reporting for duty."

Jace nodded and smiled. "Join the ranks."

With another war whoop, the four were off bringing up the rear.

Crescent sounded pleased. "Four more."

Jace glanced down at his patron. "In fighters, those three males are worth twenty-four more. Even little Ana is becoming formidable." Star stood regally, an exotic queen surveying her invincible troops. She appeared transfixed by Jace's mighty army, by the Gods, he did not want to lose that look of pride in her eyes. And by the Gods, he would mount her this dark!

Later, out of sight of the locals, they would stop, send out scouts and reorder the march line. Star and her sisters would come after the forward columns, before the carts. Still a dusty position but safer if they were attacked.

For where the Silvers saw an invincible force, Jace noted raw recruits that were having trouble trying to march at a measured pace. They needed drilling, not a war march. When they were past showing off for the bazaar folk, he would have Sandi pull out the green troops and pair them with an experienced marcher. The feast cart's wheels wobbled precariously. Urzi could work on it–no, Urzi was no more. Willow carried her young filly on her back with her colt trotted alongside her. If Jace was not mistaken, Reet's flanks were twice what they had been before. What did they forget? You always forgot something on a march.

As Rufus and Abel had drawn abreast, Jace indicated that Star and her sisters were to join the line before the last scouts. To his surprise the Silvers traveled with neither harnesses nor cart, just trotted off barebacked with just a few grooming tools woven into their hair and a pouch slung off their shoulders. He found himself watching those cream dabbled flanks as they took marching position. Then Jace pulled up that long, braided cord he had tied to his battle harness. First sun marching, he tied a knot into it. Then he flicked his tail and Garrison followed as they loped up to the front of the column. "Reet's flanks grow bigger every sun."

"Aye," Garrison said regretfully. "Sandi spoke with her. Reet is with foal, and she is due in three moons. They have told no one because in the past she lost all the others."

"Hopefully we will slay our dragon before she drops the babe."

Garrison shook his tail. "If we have a battle, she will drop it."

Reet signed on. It was her choice. The Regiment was her kin. She was better off on the march, but what was Jace marching them off too?

They reached the top of the foothills before mid-sun. At the crest, Jace looked back. The dealers had all returned to their stalls; only one lonely figure still watched the Regiment. Urzi, Alone. Jace waved one last time.

The Regiment needed Urzi to fix those dunging wobbling wagons and to mend the signal drums, yet Jace had left him behind. Were all his decisions so rotten? Even with two of Merdi's yellow cakes, the pain was sapping his strength and sinking his spirits.

Out of sight of the Bazaar, Garrison and Sandi reordered the marching. With Scarlur about, Jace told the forward scouts to keep just out of sight. The Regiment marched at a steady pace–usually. This time, they did at the beginning, but soon the new recruits were slowing the columns.

Sandi had lifted Willow's colt up on to her back. Crossing the river at a stony, shallow ford, the second cart fell over. Time wasted righting it. The water barrels needed retying. Again, they stopped while Sandi and Abel rigged a temporary hold to the flopping wheel on the festival cart. Jace hurried to her. "Will it hold?"

Sandi shrugged. "Wish Urzi was here. This is a job for his magic."

"You can do nothing with these carts?"

"Chop them up for kindling." She saw the flash of anger on his face, she did not quail but added. "Sir."

"Just try–we need them!"

When he trotted off, he could hear Sandi muttering. "Should not have let Garrison go off buying by himself."

Ardon was headed his way. "Sir, we must talk."

"Now?" Jace stopped.

Ardon started loping away from the lines. "Privately."

He loped after Ardon. Where was he going? Finally, Ardon halted quite a distance from the line. "Jace..."

"Hold." Jace was untying his pouch from his harness and handing Star's bag to Ardon. "Lady Star gave me more metal at the feast."

Ardon opened it and poured some the contents into his hand. "Gold and silver coin. I will count it, but even with this, she is not making her promise of two silver coins, per sun for a moon cycle."

"She had two bags, and we had some metal salvaged from before..."

"Jace, you have five double officer portions, and twenty-five regulars pulling shares."

"Arnfinn and his have rejoined, and I promised quarter shares to Sandi's colts. Ross and Kent are training recruits."

That deepened the look of concern on Ardon's face. "Jace..." He shook his head but did not finish.

"You counted all that was in the sacks?"

"There has not been a time to do a full count. The first sack had unrefined gold, silver coin and gold veined quartz nuggets. I have not put the refined metal on trader's scales, but I can do a fair estimate."

Probably exactly within seed grains of measure. "Your estimates have always been quite accurate."

"The first sack will cover 15 suns marching."

"The second sack?"

"Mostly silver coin–another 7-10 suns at best."

"There was jewelry?"

"Aye. Exceptionally fine pieces, worth much. You will have to apportion it, mostly to the shes but, Jace, there was only half a moon's march metal there before we provisioned. Not the whole moon the Regiment was pledged."

"She has promised more when we open her mines."

"*If* we reach her mines. *If* she has told us the truth about her piles of gold. *If* we can defeat the dragon she claims guards it. Jace, you and I have covenanted her word. If our troopers march for nothing, they will tear Lady Star and her sisters apart–after they finish with us!"

Jace well knew that, but Lady Star was trotting to them, and he truly believed she was not hiding coin from them. Jace could halt the march now, yet there was nothing for them back at the bazaar. "The Regiment is marching, and we will open her mines. There will be gold." Ardon looked from Jace to Star. He looked as if he wanted to say more, but the lady was joining them. "Ardon, we will talk on this another time."

Star bounded up. "Jace, what is the delay?"

"The carts, my lady."

"Can not we just leave them here?"

"Water casks are necessary."

She looked helplessly about. "We must leave the caravan trail here."

Here? Where? Jace reached to untie his chart of the caravan route as he looked across gray-green prairies. What landmark had she used? He did not see anything: hills to the side and ahead; clumps of shrubbery and trees in the distance; ravines and fetlock high brush. The way Star pointed was just more prairie, not even a game trail. They would be tramping on just grass, brush and rock. He signaled to halt the column and loped to where Star's sisters had left the trail.

Star's unencumbered sisters were already taking the lead, moving briskly, jumping over dead trees and rocks and cantering off to nowhere.

Garrison trotted to Jace who said, "We leave the caravan trail here."

"Here?" Garrison looked in all directions.

"Follow her sisters."

"Is there a trail?"

"Does not look much like it." Jace stamped his front hoof impatiently.

Garrison just shook his tail as he looked down the line of troopers. "Nay worrying about the carts being stuck in trail ruts any more. Nay trail. It will be hard going, we will have to shorten the pulling rotations." He frowned. "What if these fine ladies have no sense of direction? Are we to wander aimlessly?"

"Order the change!" Jace regretted the shortness, but the trampled down caravan trail had been hard on his hindleg. This rough ground would be worse.

Garrison backed slightly. " Ross! Catch up with the front scouts. We are changing direction. Kent, tell Deadrick! Follow the ladies!"

They went from a dusty, beaten dirt trail to grass, rocks, and nothing ahead. The rough going was hurting Jace's leg. He chewed three of Merdi's cakes as he galloped the line to Sandi. "How were the new recruits were doing?

"Barley disappeared. Bugged out I guess." Sandi said with contempt.

"Barley?"

"That new recruit with the two colored hair and tail."

"Oh, the odd white and brown one?"

"He said he had hoof stone and dropped to the back of

the march line. Out of my sight, he must have run off in the bushes to high tail it back to the bazaar. Do you want us to go after him?"

"Nay. We always lose a few. How are the rest holding up?"

"The green troops? Sore of hoof, but they can be whipped into shape."

Garrison galloped up. "Your Silver ladies are overriding our new scouts."

The pain in his back leg grew as Jace hurried up to Star. "My Lady, please. The Regiment marches with order. Our scouts must lead with only one of yours to guide them–let Silver Sunny do that. Then comes the front ranks. Then yourself and your other sister." How many times must he tell her this?

"We must hurry."

"We make progress. Now, let Sunny guide us..."

"Nay, I do!"

"Fine! Let Sunny and Crescent return to their place in front of the carts. To make progress, we must march!"

The sun was sinking closer to the horizon, so they would have to make a camp soon. Not in a soft grassy meadow, but in scratchy, fetlock high bushes. Seeing the carts were halted again Jace loped back to Garrison. "What is the problem?"

"These carts need tying up. Ye looking for a campsite?"

He looked about disgustedly. "Aye."

Jace's leg hurt, but he already had more pain cakes then he should. Did he have enough for the march? The way he felt now, he would not be marching long. This sun's tramp was much slower than he planned, but soon they would lose the light. Only they had not found water, so they made a dry camp in the gloaming. Warriors separated by the branches and thorns. Mostly sleeping standing up. The water-casks were being depleted. Jace spoke to Star. "My Lady, you said there would be water?"

"Your warriors travel so slowly. The next sun we should reach water." She promised softly.

Should? That did not inspire confidence.

At sunrise, the leading centaurs slashed brush out of their way with long swords. Garrison had four centaurs hitched to the water cart, with two aside to help keep it from falling. Two pulled the provision cart, with two more assigned to push from behind.

A long sun, but they made little progress, and Jace started to look for their next camping. Jace trotted to Star. "My lady, we must halt soon. We have not found water yet."

She nodded. "There is some ahead. This brush will give way to short grass. You must keep going before we lose the light."

The brush did give way to a small ravine of shorter, thick grass clumps, a fair spot to camp. Star had said they would find water here but where was it? He inhaled a weak wet smell, but he saw no weeping trees, water reeds or water birds. Yet Star said there was a waterhole on this trail. Where was it? Jace trotted up to Star.

She looked at his leg. "Sir, you are limping."

"A stone bruise on my hoof frog."

"When I was but a filly my Aunt Crystal, our healer, chose me as her apprentice. From her training, I am very skilled. Please let me look at it." She reached out to his sinister hind quarter, but Jace shied to the side.

"My lady, where is the water?"

She looked up from his leg. "You can smell it."

"I can...weakly. How distant is it?"

"It is right here." She turned and trotted away from him. He looked from those shapely black stocking legs to those glossy, cream dabbled gray and black hindquarters. As she pranced, she arched that long, glittering whitetail. He inhaling her aroma, followed her graceful lines with hungry eyes and knew he would mount her this star rise. Harness jingled behind them, impatient hooves stamped, returning him to duty. "Where is it?"

Star trotted over to a boulder and pointed downwards. At what? Jace strode up. Before her was a large boulder, beneath it a puddle of water no bigger than the mouth of his cart's bucket. "That is it?!"

She appeared surprised at his harsh tone. "Aye."

He scanned the hillside of yellow-green grass. "There is no more?"

"No." She pawed nervously with her front hoof, backing away from his anger. "It is clean and drinkable."

"My lady, look at those warriors." He pointed angrily. "On the march, each one drinks three, maybe more of that pool a day. The first one here will drink it out!"

"When you dip, it will fill up again." In fear, she was backing away from him.

"By the time it fills up, five more troopers will be thirsty. How long will it take to sate our thirst? How long to refill our water casks and harness bags? Are we to camp here for another moon?" He stamped hard about the piddling puddle.

Recoiling from his anger, she shook her head. "Nay. I thought..."

"Is there other water near here?"

She looked helplessly about. "This basin was always good enough for us."

"And how many were you?"

"Never more than six."

"And your breed drinks much less than ones of our size." He said disgustedly.

She looked terrified. "You will not turn back?"

"Axel! The water wagon!" He looked back at Star. "These other water holes that you have drawn on my chart." Her face looked blank as Jace fished the awkward scroll from his side carry pouch. "This was the way you said we must go. I asked you where the water stops were. Are they all like this?!"

Frightened, she shook her head, backing away more. "You leave us?"

With effort, Jace quieted his voice. "My lady. We are not talking of abandoning you. The water cart will help us a bit, but I must know–truthfully–what lies ahead!"

Sandi had cantered up with Garrison. She looked down at the small pool. "Dung!" The squeaking water cart was rolling up drawn by Kear and Wheat.

Garrison looked down at the small pool and shook his head in angry disgust. "Our watering today?"

Jace raised a hand to silence them and then turned to Star, speaking quietly and firmly. "The caravan route, the one I showed you on the chart, why did we not take it?"

"This is faster."

"Not if we have to wait for rain puddles to refill."

"It is safer..." Her voice trailed off.

Jace looked at the fanciful drawings of dragons on the scroll in each of the directions. She could not be afraid of mere artist's embellishments? Or was this dragon of hers real? "My lady, what is the danger?" She looked to bolt. "Star, you must tell me!"

Star looked up him guiltily. "Robbers lay in wait on the caravan trail!"

"The ones they call the Scarlurs?" Jace asked, now he might get the truth. "They wait along the caravan route and attack. That is why you have hired us?"

"Partly..."

The 'partly' bothered him but with her so terrified of his anger, this was not a time to pry out more of her secrets. "The caravan route has more water holes?"

"We cannot take it!"

He unrolled the stiff chart with both hands moving towards her, but she shied away "Please." He stopped, as frightened she still stepped back. "Where do you think we are on this chart? Please, come here." It took the military discipline of a lifetime, but he just said quietly to her, "I will not hurt you." She tentatively stepped out a polished front hoof towards him as Jace held out the scroll. "Are we here, do you think?"

Silver Crescent had trotted over, followed by Star's other sister, Sunny. They could see Star's lowered tail and head. Crescent asked, "What is the matter?"

Star looked at her with tearful eyes. "The spring is not enough drink for them."

Sunny looked puzzled but Crescent just nodded. "I told you!" She stepped toward Jace. "The other holes ahead will be less."

Jace handed one end of the scroll to Crescent, freeing his finger to point, then rolled the scroll end back to the Bazaar. "We started here near the sea. These red hoof marks show the ancient caravan route."

"Poorly." Crescent studied it some more.

"I know." He rolled up the bazaar end and pulled at her spindle, unrolling more. "Do recognize the land markings?" She wrinkled her forehead but her tail was rising, and he saw understanding in her eyes. Crescent pointed her finger to a single arrow point that was labeled 'the Blue Hills.' "What is this?"

"The drawing indicates a foothill. You do not read the script?"

She shook her head nay.

"It is labeled "Blue Hills.""

"Yes." Crescent smiled in recognition. "There is large outcropping of blue rock called 'slate.' It pokes out of the ground. There is a large drinking pool were we may bathe." She nodded.

"Then those blue blotches are water holes that you know of?"

"I think they are." She spread her slender fingers on the parchment, pointing. "One here is half a sun lope from the bazaar, with a deep pool that has sweet water. Further on, a wide stream crosses the trail, where there is another blue rock outcropping." She pointed to the drawings of each. "Sometimes that stream near it is dry, but this season, it should run well."

"We must not go that way!" Star protested.

Star had drawn closer as if she could not bear Crescent standing so close to Jace's flank. "We cannot take the caravan route! The Scarlurs will attack." She looked to her other sister. "Sunny, we should not go that way!"

Standing a little away, Sunny looked to both of them and then looked back, with proud eyes at Axel's mighty height and muscles. "They are warriors, they will protect us on the caravan trail."

Star just looked miserable.

Crescent nodded again, studying Jace's scroll. "The water holes will be larger. The trail flatter for the carts, but look, over to the sky, there is dust. That could be Scarlur?"

Jace studied the sky. "Or the caravan that left before

us. We will have to go back to where we left the trail." He said looking backward.

Crescent looked to the rocks. "We do not have to go back. Ahead, the low hills run between us and the caravan trail. There is a dry river bed, we can trot it and rejoin the main trail."

"My chart does not show this." Protested Jace.

Crescent shrugged her shoulders. "Mayhaps it is wrong?"

They had lost two suns marching on Star's side trail, and it would take two suns to go back to where they had left the caravan trail. Crescent's route would be shorter if she was correct, but if she was not, they would be just wandering out in the brush. "We take rest camp this stars."

Star was agitated. "Nay! We can still trod in the gloaming ."

"My warriors need rest and water." Jace strode away, trying to lay off that hurting hind leg.

By sunrise, he would have to make a decision on their route.

After dropping his cart harness, Kear was stepping in a measured pattern. Head down, he seemed to be feeling the ground with his fore hoofs, as he circled outwards from the small pool. Finally, he looked up and called. "The grass is slightly greener here, and the soil sinks a lot more under my hooves. If we dug a hole here, we might get more water."

Jace looked about. "Axel, Wheat, dig where Kear says." He remembered that Kear's kin hailed from the mountains, wherein the snow melt they mined for copper. His kind studied the ground. Using spears and buckets to dig and throw away dirt, his warriors soon had a pit ten hooves round and about five deep. As dark liquid rapidly filled it up, Sandi sieved the muddy water through her head cloth into buckets. It was discolored, but drinkable. Jace gave more orders to set up the rest camp.

The next sunrise they marched on Crescent's directions, and at mid sun, Jace was relieved to come across her dry stream. Star's sister's navigational sense soon proved much better than Jace's chart, and they rejoined the trampled caravan trail by before sunsink.

Out of the brush and on a hoof packed trail again they finally made progress. Jace trotted up to the front ranks alongside Garrison. "Those low trees far from the trail. You could hide the whole Bologian Valley troops behind them."

"Aye. It like walking into one of your trap jars." Garrison looked down at the hoof prints in the dust. He trotted off the trail to a pile of dung of ahead of them, poking at it with his spear. "Not quite dry inside. Someones not far ahead."

"That caravan that left the Bazaar before us?"

"Them." He nodded. "But I am also smelling something else, too."

"Scarlur?" Jace enquired, as he looked to the trees in the distance.

"Scouts. Probably going off trail. Sticking to low growth."

"Hunting?"

"Game or us?"

"The caravan ahead?"

Jace nodded, soon he would pick a rest camp and get that weight off his back hoofs. After high sun, the trail wound through a long ridge of trees, which as he suspected covered a meandering stream. Camp here? Jace raised his head to smell the wind. He would like to get farther this day. "Crescent, this other small stream on the map? How close is it?"

She shook her long tail. "There is a shallow stream,

two centaurs wide, three furlongs away."

Garrison returned from a splashing lope across the stream. "The caravan did not stop here. Either they hit this spot too early in the day or they know of a better camping further on."

Jace sighted the sky, then raised an arm, giving orders. "Not a sleep camp, just brief rest only. Refill the casks and water skins."

Star was at his side. "We must hurry."

"We need water, my lady." He spoke firmly, but gently.

Deadrick loped up. "You heard we lost Barley?"

"Aye. The new recruit with the brown and white tail."Jace nodded. "The others?"

"Well, the other three are sticking, but visions of plunder and glory is giving away to the reality of sore hooves."

Again Jace just nodded. These new recruits were with them, but they were not being trained. The pace of a constant tramp was hard enough for those unused to it. Harder and harder for Jace, with his ever-diminishing box of yellow pain cakes.

As they regrouped to march again, Deadrick trotted to Jace. "Scouts reporting your Scarlur friends are showing themselves along the trail."

"In force?"

"Nay, just a few. Mayhaps, just a foraging party?"

"Tell our scouts to keep them in sight."

"You want to send a raiding party after them?"

Looking long at the short scrub growth, with its dangerous, taller concealing foliage beyond, Jace considered it but then shook his tail. "They are not our objective."

"Aye, sir." Deadrick trotted off.

Just two fingers from sunsink, Jace could smell water at the rise. It would be a good place to camp, but as they came over the ridge, he saw others had found it earlier.

In the distance, Jace could see a swarm of dun centaurs. No fires. No females. No younglings. Just hes. Waiting. Spread loosely ahead across the trail. In the center was a familiar figure, Silver Belle, standing between two fiercely painted males. One of the males besides her waved a purple cloth banner. Universal signal for peaceful parlay.

Two Spot stopped next to Jace and spat on the dirt. "Like the parlay a bit better if they unstrung their bows."

Jace looked at Sandi. "Do we have a purple flag to answer?"

She shook her tail. "Did not replace it. Should have."

Deadrick pranced nervously. He hated to talk. "Why not charge?"

"Should we not declare war on them first?" Jace asked.

Silver Belle was stepping closer to them, her males only a length behind her. Jace twisted to the back. "Bring up Silver Star!"

She was already hurrying up, but Star halted abruptly when she saw her sister. From the look on her face, it did not bode to be a warm reunion.

"They wave a purple flag. They wish peaceful parlay." Jace explained to her.

With a stormy face, Star looked at him. "Why?"

"That we must ask them."

"Nay! We do not talk to the likes of her!"

"My lady, we must parlay!" Jace noted they had two males and a she under their flag, so he ordered. "Two Spot, join me. Garrison, take command. Pass the word to untie weapons but remain standing down."

Two Spot started to line up with Jace so they could step forward in unison with Star between them, but she bolted ahead. Widening their strides Jace and Two Spot was able to catch up to Star. Mid-way, Jace reached for Star's arm and commanded: " Halt!" He continued in an undertone. "Let them come to us."

The three of them planted hooves in the ground. Silver Belle hesitated, waiting for them to come to her but Jace moved not. Lifting her tail, Silver Belle pranced towards them with her two escorts following closely. Jace noted a hard-faced, older male with that younger prancing fool from the bazaar. So Jace knew at least one of them had nay sand for a fight.

Coming closer with her jingling of gold chains, Belle smiled brightly. "Sister..." she began warmly.

"Grandmare's goddess cup! You stole it!" Stamping her hooves Star moved forward.

Belle swung her body to the side and held her head higher. "Star..."

"You stole from your own blood!"

Jace could see the two dun fighters behind Belle quietly closing in, as were some of the Scarlur behind them.

Heedless to the danger Star kept hammering. "Our mare's gold chains. Aunt Crystal's ruby pendants. Sunny's pearls. How dare you flaunt them?!"

"They were my ransom." Returned Belle in a wounded tone.

"Grandsire ransomed you, but you came back and robbed more, then returned to run with those dung heaps!"

Great. Obviously, Silver Star had Deadrick's bludgeoning touch for diplomacy. "My lady, please. We are here to listen." Jace quietly counseled.

"I want Grandmare's goddess cup back!"

"It is now mine."

"It is not yours!"

"My mate, Nine-Kill acquired it."

"Stole it!" Both grays' tails were swishing, as the sisters locked eyes.

"Ransomed it. Then Nine-Kill gifted it to me for my death cup. Silver Beard can craft another for Grandmare." Belle finished smugly.

"Grandsire is dead! Your Scarlur beasts killed him!"

Obviously shocked, Silver Belle twisted her head to face the impassive dun behind her. She started to say something, then dared not, as she lowered her eyes and turned back to Star.

"I want Grandmare's cup. You can keep the rest of your robbings!" Star hammered on.

Belle raised her head imperiously high. "I keep all my gifts from Nine-kill!"

Jace had been quietly estimating the number of fighters ahead of them. Thirty and growing, all males. The duns' scraggily line continued in patchy groups to the tree line, how many more were behind brush cover? At least the purple flag of truce would allow them to return to the regimental position before they were attacked.

"Warrior!" An older dun stepped up from behind Silver Belle to command Jace's attention. "I be Nine-Kill of the Scarlur. This is my brother, Bloody-Ax." Both of Nine-kill's arms were hung with centaur tails. Dried Blood had run down from one, it was a rare two colored tail. Sickened, Jace realized what had happened to his recruit, Barley. Had he really deserted or had he been ambushed trying to get back to the Regiment?

The harsh-faced dun was continuing. "Warrior, leave the Silvers to us, and we shall allow ye to return to the

Bazaar."

Jace smiled. "I doubt if that is what my patroness wishes..."

"Then you die this day!" Not even waiting for his answer, Nine-kill raised his arm—suddenly the Scarlur were attacking!

Chapter Eleven

Mount in haste a skiddish she

Get ready for a hard fall!

Common Centaur Sense

Silver Belle jumped forward and reached out to grab her sister, as a shocked Star reared to fend her off. Jace barely unsheathed his sword before the second peace talker, Bloody-Ax, tried to spear him. Twisting aside, Jace managed to grab the spear shaft, giving a mighty pull that shoved the second dun off his front feet. He stumbled before Nine-kill, who kicked and cursed his brother.

Screams from the attacking Scarlur line that was galloping towards them, as yells and hoof beats from his warriors came from behind him. Two Spot wedged himself between Belle and Star, shielding Star with his huge body as he slashed out with his sword at Nine-kill. Jace lunged his sword over the fallen Dun, stabbing Nine-kill's lower shoulder. Jace's long sword arm gave him a definite advantage. Nine-kill gave no aid to his fallen brother as he grabbed Silver Belle and retreated. Frustrated fury strengthened his blows as Jace slashed his sword through Bloody-Ax's neck.

Then Jace grabbed at Star's arm, pulling her back. **"Two Spot–withdraw!"**

But Two Spot was surrounded as the Scarlur line overtook them. Behind the Regiment's front line opened up to allow Star and Jace through. Star looked to him in wide-eyed terror, reaching out to grab him close. He shoved her yelling, "Get behind the line!" Then he twisted on his hindquarters to face the enemy, pain shooting throughout his body, but he ignored it. And charged.

The Scarlurs slashed and screamed savagely, but Regimental arms were longer, with a solid line that held. Deadrick, with three warriors, was slashing a path to Two Spot. The Scarlur attack was faltering in the face of the Regiment: trained strokes were deadlier; large stamping hooves heavier; warrior spears longer. Still waves of Scarlur trampled out of the woods, causing Jace's warriors to bound over a growing barrier of dun bodies. To the sides, Garrison had managed to get two Regimental archer wings in place, soon their practiced shots were dropped charging Scarlurs, who did not seem to have a leader.

Deadrick's thrust reached Two Spot, as Jace fought to keep their path back clear or rather he tried. Everywhere he turned there was a warrior in his way. Sandi and Axel on one side, Nighthawk and Abel on the other. He wanted to kick out, break clear, but every time he turned, one his own was blocking his path.

The Scarlur's solid line broke, they seem to swarm into smaller tribes...some abandoning the field, other stragglers milling in groups as if looking for a leader. With no sight of Nine-kill or Silver Belle, it was over fast as the last fighters on their hooves retreated, without any attempt to aid their wounded.

"Halt! Ardon, sound recall!" Jace had no idea of the full force they were facing, and he did not want his centaurs running into a new trap. "Garrison. Set a defensive circle with our carts and wounded inside. Deadrick! Make certain all our enemies are dead before you strip the weapons!"

Jace found Willow, aided by Star, cleaning Two Spot's wounds.

"How is he?"

Two Spot glared at Jace. "The dungheaps slit my battle harness! Got their blood all over my pouches."

Willow nodded. "His wounds are shallow."

Relieved Jace ordered. "For saving our patroness, you get first pick of the loot." Jace looked about the field. His warriors speared the Scarlur wounded, putting them out of misery, while he tried to ponder an enemy who waved a purple truce banner as bait for an ambush.

As Willow started cleaning blood from Deadrick's shield arm, Jace pulled Star aside. "Why did you not tell me of your sister, Silver Belle?"

"I did not think she would show her face."

"She is one of them now. Silver Belle is Scarlur."

Star lowered her head. "She shames us...she..."

"I want to know of her males? Who do we fight?"

An enemy screamed as Rufus ended his life. Star shivered, then recited. "There are three main clans of the Scarlur. Belle's mate is Nine-kill, he heads the largest clan. There is his brother, Fire-tail and the third brother that you just killed, Bloody-ax."

"Shields on the field show yellow moon and 2 yellow stars and a yellow moon and one black star?"

She shrugged. "There is also a yellow moon and three blue stars, but I do not know who leads."

"Nine-kill and Fire-Tail are both clan leaders now?"

"Nine-kill is younger, but Silver Beard said he had more followers. They usually fight among themselves over shes..."

Jace looked over the field. "But they are together now. Any idea how many fighters they can pull?"

"Many."

"A count would be helpful, my lady..."

She shook her head hopelessly.

"What does the Scarlur want of you?"

Star looked away from him. "They are thieves."

"They have taken your mines?"

"Nay–mayhaps–I do not know. They were attacking as I galloped to get help. Not this tribe, but others. Mayhaps Fire tail..."

"Do you know what figures Fire tail paints on his shields? What images?"

"The moon and two blue stars?" She did not sound certain.

"Can your kin hold them off?"

She shook her tail. "We are not fighters."

"Then you think your kin surrendered and were taken as slaves?"

"I do not know. As we were running, we heard a cave in. They may be trapped inside."

"Or dead?"

"Do not say that!"

"Then our job is to fight these Scarlurs? Get them away from your mines and try to dig out your kin?"

She looked at him, her eyes pleading. "Do you abandon us?"

"What of this dragon?"

She gave a dismissive shake of her tail. "You must pass the dragon to free them. Do you abandon me?" she begged again.

"Nay." Jace kept his voice firm. "The Regiment marches for you, but it helps to know who and what we are fighting?" He looked intently at her, she dropped her gaze. There was something else she was hiding, he was sure of it. But this was not the time to push her further.

Having finished the last Scarlur wounded, his warriors ranged across the battlefield, collecting arrows and captured weapons. Garrison reported that there was only one Regimental death, that of a new recruit.

"Which one?"

"Horn. A spear through his chest." They came out relatively unscathed. The Scarlur must be used to attacking only the weak and untrained. Jace sent forward two scouting parties, lead by Arjuna and Deadrick. To the rest he ordered. "Carry the spoils with us, we will choose at sun rise." Under a bright moon the rest of the Regiment would march away from here; those bodies would be stinking greatly at sun rise.

Jace was at the head of the columns, when the scouts came back, with Arjuna reporting. "Two furlongs ahead there is another watering place, several pools, tied by a meandering stream, with heavy tree covers. It will break any charge."

"We camp there. Tell Garrison he is to set double sentries."

Reaching the planned encampment, Jace limped openly. That his hindquarters burned like fire only added to his gloom: Silver Belle and her cohorts had dishonored a purple flagged truce; his own patroness had not been truthful; the remains of his vaunted Regiment walked into a trap; nothing could be trusted from any of them of this march!

Sandi came over with a cut of skewed meat. "Not a bad showing."

Biting in singed meat, Jace slowly chewed. It would have been better if every time he had tried to turn there was not one of his own under his hooves. When Sandi started to move off, Jace gruffly ordered. "Stay!"

"Jace?"

"It is sir!"

At his tone, she stiffened. "Sir."

"You, Axel, Abel, Nighthawk–you were my *honor* guard in battle." He spit the words out like poison.

Sandi winced. "Jace..."

"You were protecting me!"

"Your leg..."

"A warrior is not to be coddled like a foal!"

"Jace..."

"It is sir!"

"Yes–yes, sir."

"That 'guarding' will never happen again, understand!"

She spoke reluctantly, obviously not wanting such an order. "Yes, sir."

"Tell the others–nay, I will." Dung! It had come to this, his own Regiment guarding him. Slowly he cooled down, as the moon rose higher. He took two more of the pain cakes, but they were not working as they should have, the pain still grew deep within his hindquarters.

Should he get a fire branch torch and study those prettily decorated, but worthless charts? Where was Star? He should question her. Talk with her. Just stand near her sweet smelling warmth. Jace looked over the camp. Should he try to question Crescent, to find out what Star was hiding? Finally, he limped to Sandi. She looked at his leg and said nothing, as she handed him the last of her wine bag. He swallowed it fast, then looked around. "Where is Axel?"

"I think he sleeps in another part of the camp." At Jace's unasked question she continued, "Axel is enamored with Silver Sunny."

Jace smiled. "He will learn much."

"Ah, yes. Experience."

Jace was trying to be casual as he looked about. To the side he could see silhouettes of Axel near a fire, looming over Sunny as they both stared rapturously in each other eyes. Jace turned to Sandi.

She only shrugged. "Young love. Only Sunny's teeth are a bit worn."

Jace looked about the camp, if bedding arrangements were to be set up, he had better work on his. He saw a graceful, gray shape, Star?

Sandi smiled crookedly and said too sweetly, "That is Crescent. And what a surprise, no one is mounting her-- usually, there is a line."

His old comrade could read his mind, but he did not care anymore. "Have you seen our patroness?"

She looked up with bitter amusement in voice. "Ah. You wish to discuss strategy with her, in the dark no doubt." She shook her head. "Those cloven-hoofed Silvers are very dainty. They leave us for screening when they wish to dung, and they hide in yon shrubs when they wish to bathe."

Concern darkened his tone. "If there are lurkers following us?"

Sandi dismissed it carelessly. "There are enough of us camping about. She has gone into the shrubbery around that small water pool over there. You should find her and speak to her about our marching and many other things."

Beyond pride, Jace stepped past Sandi's taunting eyes as he headed into the trees. This painful march was over for him. He could not face another battle, especially with his warriors protecting him, so he must give up leadership. His life was finished, but by the Gods, he would have just one night with that starry dabbled one! This night he must mount Star.

He stopped in the dark trees inhaling deeply. Scent of water, leaves, then the beautiful warming aroma that was her. Jace came out in a small, moonlit clearing and just stood watching. Star was bathing in the center of the shallow pool. White light shone on her long hair and dripping tail. Soft light on those smooth hindquarters, the slender legs were hidden in darkness. With growing excitement, he unbuckled his travel harness and dropped it to the earth.

Startled at the sound, she looked back. "Jace?"

He was breathing deeply, taking in everything of her, as he said softly, "My lady, you should not go off by yourself."

She stepped closer. Her hooves were not even splashing. "Your warriors camp all around us."

"Aye, but it is not safe." How should he proceed? Just kiss her?

Slowly, almost silently, she stepped out of the pool, not having to raise her head much to look up at him. "Jace." She put out her hand on his arm. "I wish us to be one."

No need for soft words. Promises. He could smell she was ready, but he sensed she might mean more than just a night's pleasure, still, right now, he wanted her more than anything. "I wish it too."

In eagerness, she moved forward towards him. Her hard, upturned nipples pressed against his chest as her warm, soft body pushed against his. He could smell her excitement. He could certainly feel his hardening. Jace kissed the top of her head. Her lips. She put her arms around his back and urgently kissed him back. Finally, she laid her head on his chest, totally contented. A troubling thought came to his mind. Finally he had to ask, "My lady, is this the first time?"

She looked up sounding distressed. "How do you know?"

"My lady, with us standing here, holding each other, as wonderful as it is, I can do nothing."

"Oh." As her arms loosened, she stepped back, sounding embarrassed.

"I must get behind you. Mount you."

Looking relieved, she smiled radiantly as she stepped back. "Then do it."

The first time? Nay, it should not be fast. He should take the time to kiss her lips, rub her flanks and stroke her long back until her tail started to rise. Yet as his leg pain grew, his strength drained and any moment another might stumble into the clearing. It had to be now!

In the full moon's light, she was looking at him with eyes of love, and he wanted her so much. With a wild charge, he galloped away from her, circling the pond coming up behind her. She stood and watched him. Just waiting.

An experienced centauress would have widened her stance, bracing herself solidly to support his weight then whipped her tail aside. Jace shortened his stride, knowing he should stop. Yet he could not, for Star's smooth flanks had their bright dabbling that almost glowed in the dark. Charging wildly Jace used his hand to brush her tail away, then reared above her hindquarters.

That was when it really went bad. Star twisted around to see what he was doing, putting her at a tottering angle. His forelegs anchored on her back, but he dared not put his full weight on her as his pained back leg buckled, pulling them both off balance. He shifted his whole weight to his good hind leg. Off-kilter, it twisted as it started to collapse. Reared above her, he would crush her hindquarters when he fell forward. Jace painfully twisted aside, falling down. Trying to protect her–still, they both crashed painfully on to the muddy grass.

Star rolled into the pond, sending a wave of cold water on him as she whimpered in pain. Rolling with his fall, Jace found himself on his back, kicking his legs high. "Are you all right?"

When she stepped back out of the waters' edge, Star

cried out. "Did I hurt you?" She folded herself down beside him.

"Nay, my lady." Gods, now resting on the grass his back was in as much pain as his hindquarters. Even his head hurt.

She looked at his male sword, half lowered. "That is so big. You were to put that in me?"

His passion shriveled as it did. "Some shes like it very much." He had to stand up, but everything ached so, he just wanted to stay on the ground.

"Can we try again?" She was pleading.

Her she smell was so strong. He wanted her so much, but his leg and his back and his arms hurt. "Not this night." He must have Sandi or maybe Willow explain things to her. Obviously, her kin had not.

Star still looked at his retracting sword. "Can I touch it?"

"Please do."

She reached with hesitant, warm fingers. Touching him so lightly, like the kiss of a butterfly.

"Oh, it likes to be touched, strongly touched, my lady." He encouraged softly.

She stroked it, and he sighed contentedly. "Stronger my lady. Stronger."

"It grows again?" She said in surprise.

"Come here." He reached out his arm to pull her closer. If she moved closer to his head, they could kiss. He could put his arms around her smooth back feeling her full, taut breasts against his chest. Star shifted towards him as he bent forward and kissed the top of her head. She raised her head and looking at him with adoration. Suddenly she moved forward.

Blazing–shooting pain! Jace screamed as blackness

ringed his eyes. He cast her from him as pain thundered through his body, and he passed out.

When he came to he looked up to a ring of hooves around him. Deadrick, Sandi, Garrison and Willow. Was the whole dunging camp here?

A terrified Star was explaining. "We were lying together. I wished to kiss his lips, so I had to climb up to reach his face. As I tried, my back leg kicked..."

Garrison struggled mightily for control. "You kicked him in the balls with your hind hoof? Oh—my lady, that does smart!"

Sandi covered her mouth with her hand, choking back laughter.

His new Regimental surgeon Willow was leaning over him. "Uh—do you want a bandage or something?"

Jace wanted to kill–somebody–**anybody**! He breathed deeply to control his voice then spoke. "Go away, please. All of you!"

Sandi had tears running down her cheeks, obviously was about to say something, when Garrison took her firmly by the arm. "Leave him be!"

Even Deadrick showed a great deal of sympathy and left without a word.

"I did not mean to hurt you," Star babbled as she stood over him twisting her hands in helplessness.

Willow took her arm. "Let him rest a bit...my lady, methinks we must talk."

Jace laid back, the agony subsiding. Finally, he limped to his harness and took two of the pain cakes. He should go to Star and reassure her all was well, but it was not. His warriors defended him in battle. He let a she ball kick him. Disgusted with himself Jace just rolled back down on the grass. As the cakes worked, his hindquarter pain subsided but did not fully go away. Sleep did not come until the moon cantered from the sky.

He opened his eyes to a lighter but still gray sky, with clouds hiding the dawn. Dark day, dark thoughts, as the pain in his hindquarters burned with fury, even before he tried to struggle to his feet. Standing up, weight on three legs, he counted out the yellow pills. Jace had sixteen, and Merdi said eight to end his pain forever. Better a sleeping death than to continue a life of limping loss.

When he entered the endless darkness, would there be great battles in the thundering clouds? His valor in battle had earned his place among the Legions of Lightening Hooves many times over. Or would death be a merciful sleep that he should never wake from? No one alive knew those answers, but soon he would. Jace returned the cakes to their box, he would need all this day, but first, he must see to the proper transfer of Regimental leadership.

With great difficulty, he hauled his battle harness on to his back but did not buckle it. He dipped his drinking horn down and sipped. It was bitter tasting water, like life itself. He waited until he felt the others would have risen and eaten, then he limped out to the main encampment, past caring that his injury be seen.

Some of his warriors averted their eyes and laughter was choked back. Ah, on top everything else, the word was out about his escapade with Star. Dung. Jace scanned the camp and saw Axel. He hand signaled him over.

As he waited, Sandi loped over with a very disrespectful, crooked grin on her face. "Jace, Willow talked to Star. It will be better next time."

He raised a hand. "Fetch Willow."

She frowned but obediently turned tail to follow orders.

Where was Deadrick? Out scouting? He caught Garrison's eye and signaled for him. Sandi was soon returning with Willow and Ardon was also headed over. As Axel joined him, Jace untied his personal pouches, bow, and quiver and dropped them on the ground. Then he hauled off his battle harness. "Axel, this has grown too heavy for me. I wish you carry it this march. Put your old harness in the cart."

Sandi's face paled as she saw Jace hand over his long sword with the harness. "Jace, nay."

Ignoring her, Jace belatedly started to untie his broadsword but then stopped. Axel's sword blade was chipped and of poor quality. Jace retwisted the cord holding the long sword to the harness before he handed it to Axel. Jace kept only his short sword given him by his dam, Dawn. He should give it up, but he wished not to die with an empty hand.

Garrison lowered his head to the inevitable, but still, he tried. "We need to regroup. If we rested this day, you would see things differently."

Jace shook his head. "Nay. The Scarlur are behind you and ahead is a dragon that the Regiment has been commissioned to slay."

Sandi started to rear. "Jace! You can not..." Jace stared sadly at her–she dropped her front hooves and lowered her voice, "Please Jace. A bad roll with a fiddle foot virgin..."

Cutting her off, Jace shook his tail slowly. "We fought a battle where my own Regiment was protecting me! My leg injury grows worse each darkness. Sandi, for me the fight is over." He looked at the rest. "Willow, Garrison will assume command on the trail. The Lady Star and her sisters are not to know of this until then. If they ask where I am, tell Star I am rear scouting. Try to keep them occupied."

Willow nodded her head, seemingly unable to speak

as she moved off towards the Silvers.

Jace could see Star standing there, but he averted his eyes.

Garrison tried to reach out a hand, "Jace..."

"It is over for me. It has been for some time. We have both known it."

Garrison nodded. "Our trail is followed closely by the Scarlur."

Jace nodded his acceptance of the single warrior's fate.

Sandi pushed herself between them, pleading, "This is not you! Jace, you are running away!"

"Actually, on my hind leg, I can barely limp away."

Red-faced, furious nearly beyond words, Sandi spat out, "Coward!" then turned tail and bounded off.

Garrison did not protest the leadership thrust on him. He only spoke quietly. "Your rest is long deserved." Then he stepped alongside Jace reaching out his sword arm, taking Jace's at the elbow. "We have had many good fights." Jace strongly returned the clasp.

When they released hands, Jace as an afterthought, reached into the short belt on his hip-shoulder and handed Garrison his coin pouch. "Not much of a leaders' portion but you can buy charts or a few rounds on the plank."

Garrison took the pouch, nodded and trotted off. Marching orders near a likely ambush trail were done by hand signals. As Garrison loped about the camp, he signaled for battle harnesses to be lifted on, fires quenched and cooking gear loaded on to the carts. As Jace stood off by himself, a line of twos were forming. Then those dunging carts were squealing and creaking.

Axel cantored to him. "I will stay with ye."

"Nay."

"Jace, two warriors..."

"Will die half as fast. Besides, you have signed on for Lady Star's dragon quest. I will not release you. Take care of her."

"Jace–sir, please."

"Leave me my peace, I beg you."

Lowering his head, Axel stepped slowly away.

Jace wanted it all over. To just be by himself. Then, oh, by the Gods, he could see Star breaking away from Willow and trotting over toward him. Just to look at her graceful movements made him forget the pain.

"Jace, I am so sorry..." Star began.

He forced a smile. "It is forgotten."

"But Willow told me I should have braced..."

He put up two fingers to her lips. Those so firm, moist lips.

"Please, listen," she begged. "Now because of my clumsiness, your warriors laugh at you."

Those graceful gray legs and shiny back flanks, nothing so beautiful could ever be clumsy. Inhaling her beautiful seaweed scent, he only smiled gently. "It will pass. My warriors respect their leaders if not, they will be taught. Now you are assigned with your sisters to march in the front ranks. Please, you have said there is haste."

"You will give me another chance?" Her eyes pleaded with him.

Looking deeply into those lovely green eyes; that face framed by that silky seafoam hair, he could honestly say, "I will take no other but you."

Still looking upset, she obediently lined up with Crescent at the head of the marching line. Now the two lines were parading past him. Ignoring the burning pain, Jace pushed solidly back on his hindquarters. He spread his weight evenly, stiffened his back proudly and took his last review of his Regiment.

Chapter Twelve

Those who risk all

Can lose all!

Prince Roan-hoof, as he lay dying

The Regiment rapidly marched out of sight. Jace realized soon their smells would be gone too. Even that sweet, sea weedy aroma that was Star. Out in the open, standing alone, Jace was an easy target for the Scarlur. He looked to the sword and sinister sides: sunny hills and high grass but no protection. Still behind him was the stream with its shallow pools and screening trees. After picking up the belting for his bow, arrows and short sword, Jace limped to the tree cover. Leaves rustled under his hooves, insects buzzed over the stagnant pools below as he moved deeper into the shadows.

He might get away if he stayed to the trees and kept moving. Nay. He would stay on, guarding their trail. Jace moved deeper into the trees. Something small ran through the branches above. As long as creatures stirred boldly, Jace could be sure Scarlurs were not moving in. He must rest. Mayhaps his leg would heal, and he could catch up with his Regiment. Mayhaps after the lady's dragon was slain, he could cover her.

He smiled crookedly at his fool's fantasies, then took a step forward. Shooting pain up his hindquarters as his sinister hind leg started to buckle under his weight. Jace had to find a resting place. Some place where he might be concealed, yet he could see the trail, a place he could still guard Star's passage.

He tried to hop on his three good legs. How could

Urzi do this for full marches? Jace gritted his teeth to keep from screaming–pain must be endured. The caravan trail crossed the stream near here. The embankment looked steep but below was a shallow pool. If he could just rest and cool his burning body. Lifting his carry pouches and bow high, he started to climb down the moss inflicted bank. This quickly turned to an uncontrolled slip and half fall. At the stream, cold water shocked his hooves and his hindquarters radiated pain as he limped deeper into the slimy pool.

The fishy smelling water rose only to his fetlocks, but its coolness eased his pain. He planned to stand on the other side but midway, Jace just gave up and rolled his body down into scummy, green water. He would not be getting up again. By twisting, he managed to get his back and shoulders resting against a half-submerged tree. He reached over and placed his bow, short sword, and pouches on a flat rock just above the water.

With the weight off his legs, the total pain dulled but still, that deadly pressure within his leg grew. He reached out for his carry pouch with Merdi's pain cakes. Take eight, and it would be over. Nay! If the Scarlur vermin crossed here, he still could be of some use. Jace pulled two small yellow cakes and chewed them, when the pain started to lessen, he strung his bow. The woven leather cord creaked as he did a test pull. He took his last sharpened arrows and laid them out on the rock. If he must die, it would be on guard.

Behind him, yellow sunlight shafted down through the leaves onto the soupy, green water. Soon Star would know he was gone and that was for the better, for she must forget him. Glittering dragonflies flitted over the pool, as small black fish nibbled at his under stomach tickling him. Slowly the sun shifted overhead, and his eyelids grew heavy.

His eyes snapped open. A splash, a small fish? Pain

rushed back as he rolled a bit, so he could reach the rocks and pull one of his worn leather pouches closer. Awkwardly, he struggled to keep it from the water as he reached inside. These were the last of his personal treasures, the ones he kept tied to his harness even in battle. Inside the pouch, he felt for an old, worn scroll, Dark Moon's poetry. Master Redson was the Emperor's greatest battle arts instructor. The Master had constantly repeated, "A warrior must read as it schools his mind. A warrior must practice reading as often as he shoots his bow." Jace unrolled the scroll of Dark Moon's poetry, soft words to quiet the mind. Words that Jace laboriously copied from Master Redson's own scroll. Jace should have been teaching Axel how to read, getting him to copy this scroll.

When Jace focused on the faded script, the heat, stink, and pain drained away. He read for a long time, then carefully returned it to his pouch. He dug deeper. At the bottom was a soft golden velvet sack. From inside he withdrew an elaborate chainlink headpiece. It was of silver now blackened with age. Stretched out it resembled a dew-dropped spider's web with the dew drops pierced, polished crystals and a crouching spider of dark emerald.

To obtain this for Ginger he had bartered two fine swords and all his coin. Of his massive breed, Ginger was tall, with cream skin, dark chestnut hide and white feathers over her hoofs. A she with a pride straight back and laughing eyes. She wore his headpiece as she cooked their meat and wore it into battle under her helm, as Ginger fought beside him. She even wore it as he triumphantly mounted her and they screamed their ecstasy together.

As foals, they had sparred and chased each other over the fields. With saddened eyes, Ginger stood beside his mare, Dawn, as they had watched him gallop away from their band that last time. Young and foolhardy he forgot all, so excited to see what was beyond the next hill!

Yet at night when the stars shone high, a part of him ached to feel her soft hide pressing against his, to cup her full breasts in his hands again, to sleep beside her. When he had started gathering mercenaries for his Regiment word of his exploits spread. Then one bright sun, Ginger found him, and for many a campaign, they galloped beside each other.

In the misery of unending pain, Jace remembered her last battle. Bleeding, with two legs broken, her eyes pleaded for mercy from him. He covered those eyes from his killing blow. A nightmare of twisting and then it was all over. Jace stripped the headdress from her so no other could steal it. He never wanted to care about another she, for there was no other Ginger. He never wished to offer the headdress to another, but he should have given it to Star before she marched away. Too late. Time and warriors march on. Jace carefully folded the smooth links back into their velvet bag.

Sounds of flies buzzing and birds calling in the trees. Time, an endless time where there was nothing he could do. He dug back into the pouch and took out Dark Moon's poetry again. All that was left of his personal property when the rest had been lost with the officers' cart at the Yellow Hided Dominion.

Again he studied the cramped script. Dark Moon had been an ancient fighter who distilled the beauty of the wind, trees, and moon into flowing words. Very few centaurs learned to read and fewer still warriors but Master Redson believed the mind must be as agile as one's throwing arm. At first, Jace found the reading practice a waste of time, but gradually he had grown to appreciate the flow of words and mind pictures from a distance of land and time.

Was his pain subsiding? Jace shifted in the water. He had had a long life for a warrior. A good one. Known many fine comrades. Lost many. Never had claimed a land run somewhere, with a she of his own and colts with his white feather hairs. He wistfully thought of Star and what colts he could have gotten out of her.

Water spiders skipped in tiny rippled circles across the water. Dying was damned boring! He hated waiting. Always. After all the battles, the wounds, leaping the firewalls and smashing down shield walls, he would die stuck in the mud. Near tears of frustration, he put his head back against the tree trunk and closed his eyes again.

Jace woke with a start. Something was wrong. He opened his eyes just a slit, cursing himself for sleeping. The trees to the Red were shady as the light now came from the Green. He must have slept most of the sun's light away. The pain in his hindquarters was growing again, so he tried to shift his hind legs to relieve it. Sweat poured down his body, and he was shivering along his flanks. What had awakened him? What was wrong? Out of place?

No enemy smell. No sound of hooves. Nothing. No bird callings from the trees. No animals scrambling among the bank leaves. That was what was wrong. Something big was near and moving in. Silently he reached out and picked up his bow and began notching the arrow fully back, silently cursing the warning creaking of the stretching hide. Soft hoofbeats from the river bank above. Single Centaur? A scout? Did the Scarlurs already cross the river downstream? Had they picked up the trail? Or were they backtracking?

The soft hoof falls stopped. Someone listening or smelling him near? Then movement again. One? Or more? He slung on the straps of short sword and quiver over his shoulder. Jace rolled upwards, getting his legs underneath him. Pain be damned, fighting was the way he wanted to go, and he would take them with him! Movement closer.

Someone tall was parting the saplings on the bank. Swinging the bow to point high, Jace forced himself to wait until he could see a clear target.

Then he would shoot. Reload. Keep shooting, and when he ran out of arrows, he would have the short sword. His arm muscles trembled with tension, with discipline he stiffened them. It would not be long. Saplings parted. A head appeared. Wide green eyes. Flowing bright hair. He released but managed to swing the bow wild, sending the killing arrow just past her cheek.

Ignoring the shaft that nearly killed her, Star was scrabbling down the bank in a shower of moss clumps and pebbles. "There you are!"

Collapsing down, Jace felt nauseous from just how close he had come to killing her. "You fool!"

She was splashing across the stream. "How badly hurt are you?"

"I nearly **shot** you! I should have!"

"Can you stand upright?" She reached out, grabbing his arm and trying to drag him up.

He rolled back in the water and unfolded his legs but did not try to rise. "Are the others with you?"

"Nay."

"You should not have left them! You will race to rejoin them!"

"And leave you?"

"I am dying."

She raised a skeptical eyebrow. "Of one injured hoof?"

"Of the burning. Pain. And the vengeful spirits of those I have slain."

"I have some herbs..." She reached for one of the regimental surgeon's pouches, now slung over her withers.

Annoyed, Jace reached out to put down the bow on the dry rock. "I have medicine. It worketh not."

"What is it?"

"Pain cakes."

"Let me see."

From his pouch, he fished out his wooden box of yellow cakes as he looked at the riverbank behind her. "You may have been followed by the Scarlur."

She ignored him. "You got this from Merdi in the bazaar?"

"He knows all about herbs."

Only enough to trade in stew spices." She was fingering one of his last pills to smell it.

"Those are mine," Jace said.

She was licking one of his medicine cakes. "These are distilled from the red flower? "

"I need those to heal."

"Nay. It only takes away pain...for awhile. What instructions did he give you?" She demanded firmly.

"To take two for pain and eight to die. I have just enough to finish me off."

"Two?! For the size of you? No. Maybe four. You could handle that easily. Eight will probably just put you into a deep sleep." She said before biting her bottom lip. Stuffing his cakes into her surgeon's kit, she commanded, "Get up!"

Too weary to argue, Jace started to painfully unfold his legs to rise, but Star was pulling at his arm again, overbalancing him. "My lady, you are not helping." He complained. Water rivulets ran off his back hide as pain shot through his hindquarters.

She had waded in water up to her hocks and the closeness of her warm body made all his longings return. "It is this hind hoof, is it not?" She was probing his leg with her firm fingers. It hurt, but he did not care. "Your leg is too warm. Your body must be fighting a blood poisoning that grows." She rose and pressed her fingers against his throat. "But there seems to be good blood pounding, and your chest is of good color. What happened to your leg?"

"A battle two moons ago. I was struggling with a fool, then cut off his head."

"And?" She asked unimpressed.

"I stepped on his spear, and the shattered shaft went up my hoof."

"Do not warriors have hoof covers to protect their frogs?"

"I did not wear any."

"Why not?"

"You can not gallop out on to the field, with boulders on your hooves. You have swords, harness, bow, shield, spear, calling-horns, helmet..."

"The spear haft, was it metal?"

"Wood." The memory was bitter.

"Wood that splintered?" Frowning she bent down to look at his leg.

"The regimental surgeon cut it out, that was Whitlock. He is dead now."

She looked perplexed, running her probing fingers down his leg to his feather hairs.

Jace shifted his weight. "The pain is high in my back thigh."

"Nay, it is rooted deeply in your lower leg. Probably just above your hoof, lift." She forced him to raise the hoof. "He may not gotten all of it. The wound has to be reopened."

He winced at the thought of knives cutting into his hoof frog again. "Nay, just let me die in peace."

She was rapidly looking up and down the stream. "I

must have you lying down in the sunlight. Over there on that sand spit. Come." Star pulled at his arm, pushing him with her withers and hindquarters. Her soft fur felt so good. She pushed harder, and Jace found himself first stepping, then limping over to the sand.

"When I go down, my lady, I will not get up."

"Good. Go down here!"

Jace folded his legs down on to the sand. She dashed back into the stream to bring both their pouches.

"Fetch my bow." He commanded.

She did but laid it out of his reach. Quickly she moved to raise both his rear hoofs, folding her front legs down to examine them, looking from one to the other. "The bleeding healed within your sinister hoof, but your fetlock is too warm above it." Her fingers pushed painfully into his hoof pad.

"That hurts!" He shouted.

"Your sinister frog pad is swollen within the hoof. It has to be reopened." She was reaching into the surgeon's pouch, bringing out hoof picks, and several long, thin blades.

"Nay, not that!"

Star looked at him with pity. "First you must chew your medicine cakes." She reached into his wooden box and started counting out yellow cakes. "Here, two will dull pain, and four will end it. You will take seven, no eight for me to cut."

"It will kill me!"

"Nay. Your body is larger than Merdi normally deals with. Eight of those potions would not even kill one of my breed."

"But if you cannot heal me, I will not have enough to kill myself!" He finished dramatically.

She gave him a contemptuous look. "You can always beat yourself over the head with a rock."

The thought did not appeal. "I would rather not."

"Chew!" Star demanded.

Jace took several cakes into his hand. Star looked like she knew what she was doing, but, "When the regimental surgeon worked on me, he had thick poles stuck deeply in the ground to tie my legs to. There were huge, strong centaurs to aid him. My lady, you start cutting into my hoof, a kick of mine will kill you."

The thought must have already occurred to her. She was looking helplessly about. "We have no poles, nor rope nor help. Chew nine cakes."

Jace chewed as she was gathering dried branches. He objected as she chipped a flint for a fire spark. "Nay! It will give our position away."

"Your screaming will give it away. Just chew! We will lose the sun's light soon."

First, the pain dulled and then his eyes seemed to fog. Groggy, Jace leaned an elbow on the sand. He remembered her pushing cushioning pine boughs behind his back and lowering his head on her soft leather pouch. Jace closed his heavy lids as he slid into darkness.

He was galloping across a white-flowered field with Star at his side. No, galloping in battle. A long-dead warrior grabbed his leg. Holding it. Jace wanted to kick out but could not. The leg would not respond. The sounds of loud scratching. His enemies would find them. Sharp pain. He must move, but he just could not move. A soothing voice. His Dam's murmurings? Ginger's? He could not understand what she was saying. Sharp pain. He kicked out. Someone held on to his leg. He must be in battle, but he did not care. Searing pain, then something warm wetting the frog of his hoof. Smell of rotten meat. He shivering uncontrollably as blackness came again.

It was cold, and a fly was biting his shoulder. With his eyes closed, Jace scratched at it. There were no smells, but he heard the sound of small animals scurrying about. Cautiously Jace opened his eyes to a slit, finding himself looking up into trees tops under the midday sun. There was the feeling of warm pressure against his back. He opened his eyes fully and twisted to look to his side.

Star was asleep against him. The sand and the rocks pressed him uncomfortably, but he did not want to move. If he woke her, she would take that soft, sweet, warm body away from his. Sunlight glinted on her snowy hair and the cream dabbles of her hindquarters seemed to glow. Next to her hand was his bow. She must have been trying to keep guard all night. He reached over and gently stroked her silken hair.

She had to go back and rejoin the Regiment. He would make her run and catch up with the others. Jace shifted his front legs then slowly started to move his back legs. To his surprise his back leg hurt; only hurt; but not that deep, killing pain and crushing ache. Did the eight medicine cakes cure him? No, he could still could feel soreness, so it was not Merdi's medicine.

He rolled away from her and carefully tried tucking his legs underneath him then rising slowly, out of habit trying to keep the weight off his sinister back leg. Finally, tentatively, he set the last hoof down hard. It felt squishy. He looked down. She had it wrapped in some wet fool's sack tied above his feather hairs. He kicked his back leg out. A poultice? Jace shifted more of his weight on to it. Sore, but no longer that deep burning pain. He took a cautious step.

Star had rolled to her feet seeming to fly up, asking anxiously, "How do you feel?"

He tried to inhale her aroma. "I can not smell

anything."

"The pain-flower cakes do that. It might wear off."

"Might?!"

She moved closer, running her hand down his buttock hide. Lord of Lightening Hooves that did make things grow. She probed her fingers, into his gaskin, hock, cannon, and fetlock. "The hotness is gone, and the flesh feels dry, firm. Try putting more of your weight on that sinister leg."

Jace did not want to. He wanted to put his weight on her.

Star briefly looked down. "Oh, you are feeling better but no time for that now, sir! Try walking slowly around me." She reached down and picked up the surgeon's pouches.

Jace stepped out on his front legs, then he stepped forward, putting his full weight on his injured back leg. That squishing bag interfered. Soreness. But he could stand, touching it to the ground without wincing, walking into the pool with almost no pain.

She watched his movements carefully. "Your surgeon did not probe deeply enough." Star reached into her carry pouch and held out a long, dark stained splinter. "I found this deep within your foot. It was poisoning your blood."

He looked at the piece of spear shaft that was a long as her hand. No wonder it hurt. "You got it all out?"

"I do not know what was in there." She bit her lip, watching him closely. "I wish not to cut too much good tissue. We will see if it heals or I may have to open it up and cut again. You will rest here a sun, and then I will see if you have heat in your leg."

Jace stiffly walked out of the water. Bending down and stretching back he ripped her sack of wet herbs off his hoof.

"Nay! Leave the poultice..." She pleaded.

"We must start moving because alone we will not have a chance if the Scarlur attack. The others must be far ahead. What was I out–one sun? Two?"

"One. The others will not be far off. When I left, I ordered them to camp..."

He turned on her in shock. "You give orders to warriors?!"

"They are in my hire."

"They listened to **you**?!"

" I told them I had a chance to heal you but that we needed time."

"They obeyed you?!"

"That white-haired, yellow hided one ordered them on."

"Deadrick."

"Some started to obey him..."

"Garrison was in charge!"

"But the others objected and planted their hooves solid. Most like Garrison wanted you to have that chance. It was decided they were only to wait for one sun ."

"You fool!" Jace gathered his weapon straps then started climbing up the bank, using tree trunks to help pull himself up. "The Scarlur will drink the blood of your sisters!"

Star followed, helplessly protesting."You must heal!"

"We must march!" He did not order her to gallop ahead and join the others. He knew she would not obey, but he set a steady pace. First walking, then loping on open ground as his soreness seemed to diminish. There was pain, but he had lived with pain for so many moons.

Back on the caravan trail, the tracks were easy enough to follow. What was the matter with Garrison and Two Spot? They seem to be making no effort to brush-sweep their back trail. "Did you order them not to cover up?"

"They felt we could follow easier."

Balls! In anger, Jace lengthened his strides. He would put the coals to them all!

At sunsink, they were still following a cold trail, and he could not smell anything. "Star, smell for the Regiment."

"Very, very faint."

"Can you smell Scarlur?"

"They stink horribly."

"Just tell me if they are about!"

She avoided his eyes.

"Star!"

"When the wind comes from ahead, I sometimes smell them, but the warrior scent is also there."

"Tell me when you smell anything closer!"

She seemed to be ignoring his words as she studied him. "You are limping again. How does your leg feel?"

"It needs rest, but we cannot take it now." The Scarlurs would know the caravan trail, know mayhaps where they could run over rougher country and cut off the caravan route ahead of Garrison. Even with the deep pain gone, his hindquarters were hurting from the relentless pace. With no sense of smell in the moonless dark, he could lose the trail or stumble into a Scarlurs' camp. "Did you bring food?"

"Nay." She lowered tail in shame.

If he sent her to hunt for food, she would be helpless if attacked out of his sight, but his legs were trembling with weakness. Jace slowed and looked about.

Ahead were several low trees with bent low branches, light green leaves, and flashes of yellow. He left the trail and trotted to them, finding they were laden with ripened fruit. If they got down on their knees, the lowest branches would offer a little cover and something to eat. He trotted further into the grove and selected the largest tree. "We rest here tonight."

"Please..." She ran her hand down his leg. "Does this hurt?"

"The deep pain is gone."

"So is the heat in your leg. That is good. Lift your hoof for me." He did, and she studied it carefully. "You heal fast, I expected more bleeding."

"We eat and rest."

She reared up, picked yellow fruit, giving it to him first and then they ate in silence. When Jace limped into the cover of the low branches and bent his legs to the grass, Star wordlessly followed him and pushed her flanks against his. He put an arm around her shoulders, and she rested her head against his chest. Too tired for anything else, he closed his eyes.

The earth dropped beneath him. He struggled as he fell down. He was trapped in a pit above his head. Screaming enemies taunted him with spear thrusts...no water. The stink of his dung. They laughed as he was dying. They were covering the pit so he could not even see the sun!

"Jace."

A she voice–Ginger? Nay, Star. What was Star doing in the pits of the Salt Plains?

"Jace! Jace, wake up!"

Cold sweat ran down his chest. There were branches above his head–that suffocating pit. Someone was shaking his shoulders. Where was he?

"Jace!"

He raised his shoulders, suddenly a solid, pale fruit hit his head waking him from his night horror. They were under tree branches where he could see darkness but graying, soon the sun would rise.

"Jace, what is it?" The soft voice beside him pleaded.

"Did I make noise?" He asked harshly.

"You cried out '*the pit*'?"

"We must move from here. Gather what fruit can fit in the surgeon's pouches."

"Your leg needs rest."

"Hurry!" He started picking fruit with one hand, using his other hand to bite the sweet and juicy fruit. They would need water soon, but at least she had taken a small waterskin.

"Jace what did you dream of?"

He picked more fruit. "It matters not."

"It might be a whisper from the Goddess. Please tell me. It is part of your healing."

"A long time past, I was trapped in pits..."

"Pits?"

"Underground holes. Sultan Iron Tooth had holes dug for his enemies. They captured me in nets and then dragged me into the trap."

"Why?"

"To enjoy my suffering as I died. How your kin can step a hoof in a cave, much less live confined in the stinking earth, I can not understand."

"You need rest..." She soothed, but still stuffed fruit into her bag.

"We must move. I still smell nothing!" Jace complained as he peered into the graying night.

"You must be patient." She counseled, but did he detect a trace of helplessness at his condition?

When the sun rose, they returned to the caravan trail where Jace picked out cart marks and familiar large, Regimental hoof prints. At one point, he studied smaller hooves steadily spaced in their markings. Tar-bel's caravan mayhaps? The hoof prints looked a bit bigger than Scarlur and seemed the result of a disciplined, steady marching? Other times, smaller prints crossed the trail, as if a scout darting across the back trail. Then an uneven rush of more smaller prints obliterated what was there. If it was Scarlurs, they were between them and the Regiment.

As the sun rose and warmed, the trail climbed to another rocky ridge. Should he send Star on ahead? She could go so much faster and tell him what was over there. With her speed, she might just reach the safety of the Regiment or be attacked and killed before he could reach her. Jace increased his lope. His sweat dark flanks were foam-flecked from the exertion of pushing hard on a leg that still ached. Yet her black and gray hindquarters were just glossy and dry as she ran close to him.

Jace complained again. "I can still smell nothing. What do you scent?"

"Your warriors ahead and others."

"The stink of Scarlurs?"

"Aye, but something else, strange like the spices from the bazaar."

"Tar-bel's caravaners were on the trail before us, we may be catching up with them."

At sun hitching, the shadows were gone, and they were reaching the top of the ridge. Ahead Jace could see rising dust. Big group. He heard shouts, was it the Regiment or Scarlurs? "Star." He held up his hand and slowed to a stop. "What do you smell?"

She gave a half rear. "Your warriors, Scarlur and spices."

Jace scanned the rock-filled terrain realizing he could hide an army out there. "You stay here. When I reach that crest, anyone below can see me. If I raise my hand like this, join me. Otherwise, run."

"Run where?"

"Your best hope would be back to the bazaar. They

seem to be allowed to live unattacked."

"My kin..."

"If the Regiment is gone and I am gone, there is nothing you can do. Save yourself."

"I could not..." She sounded frightened.

Jace looked at her fiercely, and she backed away. He unslung his bow as he loaded the first arrow. She probably would follow too closely, but he had to see what was over that hill. Jace galloped to the crest.

He heard the clash of swords on wooden shields before he saw them. It was a sight worth seeing. In a bowl of low hills, the trail cut across of oval plain and at its center, the caravan carts had circled in defense. They were being attacked by waves of Scarlurs. Yet Tar-bel's centaurs were steadily sending out arrows that usually found Scarlur flesh.

Jace could see the Regiment's abandoned carts to the sinister and no one guarded them as Garrison had taken an offensive position. He was leading his troops to fight on hoof, running down the enemy as it threatened. Garrison was using his archers to scythe the enemy and then charging to scatter them before they could reform firing lines. The caravaners seemed to have recognized Garrison as an ally and in a disciplined fashion were not shooting in the direction of the Regiment's furious charges against the duns.

It took Jace barely a breath to understand what Garrison had done, as he pulled back on his bow. He could not see Star's sisters or the younglings or who directed the duns. He let fly a shaft into the skull of the nearest Scarlur. As the fool fell, Jace had the sinew bowstring pulled back for another arrow to drop a second dun.

Star's kin must be somewhere behind Garrison's charging ranks. The charges looked unstructured, but Garrison was breaking the choking circle around the caravaners. Jace shot every one of his arrows and then cursed his lack of battle harness, as he untied his short sword. Now the fun started! Unwounded Duns were fleeing the Regiment charge in front of him.

It was a fine sight and more fine to join. Jace half reared then with a blood-chilling yell, he charged down the hill, faintly aware that hoof beats drummed behind him.

Chapter Thirteen

Sometimes the hunting centaur wins

Other times the beast prevails...

Boar Hunter's Lament

Screaming like an attacking eagle, Jace charged a band of retreating duns. The first he reached was looking back at Garrison's charge, which was a fatal mistake. The unwounded Scarlur were fleeing too fast to defend properly, so with just his short sword Jace cut and hacked until Garrison and his wing of the Regiment caught up to him.

Jace yelled. "**NO PURSUIT!**" He hand signaled those who could not hear over the battle fray.

Garrison nodded, yelling over the battle screams. "**ARDON–SOUND REGROUP! REGROUP!**"

Two blasts of the shell horn and the Regiment shortened their strides and started milling around Jace and Garrison. Many faces smiled to see Jace as he reached out to hands welcoming in salute of his return. The Regiment's second line just chased remnants of the duns to the scrub growth.

"The duns will lose a lot of hide in those thorns!" Garrison laughed.

"Who was leading?"

"They were already attacking when we came over the hill." As Garrison surveyed the battlefield, their warriors were already retrieving arrows. "On that rocky crest, there was an older warrior covered in red paint who seemed to be ordering. He had a yellow moon with one black star painted on his shield and did not hang around long when we showed up.

Those Scarlur leaders seem to bug out fast." Garrison leaned down with his spear, probing an overripe Scarlur body. "Dead a sunsink or two. They must have been surrounding the caravaners for awhile. These cart pullers do not surrender."

"Thunder keep them."

"Aye. Lord Thunder keep them." Garrison echoed with respect.

Alongside Jace, a complaining female voice. "Why do you fight for them?"

Jace and Garrison twisted to see Star. Indignantly she demanded again. "Why do you fight for the caravaners? We are paying you to fight for us!"

With a tight, bitter smile, Garrison turned and trotted off as he ordered, "**CHECK FOR WOUNDED! RECOVER WEAPONS!**" He pointed sword side. "**PLUNDER PILE OVER THERE! GUARD DETAIL HERE!**"

"**WE NEED SHIELDS!**" Jace also yelled and then he turned back to Star. "My lady, any of the caravan route robbers are your enemies. So we attack them for you."

She looked across the field, obviously sickened at the sight of the dead. Wheat had found a wounded Scarlur and was spearing him. As he screamed, Star looked away.

From the distance where they had been hidden, Sandi trotted up with sword in hand and Willow's colt's long legs sticking over her flanks as he rode her back. He was really too big to be carried. Star's sisters were following Sandi, with Silver Sunny carried Willow's filly in her arms. In battle helm, Willow brought up the rear with her sword unsheathed.

Moving through the field of dead, Garrison reached down and pulling up a painted shield trimmed with green feathers. It was painted with a yellow circle, a moon perhaps with a two yellows stars alongside it. "Clan badge?"

Jace nodded with his tail. "In the bazaar, the ones I

faced carried shields with a yellow moon and two yellow stars. That peacekeeper I killed last battle had such a shield."

"The older dun with Silver Belle had a yellow moon with a black star?"

Deadrick joined them. "So you return to us old one?"

Jace gave him a grim smile. "Aye." At first he expected Deadrick to challenge. Instead his officer just continued with. "Some of these warriors on the sinister flank held shields with the yellow circle with a black star."

"So you think we are fighting clans of the same the tribe?" Garrison asked.

Jace answered. "All are duns with black stripes down their back. Their warriors sport centaur tails for decoration, and they are called the Scarlur."

A drum of hoofbeats towards them and as a unit they twisted torsos. The dark hided caravaner, Tar-bel, was approaching and Jace noted all of the other caravaners remained behind their cart barricades, with arrows still notched.

Tar-bel trotted up before them. His mouth was set in a thin line, and his yellow eyes were glaring. He slammed to a spread leg stance before Jace, loudly proclaiming, **"We do not pay tribute!"**

Dung! His patroness was pissing her anger all over his hooves, and the fools they just rescued from slaughter were preparing to fight them. As his sire, Jachom would have pronounced, '*Some days it is hardly worth rolling up to stomp a snake!*' Jace moved to take a solid stance before Tar-bel as formally Jace intoned. "We demand no tribute, and we share none of the plunder!"

Tar-bel looked to Rufus who was yelling he had found a gold pendant. Straight-faced Tar-bel turned back to Jace and replied, "Sounds honorable." Tar-bel relaxed a little, wiping the sweaty dirt from his dark, thin face. He twisted and gave a hand signal to his caravaners, they lowered their weapons.

"How long were you under siege?" Jace asked.

"Two Suns."

Jace nodded admiringly. Forming defenses under an ambush and holding out in a hopeless situation boded well for fighters. "How many more do you think they have?"

Tar-bel shrugged his shoulders. "This was just one of the clans. More could come."

"Why not appease them by abandoning the carts?" Garrison asked.

"They would have hunted us down for the sheer sport." Finished Tar-bel grimly.

Jace looked at him. "Do you think the Scarlur will regroup and attack this sun?"

Weary-eyed Tar-bel looked out over the dead. "I did not expect such a bold attack. Usually, in the darkness, they try to sneak in and steal, but this time they attacked in full sun all yelling '*Death!*'"

Jace nodded. Trying to terrify their victims into surrendering, yet the caravaners still formed their circle as they fought off the screaming attack. "Did they break off and parlay for tribute?"

"Nay, the Scarlur know their word is worthless. If we parlayed, they would take the tribute and then kill us.

Jace shook his tail. "It is poor when thieves so dishonor themselves."

Tar-bel looked back over the field. "You are with Silvers. You travel this trail to the Black Mountains?"

"Aye."

"We do not do tribute, but it would be to both our advantages to travel together."

From behind, Star spoke up. "Nay, we must hurry on."

Jace gave her a silencing look and then turned back to Tar-bel. "Your kind offer is accepted. You rest then regroup, and we will stand guard."

Tar-bel nodded with his tail. "Let us move from these stinking bodies." He looked to the sun. "There is a sweet spring about five furlongs from here. We can reach it before sunsink."

"Sweetwater is fine purpose to trot for."

"My caravaners must briefly give blessing, and then we tramp." Tar-bel lifted his waterskin above his mouth, only a weak stream dribbled out, this he finished and wiped his still dry lips with his hand.

Garrison unhooked his water skin and passed it to Tar-bel, who seemed surprised, but after a hesitation he accepted it. Garrison also offered. "We have water in barrels we can share."

Tar-bel nodded his tail in thanks and then trotted to his cart ring. Jace shifted his weight off his sinister hind leg. It hurt, but not that deadly pain that kept growing. He would like a rest, but he must take the leader's first pick of the loot pile, so he started to move forward.

Star stepped determinedly in Jace's path. Realizing this could take a while, he wished he had his harness and a waterskin.

"My lord, you are in our hire!"

"Yes, my lady."

"Then you will do what I say!"

"Nay."

"Jace?!"

"My lady, I have sworn to fight for you. Die for you. But never would I have sworn to obey you."

Frustrated Star stamped a front hoof and looked from him to the caravan. "They will slow us down. Jace, please."

He was much thirstier than usual probably because of the loss of blood when Star cut into his leg. What he wanted was a long drink of water, but he was mired into softly explaining. "My lady, there is a formidable robber force out there, and we do not even know how many. Aye, we are more protection to Tar-bel's fighters than they are to us, but they know the terrain, the water holes, and the best ambush spots. They have fought your Scarlurs off before and survived. There is much I will learn from them."

"But..."

"Will, their route take us to where we must go?"

"Aye, but it splits before our mountain!" She shook her tail. "And..."

"We **shall** journey with them!" Years of leadership had given a finality to his tone that even Star did not dare dispute. Jace trotted over to Garrison who was recovering his spear from a slumped down centaur. "Report."

"None of ours dead. Several hide wounded but all can trot."

"Looting must finish shortly."

"We leave here?"

"We journey with the caravaners to a new camping. Scouts ahead and behind, half the troop before the caravan. Younglings and carts behind the caravaners. Rest follows. Give orders, the looting and apportioning must be finished before the caravaners pull out."

Garrison nodded with his tail. **"ARDON! DEADRICK! SANDI! TWO SPOT!"**

Jace did a lope around the field of battle noting the paint markings on the shields. Most were moon and yellow stars, but some of the older, strong bodied fighters had shields that bore the moon and a black star. If Nine-Kill had not been on the field, he might still have directed this attack.

At the sounding of the shell horn, Jace cantered to where their plunder was spread on the ground. He chose for himself a short sword of wavy river metal.

Star was watching. "Forged by my kin. It will serve you well."

As the others began making their first choosing, Jace cantered over to the caravan carts and saw Tar-bel's centaurs had bound their wounds. They were now forming a silent circle of attention, and none appeared to notice Jace as he quietly moved to a position behind Tar-bel. With his superior height, he could see over their heads to the center.

There on the ground before them, one of the dark caravaners lay dead. All the others bowed their heads silently waiting. Finally, in a deep voice, Tar-bel intoned in Hamish. *"Ye be free. Ye have served well."*

Jace silently agreed. '*Ye be free. Ye have served well.*', a fine eulogy for any centaur.

Silence reigned again as the second in command, Eli, stepped into the center of the circle. Unsheathing his sword, he reached down to the fallen centaur and began chopping off his dark tail. When he finished, Eli walked stiffly to hand the tail to Tar-bel. To Scarlurs the tails of the fallen were battle trophies, but to the caravaners, Jace suspected they were treasured as mementos of a fallen brother.

Jace bends his head in respect as the circle moved to form around the next body. Again Tar-bel repeated, *"Ye be free. Ye have served well."* and the tail chopping began. Finally, the dark centaurs moved to the last of their fallen as Jace followed in respectful silence.

The chopping sounds ended, and the caravaners wheeled about, headed toward their carts. They were beginning to take up cart harnesses. So much for rest. Tar-bel carried the three tails to one of the carts as he explained to

Jace. "It is our custom. We will return their tails to their kin."

Jace nodded approvingly. "To die fighting is to die with honor."

Then Tar-bel's face hardened as he spoke again. "We lost three. We will have to abandon two of our carts. Normally we would burn them to keep them from robbers, do ye wish them?"

"What metal wish you?"

"Given in gratitude."

"Accepted as such."

"Our caravan will march as a unit. Will your troops march before or after?" The smaller centaur spoke as if he ordered.

This would be tricky. "You will be more protected if we march some before, the shes and youngsters just after you, and the final body of warriors behind." That would leave Tar-bel tightly surrounded, something that made his shoulders and tail stiffen. It was not to his liking, but he was aware that both the Scarlur and the Regiment outnumbered him.

"Or you can continue on your own, alone." Jace quietly finished. Tar-bel must trust Jace or not. If the caravan traveled with their guard, they must take Regimental orders.

Ta-bel nodded his understanding. If he directed his caravan to leave, they would not be robbed by Jace's Regiment but neither would they be protected. It was not his way, but Tar-bel could see his centaurs were weakened from battle and another attack might come at any time. After a few moments of obvious struggle, he nodded his tail. "We will march at the center if yours can keep ahead of us."

Jace continued. "The Regiment sends out scouts behind, some will range on the sides and two ahead."

"We send out ahead with none behind."

"Since your kin knows the trail, I suggest we rotate

one of your point scouts with one of ours."

Again Tar-bel nodded his tail in assent. "We gather now."

Jace loped back to the Regiment where Deadrick was loudly arguing with Garrison. With a whip of whitetail and golden hide, he twisted to confront Jace. Deadrick's eyes narrowed his chest reddening. "There was to be a drum tonight. Garrison accepted my challenge for leadership!"

Garrison commented mildly. "It seems we do not need it since the Regiment's chosen leader has returned."

Deadrick glared from Garrison to Jace. "You come back and just take over?"

Again, Garrison took the point. "Our patroness has chosen Jace. It is settled."

Undoubtedly Deadrick already saw himself as the new First, a position he was not about to give it up. He glared at Jace and pranced angrily to the side. "You canter stiffly, so your leg is still injured!"

"But it heals." Jace just smiled and started to move off. "They are calling thirds on the loot."

Deadrick stood rock still as Jace and Garrison moved off to take their places at the head of the plunder line. "You did not decline a challenge from him?"

Garrison smiled. "If I declined, I would have had to serve under him."

"He is younger and stronger."

"Oh, he is a fighter. A good one but not a great one, just watch his movements, his eyes, his shoulders and you know where he is going to strike next."

"We have warned him of that."

"But he knows too much to listen to the likes of us."

Jace shook his head, feeling vastly tired. "He will challenge me this sunsink."

"Nay, he will not, unless enough of the comrades are following his tail."

"You think he will get them?"

Garrison looked over the field of centaurs carefully. "Many would have sided with him against me–but with ye, nay, he will not challenge this stars." He reached down and picked up a bone-handled dirk from the loot pile. "But to be on the safe side, I had better start talking to some and feeling out the ground." With a frown, he looked into Jace's eyes. "If he does challenge, you could decline. Stay with the Regiment until you get stronger."

"Nay, I march not under Deadrick." Jace found himself smiling slowly. "One day, one of us may kill the other..."

"My metal will be waged on ye." Garrison smiled. "Old age and treachery will always win out."

Axel loped up, a wide grin on his face. "Ye ready to carry your own battle harness again?"

"Aye." It felt good to slip on the worn leather and feel his long sword by his elbow.

His Regiment had not rested or eaten, but pairs of caravaners were already throwing their cart harnesses on. Tarbel's hes would not be slowing them down.

A shadow cooled Jace's withers, and he looked up. Above him, wide black wings were circling as those dunged vultures were coming in for centaur meat. Without thinking, Jace hauled his bow up and pulling back on the braided cord. Instantly his scavenged arrow sped, shooting down the closest bird, as its nest mates shrieked in protest and flapped away.

When the black feathered body hit earth with a thump, Sandi quickly trotted close. "Waste of an arrow. Kent, retrieve the arrow and bird. It might taste good on the spit."

"Nay! Bring back the arrow only! Those dung heaps

feast on centaur flesh!" Jace looked to the caravaners. They were pulling two carts over to his warriors, those carts were piled high with their trade goods, more gifts from ones who would not pay tribute. "Ardon! Those carts are ours, assign pullers. Sandi, this sunsink, pick any of the goods to keep and burn the rest. We must line up now, methinks these caravaners will trot fast." Jace looked to the side. "Garrison, hurry that loot line!"

"Jace!" A frightened Ana was racing up. "Reet is down!"

He wheeled and followed her to the edge of the battlefield. There a helpless group was looking down at the dark, sweating flanks of Reet whose entire body shook as she took each painful breath. Per Ben knelt behind her on bent legs. Square faced Per Ben, who could face a full charge with only a bitter smile, looked terrified as his mate lay on the grass. Reet's flanks were flecked with yellow foam as her huge-belly muscles contracted. She grimaced in pain, but she stoically remained silent, except for her labored breathing.

With the surgeon's pouches open, a hovering Willow bent over her. Reaching to touch Reet's back, Willow was shoved aside by Per Ben. "Leave her be!"

Anguished, Reet pleaded with Jace. "It is too early. The baby comes too soon–it will die!"

Per Ben covered her eyes with his big hands, as if he could keep death away if she did not see it.

"Willow." Jace moved away, signaling for her to follow him. "Report."

"The battle started labor." Willow sounded helpless.

"Can you stop it?" Jace ordered.

"Nay. The foal will be born and then die. Reet may keep bleeding and die with it."

Sandi pounded up. "The caravaners want us ahead of

them. They want to move out now! What is keeping you?"

Ana was at Jace's withers begging. "We can not move! She will die."

Sandi looked down at the heaving Reet. Reet was a long, close friend and comrade but Sandi lived by duty first. "Jace, will you halt the Regiment for a she in labor?"

He could not. With another attack impending, they had to move with the caravaners, but if Reet could not walk, Per Ben would not leave her. Ana darted to her brother Arnfinn. She was clearly begging him to stay with Reet. Arnfinn and Per Ben camped together if Arnfinn added his four to Reet and Per Ben, that would lose the Regiment six fighters. Left behind the six of them could not hold off the Scarlur coming back for their dead.

Again Sandi demanded. "Do we march?"

"Fetch the Lady Star. Now!"

Sandi bounded away. Jace walked stiffly back to Reet. Her face was dripping with sweat and the tears of her mate.

Per Ben looked up defiantly at Jace. "She cannot move. I stay with her."

White hided Arnfinn trotted up to Jace. "Ana will go with the Regiment while Arjuna, Aneurin and I will stay with Per Ben."

Not a request, just a simple statement. So much for disciplined troops. A soft beating of hooves and Star was brushing past Jace. She folded her long front legs down and was gently reaching out to Reet, speaking in a soft, crooning voice. "Reet, what is the matter?"

Reet opened her agonized eyes. "The babe comes..."

Behind her, Per Ben babbled. "It will die! It will die! Reet will die! She bleeds!"

Star ignored him and gently cupped her hand under Reet's chin, forcing Reet to look into her eyes only. "You were frightened by the battle, but the battle is over." Star's voice was low and compelling. "The pains already lessen...they will weaken... they will stop."

Per Ben cried out. "Nay! They grow worse! The foal will die!"

Frustrated, Star looked from the anguished eyed Reet to Per Ben. She spoke in a low, but determined voice. "Per Ben, Reet needs wine. The strongest you can find. You must leave to fetch it!"

Still holding Reet's shoulders, he raised upwards, starting to lift her.

Jace stepped forward, in full command voice. "Let her lie! Per Ben, just leave and find wine for Reet."

Per Ben looked desperately about. "There are no merchants here."

Star's voice continued in a soft, reassuring tone. "Someone in the Regiment will have wine. Find it!"

"I cannot leave her." He said defiantly.

Reet reached up to him, taking his big hand in hers. "Benna, listen to her. Do this for me. For our foal."

Per Ben raised himself, stood on stiff legs for a moment and then bounded off. Star just smiled confidently and gently ran her hands over Reet's flanks. Reet forced a weak smile back, but Jace could see her huge flank muscles tightening again.

Reet spoke in a weary voice. "Can you stop the cramps?"

Star hesitated for a breath, then replied firmly and confidently. "Of course I can, but you must help me. You must try to relax. To rest." Star signaled to Willow who moved in. "Willow, come kneel behind Reet and support her head and shoulders. Rub her back slowly in a circle. Reet, close your eyes and think of a beautiful...orange sunset over a quiet lake. You will bathe in the lake, and it will cool your body. I will get a wet cloth for your head, soon all will be well..." Reet obediently closed her eyes and laid her shoulders down on to Willow's breasts.

Sandi was trotting to Jace announcing, "The caravaners are marching."

Jace moved to her. "Any of ours before them?"

"The fastest Garrison could find. Those lads step sprightly."

Silently Star joined them looking up at Sandi's head. "I need your headscarf dipped in water." Sandi looked to Reet on the ground and pulled off her white linen head cloth. Wetting it from her water bag, she took Star's place as the tall she moved to Jace and spoke lowly. "I know Rufus has wine left..."

"If he does not, Snake does. But you sent Per Ben to get wine?" Jace questioned.

"Per Ben increases her terror, and he must be kept away! Jace, you must keep Per Ben busy."

Jace looked at Sandi. "Get wine from Snake or Rufus."

Star still looked to him. "Your yellow pain cakes. They may help Reet."

Jace reached for one of the pouches back on his harness, as Star still looked about and seeing Ana, she signaled her closer. "Tell my sister Crescent that she is to pick the Cloud-tears, those purple flowers by the trail. You both pick them and bring them here."

In the lowest tone, he could manage Jace asked. "Can you stop the birth?"

Star looked back to the heaving Reet and lowered her tail, speaking so softly he could barely hear her. "I will try, but she is far gone. And you will have to keep Per Ben away from her."

"Reet must rise. We march."

Star shook her tail. "She cannot. She must lay. Perhaps next sunrise..."

He shook his head.

Star pleaded. "Even a short time might help."

"Can she not make just a few furlongs?"

"Nay, she has blood on her tail. She will drop the babe if she tries to rise."

"We must leave. The Scarlurs will come back for their dead."

"They do not care."

"They will, if just to scrounge for weapons."

"Reet cannot move. I must stay with her." Those green eyes searched his, pleading mercy.

He could give only one answer. "The Scarlur will come. They kill her and those that stay behind with her."

"I can outrun any Scarlur alive."

"Even the wind cannot outrun an arrow."

Star bit her lower lip as Reet moaned. "Forget the caravaners. Cannot the Regiment camp here? Soon it will be dark."

"You are willing another attack on us all. If she must stay here, then Arnfinn and his brothers will guard her and rejoin us later." He did not add there would likely be no later.

Her lips formed a stubborn line and then she spoke with finality. "Reet must rest. You will march."

"You march with us!"

"I stay with Reet."

"Nay."

"I am your patron, and this is my order, Jace." she put her firm fingers on Jace's flank. "My sisters will take you to our mines, and you will fight for us. My duty is here." Then on silent hooves, she wheeled away from him, going back to kneel in front of Reet. The stricken she's sides were still heaved powerfully, but Star crooned. "That is it. You are doing better, see already the cramps lessen." Star opened Merdi's wooden box of pain cakes and from Willow's pouches dug out a drinking horn.

In the distance, Jace could see Garrison ordering the rest of the Regiment behind the last pair of caravaners.

Sandi bounded back with a wineskin. "Strongest we have."

Star rose, her grace making a fast movement seem unhurried as Sandi poured the wine into the drinking horn she held out. Then Star crumbled two of Jace's yellow pain cakes into the wine. Silver Crescent closely followed by Ana ran up with a handful of purple flowers, which Star crushed and stirred into the wine with her finger. Reet cried out as the contractions began again.

As Star continued to stir the mixture with her finger, she called out gently. "Aye. They will appear stronger before they weaken. That is good. Now, Reet, open your eyes. Willow will hold up your head, and you will drink this strong potion that will stop your cramps."

Sandi turned to Jace. "Scouts are out, and we are barely keeping ahead of the caravaners. Is Reet marching?"

Sadly Jace shook his tail, looking back to Reet on the ground.

Reet drank desperately and then started choking. She tried to hold it, but threw up, spewing red wine all across Star's breasts. Horrified Reet started to cry, hopelessly reaching out to wipe the wine off but Star just continued to croon softly. "That is fine. Your body is gaining control. And this is good. Try to drink again, more slowly this time....sip just a little. Soon your lips will numb, and you can drink more..."

Obediently Reet sipped. There was the sound of hooves drumming closer.

Star handed the drinking horn to Willow to feed Reet. "That is it. Sip slowly. Aye. Do you not feel the cramps lessening? Aye, they are growing weaker..."

Per Ben was galloping back with two huge goatskin wine bags. Lounging fast Jace intercepted him and grabbed his arm. "Your Reet has medicine! Now we must move out, you are needed to pull a cart!"

"Nay. I must...."

Star hurried to them. "Reet is resting, but Jace needs you now!"

Per Ben just stared beyond them to his downed she.

Jace pulled at his arm. "Your Reet will be fine, but I am down fighters. Per Ben, you must carry the slack for your sickly mate! Sandi, see that Per Ben is harnessed to one of the new carts that must roll out."

Sandi rolled her eyes but valiantly stepped up to stand beside Per Ben. No one of her small stature moves a heavily muscled mass like Per Ben when all four of his hooves were rooted to the ground. Still, with both her hands, she grabbed his other arm and started to pull him away, or tried to as the effort to move him lifting Sandi off her front hooves.

Jace also shoved at Per Ben. "Move! You must report to your position!"

Even with Jace's strength on his other arm, Per Ben moved not as he stared to his stricken mate.

Star crooned lowly. "Please. You must let Reet be quiet."

"Per Ben..." A weak voice came from behind them all. They looked down to see Reet's eyes were open. "Benna, you must listen to Jace. I will rest." She looked about. "Arnfinn and his brothers will guard me. You must take both our places in the Regiment. Go to the cart."

The muscle mass between Sandi and Jace moved not. Jace was sure he would rebel but years of discipline kicked in as a bleary-eyed Per Ben turned and allowed himself to be led away by Sandi.

Reet stretched back on to the ground, her shoulders were now covered with a green leather cloak of Willow's. Ana was carrying Reet's weapon harness, she now offered it to Jace. "Others must carry this."

Since Ana would offer little in battle with the Scarlur it was better that her life not be wasted, Jace looked to Arnfinn, who shook his head his with mouth grimly set. Jace turned back to Ana. "You will carry it. You march with us."

In protest, she looked to her brothers but Arnfinn just flatly stated. "We will guard Reet. You will go with the Regiment!"

Ana turned to plead with Jace, but he just reached down and slapped her rump. "March!"
Jace turned back to Arnfinn. "We would come back for our wounded and weapons, so may the Scarlur."

"Aye."

"Do you need water?"

"Nay." Arnfinn indicated two huge goatskin sacks on his flanks. "More arrows would help."

Jace reached behind into his harness. His stock was depleted, but he grabbed what battlefield scavaged ones he had. Not many, but he handed all to Arnfinn. "See if your brothers can get some from those last pulling out."

Arnfinn nodded to Arjuna, who took off with Aneurin.

"We head due Blue, following the trail. We will try to camp at a waterhole before sunsink. At sunrise we must march and can not wait for you."

"Aye." Again Arnfinn spoke without bitterness at the Fate Weavers, but they both knew how small were the chances of them living to rejoin the Regiment.

Still, Jace finished. "If Reet can move, try to get her off the trail and into those clumps of trees by the rocks. It might hide you and give you some sort of defense."

Arnfinn smiled crookedly at the notion of a defendable position there, but he just nodded his tail as he stepped to Reet. Star now walked to Jace as she was pressing more purple herb into carved drinking horn. He already knew what she would say, but still, he spoke. "Those who stay will most likely die in another attack."

Star looked up at him, those green eyes, clear and tearless. "Willow must go with you. We will rest here, and when Reet can move, we will catch up."

"My Lady, you lead us."

"My sister Crescent will lead you to our mines."

"To your dragon?"

Reet moaned as another contraction grabbed and Star looked back to her. "Duty is very important to your kind?"

"Above all else."

"To be trained as a healer among my kin is an honor. It comes with great responsibility." She looked back deeply into his eyes. "Jace, I wish it was other for us, but I must stay."

He should command her, have her roped, and dragged away, but he well understood duty. Star had found hers, and he had his. Signaling Willow to join him, Jace turned and trotted off. Only when they rejoined the last of the Regiment did he look back.

Chapter Fourteen

Those who poison the water Soon drink blood

The Ancients

In the distance, he could see Star kneeling behind Reet as the three white hided brothers stood at attention waiting for the Scarlur attack that would surely come.

Still a bit sore of leg, Jace found it hard going to maintain his usual loping alongside the line as those cart pulling caravaners forced a rapid, bone-wearying pace. Tar-bel's caravaners would not be slowing the Regiment down. As Jace trotted past his own weary warriors, he grabbed arrows from whomever he could.

Garrison had gotten the other Silvers, the young and their carts marching behind the caravaners. Willow was paired with a caravaner as the first scouts, while Sandi and Silver Sunny carried Willow's foals to speed passage. As they marched, the sun started sinking beneath the hills, gray gloaming came, then the world darkened. They could barely see the tail of the warrior ahead of them, and most must be following by smell only as pressure from the caravaners kept forcing his leaders ahead.

Out of habit, Jace kept raising his head to pick up scent. Not being able to smell was driving him mad. He trotted to Sandi. "Any smell of water? Scarlur?"

She shook her head. "Too much dust and nose wind. By the Winged Lady, those caravaners can move! Those yellow eyes must see all in the darkness."

A thin moon was rising, lighting up the sky a bit and ahead Jace could see the outline of a taller, dark band of trees. Mayhaps growing around that spring of Tar-bel's? When the first of the columns reached the trees, there must have been a signal from Tar-bel's scouts because soon the lead warriors stopped and the caravaners circled their carts.

"Warriors! Circle outside them!" Just as Jace gave the order, Per Ben dropped his pull harness and, without a word of permission, charged off. He would be galloping back to Reet. On a dark track into enemy territory. Would he find her and Star with their throats cut and tails chopped off?

Ardon looked at Jace. "Should I try to pull him back?"

Jace shook his tail. Per Ben's duty was completed and now he must hunt his mate, even unto Lightening Hoof's dark bone grounds.

Flames would show far in hostile territory, yet the Scarlur would know where they were, so Jace ordered fire pits dug. They should eat well and rest as long as they could, he expected those caravaners would step smartly with the sunrise.

Exhausted Jace just rolled down, taking the weight off his aching hindquarters. Later Kent brought him a bowl of Sandi's stew, but without being able to smell it, the food tasted like clods of dirt. The night air grew chillier, and he wondered how was Star doing? Did they leave her any food? After a time the moon came out of the clouds. That would help if she were trying to rejoin them.

He should sleep, but Jace kept looking to the trail behind them for that graceful she that always moved as if she cantered on clouds. The others settled into snoring but no sign of Star. He could order a rescue party with torches. Lead it himself with torches. Go back and find them all dead, in his mind he saw a vision of a butchered Star, her tail hanging from some Scarlur's spear.

Angrily Jace rolled up, trying to shake the bloody visions from his head. He was sore, restless, he must do something! He trod to the caravaner's camp. Deep within the Regimental lines Tar-bel still set guards, now one stepped into Jace's path, sword in hand.

There was no challenge, just a silent stare in the moonlight by a rather long swordwielding centaur.

Jace waited and then spoke. "I be Jace of Thunderhoof Regiment. I wish to speak with Tar-bel."

No flicker of recognition on the guard's shadowed face, nor did he look back for orders from superiors. This guard probably already had his orders to kill any intruder!

Jace raised a tentative hoof but at his movement, the guard's shoulders stiffened and his curved sword point slightly raised. He would not be allowed to pass. Out of the corner of his eye, Jace could see another caravaner guard drawing close on quiet hoofs. A few words with Tar-bel were not worth getting into a double sword battle. Still, Jace decided to try another tactic as he repeated in Hamish. *"Wish I speak Tar-bel. Be Jace of Regiment."*

At this, the caravaner nodded his tail in understanding and lowered his sword point. After nodding to his comrade, he signaled for Jace to follow him into their camp. So some of these caravaners understood universal hand signals and Hamish but not common speech. Were Tar-bel and Eli the only ones his warriors could communicate with?

Inside the circle of carts, a lowering fire lit several groups. All were standing, but some, with hands, hung down and heads bent, were snoring softly. Yet other yellow eyes shining in the firelight stared at him. Tar-bel had taken off his headscarf and was moving toward him. Jace slowly raised both his hands palms up in front of him so they could be seen to be empty. Another gesture universally understood.

Nodding to the guard who hurried back to the patrol perimeter, Tar-bel then asked, not unkindly. "Ye dare to come into another's camp after dark?"

"I am a stranger to your customs. Do I offend?"

"Nay. In fact, we cook too much. Perhaps ye can help us avoid wasting?"

Jace nodded and followed Tar-bel to the fire pit where one of his caravaners immediately filled a wooden bowl with shredded meat for him. There was not much, but these proud rangers must feed a fellow traveler first. Jace took his bowl first and then waited for Tar-bel to receive his. He was careful to lift food to his mouth at the same time Tar-bel took his, and they chewed in silence for a long time.

Jace still could not smell, but he tasted strong spices. It was a meal he would loved to have savored under better circumstances. When they finished, Jace was offered more; which he would have liked, but he politely refused. As he expected others were waiting to see how much he would eat before they took theirs.

Tar-bel finally spoke again. "It was a poor meal to offer."

"But very filling, fine for the trail." Politeness dispensed with Jace asked, "I have come to talk about our next marching. We leave at sunrise but will need to find another waterhole before sunsink. Do you know of one?"

The caravaner looked past his carts, over towards Willow who was feeding her filly. "With shes and wounded the pace seems hard for yours?"

"We will keep up." Jace stated firmly, then said, "I bartered for a chart at the Bazaar." Jace reached back into his battle harness, slowly, because with his sword close Tar-bel never seemed to let his guard down. They moved closer to the light of the fire pit, lowering themselves down as Jace unrolled the scroll. "This was from Var-tee in the Bazaar. It is the caravan trail."

Tar-bel traced the trail with his finger. "Var-tee has seen many winters, but this scroll is much older." He pointed to three marked water holes. "These were dry in my sire's time, and your map maker has missed water here and there."

Jace reached into his pouch for Var-tee's marking stick and re-drew to Tar-bel's corrections.

Tar-bel unrolled more of the scroll. "This is where we will part. Your warriors continue here on to the Black Mountain of the Silvers."

"Does this chart show your lands?" Jace asked casually.

Did the air become a little bit frostier? Tar-bel rolled the scroll back up, and Jace silently cursed himself for moving too fast.

Tar-bel turned to one of his centaurs speaking to him in Hamish. Well, at least Tar-bel had only asked for wine, so Jace was not be thrown out of camp but hospitality this night was winding down. They both drank briefly, then Tar-bel swung his tail. "Jace of Thunderhoof, ye will honor us again."

Back at his bedding ground, Jace knew at sunrise he would have to make a decision about Star. His legs throbbed with weariness as he sank to the grass, what was the matter with him? He always made decisions so rapidly, right or wrong. Star, Arnfinn and the others all chose to stay behind with Reet; if they could not catch up, they must be left behind! It was a simple matter yet all he could see in his mind was the vision of the loveliness that was Star. Her wide green eyes looking trustingly at him, her slain body with its tail cut off. The night was long and cold. Rest fitful. Night animals calling. Sleeping centaurs stamping hooves. Why had he let Star stay behind? Was she already dead?

As the sky grayed slightly before the sun rose, the caravaners circled for some sort of Hamish prayer. Jace expected they would eat then be harnessing themselves to their carts shortly.

Jace rolled up and ordered his officers. "Up and food!"

The deadly pain was gone, but his sinister hind leg still ached. He hauled on his battle harness and started to walk to the firepit when Sandi stopped him. "Do we march without Reet and our fancy Patroness?"

"The Regiment marches with the caravaners."

As Garrison and Sandi whipped about the camp rousting their own up Jace heard Rufus in guard position call out, "Hoofbeats!"

"AROUSE!" "STAND TO!" The camp drew weapons, immediately falling into battle lines.

They waited silently in the predawn's grayness as the hoofbeats drew closer.

Peering into the shadows, Jace figured three, four even five shapes? Not an attack force, mayhaps another murderous parlay? Six shadows closing at a slow trot. Pale hides leading: Arnfinn. Arjuna and Aneurin. Behind them were two solid bodies, Per Ben, pulling at Reet's hand. On the other side of Reet, the graceful poem that was Star that with her dark stockings, looked as if she was floating across the field.

They slowed as they came in and Jace moved to meet them. Giving a brief smile to him, Star guided Reet to the side. "Lay down and rest. I will brew you more potion."

Jace waited until Star stepped back to him, then he asked quietly. "Did she lose the foal?"

"Not yet." A concerned Star looked back to her. "The cramps have stopped for now, but she needs more rest."

He shook his tail. "We march as soon as we gather. Reet can bring up the rear, that will give her little time." Star was untying a drinking horn as she struggled to get at the wineskin strapped over her shoulder. He reached out, fingers brushing the smooth skin on her back as he helped her pour the wine. From a tiny sack tied into to her hair, Star took out the last of Jace's pain cakes. Ana was rushing over with a handful of those purple flower herbs. "Do you need more of these?"

"Aye and Reet must eat if she can." Star directed, then turned back to Jace as she mixed the crumbled yellow cake and some of the crushed flowers into Reet's wine. "Jace, while we hurried here I smelled Scarlurs behind us. It was very strong."

"Behind?"

"And sometimes swordwise."

He narrowed his eyes, searching out the danger in the dawn's grayness. "If Reet goes down again, we cannot stop. This time you **must** march with us."

Star scanned the field. "You have more carts? Could we not repack the largest and lift Reet on to it?"

"Carry her?" It was not done, but... Jace looked to the wagons. "It would be hard pulling over rough ground. She will be bounced much."

"It will be better than moving her legs. You have cloth could go underneath Reet for padding. Please order it."

He signaled to Axel, Two Spot and several others of the strongest. "We need that cart emptied! Sandi! Direct the repacking, we carry Reet in a wagon?"

Sandi looked at him. "In a cart?"

"Aye."

Sandi shrugged, and he turned back to Star. "Have you eaten?"

"Nay," she said.

Jace nodded his head. " They have kicked dirt over the coals, but there is meat on the sticks."

Ana was hurrying back to Star who ordered. "I will bring this potion to Reet, you get meat for Reet and Per Ben. Then they will lift her into the cart."

"The cart could hurt her..." Ana started to argue.

"Gallop!" Jace ordered Ana.

The wagon carrying the water barrels was the biggest, but by repacking all, Sandi managed to make a bed out of grain sacks and pine boughs in the next largest cart. It took six warriors, but a frightened looking Reet was lifted up to where she was sitting on folded legs. There were many volunteers to pull as Reet and Per Ben were well liked. As the last of the Regiment moved out, Per Ben, Axel, Two Spot, and Black Ears pulled mightily on her cart and trod slowly into line as desperately Reet gripped the cart's sides as it began to roll off. Throughout the sun's traverse Per Ben either pulled or walked stiffly alongside Reet, with Star on the other side.

As the sun rose higher, they made good time, but Jace could still smell nothing. Without scent, he was constantly questioning each scout coming off duty trying to estimate the closeness of the Scarlur. As the sun headed downwards, Sandi galloped past saying she smelled water upwind. Star was cantering up to him.

Seeing her near made him feel stronger. "My lady, how does Reet?"

"The cart jostled her much but now she is down, and trotting and the cramps have not come back."

There were things he wanted to say to Star, but a change in the stride of the warrior nearest him drew his attention to the columns. All were shortening strides to slow. Something ahead? He turned to leave but Star spread her warm fingers on his withers speaking softly but with urgency. "Your fall was my fault. Willow says I should have braced my legs and moved my tail. Can we try again?"

Mount her? What, now? With the Regiment marching and under imminent attack? With his sinister leg barely strong enough to march. This she had the timing of drunken Harlot! The forward marchers were halting, and he had to know why. "There will be time, my lady, but not this sun. I must talk with Tar-bel at the head of the columns."

"The caravaner? Why do you talk with him so much?"

"My Lady, I talk with everyone. That is how you learn the ways of others." She started to follow him causing Jace to give a gruff. "Stay here!"

The forward warriors had stopped, and when Jace reached them he found they were all standing around a pond, maybe twenty hands across lined with rough cut rocks. Jace joined Tar-bel at the edge of a pool of clear water, too deep to see the bottom. With this amount of water they could easily have refilled their drained water carts but for the two sunken bodies that were beginning to bloat below the surface. Poisoning centaur carcasses weighed down with Scarlur arrows through them. "They poisoned a waterhole?" Jace asked.

Tar-bel looked as if he could not believe the infamy of the sacrilege. "The jackals..."

"They also dishonored a purple truce flag."

He looked in horror. "Fleas!"

Jace stared toward the lowering sun. "The water in our wagons casks are at the bottom, and most of my warriors have empty water bags."

Tar-bel squinted. "It gets drier ahead."

Jace signaled two of his leading warriors. "Snake! NightHawk! Rope the bodies and drag them to the rocks over there."

Tar-bel did not look happy. "It will still be undrinkable for a moon." The caravan leader tightened his lips. "If we march on this trail until sunset, there will be no water hole for two more suns, and that too may be poisoned."

"Nothing closer?" Jace asked.

Tar-bel thought for a moment and then turned and loped back. Jace followed closely as the caravan leader reached his carts and dug under a tied down covering. From deep within he pulled out a pale leather roll that looked smooth and supple like kidskin. It was tied with yellow silk and was the length of his forearm. Jace struggled to control the naked greed on his face. A chart of these lands? What would Tar-bel be willing to trade for it?

The caravaner unrolled it pointedly not showing it to Jace. He waited patiently until Tar-bel re-rolled his scroll and looked up. "In my grandsires time, there was a deep, sweet spring that fountained out a bit off the trail more than half a sun from here. We could leave this trail and trot until sunset, camp dry this stars and then trot to it by mid sun. We spend one sun there, refilling our water and resting the wounded. Cut back to the trail on the next sun. We lose ground, but we march stronger."

Haste was important, but fighters able to fight was critical. "Is this what you wish?"

Tar-bel looked at Jace and realized the decision was being left up to him. "Aye. With some rest, hooves will be fleeter."

Jace nodded. "Your scouts lead."

Tar-bel studied him. "We will have to tramp our own trail, and my grandsires' spring may have long dried–there is nothing else close..."

"This we shall find."

"If the Scarlur has not poisoned that spring too."

Jace backed his hindquarters as two of his warriors began pulling a dripping hided body out of the water. It had once been a female. "They must have water for themselves."

"Aye," said Tar-bel sourly.

"Garrison! Set a guard, no one is to drink from this bloodied water. Order the line moving again following Tar-bel. Dry camp this stars." Jace stepped closer to study the pond. "This spring here, it is ringed with a rock wall. Centaur made?"

"The spring was natural but hollowed out and reinforced with walls, probably by the ones that now float in it. Once this caravan trail had maintained water holes every sun. There were log or rock corrals for safe sleeping, these were called caravanserai. The safe areas were kept up by those who lived nearby to keep traders trotting in their territory. The caravanserai even had food cashes, where we left goods in grateful trade." Tar-bel finished.

Sounded like a good system. "What happened?"

"At first the Scarlur demanded payment for their 'protecting the route'. Soon less traders would take it, then outright raiding began. "

"Why do your people not allay with the bazaar males and wipe out the Scarlur?"

Tar-bel only gave a wry smile. "We are the only ones who still tread this path, and after this, I do not know if I can get any other caravaners to trot this way." The Regiment's columns were passing them.

Jace looked down at Tar-bel. "If your trade is killed, mayhaps your hes should join with us?"

"Join your regiment?"

"Aye. My patroness wishes more fighters."

"For what?"

"To free her mines from a dragon."

"A dragon?"

"Have you ever seen one?"

Tar-bel shook his head. "Nay."

"Each warrior will get one silver coin per marching sun, plus plunder and a promise of bonus when we clear the Silvers' mines. Your officer's share would be larger."

Tar-bel was silent for some time. Then he said, "Nay. We are traders, if we can not get through to the Headlands Bazaar, there are five other directions to trade in."

Jace thought he might argue his case more, but Tar-bel abruptly nodded his tail and trotted to his carts. Rejoining the line himself Jace cut the length of his strides down to a slow lope as first the caravaners, then the second line of his Regiment started passing him.

"Garrison, dry camp further on. Then half a sun march and rest camp if we find water."

Garrison shook his head in disapproval. "Fine for a dragon's hunt me thinks."

As the next sun rose a thirsty line marched again. Jace he could see Arnfinn and Arjuna bringing up the rear with Reet out of her cart and marching alongside Per Ben. Jace slowed and moved alongside Reet. Her face was very white, but her thick legs strided strongly.

He spoke to her quietly. "Mid-sun if we find water we make an early rest camp."

She smiled gratefully.

Jace lengthened his strides again to reach Star and her sisters. Not ever seeming to hurry, the three Silvers easily keep the pace with their long legs Jace noted as he stepped beside Star.

She gave a critical glance to his sinister hind leg. "How is your leg?"

It surprised him to realize he had not even thought much about it. "A little sore. You are truly an amazing healer. Reet walks, and she still has her babe."

With a frown, Star looked back to her. "It would be better if she rested."

"We will soon," Jace noted that those wide green eyes were actually flecked with gold.   Star smiled to him as if he had given her a great gift. "Rest. Blessings be to the Goddess."

At sunsink they dry camped as guards were set, brush was gathered for fires and scouts sent out. Before loping the camp, he saw Sandi pouring wine from Rufus' goatskin into a large stew pot as Star now trotted to her. Again he just stopped to admire the gray she's taut haunches.

Star was offering Sandi an armful of greens. "These will give the meat a tart flavor."

Sandi bit a leaf and then nodded. "More for the pot. Will you and your sisters join us?"

"We would be proud. Crescent gathers more firewood." Star swung her long tail. "Sunny has found sweet berries."

"If the berries are very heavy, it is fortunate Axel is there to help her carry them," Sandi said tartly, as she looked to the distant couple that were obviously more interested in each other than berry picking.

Star was staring at Sandi's neck thong with its three beads. "May I see your necklace?"

Sandi stepped forward.

The taller she delicately touched the three, smoothly polished beads on the leather thong. "Tri-color jade. My kin would value these very highly."

Sandi blushed a bit. "Gift from my long dead mates, Mica and Smokey, on the foaling of Ross. This stew will take a while, but Jace returning here seems to be looking at you. Mayhaps he has a rare stone or something he wishes to show you?"

Later by the fire pit Star's beautiful face looked up to his with total absorption. "Tell me of the others you have seen," she asked.

He just wanted to look at her. "Others?"

"Your friend, Garrison, tells me you have marched across all lands."

Jace chuckled. "Not quite, but I have been privileged to see much."

"Your kin travels far?" Her eyes were wide with curiosity.

"They did. And, after I left them, I traveled farther."

"You left your kin?"

"Aye." Her pale gray hide and skin looked more polished than the marble. Mayhaps...

"Please tell me more." Her voice had an urgency that was quite unexpected in a breed whose kin stayed rooted to one mountain for generations.

"I left my dam."

"She who foaled you, what was her name?"

"Dawn."

"Did you have a sire that ran with your dam?"

"He lived with his band of fighters. Jachom of Iron Shield Clan. We followed him at a distance and, as a youngster, I eagerly watched him charge into battle."

"But he was not with you?"

"He came back. Mare tended his wounds." Jace smiled wickedly, "and such."

"Most of the time he was fighting?"

"When I was older, he did patiently drill me in war maneuvers."

"He must have been proud of you."

"He never said so, and Jachom constantly yelled: I was too slow; too fast; too foolhardy; or without a plan. But

I was the youngest he marched off to battle."

"Then he was proud."

"For a time, but as I got older, we began to fight constantly. He was used to shouting orders that were always obeyed. I did not wish to obey, and I wanted to see other lands, other centaurs that we were not killing."

"Did you?

"Finally after our sparring got both of us some serious wounds, my dam sent me away."

Star seemed not to understand. "By yourself? You went alone?"

"The young think themselves invulnerable. I did not even take a battle harness, just a short sword, and a hunting bow."

Her eyes grew even wider with wonder. "What did you see?"

"Grass." He laughed. "Mountains."

"Were the mountains like ours?"

"Wet forests on one side, high naked rocks and long, dry deserts on the other. There were furlongs of prairies where you could gallop for moons and see nay mountains or ocean."

Her eyes reflected the firelight. "Silver Beard brought me scrolls from the bazaar with all sorts of painted animals. Can you draw the ones that you have seen for me?"

"I am not an illuminator, my lady but I saw spotted leaf eaters with long necks as high as trees. Great lumbering gray creatures with tusks twice the thickness and length of my arms. Centaurs that tend vast herds of tamed animals."

"Why?"

"For meat and hide."

"Can they not just hunt game?"

"There are centaurs that grew food plants in rows like lines of warriors. Centaurs that throw tethered spears into the sea and drag out great fish. Centaurs who haul immense blue stones and set them upright in circles to track the movement of the heavily bodies."

"You tease me." She swished her tail in impatience.

"Nay. I saw centaurs who fought, those that endlessly prayed to their Gods, those that just ran free. All who spoke and painted different languages."

"I have heard some like this in the bazaar." She looked back so longingly, he thought she might bolt. "Tell me more."

"For awhile on the prairies, I ran with a herd of light chestnut colored centaurs. They were faster than most with wild golden hair and tails. The yellow hair on their heads extended down their backs to the top of their withers."

"Oh?"

"But the most usual thing was that they did not speak."

"Not speak?"

"I was with them for several moon cycles. None of them made a sound or seemed to understand any language I spoke."

"How did they share food?"

"They ate off the land, stored nothing, stayed together, mounted and bred foals, but never spoke."

"Mayhaps they had no tongues?"

"Actually they did. One day, I heard a high squealing, and I turned. The lovely young she who often ran alongside me was being attacked by a savage Rabric."

"Rabric?"

"It is a big, four-legged, low to the ground stalker, with huge fang-like teeth that hang down on either side of its mouth," Jace remembered watching the she go down, screaming as he charged to save her. "I side kicked him and then ran. He slashed at me but left her. Running before him I lashed out with a lucky double hindleg kick and heard a 'crack' as I connected. It might have broken his jaw. He fled."

"The centauress?"

"Was wounded. Bleeding, she came to me and rested her soft head on my chest, but she never spoke again."

"Did you stay with them long?"

"Nay. There was always another hill to run over and see what was on the other side."

"You have seen so much. Worlds away from here." Her eyes looking to the stars coming out in the night sky had a dreamy look.

He hated to end it but, "There is one thing I have never seen."

"What is that?"

"A living fire-breathing dragon."

Star suddenly needed to look away, down at the trail "You have not...?"

Speaking in a serious tone, he asked again. "Will I see one, my lady? A dragon to fight?"

Star stepped closer, about to say something, but then a voice called from the side. "Lady Star, pardon!" They both wheeled to see it was Per Ben.

"Does Reet need me?" Asked a concerned Star.

"She sleeps, but her stomach moves. What should I do?" He looked so lost.

Star took his hand and started to walk back with him, her voice taking on a comforting croon. "A good sign. The babe is strong and kicking."

Left alone Jace ate his dinner than before trotting to Tar-bel's camp he sought out a half-filled wineskin he could share. When a caravaner guard ushered him to the campfire Tar-bel was studying that silk wrapped scroll of his again. Seeing Jace, he put it away as Jace feigned disinterest as Tar-bel pointed out, "Soon our trails will part."

"Then it is good we can share a bit of wine as Mare sky reveals more of her star foals."

Jace held the skin high, squirting a drink in his mouth, then passed it to Tar-bel saying, "Sandor's wines are fine."

The caravaner laughed. "My friend, ye must taste the grapes of Laurel. It is the land of my sires, where the fruits grow sweeter than honey."

"Mayhaps our trails will cross. Mayhaps you will rethink joining the Regiment?"

"Nay. We are traders."

"Who needs your routes patrolled."

"We traders cannot afford your fighters, and we will not pay tribute. However, if the caravan trail were patrolled and cleared by honest guardians, the trade to Headlands Bazaar would grow again. Our caravan and others might be willing to provide trade goods, this could be bargained."

At sunrise, the caravaners marched after their Hamish devotions to the sun. Tar-bel left his caravaners and cantered to the columns' head as Jace joined him. He noted that Tar-bel carried that kid skin roll with him. By Thunderhoof, Jace would love to see what was within it, but he maintained a polite distance every time Tar-bel halted the line to study his chart.

To Jace, all the land looked the same with just scrub brush and clumps of trees in the distance, but periodically Tar-bel would stop the columns to look at his chart, seeming to sight the hills and mountain peaks around them. He also seemed to note their positions in relation to two outstanding rock croppings. Finally, Tar-bel raised his hand to stop the lines. "My friend, call in our scouts. We leave the trail here."

Jace looked to where Tar-bel pointed, just more brush

and the sandy bed of a dry river. Would Tar-bel's spring be dry too? Jace signaled, and his columns trooped off the trail.

Hot, sticky tramping trying to drag the carts over rocky, sandy soil. At least on the caravan trail, they had not had sharp branches whipping them as they passed. It seemed as hard on Tar-bel's cart pullers as it was with Jace's warriors. How much longer would Reet have to march? How much longer could she?

Letting Tar-bel choose the marching was strategically correct but uncomfortable for a leader. Now a thirsty Jace moved to the side and let the columns march past. Deadrick and Skull were speaking vigorously, but then they both stopped talking as they trod past him. A challenge to his leadership brewing? The caravaners just stoically pulled their carts over rock and sand, and his own warriors did just as well. Star passed, but Jace waited, watching for Reet. Her solid legs plodded on beside Per Ben, but there was a trembling in her croup.

Finally at the rear of the column Nighthawk was rejoining the line after being relieved by fresh scouts. Jace gave a hand signal, and Nighthawk sidestepped and halted beside him. "Report."

"Ground back on the trail too tough for hoofprints."

"Smells?"

"Enemy, but has been fading since we left the caravan trail."

"Tar-bel's scouts, how are they?"

"Can track a leaf print on the ground before it falls from the tree."

So trained scouts were leading them, but to what?

Nighthawk followed Jace back behind the columns. "Where we headed?"

"To water, we hope."

Jace was giving up on Tar-bel's directions, but when the sun left them with no shadows, his leaders sent back word of a clearing with a small but deep pool. When Jace got up there, Tar-bel was dipping his drinking horn, taking a taste and then nodding his head. His warriors took their turns dipping horns and then set to scything down brush for a resting area. Reet was the first down, but Jace noted a bit more color in her face as Star fetched her water to make her comfortable.

Sandi trotted up. "Kent and Ross have downed two fat bucks."

"Good. When Ross butchers them, take some meat to Tar-bel."

She nodded in assent. Finally, Jace drank deeply and filled his waterskin as Star moved to him, putting firm fingers on his withers. "Jace. We lose time."

"Aye. But we need rest. We need water." He looked to Axel. "When everyone has had a first drink, see that the water casks are filled."

Jace moved to Tar-bel. The caravaner had been consulting his chart and said, "We must backtrack a little but not all the way." By Thunder's bolts, if Jace's could just see that scroll. Should he offer gold to just look at it? Somehow he felt that would be a breach of hospitality. Mayhaps, if the time was right...

After gloaming, Jace decided he would lope the perimeter with Axel, but the big pinto was staring deeply into the large green eyes of Star's sister, Sunny, so Jace loped the perimeter with Garrison. "We should be training Axel. Raw as he is he can be a leader, he needs to learn to read and write Trade as well as fight."

Garrison nodded. "He still has not shaken the seeds out of his hide, but he has the potential to lead the Regiment some time."

"Not too soon, my old friend, not too soon."

With Tar-bel's scroll to guide them, they took a different route back to the caravan trail. Reet looked much better, and even Star seemed content with their progress for the next three suns. Towards sun-sink they trotted over a slight hill and Jace could see mountains in the distance. He asked Tar-bel. "Lady Star's mountain?"

"Nay, my friend. This is but a small mountain before great valleys and plains. We will part from you before it, and then you will have a tight climb up a narrow trail. Down the other side, a valley, then beyond that plains, from there you can see the Silvers' Mountain in the distance."

At gloaming, they made a dry camp. After giving march orders for next sunrise, Jace trotted to Tar-bel's camp. Eli already stirred a mutton pot.

Tar-bel greeted him. "Our last meal, my friend. Our paths will part mid-sun."

"My scouts tell me that Scarlur stink is around."

"Aye. They rub themselves in it to frighten us."

"My sire, Jachom and his fighters tried that tactic once."

"They rubbed themselves with blood?"

"Nay, they chewed herb. All sun they chewed small, white cloves of garlic for a moon cycle. Soon the stink steeped out their breath, out of their tailwinds, out of their very hide. You could smell Jachom and his fighters furlongs away."

"This chased away their enemies?"

"It chased away their shes. My dam, Dawn, and all the other of Jachom's mountings would not allow him near."

Tar-bel laughed. "It must have taken suns to get the stink out of their hides."

"Nearly a full moon!"

They both laughed and then passed the wineskin in silence. Finally, Jace asked. "When we part, you think the Scarlur will follow you and attack again?"

Tar-bel frowned deeply. "We will move fast." He changed the topic. "Now join us in our poor repast." They ate quietly, and then Tar-bel spoke again with lowered tone. "I have noticed ye seem to appreciate the smell of that lead she. The Silver with the star on her forehead."

A rude question from Tar-bel? Jace stiffened but said nothing.

"Forgive my impertinence, but my kin have long traded with the Silvers. Several times bride prices were offered for one of their long-legged shes, very high trade, even for such beauties. Nay offer was accepted. Silver Beard and the others would not even bargain." Tar-bel took a last sip. "Of course, with your warriors, ye could take her by force?"

"Nay."

"That I believe. Well, my friend, mayhaps times change. I have never seen the Silver shes without their male kin escorting."

Jace needed to change the topic. "Mayhaps we should split earlier. I see more heavy brush ahead that would cover my warriors."

"Ye wish to hide your warriors?"

"Our scouts say the Scarlur follow closely. We will part, and your caravaners will march ahead. The last of your back scouts can carry leafed branches to sweep and raise as much dust as they can. My warriors will wait patiently, and mayhaps we will have our friends in a trap."

Tar-bel looked at him quietly, then moved to his cart and pulled out the kidskin case parchment. "There is a better spot..." He undid the yellow silk ties, this time he spread his precious scroll before Jace.

Chapter Fifteen

One trail sinister

One trail swordside

Both will be different

Both will be the same

Wisdom of the Elders

Before sunrise, Jace trotted into the caravaners' camp. Tar-bel never seemed to sleep, Jace found him using a stick to stir the living coals to kill his fire. The caravaner looked up. "My friend, soon we shall part."

"Aye." Jace would miss their talks.

"The wind brings smells of Scarlur."

Jace pointed to the caravan trail. "If they are following, the Scarlur probably will not leave the trail."

Tar-bel nodded. "If my comrades move fast enough, we should be out of their territory soon."

"Hopefully they will be stopped here."

"There are many of them." Tar-bel looked to his hes lining their carts up. "We follow the trail to the Plains of Laurel. Ye might wish to trot there sometime. Ye will be welcome at our fire pit."

Jace reached out with a bent sword arm, and Tar-bel awkwardly took it.

"Thunder be with us." Jace intoned.

As Jace pivoted on his hindquarters, Tar-bel held up his hand. "My friend, before we part." He turned signaling for Jace to follow. "I have something too poor to keep. Mayhaps ye can light your fires with it." As they trotted to the edge of the camp, Tar-bel reached deep into his cart and pulled out the kidskin case with its silk ties and parchment scroll. Tar-bel hesitated and looked down at the scroll before he handed it to Jace. " Use it wisely, my friend."

"Speed to your hoofs," Jace said accepting it wishing he had something to give in return but feeling any such gesture might be misunderstood. Tar-bel just briefly bowed his head and then trotted off.

Cradling his unbelievable treasure, Jace loped back to camp. There he took just a brief time to unroll the scroll and look at it. Past the Silvers mountain there was still over half of the scroll to go, but if he guessed right, they had a battle coming. To Garrison, he passed a quiet word. "Station lookouts up on the higher rocks with the polished signaling plates, then order quiet resting. We want no betraying dust kicked up. Keep the Silvers and foals with Sandi, ahead of us."

With the sun halfway in the sky, Jace drank deeply of brackish water as Star hurried to him with Deadrick at her side. "Why do we halt? We are but a bit from the mountain path?"

He expected Deadrick to be ingratiating himself with Star. Mayhaps smooth talking her to changing leadership, at least appearing to take her side. But Deadrick's head was up as he smelt the wind. Deadrick's white tail stiffened, his bone-white front hoof nervously stamped the ground.

Star not really seeing any of this demanded of Jace. "Please, I know you are still angry with me. I know you hate the confinement of the caves, but we must move on." She looked to Deadrick to reinforce her counsel, but she only saw his eyes staring back along the caravan trail.

Before she could speak again, Jace whispered to Star. "This camp is on silence."

She lowered her voice. "Why?"

"The caravaners are gone."

"I see their dust."

"So do others, my lady."

From the hillside above, the Regimental scouts flashed their polished plates. No longer in need of quiet Jace ordered Star. "Quickly, return to Sandi and your sisters. Now!"

Footfalls on the trail as Scarlur raced over the top only to be trapped inside Jace's jar. Nine-kill was leading with Silver Belle at his side. They were not expecting a trap or fight so reacted slowly. Except for Nine-kill who pulled to the side, ordering his fighters down the path. Jace saw Silver Belle get swept forward but not as a helpless hostage. Star's dark sister was shouting orders. Directing her mate's fighters.

Deadrick led the frontal assault with Garrison and Axel leading wings charging from the brush, that closed off retreat for the Scarlur. Again, Nine-kill seeing resistance, saved himself first. He turned tail and escaped into the brush.

Jace had his hands full, even when leaderless and trapped the Scarlurs were fierce fighters. Jace cut off an arm, then had to stab its still fighting owner. They battled a smaller group then he had expected; were there more still down the trail? He saw a flash of gray out of the corner of his eye. Twisting he swung up his sword, but the sight of cream dabbling on her hindquarters halted his swinging slice.

Too late he realized that it was not Silver Star but Silver Belle he faced! He just managed to pull back his torso as the tall, gray female's sword dug a shallow, painful cut bloodily across his chest. Fast on her hooves, Belle pulled back and aimed for his chest again.

Still, his arm held for a breath. Then instead of killing her, he parried her sword. He had to kill her, but...Belle's sword rose, then fell, as her front legs buckled. Garrison's spear now thrust deep into her upper stomach. Twisting it, free Garrison was disemboweling her.

Belle was on the ground. She was alive–that would not be for long. Jace was fighting the Scarlur next to her.

In Jace's jar trap, the Scarlur died but not the massive force Jace expected. Mayhaps they had gotten Nine-Kill's honor guard, but they missed him. Chase? Jace did not wish to hunt him on Nine-Kill's terms. He ordered recall sounded. "Looting as you pass only, we head up the mountain path." Could they be over it by sunsink? They had too late a start.

As he headed up, Star was waiting staring down at the carnage. "My Lady?" He asked.

"Silver Belle?" Her voice sounded anxious.

"Your sister is gone. Dying or dead." Jace grabbed Star's arm and forcibly pulled her alongside him and away from the carnage. "There will be more Scarlur. We only slowed them and bought Tar-bel some distance."

She followed him silently for a time. "Jace, if my sister Belle is dead, Nine-Kill will have to put Grandmare's goddess cup on her body. The Scarlur have not set lands, they roam. They must have it with them."

"Do you want me to go back and strip the gold necklaces from your sister's chest as she dies?"

"Nay." She looked horrified at the thought. "We have gold and jewels, but Grandmare's Goddess cup captures the Goddesses' tears." She lowered her tail. "Silver Belle has cursed the Trail of the Goddess and will not need the cup."

Jace thought the way she died ferociously fighting, Belle would have an honored place galloping the clouds in Lord Thunder's brigade. He wanted to hurry Star away. Jace knew his rear guard would soon be stripping Silver Belle of her necklaces as the Scarlur could be regrouping. "Let Nine-Kill drink to your sister with the Goddess Cup. We must hurry."

A knot of centaurs ahead and Jace slowed his long strides. Something was wrong, eyes were averting from Star beside him causing Jace to touch her flank to stop her. "Hold, my lady."

She saw none of this, continuing, "Jace, if Nine-Kill comes back, he may leave the cup on Silver Belle. We could..."

Garrison was loping to them, and his face looked tremendously sad.

"Report."

Garrison spoke slowly. "Two warriors dead, Blue Horn and Raider. Maybe twenty or more wounds being bound." Seeing the blood from Jace's chest running down his front legs, Garrison commanded, "Willow, attend Jace!"

Star finally looked to see the blood on Jace's chest. "Jace?"

He ignored that. "Can they all trot?"

"Aye," Garrison answered. Garrison then stopped speaking, but there was more. Jace knew there must be more. The Regiment was used to death. The ratio of two dead warriors to thirty dead Scarlur was good, so what was this tragedy that seemed to have stunned even such a battle hardened warrior as Garrison? "What else?"

Garrison looked to Star and then seemed not to be able to look at either of them. "During the battle, we think Willow's filly panicked and raced up the raising trail to the mountain cleft..." He stopped.

"Is Lotus hurt?" cried Star.

"Nay," Garrison answered and then swallowed. "We think your sister, Sunny, tried to catch the babe...the path was steep."

"Sunny fell? Is she hurt? Out of my way! " Star

bounded from Jace's side, but Garrison moved fast and caught her arm. Holding her as Star tried to twist away from him.

"She is gone." Garrison still imprisoned Star. "It is not..."

"Nay!" She pulled herself free and bounded towards the trail. "If she is hurt–she needs me."

"Not anymore, my lady," he sadly called after her.

Jace started up the steep, narrow trail that leads from the mountain's base as ahead warriors moved to the side for a frantic Star to pass. The trail rose narrow and steep, it would be hard to pull the carts up. He would have to assign two more warriors to push from behind on each cart.

He kept just behind Star, soon Jace heard deep sobbing ahead as the trail turned. Here the ledge widened a bit above a steep drop off. Silver Crescent now stood there, as if frozen, looking over the side of the cliff as silent tears rolled down her pale pearl cheeks. Star was also silent as she stared down that drop-off. The sobbing came from down below the cliff's edge.

When Jace reached that point, he too looked down. The drop was steep but climbable to another rocky ledge below, then from there, it dropped off more steeply into a huge canyon. It was there on that second ledge that Silver Sunny lay.

Axel had already climbed down, now he sobbed openly over his Sunny. She lay quiet, her legs folded to her stomach as if just sleeping on the rocks. Her silvery hair faintly moved as the breeze blew it, giving the illusion of life. Before Jace could stop her, Star scrabbled down the cliff.

She bent over sister, moving Sunny's head slightly. That displayed the blood and gore that ran from her smashed skull. Star looked up to him disbelievingly. "She is cold. We must find a cape to throw over her." Star softly brushed her sister's hair back again, still talking to her. "Silver Belle is gone. And now you...."

Jace turned to Wheat. "Get ropes from the cart. Get Two Spot and Per Ben and the strongest backs you can. We will have to haul Star and Axel up."

"The Lady Sunny too?" Asked Wheat with concern.

"Silver Sunny will rest there."

Star really needed little help to climb up out of the rocky ravine, but first, she had to tie the ropes to Axel. He just stood there in a stupor, staring at Sunny, his lost love.

They hauled him up first, nearly dumping the whole line of centaurs pulling him. Wheat took him by the arm, pushing him higher up the trail, repeating, "It will be well. It will be well."

As Star reached the top of the cliff, Jace grabbed her arms and pulled her up to a stable footing for her hooves. She looked confused. "How will we get Sunny up?"

"She has a good resting place."

"Nay, we must raise her."

"And then do what with her?"

Star looked about helplessly. "Take her to our valley."

"How?"

"In the carts?"

Oh, they could cut her up and smoke the meat and load her in the carts. Jace did not think Star and Crescent could stand that. The Empire would cut off the heads of enemy princes and dead generals for honor and carry them back but either cursed enemy or valiant warrior, they soon stank.

Star was looking about. "There are rocks here. We can dig a burial niche for Sunny to sleep in."

"Nay."

"We could look for a cave." She pleaded.

"My lady, you wish to march to save your kin? Or will you have us gilding the dead?"

"You said that Silver Belle will die?"

"From that wound in her upper abdomen, I am sure she already has." He did not add that if Nine-kill truly loved his lady, he would have put her out of her misery by now.

"Silver Belle told me that she had Grandmare's goddess cup. That if she died, Nine-kill would place it with her."

"This cup—is it gold?"

"Formed like a shell with pearls for seafoam. On the stem, it is encrusted with gold sea creatures, topaz and sapphire pebbles, it is Silver Beard's masterwork. We could sneak back, see if Belle is laid out on the battlefield and steal the Goddess cup back for Sunny."

"Nine-kill will drink to his late lady with it and then melt it down for coin from the bazaar," said Jace grimly.

Horrified Star begged, "Have you respect for nothing?" She turned away from him to look back down at her dead sister.

Jace had the remnants of Regiment to move up a narrowing trail. Would the carts make it? Would his big flanked warriors be able to? And according to Tar-bel, this was only the minor mountain pass. After they crested, they would come down and start on a series of valleys and plains until they reached her dark mines.

They had just reached the crest at sunsink. Jace called a rest halt where all would sleep on the ledge trail standing up. Would Star join him? He would not walk to her or beg her. If she came, well, as the temperature dropped they could warm each other and be together, and he could kiss her tears away.

Chapter Sixteen

Never trust anyone or anything

Not even the harness on your flanks!

Vechcione of Archport

Star did not come to him, and he slept little. The sky was lit by paling star children that had not yet fled before the hungry serpent sun. Stepping carefully on the narrowing ledge, Jace worked his way back down the column of warriors. At the end, he could see a tall, gray shape against the dark mountain wall. Star? Nay. As he got closer, he could see it was the silhouette of Crescent as she stared back down into the darkness below.

Jace stepped up to her. "My lady, you should not leave the protection of our guards. Where is your sister?"

There were tears in Crescent's voice. "She is gone."

"Gone?"

"Star went to recover Silver Pearl's Goddess Cup. She wanted it to ease Sunny's last rest."

"She went to their camp?"

"The battlefield only. She felt they must have left it with Belle."

Jace too stared out into the darkness, his frustration turning to anger. "How could she be such a fool? "

"None are faster than Silver Star. She thought she could just steal it back and run."

"The Scarlur are not going to dump a jeweled cup of gold on a dead centauress unless they are using it for trap bait."

Crescent lowered her head. "We both loved Sunny so

much, but Star is the fastest of us all, if she is not back, she must be dead too."

His Second and Deadrick stepped to them as Garrison asked, "We march at light?"

Deadrick looked from Crescent to Jace. "Where is Lady Star?"

Fury choked Jace's throat. "Chasing that fool's cup. Let her die!" Dung!

"She is our patron," Deadrick said.

"The Regiment now marches for her sister." Jace felt bloodless and numb. Star was a ninny, but he could not lose her!

Deadrick half reared, trying to peer into the darkness below. "I will get our fleetest warriors. I will save her!"

To go after one so foolish was wrong but, "Deadrick, get nine of the fastest fighters. No shes, no youngsters! Then follow me!"

Garrison looked grim. "We lose all for one she?"

"You will march the rest!" Jace ordered.

"What about ye?"

Jace knew where his duty should lie, but for this she, he would chase after the wind. "I go for Lady Star. Gather the rest for the march, then head..."

"Where?!" An exasperated Garrison stomped a hoof. His second was too disciplined to disobey, but he obviously found the whole thing a mad chase after one's tail.

Chances were he would not be returning from this fool's game, so Jace untied Tar-bel's chart from his harness. "Take this and let Crescent lead you to her dragon."

"Jace! Reason!" Garrison begged.

Clattering of hooves as Deadrick gathered his band on the narrow trail ledge. He would expect to lead, but Jace would not allow it. "Follow!" Jace started down.

The sky was barely graying as they were trotting down that dangerously steep trail. Soon Jace was on the hillside where he could lengthen his legs for a full lope. Like his sire Jachom, he charged heedlessly to the danger only knowing a battle lay ahead. He had not even lightened his carry harness of cook pots and hoof picks. On flat ground, his warriors spread out in a wing with Sandi, and her Kent two lengthens behind him. So much for his orders. The graying sky finally gave some definition to the valley ahead.

He slowed his strides to let the others catch up. Jace must form a plan, not just run his hooves–but as he slowed, he saw gray shapes against a foggy landscape. What appeared to be only a line of woods way in the distance was now an advancing line of racing centaurs. Not a full camp, just eight–ten? A guard set at the battlefield no doubt.

Jace twisted back, silently signaling attack. This must be finished before the main Scarlur camp was roused. Galloping close to him were Deadrick and Sandi with the others following. As the sky lightened, Jace could make out nine running before them.

Deadrick called out. "Look! One long figure ahead!"

Jace could see more clearly now, one lone figure was leading the pack, one tall gray–faster than all the others. Long legs leaping forward, jumping across rock and ditch, not breaking her speed, almost flying. A she was pulling away from the sprinting Scarlurs.

"It is Lady Star!" Called out Sandi.

"She can outrun them!" Yelled Kear triumphantly.

Jace shook his head, in the brightening light he could already see the lead Scarlur pulling his bow forward. Nine-Kill would have his vengeance. Even the fleetest of centauresses could not outrun an arrow. Nine-Kill's warriors would drop Star right in front of Jace.

"ARCHERS HOLD!" Jace planted four hoofs solidly in the earth. "SHOOT FOR THE LEAD BEHIND HER !" Jace began lifting his taut bow up to sight.

In total disbelief, Kent stared wild-eyed at him. "They are out of range!"

Lancer obediently lifted his bow. "Jace, it is nearly a furlong away. Too far!"

Even Deadrick protested. "Your arrow may kill her! I am going down!"

Jace answered not as he pulled, bending back on his bow.

"FOLLOW ME!" Deadrick yelled taking off, followed by a few of the pack. They would never reach Star in time, but they were charging down the slope.

As he bent his bow even tighter, Jace could see Lancer's first arrow falling short. Star's whole torso was leaning forward, parallel to the ground. Her legs pumping tight and her long tail streaming out behind. With supreme effort, she had lengthened the distance between herself and the Scarlurs, but not enough. The lead Scarlur had halted to stabilize his shot and was drawing his tall bow back. She could run, but his arrow would bring her down.

Lancer, the best archer in the Regiment, bent his bow and released his third arrow and Jace saw it fall a length after Star. As Deadrick lead down in hopeless intercept, Jace's archery line loosed arrow after arrow, all falling too short to reach the Scarlur. Holding his breath, Jace drew the bow cord back even tighter. It cut into his fingers as he bent the bow to its breaking point. He aimed for the leading Scarlur's chest and released.

It did not hit his chest, but it hit! The Scarlur's head and torso whipped back as his front feet collapsed downward and he stumbled forward. His bow fell from his hand.

Shocked, his comrades halted behind their fallen leader. Star still tore across the uneven ground as Jace had notched his next arrow and was pulling back.

"By the burning fire! Pardon my disrespect." Lancer was staring. "Ye got him in the face. Why did ye aim for a small head?"

Jace let loose another arrow. "Aimed for the upper torso and just got lucky."

"Guided by the Gods." Lancer shook his head as one of his arrows hit one of the Scarlurs milling about their leader. Deadrick and his were two lengths from Star. The other Scarlurs regrouped. Star ran forward as Deadrick, and his troop surrounded her. The remaining Scarlur decided they had fought enough and were retreating back into the trees. As Deadrick looked back towards him, Jace hand signaled recall. They could not dare scavenge for downed arrows and weapons.

Jace's mouth tasted sand. Star was alive, and he wanted to kill her for the chances she had taken! He turned his back and started loping up the hillside. Dung her! If she were in the Regiment, he would have her run a whipping gauntlet! But she was his patroness. Curse her! Hearing the rest behind him, he slowed to take the load off his sore leg.

The sun was higher as they reached the mountain path and started up. Up the cliff trail, past the body of Silver Sunny. He could not look back to Star. How could this stubborn, fool-hearty she steal the very reason from him? Rip him from his duty? Even Ginger had not been able to do that. This cloven-hoofed one was a bewitching sorceress!

The Regiment was already gone when he just about reached the crest. He stopped to rest, letting Deadrick and the others catch up and pass him. He waited for Star with deadly anger. With the scuffle of hooves, the others passed, and then

Star came past the rocks. She hesitantly stepping to him, gold glinting in hand. Running for her life, she had held onto that dunging Goddess cup!

"Jace, I had to get it for Sunny, but Deadrick hurried me past the drop off to her body! If you could just send two fighters, with ropes back with me, I can place the cup with Sunny."

Jace just glared at her.

"Jace..." She held out the cup.

He reached out and took it from her. It was truly amazing. As he rotated it in his hands the highly polished golden bowl reflected his grim features. Outside, the drinking bowl was formed as a sweeping shell, delineated in fine grooves. Large, irregular pearls rested on the cup's lip as if seafoam laid there by some sea nymph. The jeweled stem was entwining, marvelously fashioned seahorses and starfishes, while the base was a mock seashore of glittering topaz sand. Truly a marvel of incomparable artistry. Jace looked down at her. "Such fine work for the dead."

"For the Goddess to accept Sunny for eternity."

"You risked your life, Deadrick's and all my Regiment's, for a pretty drinking cup? If your Goddess did not save Silver Sunny, why do you think a fancy jeweled cup will bribe her?"

Jace drew back his arm and--with all the strength that he had--threw the dunged cup into the ravine. It kept clanking as it bounced off the endless rocks below.

Star reared in horror as if he had struck her. She twisted to see it land, but even she knew no one could ever recover it.

He swung in tight quarters. "We move out!"

Soon they rejoined the Regiment now marching down the other side of the cleft pass. Deadrick trotted alongside the

Silver sisters as Star's savior and Jace did not care. This steep trail was enough to keep all his attention, for one misplaced hoof and the cart pullers or himself would be falling off that long drop. He must order shorter marches with his warriors sleeping standing up in a dry camping.

The third sun they were on prairie again, and they would have found no water, except for Tar-bel's scroll. It showed a short, side cut into a small valley. There they found a cairn of rocks, piled up by the caravaners marking a half hidden pool. It was covered by a low cave, but Kear and a work crew enlarged the opening enough to fill drinking horns, goat skins and some of the casks.

During this time, Star had the wisdom to stay away from Jace, but she lost this. As they trotted the next sun, he heard a pleading voice behind.

"Jace, please! Listen to me."

He twisted his torso back. By the gods, she was so beautiful. The heat of the trail made her skin glisten and the dust on her glossy flanks just bathed her in a look of soft moonlight. It was hard to stay angry with one he so wanted to couple with

Star moved to his side but kept her distance. Not touching was almost as much as touching. "Please, Jace. Let me walk with you?"

"Nay." He lengthened his strides.

Refused she fell silent, but she stubbornly followed close to his tail.

By the fourth sun they came over a hill crest, ahead he could see a taller, dark mountain. He turned back to her. "Star, is that your Black Mountain?"

"Aye. Still suns away," she said sadly.

That would mean a higher, even narrower trail to climb and then those dark mines of horror but for now, Star was stepping alongside him on flat grassland. They walked quietly for a while then she asked, "Do you know of the Goddess?"

Jace answered coolly. "I have heard tales of many goddesses."

"Nay, not the tail-hunting whores of the bazaar myths. The Goddess, she who created all and who brings the spring rains, the fall harvest?"

"On the grasslands where I was foaled we did not sacrifice to your Goddess, yet in spring the rain came, the grass grew, the trees blossomed, the fruit came in and then the nights grew colder. Without your Goddess, our coats and tails thickened, the days shortened and snow melted on our hides. And then the warm suns came again with no intercession from your Goddess." His voice was as icy as his heart.

She lowered her head. "I do not know this."

He continued. "Did you pray to this merciful Goddess, when the Scarlur attacked your mines?"

"Aye." She turned her head away. "She did not answer."

"Nay, my lady, she answered you, she just did not save you! Your Goddess knew her creatures were battling and she decided they must fight and win, or fight and lose by themselves."

"Then you do not pray to anyone?"

"When I was trapped in the pits in despair, I called out to every god or goddess I could remember. I even called out to my dam. She would have been so ashamed to have her colt cry out like that."

She said nothing awhile. "Is she still alive? Your dam?"

"Dawn? Mayhaps. Probably still following my sire's tail into battle after battle if Jachom still fights."

They trotted in silence then she said, "It was my fault that Silver Belle joined the Scarlur."

"Your fault?"

"I did not want to stay in our valley; I wanted to see more. Learn more. Silver Beard and my uncles would go to the bazaars each season to sell our metal work and acquire more gems. I begged and begged to go. Finally, Grandmare agreed that I should learn to bargain for us, but she wanted a she not to go alone, so at first she sent Crescent with us.

"It was wonderful! The smells, the strange colored centaurs. The food spiced with all that I had not tasted before! Each time, my uncles prepared to trade, I begged to go again. Silver Crescent and I would go, carrying some of the trade loads. Not as heavy as those my uncles carried, but it was worth anything to go to the bazaar."

"How did Silver Belle get to the bazaar?"

"One season, Crescent injured her hoof and she could not go. Grandmare would not send one she alone, so I pushed her to send Belle. Belle hated the heavy sacks. She hated sleeping exposed under the stars. Tramping the long trails hurt her hoofs. But Belle loved the bazaar. Silver Beard was annoyed that she cared not to learn the coins or the measurements of trade, as Belle just pranced from one dealer to the next. And where Crescent had just flirted most outrageously, Belle..." Star blushed and would not continue for many steps. "One night we camped outside the bazaar. She was supposed to be sleeping alongside me, but Belle slipped out to meet some fool. That night she was captured by the Scarlur."

Jace thought about it. "The daughter of wealthy miners? Mayhaps she was lured out to be captured?"

"Nine-kill came to Grandsire and told him that if we paid the ransom, she would be freed. We returned to our mountain and gathered gold, silver, gems, and wine. Nine-kill and his fighters came to our valley with Silver Belle. They accepted our tribute. It took three of their shes to haul it away, and they left Belle with us." Star looked away, her mouth set in a bitter line. "As Nine-kill left, he reached out and kissed my sister on the lips. She kissed him back in front of all!"

"Love, my lady, makes fools of us." He had not intended that bitterness in his tone.

"That darkness she must have taken Grandmare's Goddess cup from its niche. At sunrise she was gone."

"Did you have any guards?"

"Nay." She shook her tail.

"I have orders to give." He started to lengthen his strides.

She would not take a hint. "Have you never made a mistake, Jace?"

He did not answer.

She pleaded. "Not one mistake?"

He looked down at her. No matter what this one did, he could not but want her. And he had made many mistakes in his life. "Will you follow orders?"

She hesitated, then said, "Aye."

He nodded his head. "There is water ahead. We halt and rest."

Chapter Seventeen

Wind turning the leaves to their pale sides

Storm soon to follow

The Watcher at the Long Wall

The next sunrise Jace tore the bandages off his chest; scabs had formed, and he had nay need for constricting wrappings. He had ordered Garrison to assign more responsibility to Axel to train him--but since Silver Sunny's death--the great black and muscle mass that was Axel remained frozen. The massive warrior seemed not to hear, and he walked as if alone in a fog. Jace shook his head, a warrior who did not care did not live long.

Deadrick marched with Star again, and Jace just looked away. He concentrated on the Regiment which was making good progress with the wind at their tails. It was still two thumbs from sunsink, but they were at the best water stop by Var-tee's chart and Tar-bel's scroll. Jace held up his arm. "Hold." Gradually all stopped to look at him. "We make an early camp." He squinted at the sky. Clouds. Rain? " Just put a black crust on the meat. Looks like a storm coming in."

As guards were assigned and harnesses dropped Jace scanned the endless roll of grasslands behind them, now bending into ocean-like waves from the gusting wind. That sea of flattened grass was mirrored in the sky by a second sea of clouds. What had been a low bank of white behind them, was spreading across the entire sky and it had now started darkening. Purple clouds piling higher and spreading as a big storm blew in.

The warriors pulling carts dragged them into a rough

circle, with the wind picking up they would have to tie down the covers on the two caravaner's carts tighter. Kent herded the milkers bought at the Bazaar inside and tethered them to the carts. Sandi was stomping off a single firepit and ordering Axel and Lancer to start pawing it out. Not even seemingly to hear her Axel just walked off. Sandi looked to Jace who just shook his head, Axel needed more time, so they would let discipline slide a bit. She replaced Axel with Skull. Deadrick moved off sullenly, just standing up with a few of his centaurs but they would share the firepit, once it was dug.

Wind blew Jace's tail flat against his hindquarters and the unshaven hair into his face as Star cantered back to him. "You camp now? Can we not get farther this sun?"

"Look back. A storm overtakes us." She looked at that dark sky. He did not expect that look of terror on her face, that frightened raise of tail and her rearing.

"We must hurry!" Wild-eyed she looked desperately about.

"My lady, hold! In your lands, a storm like this, how bad is it?"

"We go into the mines when the sky clouds." She fearfully twisted. "We must run for shelter."

"Shelter?"

"A tunnel. A cave. A hole where we may be covered."

Jace grinned. "What? Your kin hides in caves from rain?"

The wind was now flattening the high grass. In the distance, they could see the flickering of light flashes.

Star twisted around. "Tis fire from the sky!"

"Lord Thunder throws his flaming spears from the clouds. My lady, do you feel his invigorating breath? Have you ever run before a curtain of his rain?" Laughed Jace joyously.

Lowering her voice, she pranced nervously in place. "Can we build a shelter? Run to the trees..."

"Way across the plain? That is not where we are going."

"What are they doing?" She pointed to Sandi trying to spit meat over a fire, whose smoke blew fast and close to the ground like a white battle steamer.

Sandi would have to put the fire out before it spread, this flattened grass was too dry for cartwheeling sparks. It would be raw meat this stars. "DOUSE THE FIRES! I do not think we will have much more time before this one hits." Sandi nodded and had Kent pull the meat away as she and Ross turned and rear kicked dirt on the fire. Jace dug into one of his back pouches for dried meat. He held out some to Star, but she did not even see it as she stared fixedly at the lightning coming towards them. Above the wind, Jace ordered as he pointed. "TWO SPOT! Raise the Regimental standard over there."

Two Spot trotted to the highest mound near them and took his massive spear, with the Regimental colors on it and slammed it deep into the earth. Rufus tossed his metal helm on top. Wild wind was whipping the blue and green standard.

Star looked at Jace obviously terrified. "With the sky rumbling you bedeck your camp?"

"Old warriors say that a tall pole hammered into a hill with shining metal will attract Thunder's flaming spears and protect us." She looked at him like he spoke gibberish, shrugging his shoulders Jace had to agree but said, "My dam told me to lower my head in Lightening Hoof's storms because the Skyfire always seem to hit the highest tree or the tallest centaur." He turned to his warriors. "Kear, Abel, patrol at a short distance in sight only. Before Lady Illume's tears reach us, come back fast." They gave an agreeing swish of their tails and charged off in opposite directions.

Turning his attention to Star Jace noted her flanks were darkening with fear sweat and her eyes opened too widely, showing their whites. "My, Lady. Star, settle! The clouds will bring cold rain and blowing wind. Mayhaps a few frightening flashes but we will get through it! Lady Illume's water will wash the dust off our hides."

Lightning flashed from the darkening plain behind them, and thunder rolled. Star pulled at his arm, whipping her hindquarters around. "We must run!"

"Nay! It will be dark before the clouds pass. We could get separated. You could put a hoof in a hole!" Thunder shook the plain again.

Star reared in terror. " The rumbling!"

"That will not hurt you!"

"It is the sound of death! Kryia the mountain guardian coming to claim us!"

Jace grabbed both her upper arms with his hands, and his solid weight anchored her. Struggling to free herself she reared wildly. "Star! Steady. We camp here. The rumbling comes from the clouds. I have climbed mountains with clouds. I have cantered through clouds, and I have stepped above clouds, they do not have the substance of a silk veil. They will not hurt you."

Closer thunder reverberated, she twisted in terror. "It is the sound of a rock fall! My mare was killed in a rock fall!"

"There are no rocks here to fall." Looking about she did not seem to hear him. Jace tried again. "It would be better if we had someplace to hide behind. Let us get downwind of the carts." As he looked to check at what the others were doing Star twisted free from his hands.

"Star?" Crescent was calling to her sister. "Come to me."

"Crescent!" Star dashed off to her sister. Crescent seemed calmer than Star, and hopefully, she could quiet her down. Jace gave the standard instructions to Garrison: Douse fires. Nay permission to hunt in unfamiliar territory, until after the storm. Jace loped to inspect the tying down of the carts.

Hastily dug firepits were buried again as the wind rose. Warriors were eating raw meat as stronger gusts buffeted them whipping tails. Jace trotted back to Star and her sister. Crescent did not look happy, but it was Star's hide-- dripping with sweat and whitened with foam--that worried him. She pranced sideways, whipping her tail back and forth as half rearing she stared fixedly at the blackening, purple clouds.

Jace took a firm hold of Star's, arm and she looked down at his hand. "I do not want to be held!"

Stroking he tried to divert her. "Yes, my hand must be so rough against your soft skin..."

"Please!" She struggled to be free, backing away from him.

Yet Jace would not let go. "My lady, if you bolt in this storm you might badly twist a hoof or break a leg." He knew that with her speed, none of his could catch her and he doubted that even the concerned looking Crescent could match Star's long legs in full stride.

"Star, it will be all right. Just ease." Crescent tried to touch her sister, but Star shied violently away. Crescent looked to Jace. "She has always been this way. Even in the deepest caves, she shiverers at the rumblings of the sky."

With Jace still holding her, Star circled him but could see nothing but the blackness overtaking the prairie. Some early droplets of cold wet were hitting their hides. "We must run!" She cried.

"It is only a few drops pelting your hide, like snow that melts in your pretty hair." With his other hand, he brushed strands of hair off her forehead, but the white showing on her eyes worried him. "Come to me!" He had to yell over the growing wind. "**SANDI, WE CIRCLE!**"

Hearing him, Sandi finished stomping embers and signaled for her sons to join Jace and Star as several others followed.

Around them other centaurs gathered in tight circles, huddling together. As Sandi's group joined them, Jace was relieved Kear and Lancer had had enough sense to return before curtains of rain would have concealed their way back. This storm looked worse than he had originally thought. Some of the smarter hes had put on protective battle helms, as branches and debris blew painfully against them. Jace swung his ample haunches around into the wind as he pulled Star to him, sheltering her with his body as much as he could.

Wild-eyed she stared past him as the flashing sky bolts drew nearer to them. He placed his other hand around her back, rubbing her slowly but increasing the strength of his hold. Jace spoke softly into her ear, not knowing if she heard him above the wind's keening. Finally shuddering Star closed her eyes and lowered her head against his chest, seeming to have found her shelter.

With no trees or rock ridges to break the wind, rocks, and sticks it carried painfully bounced off his hide and back. "**KNEES!**" Jace shouted above the wind's roar as he used his strength to force Star down. With much jostling all the centaurs went down on their folded legs, reducing their bodies as targets. Around Star and her sister, Jace's warriors pressed close, the tight ring of bodies warmed those in the center and protected at least one side of each centaur from the pelting storm. A blackened sky in every direction and the thick breathing air all about them boded a long storm.

Star's aroma and warm breasts pressing against him. Jace put his helmet on her head. When the rain came, it swept in like a solid line of warriors as lightning flashed all around them. Panicking, Star struggled to jump up but, Jace held her tight until finally, she relaxed back into his arms. If he were in other lands at other times, he would have enjoyed running with her and trying to beat the straight line of rain across the grasslands.

The solid, cold water wall was drenching their bodies. No guards out, but he doubted a Scarlur attack possible if an enemy could not see any farther than he could in the drummed downpour. Dark blackness filled the day with sudden, unnerving white light bursts that were seen even with eyes tightly closed. The wind pressed hard, lifting tails, streaming rivers down their hair and faces. He bends over his head to kiss her past the helmet. By bending his head over Star, he could shield her a bit more, and in gratitude she wrapped her arms around his back, curling into his chest. Even with the helmet's cold metal between them, her embrace warmed him.

The darkness did not change, but it got cooler at what Jace imagined was sunsink. Now it was soaking cold but not freezing. They must just endure.

He had sworn to fight for this Centauress and her Silvers. He would, but even without a vow of fealty, he would trot off the end of a mountain for her. If Star would be with him in this howling darkness, he would march into her suffocating mines!

Chapter Eighteen

To defeat a centaur, It is not necessary to kill him It is

only necessary to make him want to stop fighting!

Jachom, sire of Jace

Two more suns tramping. The Silvers now owed the Regiment twenty-one suns marching, and all saw Silver Star openly sleeping beside him. He had not mounted her but having her close in the darkness held a sweetness of its own. Lord Lightning Hoof's legions banked their fires in battlefields in the sky, as the clouds pinked with sunrise. Jace savored Star's warm flanks against his back both just laying there. He must get off the soft grass, get the others moving but Star had that tantalizing she aroma. Just breathing it excited him. By Lord Thunder, he wanted to cover her, but not now. Now there was something else, a faint dead smell. The stink of Scarlur?

SMELL! He was getting scent again! The pain cakes had not killed his nose! Lord Thunder be praised! Jace shifted his body and rolled, half turned his legs in the air resting more on his back. Star's silky white-blonde hair now rested against his shoulder, and it sparkled in the sunlight, shifting as the still sleeping she cuddled her head against him. Her legs were tucked under her gray body as he drank in those black, cream dabbled flanks that were so smooth, even in the pale rising light.

Movement near caused Jace to alert, as he gently pushed Star away he rolled over to raise himself. No harness. Battle sword over by the tree. His growing he-sword wanting to stay with her. Movement again. Ardon coming out of the screening leaves, he was usually quiet hoofed, but Ardon must have rustled about to give Jace some warning.

"Sir." Ardon's bronze hide stepped into the clearing.

"Report," Jace said quietly.

Star had hastily risen to her feet and was standing beside him.

Ardon walked to them in a measured fashion. He was bigger than Star but small boned for a warrior. Now his narrow sword blade was in his hand, not usually done for just trotting around on guard duty.

"My lady, stay here." Jace moved to Ardon, speaking low. "Sign?"

"Not by sight but that wind behind us has picked up again, and I'm getting stink, smoke, and paint. Our friends are drawing closer, must be a bunch for us to smell them this strong."

Jace started stepping out to the main camp. "They are still following. They know where we are, but they are not attacking?"

"They have a better place picked ahead?" Ardon asked.

"Mayhaps. They know where we are going better than we do."

Ardon hesitated, and then looked back to where Lady Star still stood. Then he looked to Jace. "Sir,..."

"Aye?"

"We should speak." His officer said but appeared reluctant to have that talk.

What was this about? If Ardon left the Regiment, who would Jace get to keep track of the shares? "Talk about what?"

Not meeting his eyes, Ardon looked downward. "The Lady Star has commissioned the Regiment to march for her at two silvers per sun. There are now twenty-six troopers with two half shares and five officers' double shares. Barley and Horn left no instructions for the distribution of their shares."

"We keep that in the bonus pool unless claimed," Jace settled.

Ardon again looked briefly in Star's direction. "We have marched for twenty-two suns."

Was it twenty-two? Jace had calculated twenty-one, but Ardon had never been known to make a mistake. Jace pulled out the cord tied to his harness and counted twenty-one knots as he tied the twenty-second knot for today's marching.

However, Ardon was continuing, "As I told you, sir, the metal and jewels from Lady Star and her sisters barely covers what we have already marched."

"Facts we both are well aware of."

Ardon still could not meet his eyes. "Aye."

"Is there another problem? Is someone else questioning this?"

Now Ardon looked directly at him. "Some warriors have come me."

"Who?"

Reluctantly Ardon looked down at his hooves again. "I would rather not..."

Jace cut him off abruptly. "What did you tell them?"

"That the Silvers have given portion towards what they will owe us when we free their mines."

Jace felt his anger raising, both that his warriors questioned his judgment in dealing for them and that they dared speak directly to Ardon. "Did you tell them how much?"

"Nay, I said they must speak with you."

"That is correct; you say no more. Tell me if they speak with you again."

Ardon looked like he wanted to pursue the matter but he just nodded. "Aye, sir."

Ahead Garrison was loping to them. Ardon looked relieved to have finished an unpleasant task.

"Want Lancer and me to take a canter on the back trail?" Ardon asked Garrison.

"Just to the last crest," Garrison ordered.

Jace added. "The Regiment will be taking food and then moving on as fast as possible."

Ardon stopped and looked to the ground curiously. "The earth trembles."

"Aye." Garrison frowned. "Has for many furlongs."

Had it? Jace had not noticed. He planted a hoof on a patch of bare dirt and Jace could feel a faint rumbling through the shell of his hoof. Huge enemy force? His mind had been too full of Star. Her suffocating mines. He had to get focused.

"Are we headed for a great waterfall?" Ardon asked.

Garrison shook his tail. "Nay, the trembling seems to stop at sunsink. A waterfall would not stop."

Ardon nodded and moved off as Garrison continued, "Mayhaps ye could ask your lady what causes the earth to tremble..." Garrison added acidly, "besides, of course, her tall warrior."

Reddening slightly, Jace lowered his voice. "I am told that there are those who question how the Silvers will pay us?"

"Aye, do they harry Ardon?"

"Deadrick?"

"Others too. It has been a long tramp."

Jace did not understand. "We have tramped longer."

"Never before has our leader been so enamored with one of our patrons." Garrison looked directly at him. "So lost in a she's aroma."

It was Jace who looked away. "I will deal with my responsibilities."

In only a furlong's measure, Ardon returned and reported not seeing any Scarlur, while Nighthawk and Finehair scouted ahead. The columns were on the move, tramping ever closer to his lady's confining mines. The wagons kicked up dirt and stones, but Sandi had managed to cut down on some of the hub squealing. They were on a long, yellow grassy plain, a plateau in the mountains. That yellow grass worried him, showing they were entering a drying land that might not have enough water for his warriors.

At the next rest stop, Jace dipped into his pouch setting out Var-tee's drawing stick and Tar-bel's chart and then turned to Star. "My lady, tell me what you know of watering places ahead?"

She shrugged her shoulders "A stream...I think"

"My, lady, try to line it up with something." Jace looked up to find Axel was just wandering about the camp aimlessly. "Axel! Attend me!"

Seemingly surprised, Axel stepped to him. Jace firmly said, "You must learn to read the charts."

As Jace spread the charts out, Star's big green eyes were on him. He could see she wanted to please so much, but she did not know how. For a brief time, Axel also seemed to come out of his deadened state. Before them, Jace spread out a virgin roll he planned to sketch on with all the near landmarks. She touched the stiff, smooth surface. "This is animal skin?"

"Nay, they take reeds and press them to a pulp. It dries in a form; then you can make a chart of how the land lies. Maxima traded me some." He looked to Axel. "You must learn to read these charts. And to write them." He saw a flicker of interest in Axel's eyes.

With Var-tee's stick, Jace lightly sketched. "These are the foothills growing on either side of us. Now, Star, where is your next stream in relation to that peak?"

With a rough map to compare against Tar-bel's scroll, they marched until the sun sank and when they halted, Star was beside him. The ground under his hoofs seemed to settle. "The earth rests."

Star looked up to him. "What?"

"Do you not feel it? When your hooves are flat on the earth do you not feel a rumbling?"

She looked down at her black, cloven hooves.

He continued. "That rumbling could be the sound of a vast army, but I do not think so. Is there some natural feature?"

"Nay."

"Then what is it?"

"I do not know."

"Perhaps a dragon?" He asked, studying her reaction carefully.

Star looked away from him. "I must go to Reet. See how she does." She loped away.

At dawn the ground rumbled under their hooves again and, as the Regiment prepared to move, Jace stepped to Garrison. "Smell anything?"

"Winds behind us."

"That rumbling?"

"Aye. Odd it stops at sunsink and then starts again."

"Scarlur?"

"Pray not. Be a tremendous mass of them to cause the dirt to tremble like this."

"Put your most experienced scouts out."

Garrison scanned the troop and then called out. "Per Ben! Clay!"

As they watched, both scouts cantered to the crest of the next hill before them as the Regiment gathered in two columns. At the crest, they both scouts had halted. Per Ben half reared to get a better smell and sight, while Clay abruptly turned and was racing back to them. Sensing danger Jace leaped ahead to find out what was happening.

Clay halted before him planting his hooves down flat. "The valley is full of monsters! Dragons!"

Axel had followed. "Dragons?" Garrison and Sandi were not far behind.

"Huge, hair-covered monsters with long, curving horns on the side of their heads. A valley of them!" Clay babbled.

Jace loped towards the hill crest and reached Per Ben, who was making no effort to hide himself as he stared at the vast yellow plateau below them. At first, Jace thought he was seeing a huge plain covered with monstrous boulders, but then he realized these immense boulders were moving. A vast herd that did not seem to end.

Per Ben calmly chewed a sweet stick. "Shag beasts, moving quietly now."

"The size of them." Jace was truly amazed. "There are not many things that make me feel small. Are they dangerous?"

Per Ben nodded his tail. "Look at the horns on the bulls and the shes."

"They meat eaters?"

"Nay, they chew grasses."

Jace looked to the hills about them, the valley narrowed to a tight pass ahead, and that was where the old caravan trail led. The endless trail to her mountain. Others were clopping up behind them with Axel leading.

"Then they are harmless?" Garrison asked. He and

Sandi had joined them.

"Not if you frighten them." As ever, Per Ben spoke from experience. "Startle a calf, frighten his dam, anger his sire and they all charge. Even one of their young can trample one of your size."

"Something that big would be slow moving," Axel said.

Per Ben chuckled. "Nay. See them get spooked and have them charging you. For a furlong, they can stomp as fast as we can."

Axel side stepped forward, obviously anxious to get closer to the beasts.

"Nay." Jace pulled out his view tube as he quietly commanded. "It looks like they range through the whole valley." On both sides, the valley spread upward with steep, crumbling rock walls. "Nothing we can climb to bypass them."

"Aye." Per Ben nodded. " Does the Lady Star know of another trail?"

"Nay and none of my charts show anything different. We have to go through this valley or go back and trot clear round the mountains. Then dig out a stone blocked trail."

Garrison nodded with a grim smile. "So we will be funneled down to that pass."

"Aye. They will be all around us." Sandi pointed out. "I have seen them before."

"Do you think we could march through the herd?" Alex asked.

Per Ben shook his tail. "Too many calves. Startle one, and you will have that whole mass trampling us."

"We might get past them stepping to the side lands." Jace pointed to the strip of grass along sword arm. "If we move quietly and appear non-threatening, we might just get past."

Per Ben studied a brown-haired straggler closer to them. "Make great eating, if we could get a young one."

"Nay. If that herd panics and stampedes, we will not have a chance!" Sandi said.

Per Ben nodded with his tail. "Shame. They butcher up to great, thick steaks."

"Or great mashers of centaur hide," Sandi said bitterly. "I have seen the remains of a centaur clan trampled by them."

Jace swiveled on his hooves and started back with Garrison. "We will have to break ranks so as not to spook them and go slowly in nonthreatening twos, maybe threes. Do not let them see you looking directly at them. First, we rest and eat, and then you assign marching order. There will be nay fires or meat eating, while we pass upwind of the herd."

"What about the carts?" Garrison asked.

Jace did not want to abandon them especially if the Silvers rewarded them with the promised treasure. "Put them at the end. We will only move them one at a time when the rest are safely past."

He surveyed the land even more carefully. A tight valley, what his sire, Jachom had called a "jar." You drew your enemy in, then cut him off and killed him. That was what they were loping into.

Hoofbeats behind him and Jace twisted to see Sandi catching back up with him. As much as he valued her strategic assessments, he did not want to hear it this time.

She knew that and just smiled. "What a marvelous crafted trap! You close off the ends and come down on your sacrificial lambs; only we are not to be the predators, we are to be the victims?"

"It is the only trail."

"Your lovely lady says thus?"

"Our patroness who was foaled near here."

"She does seem to whisper into your ear a lot."

"I am her commander." He responded angrily but really did not want the severity in his voice, so tried to soften his words. "Lady Star is interested in having warriors do her bidding, that is her interest in me."

"Oh? When you are about, her step is just a bit higher, and her tail raises oh so prettily."

He felt himself reddening and tried to side step her banter. "You sound like you have rekindled an interest in me? Or are you interested in her for yourself?"

She would not be cowed. "You and I have had some good rolls." Sandi cast lustful eyes over his muscled flanks. "We could again." Her face turned serious. "But this Star, Jace, she is different, she wants more than your warriors. She may actually want you,... but with her, her kin and her treasure mountain will always come first.

"When she ran," Sandi continued, "her Silvers where besieged. The Regiment could barely repel Scarlur attacks; untrained miners could not have. Her kin are dead, so why are we going to rescue them?"

"We are commissioned. We march and we will dig out her kin."

"The bodies?"

"And the treasure..."

"That treasure grows greater with every campfire so our warriors may expect far more than is there. When our galoots get some stingy pouches, it will be our hides they will be flaying!"

"Mine, not yours! You join the other side as fast as you can—*Jachom always said loyalty is fair, but coming out on the winning side, that is the trail to trod!*"

Sandi twisted her lips in a sour smile as she looked to

the camp. "Your high stepping lady sees us talking privately, and she is hurrying over here." Sandi's smile grew even brighter. "Oh, see how her fine blonde hair sparkles so in the sunlight."

It did sparkle, and Jace found himself just entranced by her simple, natural beauty, as he is watching Star's graceful, effortless pacing towards them.

Sandi continued. "I followed her last morn. She stopped, bend way down and picked up something from beside the trail. After she hurried on, I checked to see what it was."

"A healing plant?"

"Nay. It was rock ledge. A ledge studded with large pieces of mica ."

He did not understand. Mica was a mineral that can be split into thin, clear sheets sometimes used for compass covers.

Sandi's voice dripped with contempt. "Oh, you hes are so dense! She takes the mica, hammers it with a rock into the tiniest, little flakes, then she sprinkles them on her flowing locks and abundant tail. Then she sparkles so attractively in the sunlight. She uses beet juice to rouge her lips, too."

Jace felt his chest expanding and found himself grinning.

Sandi moaned. "Oh, you besotted fool!"

Star was half a lope from them, when Sandi butted her shoulder into Jace, grabbed his arm and half rearing, gave him a fast kiss on the highest spot she could reach. Star halted in mid-stride, then continued towards them, with a more constricted lope, and a tight smile painted on her face.

Under his breath, Jace muttered. "You will pay for this, Sandi."

"I am being led by a smitten sog, who tags after the

glittering tail of a deceptive she who takes us to fight a dragon. What else can be done to me?"

Jace swung his arm for a hard whack at Sandi's rump, but she was too fast, bolting away. With a wide, friendly smile, Sandi nodded to Star as she loped past her to camp.

Pleased Jace noted that Star positioned herself protectively between himself and the departing Sandi.

Soon the Regiment was marching in groups of twos and threes, with a careful distance between. A regiment of snails marching from a cage into a tighter trap. By mid-sun, only a third of the camp had crossed over, with the rest lined up impatiently jingling their battle harnesses, as they waited for Garrison's hand signals.

Finally, with the shadows growing long, the carts started. The last of the Regiment was reaching the narrow cut between the hills and reassembling. That was when Jace smelled the smoke! Alarmed, he first scanned the remains of his camp, had someone broken his 'no fires' order? Jace shifted weight to his hind legs and raised his forelegs in a half rear. Higher up the air smelled clear but closer to the ground; it was acrid from smoke.

Already expecting the answer, Jace twisted to look behind. Low waves of black smoke were streamed on the stiff breeze. The great valley funneled towards them, but now the hillside of brown shags was edged with black. Jace tugged at his harness' side pouch and pulled out his view tube to see in the polished lense the brown ocean of shag beasts. Behind them, racing centaurs, short and dun-colored--Scarlurs--racing ahead of the fire. Nay! They were pulling ropes tied with burning branches as his enemy set the prairie on fire behind the shag beasts.

Already the beasts were bellowing in fear. Milling in terror. The lead bulls were charging forward down the valley toward the Regiment, and a quick look to both sides showed what Jace already knew. They were caught in a trap. He bellowed, "Abandon the carts! Garrison! Lead the shes forward!" At full gallop Jace loped into the ranks. "Finehair! Lancer! Kear!"

Axel bounded to him.

"Nay." Jace continued. "I need fast-footed scouts to try and turn the herd! You and Two Spot bring up the rear of our troops." Like even those two massive centaurs could stop a single stampeding shag.

A fast look backward showed the whole herd was running away from the black smoke towards them.

Sandi galloped up with young Ross and Kent following. "Sir?"

Jace ordered. "Sandi! Race ahead of the columns! Try to find a side ravine! A rock wall to hide behind! Anything! Nighthawk!" Nighthawk ran up as Jace yelled. "I need runners to turn the herd. Get a spear!"

Sandi was twisting away, but beside her, Kent yelled. "I can run!"

Jace looked at Sandi, and she nodded. "He's the fastest!" She tossed Kent her spear.

Surprised by his proud mare, Kent grabbed the spear, looked as if he would kiss her and then bounded off to the group converging on Jace.

Jace unhooked his own spear from the cart; then as he ran forward, the others fell into two lines beside him. "We must turn them! Go sinister! Get the herd to mill swordarm! If we press the outside leaders, they will circle! Spread out! Try to turn the leader bulls!"

As they charged off, splitting up, Jace was aware Nighthawk was to his sinister with Kent right alongside him. Under the beasts' terrified stampede the earth shook beneath each hoof fall, as running from the fire Shag beasts were trampling their own bellowing calves. Thick clouds of dust hid the sky as their brown furred hides seemed to spread across the horizon. If the stampede reached the narrowing valley mouth unstopped, Star, her sister, his warriors--they would all be trampled to a pulp!

The terrified, bellowing herd drew closer as Jace angled to the edge. By the Gods, these beasts were huge and fast. Jace had to get to the outside edge of the herd that was coming straight at him!

Galloping madly, he turned and twisted to where he was now running alongside the herd. Beside him terrified Shag beasts ran with white rimmed eyes and foam-flecked, blue tongues. Jace used his spear as a pole to stab and prod an outside beast. The beast probably did not even feel his spear point as Jace harried and hollered but a second beast ran into the first, the herd was turning inward! Jace stabbed at another one.

All the beast had to do was lower its head and swing its curved horns to kill his tormentor, but the panicked monsters were running from him. The bellowing shags were maddened by smoke, blood smell and fear of the centaurs herding them. It was working!

Until Jace looked over his shoulder and realized he was trapped! A wing of shag beasts had widened behind him and were running him down. Pivoting, Jace tried to leap to the side, but he was lost!

A whoop from behind as Kent raced in, spearing the beast closest to Jace. Stabbing through its eye, Kent caused the shag beast to stumble sinister. Kent's fallen beast drove the following flank inward, as Jace raced to the side. Victorious, Kent was pulling away, but he stumbled on a front hoof, and as Jace ran back alongside the herd, he saw Kent fall under another bull's hooves.

In a mad fury, Jace leaped back into the fight, hollering wildly as he stabbed at the shags near him. In the clouds of dust and smoke, he could not see Nighthawk or the others, but it was working. The herd was running into itself, circling and milling down. The edge beasts were trampling the inner herd. The rearward beasts were actually trampling out the fire.

Taking painful breaths from his upper chest, the stressed vascarello vents on his point of shoulder opened up, sending needed air to his lower body lungs. Finally, Jace could halt before the valley mouth. By his count six of his own had charged the stampeding herd, now he could make out one--no two--loping towards him. Lancer. Kear. They joined him, also catching ragged breaths, looking around in vain for the others.

Finally, Jace raised his arm, and the three took off in a long lope towards the waiting columns. Fighting held little fear for him, telling a mare, he had led her son into death was another thing.

Chapter Nineteen

All too soon the dark wings of death brush flanks

As the vultures feast on the most valiant of centaurs

Redmon, Empire Drill Instructor

As he raced to rejoin the troop, Jace saw Star ahead just standing there staring at him, with Deadrick standing protectively beside her. Someone ran close behind him. Ahead, he could see his troops as they were wheeling around towards him. Why were they not moving out through the cut? Per Ben, Skull, others were unsheathing their swords.

Still hurling forward, Jace risked turning his head to the savage yells erupting behind him. Across the smoking plain, a full eighty red-painted duns were racing at them. They must have believed that the stampede would leave his warriors disorganized and broken. Jace slowed his massive strides, already reaching for his bow, as ahead battle-hardened fighters were forming a disciplined line, taking advantage of a hill lock that would give momentum to their charge.

Reaching it, Jace turned and surveyed his ground. The shag beast stampede had broken, with the main body milling and circling into itself. The charging beasts had trampled the fast burning grass flames, but the beasts could recharge at any time. On the sword arm side, two of the attacking Scarlur were charged by a Shag bull. First causalities of this battle.

Jace yelled. "NOTCH BOWS! SHOOT WHEN IN RANGE! DRUMMERS!" Let these vermin get a taste of organized fighting! Lancer blew the shell to call attention, and the drummers hooked their rounds either side of their hip/shoulders. Star raced beside Jace as he yelled to her.

"Form behind Willow! You and your sister! Gather wagon supplies you can carry, be ready to race through the gap. ARCHERS! "

Regimental archers scythed down the front-running Scarlur, while the back Scarlur lines jumped over their fallen and charged on. Jace took his place in the front of his line of fighters. "CRUSH LINE!" As best they could under attack, his younger, faster centaurs had taken the outside wings with the older, more experienced fighters stomped their hooves in the central position. Jachom's vulture formation. The slower, central warriors would take the brunt of the attack while the faster, greener troops would surround the enemy with two wings. Both armies would just have to pray the shag beasts had their fill of stampeding as Jace ordered. "ATTACK!"

As the Scarlurs ran screaming toward them, Lancer sounded 'forward' blasts on his shell as the Regimental drummers pounded the marching beat. An imposing line of Jace's massive fighters started down the hill with each solid warrior hooves' stamping down in unison.

Half of the Scarlur broke ranks and ran proving that they were not all mush-brained. The center dun core shortened their strides but kept on. The Regiment met them on the field, first with spear and then sword as each of the Regimental warrior's shield guarding the fighter next to him sword-side.

The duns left were valiant fighters, they were fast and agile, and they outnumbered the Regiment. For a time they even had two strong leaders, until they were finished by Deadrick and Snake. The Regiment was disciplined, oversized and well drilled, while the Duns--with their leaders dead--broke ranks and attacked randomly. They fought hard, but the Regimental arms were longer and more experienced. The Scarlur were fast, but that just meant they died faster.

It was a short battle, with what was left of the defeated duns running back through the shag beasts and getting gored for their efforts. With the duns retreating, Jace called a halt; if his warriors followed, they might restart the shag stampede. They also would be going in the wrong direction for Star's mountain loomed behind them now. "HOLD! SOUND RECALL!" Garrison raced along the line, hand signaling recall. Deadrick's wing was the last pulled back. They should move through the gap ahead immediately, but Jace knew his warriors. "ONE PASS FOR LOOT. WE WILL HOLD THE PLUNDER LINE NEXT CAMP!"

Jace and Garrison trotted across the battlefield, studying the shields. Garrison noted, "Yellow Moon, three blue stars. That leader Deadrick got was a moon with a black star. Nine-kill is the moon with a black star. Did you see him on the field?"

"Nay." Jace grabbed up a solid looking short sword. "That one I killed at the peace parley was moon with two yellow stars."

"None of those here so at least three tribes."

"Aye. A third of these got away this sun."

"Ye nay wish to pursue? " Garrison stood with his scarred body tight and ready.

"It would be on their ground, back over our tracks and we are commissioned to open up her mines." And pay his warriors for twenty-three suns marching. Shoddy Scarlur plunder was not the stuff of great treasure dreams. "Get a count of our dead then move the Regiment out through the gap. Try to get as much ground covered as we can before sunsink."

Axel was loping to him as smoke drifted over the field as the shag beasts milled restlessly in the distance. Jace heard the sound of birds–vultures? He scanned the field.

Many centaur bodies but mostly Scarlur, thank Lord Thunder. Bellowings of crippled shag beasts. A centaur crying out in agony? It could not be Kent. He was gone. Any more of his out there? Jace turned back to take a fast count. Garrison. Per Ben, Reet...

A stiff-backed Sandi trotted up to him. "Kent has not reported."

Jace would rather face a spear than this. "Your son fought valiantly."

He let that sink in. Her tanned face did not change, and she seemed to be waiting for more.

"Kent died saving others."

She nodded. Lips thinning, but she stayed dry-eyed.

"I was turning a leading bull and became trapped by oncoming shags behind. Kent raced up and stabbed the beast on my tail. He dropped it. The ones following were blocked by its body. Kent leaped after me and would have been clear, but he must have caught a hoof in a hole. Stumbling he went down. It happened so fast..." Yet replayed and replayed in Jace's mind so slowly.

Sandi looked to where the Scarlurs had retreated. They both knew the duns could reattack at any time, yet she spoke levelly. "Permission to break ranks and retrieve his harness."

Harness? After those monsterous hooves had crushed him? There would not be much if she could even find him. "Axel, Ardon and I will go. I owe him."

"Nay." That tanned face of hers still showed no emotion. "I suckled him. I trained him to be a warrior. It must be me that reclaims his war harness, he would expect it."

Jace swished his tail with permission granted. Sandi walked stiffly off. At a distance, Ross had been watching, and he now followed his mare, with a resentful glare back at Jace. Ross would blame him for his brother's death. Did Sandi blame him for her son's death? Kent was too young to be on the field, but if she blamed him, she would never let on.

They had little time for a bone search, but must. "LANCER!" The fast brown, with black spotted, white hind looked up. "ARDON!" He trotted to Jace. "We must walk the field, but we may have to retreat."

Deadrick trotted up. "Two dead from the Scarlur, Red of the Ring and Kell. Three missing. Nighthawk. Finehair. Kent."

"Kent is dead."

A stricken Deadrick looked in Sandi's direction and then looked away. Finally, he looked back at Jace. "We must move before they regroup!"

"First we must check the field for Nighthawk and Finehair." No one should be left legless to suffer an agonizing death on the field of battle. They owed their own, mercy.

As Jace started to move, Deadrick grabbed his forearm. "Where are you leading us now?"

"Deadrick, you scout for Garrison. Before sunsink find him a more sheltered area on the trail ahead to camp and tend our wounds. I will hunt our comrades."

By the gods, it had seemed an endless battle against fire, shag beasts and Scarlurs, yet so little distance was covered this sun. Jace's back leg was hurting, but still, he did a fast trot over flattened grass to where mashed shag beasts clumps littered the plain. Still a field of confusion with the main herd milling dangerously close, unsure which direction to run next.

Heavy, choking smoke swirled in the wind from the blackened grassland. Closer to them were the dead and dying shags with wounded beasts bellowing in pain and fear as they tried to struggle up on their broken legs and no sign of uninjured Scarlurs. Would they come back for their injured?

Or were their dead now bait for Jace?

Jace turned to Ardon. "Take position at this high point. Keep sounding 'return' blasts on your horn as you look for any of our own and look wide for attackers. Keep your spear free." Ardon blew his loudest shell blasts, but still, it was hard to hear over the bellowing of dying shag beasts.

Sandi and Ross had bounded into the central mass of slaughtered bodies as Axel, Lancer and Jace loped in different directions on the perimeter. Jace heard a cry and stopped, rotating his head as he listened. A centaur moaning in pain. He turned to signal, but Lancer was already racing to it, bounding high over dead shag beast barricades. Who ever Lancer had found, the centaur stopped screaming when Lancer repeatedly speared him. Friend or foe, it was wrong to let a helpless, broken-legged wreck suffer needlessly.

Ross called out. "There is a broken bow over here. Not Kent's." He circled the area closely. "Nothing else."

Looking around the valley, Jace tried to reckon the general area where he had seen Kent fall. He galloped closer to the back end of the plain finding trampled ground, blood. Several Shags had died, piled upon one another. In their center, Jace saw the broken shaft of Kent's carved spear sticking up out of dead hide, and slowly he worked towards it. In the pile of beasts, his eyes picked up a gleam of ivory. He bent closer. Remains of a carved drinking horn in the clump of shag calf, matted in the blood muddied grass.

Kent's drinking horn. Sandi carved it for her youngest son when he won his first tourney. Jace reached down to pick up the shattered pieces. It was caught in a muddy vine—no, not a vine, it was trapped in twisted leather. Jace was untangling the horn from Kent's mangled harness, that sodden clump of grassy plain before him was the trampled body of Sandi's son.

Jace had to raise his head up and shake off the

unbearable blood smell. He looked up at the sky's smoke hazed blue and wanted so badly just to run from this place. Sandi was there at a short distance, watching him. She must have seen him bend down to pick up the drinking horn. A mare should not see this. He had to keep her away, but...

Sandi came bounding over as Jace back stepped as if he could just push it all away.

When she reached him, she stared at the trodden lump and said nothing. Seeing the broken drinking horn in his hands, she reached out and took it from him. "Kent's." Her eyes followed his to the trampled harness. Then she deliberated turned tail to him so he could not see her face as she gazed down on what was left of her youngest son. Sandi stood facing away from Jace for a long time. Then she bent down and gently replaced the ivory drinking horn next to his body.

Should Jace stay? Should he go? Still facing away, Sandi called out, "Ross!" Her eldest son twisted and then trotted towards them, his eyes darting about as if looking for his brother to rise. Sandi was reaching up to her neck pulling at her throat, pulling her precious jade necklace over her head. When Ross reached them, she pointed down, and he blanched. Again, Sandi bent forward with a soft croon as she was laying Mica's necklace on the sodden mass that was Kent.

Jace could not stand it anymore. He turned and stepped away from that death ring. As he did, he thought he could hear Ross sobbing.

Lancer bounding up. "That was one of Scarlurs with three of his legs were broken. He thought I was one of them and was begging to die."

Jace nodded.

"They will come back." Lancer looked at Sandi and

the sobbing Ross. "Kent?"

Jace nodded with lowered tail.

Lancer looked at him. "Then he did not suffer."

Axel joined them, carrying a stained regimental banner. "Found one of ours."

Jace and Lancer wheeled. "Who did you find?"

"Nighthawk, or Finehair."

Nighthawk is or had been, pure blue-black, from hair to his skin to his hide, even his dark eyes while Finehair was red-haired, yellowed-hided and white-stockinged. But having seen the muddy, grass embedded, bloody purple meat that was now Kent, Jace knew how Nighthawk could look just like Finehair. Feeling defeated Jace just stood there.

Axel scanned the field. "If any others were alive and in pain we should have heard them."

Lancer nodded with his tail.

Jace took a long look from the burned grass foothills to the milling beasts in the distance and back to the narrow notch ahead, where Garrison must have herded the rest of the troop.

Lancer's voice sharpened. "Jace, they will come. The Scarlurs do not seem to count their losses."

Jace reluctantly swished his tail in agreement, his strength returning. "But we lessen their ranks each attack."

"By the Gods, I hope so," said Lancer.

Again Jace surveyed the field of beast bodies. Ross' head was bent down, his shoulders heaving as Sandi had put her hand on her son's withers.

"Ardon, attend!" Jace turned to Lancer. "See if you can find some shag meat not splattered by our blood that we can put on the spit."

Lancer looked sharply at him. "A fire in camp on this dark?"

"Why not? They know where we are."

Lancer nodded and pointed in the direction he came from. Soon he and Axel were struggling with a dead, heavy shag calf slung between them.

Jace still waited at a distance from the stampeded body of Kent, while Sandi reached out her arms to hold Ross. The wind blew smoke across the field, veiling them from Jace's view. It cleared as Sandi was reaching down, just one more time to caress Kent, then head held stiffly high, she started marching Ross away.

Jace followed Lancer and Axel as Ardon kept a rear guard and they trotted to the gap. Garrison had made nay attempt to cover their hoofprints. With the valley narrowing into a tight neck they could only go one way. His Second was trying to get as many hoof falls between them and the shag beasts as possible. Lengthening their strides to a quiet lope, they soon passed back guards and rejoined the Regiment's remnants.

A frantic Star was treating wounded warriors with Willow. Her gray hide foamed from nervousness. Finishing on Orson, she bounded towards Jace who was headed to Garrison.

Sandi trotted past them into camp, with eyes dry and head held high. Ross was trying to follow her hoofprints but had not yet developed control when losing loved ones. If he stayed with the Regiment, it would come with practice.

Star looked past Jace at Axel and Lancer's burden. "Is that one of yours?"

"Just beast meat, my lady." Jace met Garrison's eyes. "The darkness overtakes but we camp in a tight ravine?"

"Deadrick says it is not any safer ahead." Said Garrison looking over the ground. "Here we have a swiftly running stream."

Jace swished his tail in ascent. "Allow fires."

Silver Star looked from him to Axel and Lancer. "You were going to get their harnesses?"

"'Getting their harness' is more of an expression. We did not expect to find much, but we wished to leave none of our comrades wounded and suffering."

"Then all three are gone?"

"Five, counting the two in battle."

"Sandi's colt?" She asked anxiously.

"Aye, Kent."

Her eyes showed agony. "It is my fault..."

"Nay."

"I should never have commissioned you." She started to turn away.

Moving forward, Jace put his hand under her chin and turned her head towards him. "The Regiment committed to fighting your dragons, and each warrior chose to walk this trail." That sounded hollow, even to him. Tail lowered, she stepped away, and he quietly followed her.

Ahead they both could see Brandy and Reet crowding close to Sandi, putting their arms about her shoulders with Sandi bowing her head.

Jace had to look away. "My lady, we lost six. On the field, there are over thirty, mayhaps forty Scarlur dead. In battle, that is a good toll."

Next sun the narrow ravine widen out to a wider plain before the Silvers' dark mountain. When the sun rose high above and shadows shortened, Jace could see a light-yellow pile of rocks in the distance, an ambush spot? He pulled out his view tube and focused it; aye, not a natural rock outcropping. A flat-topped wall of yellow stone and within that another even higher wall. The Regimental columns moved closer in the high grass before the dark mountain's base as they still trod on traces of the ancient, hard packed caravan trail. Jace loped to Star to see her smiling to see him.

He asked her, "This rock pile ahead, is that the caravanserai that Tar-bel had spoke of? He once said there were caravanserai every sun's trot along the caravan trails."

"Aye." Star answered. "The others built mostly wood enclosures; they are gone now. We built with stone."

"Your kin built it?"

"It was the responsibility of those who lived along the route to care for travelers."

"A fair exchange. Aiding the caravaners brings trade to your lands."

"Before Silver Beard closed off this route to the caravans, we would rebuild the caravanserai and sweep it out and leave food in cache pits. Travelers would take the food and leave coin. All were mostly honorable."

"What happened?"

"The Scarlur said this was their runnings. The caravanserai guardians would have to tribute to them."

"Did they?"

"Some. At first. But the Scarlurs always wanted more, and the other caravanserai guardians drifted off or were killed."

"Why was your leg of the caravan route closed?"

"Grandmare Pearl felt we should leave it open, that the caravaners would help us, but Silver Beard and the uncles felt if we could cut ourselves away from all, the Scarlur would leave us alone. So Silver Beard and the Uncles went to the Blue across the mountain cleft, and at the pass' narrowest point they built a rock barrier. The caravaners were forced to take a longer route to the Green around the mountains. "

"Garrison!" Jace signaled to him and then turned back to Star. "We camp here this sunsink."

She followed him. "Nay--we are so close to our valley. Half a day trot, maybe less!"

Only the water cart and two others had survived the stampede, so now warriors carried the scavenged weapons and provisions. It will be hard climbing with the darkness coming on. "The Regiment needs rest."

Star lowered her head and bit her lip. "We must hurry!"

He lowered his voice. "To what, my Lady? Do you truly have treasure?"

She looked up at him surprised that he disbelieved. "Much gold, many jewels in the mines. Well, we did. I do not know what the Scarlur stole–if they got into the mountain, it may all be gone."

Jace quickly looked around them to see if any of his warriors had heard, then lowered his voice to caution her. "My lady, speak no more of that! We have a force behind us, and there may be a force occupying your valley so this stars we must rest to go into your valley strong to face all your dragons."

She seemed about to argue, but Jace loped off. While Garrison's signal halted the columns before the caravanserai, Jace noted a faint smell of Scarlur and water. He stepped about looking carefully noting the grass here had been trampled but not recently. What dried dung piles he saw looked to be over a moon old. He loped to an opening in the first ring of the caravanserai, seeing the outer walls were withers' high for him, but it would be higher for smaller centaurs. The wall was of quarried rock, cut in flat, rectangular, same sized blocks that were laid ingeniously in overlapping rows. In the center of that ring was a higher wall built above Jace's head, truly these Silver centaurs were amazing builders. But what was hiding in that central tower?

"Two Spot! Deadrick! Abel!" Jace unsheathed his sword, and the three others slipped in behind him. They trotted into the low ring, moving past a foreleg high wall that Jace saw enclosed a well. Drawing his sword, Jace trotted around the taller, central rock ring where one could hide two dozen Scarlurs. Jace started quietly loping around it, noting the central tower's overlapping opening was opposite the front opening which was good defensive move on the Silvers' part. Halting only briefly--to let the others catch up--Jace charged into the small inner courtyard finding it empty of enemy. He resheathed his sword ordering, "Set up camp outside the rings."

Jace loped outside to the well seeing the sun reflected clear water inside, four hoofs below ground level. The walls were set to protect it from dunging. With his long arms, he easily lowered his drinking horn on its throng down into the water and hauled it back up. Smelled good. Jace touched it with his tongue. Did not burn. He took a short taste, a bit metallic, but then he drank the whole horn down.

Garrison stood beside him. "How is it?"

"They have not poisoned this one."

"Mayhaps the Scarlur plan to drink of it shortly?"

Jace looked up at Black mountain. Were they waiting up there? "Camp the Regiment outside the walls of this place." Jace never liked being penned up. "Start each warrior at the well with just their drinking horns. We will fill the water skins and the cart barrels later. Double guards."

Soon they were lined up to fill the water skins. Jace saw Ross was coming in with a leather bucket getting water for the milkers. Had any survived the shags? Caring for them would have been his brother Kent's task, seeing Jace Ross turned his eyes away.

Near gloaming, many worked on their weapons by the

firepits. Jace tried to sleep. But could not. He rose and studied his charts, by his reckoning next sunrise they faced Star's dragon. Should they take what was left of the carts with them up another mountain trail? Or abandon them and have his warriors carry the Silvers' bags of gold and what was left of their supplies?

A tired Jace looked up. Axel stood there, just staring back down the trail. Battle should have fully awaken him from his stupor over Sunny's death, but it had not. Ahead were Star's accursed caves. Whether fighting dragons or Scarlur or digging, his warriors would soon be expecting their vast ransom.

Black wings above. Vultures! Jace started untying his bow. He would get those dunging...

"Nay!" It was Star, staying his hand as he swung up the bow.

"My lady, I just shoot..."

"Not at the vultures. The black birds, they are the Goddess' messengers, her children. When we die, our bodies are taken out under the sun. The vultures come clean the flesh and take it to the Goddess. Then we gather the bones to be wrapped in velvet and laid in a cedar wood chest. These chests are placed--with the Goddess cups--in the cave for the dead. Sunny should have been placed there." She finished sadly.

"My lady, we must talk."

Star looked about the camp. "Not here." She walked within the caravanserai.

He followed. "Star..."

"Please." She held up her hand, then walked past several warriors filling their goat skins from the well. Star kept walking around the high central wall until she could step inside and they were hidden from the rest of the troops.

"When I was very young, Grandmare would lead us down here to fix and clean the caravanserai. There were poles over there in the ground. We had leather tent tops on them so that the caravaners could hide from the rain."

"I am sure they appreciated that. Now my lady, about your dragon quest..."

Star placed her firm fingers on his withers and looked deeply into his eyes. "Jace, make us one." She half reared and kissed him on the lips. Soft, firm pressure. He returned it. Wrapping his arms around her, pulling her towards him. They kissed for some time; then she pushed his arms away.

Star stepped back from him, then pivoted on her hindquarters, before as she bounded to the center of the tower. She spread her four legs and braced her body, then whipped that long silky tail to the side. Finally, she looked back over her shoulder, waiting. Even in the gloaming, he could see her face, so beautiful, so trusting.

Her tail lifted slightly, invitingly and his excitement grew.

Jace wanted to yell of victory, scream his lust, but they must be quiet. He lined his front hooves in to place, then trotted forward. She turned her head forward, good for balance. He rose above her, his front legs bent, covering her. Trying to keep it going as long as he could, but bursting with joy. Finally, she moaned in ecstasy.

"Go forward!" he said. She did, and he lowered his forelegs. Then he moved alongside that sleek body, reaching down to kiss her again. She put her arms around his chest, kissing him back. There were tears on her cheeks.

He was concerned. "Did it hurt?"

"Willow said the first few times I would be sore, but that flood of feeling, it makes it so good. It is good, this coupling of yours but why have you stopped?" she asked anxiously.

He laughed. "Even the wind must rest." Then he reached down and kissed her lips. They slept warmly that night.

Chapter Twenty

The sweetest honey hives

Are guarded by the most stingers!

From the poetry of Running Hoof

This sun's march was hard. His columns easily covered the grassland to the mountain trail that cut deeply into the cliff side, a bit narrower than the last mountain's pass but not as steep as Jace expected. Room for carts to haul treasure back that might not be there.

The glow from last night's coupling still warmed, but the thoughts of the dark, snaking-holed mines ahead sickened him. Star and Crescent wanted to trot at the head of the Regiment, but Jace would not allow it, keeping them protected back in the columns. Here on the paths cut from the rocks, they marched in a single line except for the carts at the end.

Now endlessly the hot sun, the smell of dirty, sweaty centaurs, the scratch of hooves on rock and faint, distant stink of Scarlur. Up ahead, the trail widened out to a flat plateau so they could relax a bit before it narrowed again, cutting tightly between two ascending cliffs. A narrow stream ran alongside the trail and then dropped steeply into a white waterfall.

That water might have cut the original cleft, but Jace could see tool marks where the Silvers must have enlarged the trail. However that trail went up, and he could not see the other side. Was it an ambush point? Jace signaled a halt and called over his shoulder to Star. "Those Cliffs, are they reachable by fighters?"

"From our valley, there is one trail up to the cliff for

the uncles to look over."

"Which one?"

"Sinister side." She strained to see, raising off her front hooves to rear slightly.

She would be telling him sinister side from her valley, which makes it sword-arm side from this trail. "Point to it." Star pointed sword-arm side, and he nodded. "Can they throw anything down on our heads?"

She moved perilous close to the steep drop off, as she tried to peer up. "Nay, the trail undercuts the lookout."

Did the Scarlurs leave any fighters back at her valley? He would have, but they did not seem to be fighters who are concentrating on 'long' strategy.

His warriors waited, and Jace hand signaled for the first six to be a recon party. Deadrick, Abel, Axel, Snake, Skull, and Sandi. They cleared shields and weapons and stepped forward as Star was eagerly pushing past him.

"My Lady, please!" He moved to block her.

"Our valley is ahead." She said impatiently.

"And so might be your dragons." With a rise of their tails, his scouting party signaled their readiness, and he signed for them to go in. As Jace watched, the scouting party reached the top.

Deadrick charged first. Jace had to admire Deadrick's reckless courage, with his bright yellow hide a shining target; he would ride into Hades and savor the thrill of it. Abel looked grimmer, taking time to lower up his spear before he charged in and disappeared. The last one, Sandi stayed in sight, at the high entrance gate.

They all waited. Sandi was rearing to see better but signaling nothing to them.

Sounds of birds on the cliffs. Jace looked up. Vultures. He looked back to his warriors, hot sun on their backs, restless with dunging waiting. Carts creaking. Harnesses jangling. Some nervous warrior kept loudly passing tailwind. Just more waiting.

Then sheathing her weapons, Sandi raised both her hands above her head, waving them back and forth. All clear. She stepped out of sight, and they were marching into the Silvers' mines. At least his Regiment was. Jace found himself standing on the plateau before the gap just directing his columns' march. Finally, he stood watching the last ranks go up. His Regiment is marching and he was not at the head. Those dark, dunging mines. He must march in there. Yet he waited until the carts and rear guard disappeared over the crest. Then reluctantly he followed them.

Through the cliffs, the mountain opened up to a wide, green valley that had a good-sized stream running down it. There was a small orchard and then forest about the edges. High ravine walls with no other entrances showing. A tremendously defendable position with minimal fortifications, defenses that the Silvers did not have. There were no gates or logs on this entrance from the trail.

Star trotted to him. "We must start digging."

"First we must find out if there are Scarlur in your caves."

Deadrick and his were returning from their lopes around the valley.

"Report."

"A bit of smell about and a dropped shield. They were here but gone now," said Sandi.

"Did you check the caves?"

"Just looked in the holes and took a whiff." Deadrick's eyes were unusually large.

Star pointed. "Over there is the main mine entrance. You must go in there."

Deadrick twisted and pointed to the Blue. "What about that cave, over there?" He pointed to a hole near the entrance trail. "There are metal gates without locks, and inside there are wooden boxes covered with gold chains, jeweled cups and silver armor!"

Star shook her tail. "Jace, none of your warriors must go there! That is the sacred cave of our dead. The gems and metal within are gifts to the Goddess; they can not be touched!"

Deadrick shot him a look that Jace ignored, as he asked, "Over to the Green, those wooden gates, twice my height, what do they hide?"

She followed his gaze impatiently. "Those are not gates. The stream comes down higher from the mountain and there is a deep stone cleft behind the wood. My Uncle Black Thorne thought if we could dam it up, the water would rise and they could put leather hoses on it and use it to wash away the gravel and rock. There are sluice boxes at the bottom to let out the stream. Higher up there are plugged openings for the hoses. The stream filled high, but the hoses never worked very well. Jace, please, you must dig!"

Jace felt cold even in the hot sun. "Deadrick, have Lady Star lead you to her caves. Check smell and sign before you go in. See if our friends hide there."

Star was already hightailing away before Deadrick could take his eyes off those gated burial niches with their promise of vast looting.

Garrison trotted up and joined Jace trotting the valley, where Jace saw wooden tents built against the mountain rock. His Second pointed out as they trotted the perimeter. "Lady Crescent tells me those are cooking and food storage areas. Those over there are the sun covers for the furnaces and forges for the Silvers' metal working. That ones with the stacks of wood are where they did their carpentry and sawing of wood timbers for shoring their mines."

"Did? You think they are all gone?"

"Aye." Garrison nodded to a broken spear in the grass as they loped to the edge. "Under those apple trees, bones of a large male, probably her kin. Looks like a Scarlur spear through him."

"Why did Nine-kill not just sit up here and wait for us to canter in?" A puzzled Jace studied the valley. "Why did he leave the burial treasures?"

Garrison shook his tail. "Why did the Silvers not build some sort of fortifications? Set gates where the trail comes into this valley, and it might make it defendable."

"There are iron gates on the burial niches over there."

Garrison shook his tail in disgust. "Get closer."

They loped up to the solid mountain rock. There, Jace saw a shaped carved entrance, two hands taller than his head with an ornamental gate across it. The gate was wrought of long black, curved bars set at careful widths and on it were three black metal, life-sized centaurs. On the sinister side was a strong looking male, sword side a female, the exact image of Star or any of her sisters. In the center was an older, gentle-faced she, with laurel leaves surrounding her hooves and a pronged crown on her head. Star's Goddess. Behind the Goddess' shoulders, Jace could see soaring, sculpted vulture wings of iron that stretched out behind her. Jace put his hand on the gate. It was solid and strong, a defendable gate, but... "It has no lock?"

"Aye." Garrison shook his tail. "With all the ornaments and scrollwork, it has no holders for wooden bars, no hole for locks, how can it bar any centaur? Take a look at what is inside."

Jace pulled at the gate, and it split in half, with the

central Goddess figure being built into the sinister side, with one of her vulture wings on sword arm. Jace stepped a front hoof on the cold stone within, and he froze. The black constriction of the pit pushed the wind from his chest. He half reared as he backed out.

Garrison looked at him with pity. "I forgot. Inside, the tunnel splits into two; then I think there are more branches like a tree. On every side of each tunnel are niches cut fetlock high from the floor that are filled with large fancy wooden boxes..."

Shamed to be seen as weak, Jace finished. "Star said the Slivers let the vultures clean their dead, then they gather their bones and put them into chests."

"Jace on top of those chests are gemmed goblets of gold. Helms of silver and shields of onyx and ivory. If our warriors see..."

"Deadrick has seen already."

A look of worry creased Garrison's face. "Hopefully, if we open her mines, we find enough treasure to satisfy all the gold-hungry."

"This burial place must be covered. Guarded well from our own."

"First we need a defensive entrance gate." Skull was galloping up to them. Garrison demanded. "Report."

"We went back down the trail as far as you ordered, sir. Down in the valley below there is movement around the caravanserai.

"Troops?"

"Nay, just three of those duns. Looked like just scouts."

Jace looked across the valley to the main mine entrance where Deadrick was stepping in. Star stood at the entrance looking directly at him, and Jace could not move.

She looked away and then trotted to his warriors: Kear, Two Spot, Abel, Lerestra, Titus. Star was herding them all into her yawning maw of darkness. One by one, his warriors were stepping into that black hole, like a huge snake's jaws. Jace moved away, needing to do something. Anything.

Garrison was at the wood piles. Organizing something? Axel had loped out. Was he off scouting? Sandi was laying out fire pits and bedding areas, but there seemed to be nothing for Jace to busy himself with. Nothing to save him from that dark, dunging Hades.

It was a warm day, but Jace found himself shivering as if with fever. His love, his patron, was eaten up by that cursed mountain. Jace should be in there leading. Instead, he shivered outside the mines like a claw-cat terrified colt. He stared down at the grass beneath his hooves. He had to get control and stop his trembling flanks. What about the pain cakes? Were any left?

Soft, light hoofbeats and Jace looked up guiltily. Gray dabbles smooth dark legs, but not Star. Silver Crescent was stepping up to him.

"Are you all right?" She asked.

Jace shook his head and pretended to be studying the walls. "Checking your perimeter here. If the Scarlur makes a frontal attack, we must have defenses."

"Defenses. Oh, yes..." She nodded.

Finally had to face her. "How goes the digging?"

Her tail lowered. "Not well. No one seems to be in charge. My sister is leading, but..." She wanted him to go inside the tunnels. Her eyes begged, but she would not ask it.

Jace thought a moment. "Star is in charge? Someone else should be in charge of the warriors." He looked about. Usually, he knew where all his warriors were, but now his mind seemed clouded. Where was Axel? Arnfinn?

"Garrison?" He spoke to himself but spoke out loud.

"He works getting mine timbers to build a gate. They are pulling down fruit-bearing trees. Grandmare will be so angry–but..."

"Only if we dig her out." Jace looked about. "Mayhaps Sandi can order the digging?"

"Nay–Star will not listen to a she." Crescent beseeched him. "Your warriors do not listen to Star. Some of your warriors have found our burial caves. They are in there talking of taking the treasures and leaving."

His warriors were inside looting his patrons, Star was directing the digging, and he was outside, unable to move a hoof!

Jace twisted to the side and pained his still weakened haunch. He closed his eyes, and all the terror of the Salt Plain's pits came back. Even the stink of the dead as he could feel sweat breaking out of his forehead and along his spine to his tail. Unable to stand the blackness, he opened his eyes

Crescent should condemn him for his cowardice instead she just stood there quietly watching with sympathy in those green eyes. She reached out a gentle hand, stroking his withers. "In one of the rock falls, my Uncle Patch was injured. He could not go back in to the caves. He tried but kept bolting out. Silver Beard said he should not be faulted, we must find other work for him. It was two harvests before he could even step back in the mines, but your leadership is so needed now!" She looked about helplessly.

He stood there, saying nothing.

Crescent looked about the valley and then back to their shops. "Wait. I know what would help."

She dashed off. In pain, Jace watches those dabbled hind legs–not Star, but so like her sister. Star, whose love for him would soon turn to contempt for his cowardice.

Crescent came bounding back, struggling with a large wine amphora. "This will help."

Blue tail courage? Jace lifted the heavy pottery vase from her as she pulled off the waxed, cork seal. He lifted it high to his lips and the liquid burned down his throat. He expected a sweet, grape wine from the Silvers; this brew had the fire of peppers! Aye, gut fire that could give strength to a stone. Jace could already feel his tongue numbing and his trembling flanks settling.

"Jace! The dragon! It is there!" Lancer bounded towards them, carrying a small, metal box in his hand.

Jace twisted around, facing the tunnel entrance. "What?"

"The dragon! You have to see it!"

"Dragon?" Jace looked to Crescent.

She only slightly nodded as if it were not at all important. "It is the Silver dragon in the cave."

The mines held constriction, horror, but astir in Jace was that eternal curiosity that had always whipped his hide over the next hill. He had to see this dragon!

Lancer turned and started galloping back to the mines, and Jace found himself following. Then he halted before the darkness at the cave's entrance. Crescent alongside him also stopped running, and she said nothing. Just waited with him.

Dragon? He had to lower his head to step in, but in two strides the roof receded, and he could stand upright.

The metal box in Lancer's hand gave off light, and Jace smelled burning from it. Lancer explained. "Kear thinks this is a natural cavern, that they enlarged in places."

"Wait." Crescent had stopped and was hammering a thing to the side. As his eyes adjusted to the gloom, Jace saw sparks by her hands. A sizzlling sound and then fire showed, oddly illuminating her face and, for a second, again he thought it was Star standing there.

He looked at the box in her hand. "What is that?"

"Mine lamp. It is cotton thread twisted with wax placed in oil in the box. My Uncle Black Thorne fashions them. It takes the blackness away."

Suddenly realizing all that suffocating blackness was pressing down on him, Jace felt himself starting to rear.

Crescent reached out and grabbed his arm. "Nay. The tunnel is not that tall here! You will hit your head. Here, take this." She pushed the wooden handle of the firebox into his hand and picked up another for herself from the pile by the entrance.

His throat constricted, Jace was having trouble breathing. He wanted to bolt, to tear outside, race away from this dunging hole! Jace focused on the bright, flickering light ahead, the warm yellow cast on her glossy gray hide, black stockings, and shining tail. It was as if he was following Star in the moonlight, into some leafy glade.

If he could just focus on her light dapples and following her. Jace planted his four feathered hooves solidly on the sandy floor, one by one, as he forced himself to take deep breaths. His chest was tight, but he could still breath. Lancer seemed to be waiting for him to move. Jace lifted his front hoof and started to walk towards Lancer.

Ahead he could hear murmurings, soft and amazed. The tunnel turned into a larger cavern. Jace could not see the top but he could hear his muffled hoofbeats echoing slightly. He lowered that lamp near his body–Dung! Its hot metal frame burnt his under stomach. There were small circles of light ahead, down a long path. His warriors were holding their lamps up, studying a dark, rock wall. Why were they not working? Reet touched the wall reverently. Per Ben paced in front of it to take its measure.

Per Ben spoke with awe. "Seven centaurs length from nose to tail."

Lancer spoke rapidly. "There! In the wall! It is a dragon! Look, Jace, you can see the jaws. The neck. " Lancer bent low to point out a leg bone that gleamed white with glimmering red and yellow lights. "It is in some precious stone embedded in the rock walls."

Per Ben nodded. "The back would have been taller than your head, Jace. The Silvers must have found it while digging and then chipped it out carefully. The bones are of opal. Each one of these bones could be sawed into jewels that could be polished to adorn a Sultana."

"It is only fire opal," Crescent spoke indifferently. "We have much such rock in the Blue tunnels."

Jace saw a huge skull head with gaping jaws. It looked like the beast was twisting out of the rock wall with its long boney back, and tail swept deep into the dark tunnel. In the front, the neck stretched out as a massive front leg lifted towards him. The other must be still buried in the mountain. The front foot had huge, three-clawed toes, each curved claw longer than Jace's hand. Fiery ribs bowed out from the rock wall. Jace drew the lantern closer as he walked alongside the immense creature. Its ghastly bones danced with color–as if flames of red, black and gold were frozen within the rock.

Crescent nodded. "There are others in the cave we have cut into. Those were cut up for opal ornaments, but Silver Beard forbade hacking this one up. He wished the beast carefully chiseled in outline, then left. Silver Beard called it the 'Silver Dragon,' and he said it would guard our mines and bring us fair fortune."

Jace could move back because fortunately the cavern had been cut wider here. The beast's skull twisted out of the wall, with gaping jaws and its massive head was mostly carved free from the stone. The beast's head was huge, larger than Jace's flanks and Jace could make out a long snout with wide, solid jaws. Jaws spiked with rows of fangs bigger than Jace's hooves, how would you fight this thing? "Crescent, are there other dragons in these caves?"

"Bits of them in the walls."

"I mean live dragons?"

"Nay." She shook her head. "But Jace, your warriors must dig!" Saying that his shining star of protection was disappearing deeper into the tunnel. Jace could not follow, at least not alone. He ordered. "Lancer, come with me." Then he followed Crescent into the darkness to a scene of more chaos than that of any shag beast massacre.

Chapter Twenty one

I do not know if we will prevail

Or if we lose

But I vow we will fight!

Jace of Thunderhoof Regiment

Nose choking dust. Oil lanterns giving poor, bouncing light that created grotesquely menacing shadows. Too huge warriors trying to dig on top of each other. Titus throws back a rock that hits Kear and huge Two Spot stumbled over the mound of stones Clay has piled in back of him. Lerestra scoops up a boulder, but in the tight tunnel, he can not turn around to throw it.

At first, still wrapped in his own horror, Jace stood back, just helplessly watching the chaos in the flickering lamplight. Each warrior blocked the other while at the front, in pathetic desperation, Star stabbed at the rock fall with a narrow lance.

Jace's tight breathing, or not breathing, consumed him, but then old training reasserted. The Regiment--his Regiment--worked not as individuals but as a unit. They were not rabble! "Halt!" He bellowed echoing horribly down endless tunnels.

Only Star kept frantically digging as the others turned to look at him. "Two Spot, you will work out in the valley building defenses under Garrison. Back out of here. You and," he looked about, who was the next biggest one to get out of the way? "Lerestra, go back with Lady Crescent. There has been a misunderstanding since I have not given the order to procure treasure yet. Our commission is not completed until we have cleared the Silvers' mines. Lady Crescent will show you the burial caves to be protected. You will have Garrison assign you a guard detail and set up continuous patrols to see my orders are obeyed!"

"Aye, sir." For Two Spot to turn in such tight quarters, it took some time and massive maneuvering by all of them. When he could, Two Spot gratefully pushed past Jace. Lerestra followed.

Star was obviously upset. "We need all to dig!"

Jace moved forward gingerly trying to step over the rubble while getting a hard gravel chip painfully stuck within his hoof pad. He gently caught Star's arm, stopping her. "Nay." As Jace moved in closer, her short hide brushed against his withers. "My lady, you work valiantly, but you hinder our efforts." With his other hand, he wiped the streaming sweat from his eyes. "We need clear water for my warriors to drink before we roast in here." He called out. "Crescent!" Again it echoed horribly in the tunnels.

Her voice floated out of the darkness. "I will bring buckets and dippers."

It was Kear speaking behind Jace. "We can use some of that water to dampen the dirt, keep down the dust. More breathable for the diggers."

Suddenly, Jace remembered a long cold night about the fires, hearing Kear regale them with tales of digging for copper in the mountains above the Salt Plains. "Kear, your kin dig in the earth?"

"Aye, sir," Kear answered in a low tone, his voice echoing less. "In the dry season, we dug in the mountains. We found copper, gold, even iron to trade."

"Good. You will stand back and be in command. I will send you teams, from them you will select two more to command. You three will do nay guard duty, just keep the digging going. We will run three rotations each sun to sun."

"This digging will be rough..."

"If shorter rotations are needed, you will tell me."

"Two diggers and a line of warriors to carry loose rock away would be good." Kear pointed to the cracked lance Star was still digging with. "We could use better digging tools and leather sacks to carry off the rubble."

Jace was gently pulling Star back from the rockfall. He did not want her asking questions about that odor that fighters knew so well. "Star, your people are miners. Have they not better tools to dig with?"

Star's eyes were dull in the lamplight. At first, she resisted his hold, half rearing to argue and then as his calm reasoning sank in, she bit her lip and lowered her hoofs and her tail. Like waking from a dream, she looked about in darkened corners as if to find something that should be there. "Most of the digging tools will be behind the rock fall...but I think some of the worn digging poles were taken for repair down into the valley. They are wooden posts sheathed in iron. Aye. They would dig better."

Kear asked. "Do you have wooden wedges?"

Star nodded. "And iron wedges too. I will find some."

Jace spoke. "He also wants leather sacks to carry rocks."

"We have baskets. Strong wood wove baskets."

"Excellent." Jace nodded. "Fetch them, tell my warriors to carry them for you under my orders." Jace give her a reassuring smile, she probably could not see in the shadowed darkness. "And bring up torches."

Star stopped. "Nay, not torches–I will get oil lanterns, they give less smoke and breathe less air."

Jace wondered if there would be any air left in this

dunging hole.

Glad to see him back in command Star trotted off. He turned his body to watch her, as Kear began giving orders. "Titus and Clay will keep digging with spears until we get better."

Jace watched her leave the lantern light and meld with the gloomy gray, those white dabs on her hindquarters disappearing last. Could he get out of here himself? This stinking hole, every rock turn looked the same. Nay sun, nay wind, how did her kin stand it? He felt the sweat foam running down his flanks.

Panic was rising, but like in battle, his centaurs were looking to him for answers. Jace would find them. Kear had stopped the work and was studying the rock fall. He would hit the solid rock wall with the lance, then press his ear against the rock then he reared, hitting the lance higher.

Jace trod carefully over to him. "This cave collapsed?"

"Nay." He reached down and held up a rock to the lamplight. "These have been cut out. There see the tool marks." He threw that one down and reached for a slightly paler one. "Look at this one. White lined with mica, it did not even come from this bedrock. This was cut from an outcropping like the one just below this valley."

"They hauled rocks into a mine?"

"To make a deadfall trap. Probably stored tons of rock in some sort of cavity above that connected with another higher up tunnel, then down here they constructed a roof that could be pulled down." He stabbed at what looked like a dirty, cylindrical looking rock. "This was one of the logs that held it up." He thrust a spear at the timber. The spear haft bounced back. "Mayhaps ironwood. Well dried. Might have been here for twelve winters or forty-eight."

"The Lady Star said her people had timbers they

pulled down to release the fall in an attack. It was their defense."

"It was trap alright. You smell the death stink?"

Jace wrinkled his nose. "Crushed somebody."

"Star's kin? Or her enemies?"

"Keep digging, and we will find out."

Kear ranging his lamp light high over the rock fall. "That is the original tunnel wall, solid sleeping rock. Those Silvers are some miners."

"Is there is a hollow space above?"

"Mayhaps but we will be drilling through solid rock to get to it. I think we are better off clearing broken rubble than drilling virgin rock."

"What if there is more to come down on your heads?"

"Then we too will stink, but we need timbers to shore up as we go. I saw some in the valley?"

"I will have some sent in and assign of the line of rock carriers."

Kear looked to the rocks. "Try to keep Lady Star and her sister away, what we dig out will not be pleasant. Titus, use the lances to pry off rocks here. I will carry it over..." he looked about. "to that tunnel over there."

"How long before you break through?" Jace asked Kear as Titus and Clay started to move up.

Kear shrugged his shoulders. "It is loose boulders, gravel, and dirt. It will dig fast, but I do not know how deep it goes. And there is more coming down as we clear."

Crescent came back with two wooden buckets of water. Kear passed the first to Clay and Titus to drink. Then he took the second and splashed it on the dusty cave floor. It was muddy, but soon it was better breathing.

Jace spoke to Crescent. "Ross is to carry water in. You must show him the tunnels." When her hooves stopped echoing, Jace lowered his head towards Kear. "Do you think anyone can still be alive in there?"

Kear shrugged. "Coming in, I felt two air shafts in the tunnels. There might be more beyond the fall." Kear raised his lamp arm, rotating before the rock fall, here the flame burned straight up. "Here the air is only behind us." He raised the torch high, and the flame slightly blew to the side. "There is a tiny escape of air from within the mountain, if we keep tunneling through loose debris, we might find someone in there alive."

Star was already back followed by Per Ben, struggling with three massive poles with pointed iron ends. Kear passed them to the diggers as Star just stood there transfixed.

"My lady, you said you had baskets to carry dirt away?" Kear asked.

"Aye." She just stared hopelessly at the rock fall.

Kear tried to awaken her. "Can you get them?"

"There are some alongside the weaver's tent in the valley." She still stared at the rockfall.

"My Lady, could you fetch them?"

"Then," Jace finished, "You and your sister will be in charge of preparing food. That will free up our warriors to guard, dig and fortify."

Per Ben and Star went for baskets as Jace followed them out. When they reached the sunlight, Jace took deep draughts of grass smelling air. That diminished the panic left from the dark caves, yet even this tree-ringed valley was still overshadowed by massive dark cliffs that seemed to press down on him. He felt his chest tighten as if he was trapped in the pit again. He loped out, breathing better and he signaled Garrison. "Call a drum for all not working in the mines."

Ardon gave the command blast, and soon all were standing immediately before Jace. "Garrison will assign you into work crews. For the crews, there will be three rotations. A crew will stand guard, then dig, then rest. There will be no looting here! Return anything you have mistakenly found!" Deadrick and a few of his glared at Jace, but he just continued. "We have not finished our mission until the Silvers' mines are clear! Then I will order a fair portioning for all!"

Garrison stared at Thunder and Snake as Thunder spoke up. "There are gold goblets in those caves..."

"Lady Star's burial caves?" A warrior asked from the back.

"Is that our portion?" Thunder demanded. "We should secure it now..."

Jace glared at him. "I have given my instructions! If you nay longer want to follow Regimental orders, I will order Ardon to pay you a reduced portion. Then you and any other can be on your way."

Thunder looked to Deadrick and others but said nothing. Jace turned and walked away, ignoring the angry mutterings. He was leaving Garrison the dunging job of enforcing his orders with openly rebellious troops.

Garrison soon trotted to him, and Jace asked. "Think can you keep them in line?"

"Aye, this close no one wants a reduced portion. We have another problem. Down on the plain at the caravanserai, the Scarlurs are gathering."

"Readying an attack?"

"Not yet, they have shes. Fillies and colts with them. They camp. Mayhaps they will move on? Mayhaps they wait for reinforcements?"

Jace looked to the sky. If they marched down the trail as a single column, the first down would be slaughtered, and they might never get enough fighters down in time to turn the tide of Scarlur. "This valley is more defendable."

Garrison made a wry face. "I am building a barricade at the entrance to the valley. It might hold for a while."

"How would you attack it?"

"If I were the Scarlur? They seem to like those suicide attacks. I would send scouts to set fire to the barricade while I was filling up that small plateau just below us. Then it would be a matter of throwing sacrifice after sacrifice at us. Soon they would be through the gate." He looked up the steep-sided mountain around them. "Looks like we are trapped here."

"Mayhaps if we break through into the mines there will be another way out?"

But two suns went, and his warriors were still chipping and scraping against hard rock. Boulders still tumbled down from the top, so it was no wonder that Silver Star had known she could never dig her kin out. His warriors could dig, but what would they find? What would they do with the Scarlurs cutting off their retreat?

The next sun, seeing Kear going on to his rotation, Jace stepped to him. "You are in full stride. How does it look?" Star was joining them.

Kear shook his head, sounding discouraged. "More rock. My Lady Star do you have any idea how long that deadfall is?"

She shook her head.

"How long did it take them to build it?" he persisted.

"It was always there."

"Always?"

"Since before I was foaled." Star moved restlessly.

Kear stepped into the mine, his hooves echoing on the stone. Wanting to gallop in the other direction, Jace followed.

It helped that Star's warm body was beside him.

Jace asked her. "Your kin, they must have made some sort of a chart of the tunnels? To guide them around?"

"Nay, they knew them."

"Think Star. Did Silver Beard have a parchment with grids? A land chronicle?" She only looked at him blankly. "A map?"

She frowned. "Like your parchment rolls?"

"Aye, like the drawing I made of the caravan trail we were taking to your mountain. A map to show the freshwater springs or to show your kin where to dig?"

She obviously wanted to help him but could not.

He looked back and forward. Beyond the dancing lantern light was deadening darkness and those cursed walls that seemed to push in on him, leaving him with nothing he could use for a sighting point: not the sun's path nor the wind's direction nor streams of water to follow in these dank pits. Jace looked where the weak lamplight washed the rocks. Suddenly he wrapped his fingers around hers and raised her hand holding the lantern. He pointed it to some darkly shadowed symbols cut into the bedrock. "What is this?"

"Tunnel markings."

"Are there more markings on the other tunnel walls?"

"Aye. The tunneling weakens the mountain so we must mine without breaking into the other tunnels. The wall carvings told Silver Beard where the other tunnels were."

"Reckoning markings? Then there must be a master map ...or pictures or lines that show you where the tunnels go?"

"Silver Beard knew this."

"You mean he carried it all in his head? What if he died?"

"Then my Uncle Silver Thorne knows. "

"You are saying there is no map, no chart?" He demanded, frustration fueling the anger seeping into his voice.

"Chart?" She showed attentiveness. "Silver Beard's working area was called the 'Chart Chamber.' It is this way." Happy to please him, she twisted past him, brushed his hide with her warmth and as she passed, he stroked the top of her tail. Why was there never time?

Star darted ahead with the lantern and Jace followed, putting up his forearm up to protect his head. These rough walls lowered unexpectedly. "Wait for me!"

But she just kept hurrying ahead, her hooves thudding on sand as she headed down a smaller side tunnel, and then they crossed a stone bridge over a stream flowing out of the rock wall. It was oppressively hot here. This shrouding darkness made Jace feel the vultures hooked talons reaching out for his hide. A turn in the tunnel and Jace banged his elbow against raw rock. "Dung!" It was scraped and bleeding.

"Are you hurt?" Her voice floated back.

Foolish question. "Keep moving!" By the Gods, he had to get out of this stinking snakes nest.

She was calling back. "Here the cutting is newer and the sides of the tunnels narrow.

"Thanks for the warning."

She hurried ahead and then abruptly stopped. Jace could smell water, and a faint rotten eggy smell as shad halted before an elaborately carved, stone entrance.

"This is this Sliver Beard's chamber?"

"Nay, but your warriors will wish to come here."

To the side of the round portal gate that was taller than his head stood a carved wooden pole and on top of it, at her head height, was a large multi-sided carving, double the size of a big man's head. Carved into the flat surface facing them Jace could see a full moon or mayhaps a full he's face that was deeply cut. Star reached up and turned the carving; its next side was a waning moon that also appeared to be a male and female profiles merged together.

"How many sides does that have?"

"Eight." She turned. Each face had a phase of the moon, also cleverly carved as combinations of male or female faces. The full moon was a male face, the new moon female, there were two lovers kissing, two males looking away and then two females. Star reached up and kept rotating the octagon, showing more faces. "It is the moon guard. This face is empty, like the dark moon. All can go in." Star rotated the plaque around to a feminine face. "This is for the shes only." Then she rotated it again. "Two faces together like the half moon. For a she and he together, privately."

The octagonal turning was polished so finely it rotated silently with barely a touch of her two fingertips. The next face of the moon was definitely two males. "When your male warriors come here as a group, they will turn the marking to this."

Then she moved ahead of him, through a tall, carved stone entrance. Inside the tunnel turned and twisted, going down slightly. Jace tartly thought to himself, if the Silvers built their tunnels to guard their lives as well as they guarded their privacy, his warriors would not be here digging. To his relief, the constricting walls gave way to a tall, good sized cavern, one her lantern light could not even reach the top of.

There was thick white sand here cushioning Jace's hooves, and the ceiling appeared to rise at least twenty heads of height in the darkness. The white sand floor sloped to absolute blackness. A drop-off? This cavern appeared to have been a natural opening that the Silvers had reworked. On the wall nearest him, Jace could make out elegant stone freeze portraits of centaurs at play with some of them quite arousing.

He did not picture her work oriented kin this way. Star was watching him as she stepped backwards towards that dark pit. He moved to restrain her before she fell, but she just trod a back hoof into the blackness. Ripples spread out on the smooth surface. Was it water?

Mesmerized, Jace followed. What should have been an icy cold mountain spring was warm against his feathered hooves as the light from her lantern spread over ripples. He could hear a small water fall in the darkness beyond, that probably flowed down to the pool, which overflowed to the stream under the stone bridge they crossed earlier? The warm water on his knees and fetlocks felt good as Jace waded more deeply in. Star was in above her under stomach as he was nearly up to his.

"It will go deeper in the center." She had to hold the lantern higher to keep it from getting wet. "Our males find this very relaxing after digging in the mountain. It will wash the dirt off your warriors and the soreness from their muscles."

They would smell a bit better too. "Odd, the warmth of this mountain water."

"Do you want it warmer?"

Jace laughed, saying in a mocking tone, "My lady, you control the hot springs from the earth?"

"Aye." She stretched her arm with the lamp, indicating two long wooden handles set into the entrance wall that he had missed before. "The cavern with its pool was here naturally. The elder Silvers dug and deepened the pool as a relief for sore, dusty muscles after tunneling, but with the chilling mountain springs it was only good for short bathing."

Leaving him in the water Star headed back on to the sand, moving to the long handles. "When drilling deeper into the mountain, Silver Blacksun discovered a stinking, boiling brook a bit above this cavern. Blacksun drilled a narrow diversion shaft into the mountain and brought the hot spring to a holding pit above this. By raising or lowering the sluice gates, you can heat the pool. Actually, warmer may be better for your leg." She notched the handle on some sort of disk. Jace detected the sound of wood mechanics turning, water rushing and then slowly the pool began to warm against his hide. She moved towards him with open invitation; it felt so good but, "We have tasks to finish." Jace tramped out of the pool. "I will tell Kear each digging crew coming off will get a rest here. Now take me to Silver Beard's Chart chamber."

She led him back out of the bathing cavern gate and further down a long tunnel, then off to the side on a narrower one. "The chart chamber was originally carved out for Silver Blackstar, and each of the sires had it enlarged over the years. The shes were not to go here or touch what was inside, but Silver Beard had me sweep the rock dust away while he taught my brother Silver Storm the charting."

"You listened?"

"I did not like being in the mines, I only wanted to get outside and run in the sun. I listened a little but never understood."

Again there was a short, zig-zag privacy walk, which opened into a small, oval-shaped chamber. No other exit, just another dunging dark trap that seemed to suck his breath out. Jace looked about. "Light that lantern on the wall and the other too."

Three lanterns cast dancing shadows and filled the chamber, but Jace did not find the expected roles of parchments or piles of wood slabs with painted trails of the mountain. Nor did he see the hoped-for beaten gold scrolls that might have revealed much to him. Instead, he saw a mostly bare workshop. The center was littered with stacks of hollow wooden cubes, a huge pile almost to the ceiling. Jace stepped around them.

There was a large table built chest high to the wall but empty. The rough cut ceiling extended three heads above him and on pegs driven into the walls were coils of knotted ropes and folded, notched sticks. Alongside them were various sized metal lanterns and some metal frames holding glasses half filled with dark liquid. The chamber had a totally flat stone floor. It must have been ground down to be that flat. The outer tunnel floors were not as precisely smoothly cut. Why?

There should have been room to walk about, but in the center that wood junk was piled up. Yet holding the lantern high, on the other side, he could see slabs of polished slate stacked on wooden racks out from the walls. He started to push the wooden cubes out of his path.

That seemed to upset Star. "You are making them go out of order."

"Order? Do these cubes have an order?" Jace picked one up and looked at it closely. Thin dark wood frame slats formed the outside cube and inside them, thin to thick, peeled branches meandered. It must have taken infinite care to cut, polish and fit each of the boxes. Jace noted that almost all the cubes were the same exterior size, so they stacked neatly. All the insides seemed different. Some were empty, some had painted twigs or roots, some twigs were inlaid with tiny colored stones. A pretty toy? A hundred of them?

Some of the twigs were peeled tree boles randomly placed, held in position by dark struts attached to their box frame. Looking carefully, Jace could see a large bole that was painted blue on the bottom with a thick tan twig, blue twig and a red twig going into it. Playthings for Silver Beard's grand colts? Nay, too fragile for coltish youngsters. Making these cubes could have been an exacting hobby, to rest the mind and body after a hard day of mining, yet Jace doubted Star's kin ever wasted much effort. If he wished a pastime, why did not Silver Beard craft jewelry or weave work baskets? "My lady, did he give these to your grandmare to decorate her gardens?"

"Nay." She seemed shocked at the thought. "They were never to be moved."

He put the cube down. God, her Silver Beard had filled the place with them, but Jace had a bigger puzzle to solve. "My Lady we must find where Silver Beard kept any plans he had of the digging? Are there scrolls in another storage cavern?"

"Nay."

"Your Uncles just dug anywhere?"

"Nay. My grandsire told them where to dig, and they reported to him what they had done."

Jace's total attention focused back on her. "How did they report?"

"They scratched on the slates, those slates against the wall." He twisted fast and knocked a column of her precious boxes to the floor as he moved to the slates; an upset Star was gathering up the cubes. She seemed to be taking pains to be putting them back in some kind of order. "Jace! You must be more careful."

He realized that the dark corners of the room held several wooden racks, all fetlock high. Each held up to ten slabs of highly polished slates that were a fingertip thick. The slates easily ran half the spread of his arm--by Thunder's bolts--they were heavy! Those old centaurs of hers were strong. Jace struggled to take out first one, then the next, to look at. All were blank, but some showed marks of wiped chalk. Nothing to help him.

Star carried over her hand lantern so he could see better. Finally, he found a slate that had two elaborate sketchings on it. The top one was a flat, meandering line, probably a tunnel, with three neat columns of symbols, undoubtedly measurements. He guessed the drawing below it was the same meandering trail showing how it cut into the earth if one could view it from the side, with more symbols above it.

Jace spoke more to himself than her. "The slates were his records. But they were wiped clean. Temporary records. Star, think! You must know where his permanent records are kept?"

"Only my brother Silver Frost could tell you, and he is trapped in the mountain. We must go back and dig!"

"Silver Beard had to keep track of your tunneling to keep from weakening the mountain, and these slates were temporary records. Was it all kept in his mind? Did it die with him? Why did it not die with his sire? Star, you must tell me what you know!"

"I know the knotted ropes measure the tunnel."

He went over to the wall of orderly spikes, hanging ropes, folded wooden sticks, and boxy metal holders. "What are all those metal holders with the glass globes inside?" He studied it closer, noting there was a candle holder attached. Jace held the whole thing up to his lamp and saw inside the metal was a closed glass globe half filled with dark liquid. "How did they use this?"

She picked one up and tried to turn it. "I do not know."

"You know more than you think! Concentrate, Star. Did you or your sisters carry the ropes or globes into the tunnels?"

"We were not allowed. The shes would be whipped if

we came in here and touched anything."

"What did your males do with them? Did they carry them into the tunnels?"

She thought long and then said, "Yes, I watched as my grandsire who taught my brother. It was his first job in the mines. When they would dig a new tunnel, my uncles would measure with the folded segmented sticks or the knotted ropes. Some of the tunnels were very steep or twisted and in the dark, it is hard to know if you are going up or down. My bother had to go carry the globe. For each hoof fall, he had to place it on the floor and study it."

Jace nodded. "Segmented sticks measure tunneling height. The knotted ropes measured distance." He lifted the globe case, by holding it to one side Jace noted the black liquid slid to a visible mark on its metal case. "Your brother was getting an angle, depth."

She looked had him curiously. "That is important?"

"Aye, if you want an accurate charting. Now these cubes, you have placed them back in some sort of order. How do you do that?"

She picked out one, pointing to the corner with her fingertip. "The carvings. They are our directional symbols. Each box has its own mark that matches with the box against it."

Jace prompted excitedly. "As the marks carved on the tunnel walls. Put the cubes in order."

"You should be digging!" Star complained, but she still hurried about piling columns of cubes, which had been devised so that the large central one would still fit with the smaller ones around it. Finally, at one point the pile of wooden stick cubes had reached to the ceiling. She looked at him expectantly.

A shrewd, old centaur had spent many hours crafting

these strange cubes. There was something Jace should know but did not understand. He took one cube in his hand, revolving it and studying the outer dark wooded edges that created the rigid cubes and they were consistent of width, straight and smoothly polished. Inside some more dark wood slats appeared to be just supports for the light colored branches randomly meandering within.

Those branches were peeled and inter-twisted about like an ants' nest in the ground. Only a few, very few of the inside boxes were riddled with irregular polished tree twigs or peeled gnarled roots of various thicknesses. Of the interior twigs, some were the same thickness their entire length, some thinning to one end and others thickening and thinned as they branched and rambled within the box frames.

When he studied the polished sticks more, he realized some were not just natural root growths but trimmed and intricately joined to make each rambling branch. They were supported by the cubes dark outside frame, and some seemed to hang suspended in the air but when he placed two cubes together, often hanging internal roots joined, formed inexplicable patterns that crossed from cube to cube.

Jace bent his forelegs and then lowered his hindquarters to study the lower boxes. They had less sticks, most had none. They were just blank cubes, supporting the other cubes.

She was impatient. "Why do we waste time on this?"

He picked up other cubes, studying them carefully. Suddenly Jace understood. The pile of boxes before him modeled the mountain he was standing in. The dark wood cubes where just supporting frames to hold the peeled roots and these peeled sticks of varying thickness represented tunnels. "Star, come down here."

Unhappy, she obeyed folding her legs before the

bottom boxes.

"See, this is your mountain. That is the main entrance where we come from the valley. This swordside turn goes to the digging, and probably it is at this point here the wood bole grows upwards. That would have been the cavity that holds back the rock fall. It is huge. Now, go back to here this smaller tunnel to the left. That leads pass the large bole with blue painted on it. The bathing pools? The branch in front of it leads to a smaller bole for that is this chamber. Yes?"

She looked at him in confusion. "The cubes are small--the tunnels are big. They are not the same."

"This is like the carvings of the centaurs in the bathing cave. The carvings are smaller then the centaurs painted but represents them. This cube is only a portrait of the tunnels. Silver Beard must have done it to a scale."

"My brother, Stormy, used to love playing with the boxes. He may still be alive in the tunnels. Jace, we must dig!"

"First, help me understand this strategy." Jace turned his attention to the cube. "If that bole is the bathing cavern then that blue painted twig is for water entering it. Then the red flowing above it will be the hot spring. Only there are gaps in the red-hot spring twig, which would be impossible for a flowing stream."

"We can only guess at the waters full path through the rocks. My grandsires hunted the water by listening to the cave walls, but one time a ceiling collapsed, the boiling water poured and burned one of my uncles to death."

He needed to focus her. "On the twigs, there are tiny, inlaid stones. Why?"

"Jace, you are wasting time!"

"Look at these stones. There is a green one? A blue one? Down here–gold? Does this make sense to you?"

"Nay."

"Past the rock fall bole, there is a large tunnel that leads to a huge bole, is there such a massive grotto in this mountain?"

"The Dragon's Lair." She said not really caring.

"Your kin dug that?" He needed to focus her.

"Most of it was there in the mountain, long before we came. It must have been a dragon's den at least that is what Silver Blackstar called it." She ran her finger along a little twig that branched off and hung in the air. "Those tiny stones. We mine gems from the mountain, some we only find in special tunnels. I think that blue one is ocean's tears. We only find it at the lower levels."

And tiny ocean's tears stones were inlaid in the lower boxes. "Can Crescent measure with these slates?"

"Nay, I knew the most, because I hung around in the tunnels and was curious." She looked desperately about. "On the wall, there was a stick Silver Beard became angry when I dropped it." Rising she hurried to the wall, coming back with a dark wooded stick that had a gold inlay tip. Jace stared at it and then he understood. The stick was the measurement of a Silver centaur's hoof–probably Blackstar's. The small gold hoof print shaped inlaid on one end was that hoof print in miniature. That was the scale of Silver Beard's cubes, every small gold hoof sized piece of wood equaled a full centaur's hoof. He looked up at her and asked, "Did your kin have no run tunnels?"

She looked puzzled, so he tried to explain. " A way out of the mountain, if the first entrance was cut off?"

She obviously did not understand.

"My lady, in battle if your side is losing, sometimes it is wise to go in the other direction. Away from the enemy."

"Turn tail and run away?"

"Strategists try not to put it that way."

"Nay, we had no run tunnels. We were safe." She said, not seeing the irony of her words.

Jace picked up one of the central boxes to study it noting that it was so hard to see with the torches flaring and flickering. "Why did not your elders do this in the valley, where they would have had good sunlight?"

"Silver Black Sun and Silver Beard were always in the mines. The bright sun hurt their eyes."

Jace looked at her shining green eyes with their dark lashes. "Does it hurt yours?"

She shook her head. "Nay, we females were outside. We go gathering the plants and hunting animals for food. I love the sun warming my hide."

Jace rose to examine the top of the mountain. Here the square boxes held few of the tunnels. "Are there more boxes for the valley or side cuts in another chamber?"

"Nay." She trimmed the wick on a sputtering lantern and then waited, shifting her weight from one hoof to another in her impatience but not daring to say anything.

Finally, he backed away to see more of the boxes. "Silver Blackstar started these cubes?"

"He has been gone many warm awakenings of the land."

"Were these cubes kept up to date?"

"After Silver Blackstar, was Silver Sorrel, Silver Blaze, down to my grandsire, Silver Beard; they updated every sun of digging. When Silver Beard was killed, my younger brother, Stormy, wanted to keep going but he had not learned enough. If you understand them, mayhaps you can do it for us?" She asked eagerly.

Jace studied the cubes, turning them this way and that.

"Jace we must dig!"

"They are digging, my lady, but this must be done. Now come here. I want you to show me each of these tunnels that you know." Star's kin were trained to obey--so as much as she wanted to be away--she did Jace's bidding as well as she could.

Jace alerted to a soft sound coming closer to the grotto. Automatically his hand went to sword hilt, and he stepped protectively in front of Star. The hooves came closer. Then out of the shadows emerged Crescent, carrying two huge, steaming porridge tankards smelling of salty meat and yellow seed. Before he drank, Jace questioned Crescent on the cubes; she had not even known they existed. Finally, Jace drank deeply, never taking his eyes off the mysterious cubes. Old Groomer's proverb: stomach full of good food, makes the head run faster and the load lighter.

Star did not drink hers. Her initial impatience with him simmered to a mystical belief that he could work some magic with Silver Beard's cubes, belief he wanted to justify.

Finally, he selected the central, large one, pulling it before her and pointing. It had the trail into the rockfall, where they were digging. "Star, this Dragon's Lair, the cavern that is six times the size of this one here, which is the bathing cavern, right?"

"Aye."

"The bathing pools are at least twenty heads from water to the darkness above?"

"Aye," she said.

"The main bathing pool can hold ten centaurs."

"More."

"Okay." He gave her a large cube to hold and then pointed with his finger. "We dig here at the rockfall."

"We must dig..."

"How deep is that rockfall?"

"I do not know."

"This cavity above, could it all have been filled with stone and rocks to the top here?"

"I do not know."

"Pulling supporting logs caused a planned collapse that probably runs from here to here. But the centaurs who planned this must have known your kin could never dig themselves out in time."

"Your warriors are strong and many if they dig..."

"With the Scarlurs without, there is not time. The rockfall is too deep. Silver Beard and Silver Blackstar were fools."

"Nay, they said Silver Beard was the smartest of us." She did not seem to defend her elders, Star just said it as if it were unquestioningly true. Jace felt her kin were defensive fools but, as he thought of it, everything else Silver Beard and his sons and grandsons had laid out was most sensible. Clever in fact, except for a rock slide that would entomb them.

He looked at the cubes again. A thin, narrower peeled root seemed to represent a tunnel that ran parallel to the entrance tunnel of the bathing cavern. It almost touched in places and that narrow cave connected with an upper tunnel, and at the other end it also came out beyond the rockfall before the Dragon's Lair. "What is this tunnel for?"

She raised her hands in hopelessness. "I do not know. Silver Beard had it dug but we nay found any gems."

"When did he order it dug? Before or after your kin blocked off the caravan trail?"

She thought about it and then said. "After."

He turned the cube in his hands. "It parallels the bathing chamber tunnel, so it was really unnecessary. The two tunnels are so close, the rock must be very thin. Did you ever trod it?"

"It is a small tunnel that goes nowhere but between two main tunnels."

"Listen, Star. With the Scarlurs gathering, with little food, and warriors who do not like to dig, I do not think we can make it through the rock fall in time."

She started to protest.

He gestured to silence her. "But, if we broke into the mountain here, thirty footfalls before the bathing caravan. This area is thinner rock. It may have been a planned or just a lucky omen. We switch to digging here."

"Your warriors can only do so much. They can not do both."

"Then we will dig this one."

"Time runs out...if you are wrong?"

"I know what I am doing!" He did not, and he knew it. But she smiled weakly in belief at his infallibility.

"Get the knotted cords—we will measure the tunnel from the bathing area and from the junction with the main entrance. But by your measuring stick, it should be twenty knotted segments." He grabbed up the largest, central cube in his other hand.

"You can not take the cube from this chamber!" She cried out fearfully.

"Why not?"

"Silver Beard's spirit will not allow it!"

"Having your dead grandsire curse me is the least of my problems."

Without her lead he trotted the tunnels back to the rockfall, finding it now stank horribly. The warriors working had tied cloths to cover their noses from the dust and odor.

Jace moved to Kear. "Bodies?"

Kears nodded and drew Jace over to a digging point. A rotting corpse with some hide still intact painted red.

"Not Silvers, too small. Scarlurs?"

"The Silvers must have cut it so close, that their enemies were in the tunnel when they pulled it down."

"Or some of the enemy got inside just as they were pulling it down. We may be digging to save Scarlur hide."

"From the stink over there, it is more than one body."

"As they are uncovered we will have to drag them out." Another in endless complications of this quest.

"Insect biting job," Kear said.

"First, I want you and..." he looked, at the sweat-streaked faces in the gloom "and Titus to come with me and bring digging sticks. I think I may have another entry point."

Farther down the tunnel Jace showed them the cube. Titus did not understand, but Kear quickly picked up the measuring. He told Titus to stand at the end of the tunnel with the heavy digging stick. "It is virgin rock. Titus, swing the digging pole firmly hitting the wall every half step." Kear cupped his hand on his ear, pressed his hand and his body against the wall.

When Titus arrived at the point the knotted cords had measured, Kear nodded. "It has a less solid ring. Here we dig."

Jace's sharp hearing could detect nothing different, but he bowed to Kear's knowledge and prayed to any Gods who would listen as he gave the order. "Fetch the others, we switch to digging here!"

Star had brought the knotted cords but had a mutinous look. Then Kear reached down and behind, squirting a short burst of urine on the wall.

She looked horrified. "Sir, there are niches with sand for that."

He looked. "Sorry my lady, but I am just marking the spot to return to."

With Kear setting up the new dig, Jace had Star lead him outside. Star trotted to Crescent and spoke in a low voice. They looked unhappy.

At mid-sun, Jace joined Garrison on the line for the stew. "Where is Axel?"

Garrison thinned his lips. "He moves but not much."

Kear was coming out for food. Jace was across the tunnel, but he heard Star moving to Kear. "You have stopped digging at the rock fall?" Her tone was aggrieved.

"Nay, my lady. There is not enough room in the new dig for all of us. Only two or three of us can work at any time, and there will be others digging the rock fall."

Star appealed to Kear. "You are best of the miners, you dig like my kin. Can you not still work the rock fall and let the others do this new wall?"

Kear looked at Jace and then he turned back to Star. "My lady, I dig where Jace has ordered me. Often battles are won by the leaders who plan, as much as the fighters who slay. Jace of Thunder Hoof Regiment is renown for his strategy. I and others follow him because we trust in his lead. If anyone can open your mountain, it will be Jace."

Chapter Twenty Two

Gold gleams

But does not digest

A Poor Warrior's Lament

By the next sun, they were making progress but to what? Even Jace had just about lost faith in his grand cube plan. Since the new, narrower tunnel dig could only fit two centaurs at a time, Kear had sent more back to dig on the main tunnel. It satisfied Star but did little else. Still, if his warriors were sweat-soaked and tired, they might not have the strength to mutiny.

The main dig had produced another rotting Scarlur body to be dragged away and more and more rocks falling down on their heads. Shoring up was proving very difficult, and Kear said he smelled more bodies. Sending out scouts every sun, Garrison said that Scarlur numbers down below were growing, mayhaps it had been a mistake to not attack them immediately.

Jace came out into the valley sun to see Ross near as Deadrick was earnestly speaking to Lancer, Wheat, and Snake. Ross looked up into Jace's eyes, and he quickly slapped Deadrick with his tail as a warning. Deadrick twisted, saw Jace, nodded to the others and walked away. As Jace trotted past the rest, they did not meet his eyes. At the next drum, they would not follow his tail.

He trotted to the front gap where Garrison worked on fortifications. "How does it go?"

Garrison shook his head. "We have wood for a gate, but no place to anchor it and that stream flows through."

"I will have Kear come over. Mayhaps he can drill

into the mountain to give your wood frame purchase."

"Our scouts are seeing more distant campfires down by the caravanserai."

"Still gathering?" Jace frowned.

"Aye. Go down and fight now before they get stronger?"

"Our commission is to clear these caves. Then we must apportion." Jace loped toward a burial cave, but there was no guard. Angry, he loped back Garrison. "Who is on duty at the burial gate?"

"I set Axel. Mayhaps that was mistake, he still mourns Silver Sunny so deeply. I will get another to stand guard."

"Nay! He will stand!" Jace loped the valley looking about until he saw Axel just standing there staring into space. "Axel! Report!"

In surprise at the anger in Jace's voice, Axel looked at him. "Jace...?"

"It is 'Sir!'"

Axel reddened slightly. "Sir."

"Are you not on duty protecting the burial caves?"

"I...I was...why must we bother about the caves? The dead have no use for gold and jewels."

"You question orders you were given?"

"Nay. I just..."

"Just what?"

"Nothing matters. She is gone." He looked as he sounded, beaten.

"And you honor Sunny by leaving her sisters unguarded? Do you think the Lady Sunny would be proud of he who just gives up? This is the way you respect her memory?" Jace let that sink in. "I will inform Ardon you will be docked a sun's marching. If your dereliction continues, you will be leaving the Regiment without portion--understand?"

"Aye." Axel trotted off toward the caves.

"Aye, what?" Jace snapped.

"Aye, sir!"

Crescent was watching them. She stepped over as Axel retreated and Jace turned to her. "Where is your sister?"

"In the caves. Do they still dig at the rockfall?"

"Aye. And more rocks rain down and the Scarlur gathers below, when will Star give up trying to dig out dead bodies?"

"Never."

He could ask Crescent to go into the dunging mine and fetch Star. Nay. He had to do it himself. Ross was carrying water buckets in, and Jace followed him. By the Gods, those rocks always pushed down on him so; with measured steps, Jace came to the main rockfall. Star stood back, stiffly watching the diggers, silently willing them on with her eyes.

Jace moved to her side, letting his great flank rub slightly against her. "How far are they?"

"It goes so slowly. They must dig faster."

"My Lady, it has been nearly two moon cycles since the cave collapsed. Who can be alive in there?"

"They are alive. They must be!" Bold words but her tail was the lowest Jace had ever seen. To keep busy, to do something, Star reached down for one of the oil jugs, to refill an empty lantern, but in her frustration, she fumbled and dropped it. Jace easily reached it and held it for her to pour. When she finished, he stopped her hand from lifting another lantern. Instead, he held her hand gently but most firmly. "My Lady, we must talk."

She looked from him to the others. Rocks scraped against the digging poles, but even with the Kear's dampened cloths over their mouths, they coughed from the dust. She must have understood he did not want them to hear. Her proud head lowered slightly, but she turned and walked so slowly ahead of him, stepping as if she could not bear the weight of her burdens.

He followed until she stopped at a division of the tunnel. Here a natural cavern slightly enlarged the tunnel, and the Silvers had embedded lanterns in the walls. She had started to step into it but then must have remembered his aversion to the tunnels, so Star climbed a new side tunnel, that had the welcoming smell of fresh air.

Ahead Jace could see sunlight on the rocks. An oval the size of two centaurs had been cut out of the mountain, forming a balcony where Jace could stand in the sunlight and look out over the valley. Axel stood stiffly on guard by the burial caves, and Jace could see two of his sentries at the valley's neck. They were obviously bored but were keeping watch. A hard duty to do with nothing happening.

It was good to feel the warm sun on his hide, breathe fresh air, and for a hoof beat he just drank it in. Star did not meet his eyes. His own words tasted of ashes when he finally began. "What do you expect to find when we open the tunnel? And do not say more dragons!"

"There will be riches."

He shook his head. "You do not care for that. What else will be there?"

Silently Star looked away from him. Finally, she answered. "My Grandmare, our uncles, our aunt, my brothers, our cousins, the young hes and shes will be there."

"If the mountain has collapsed..."

"Nay, my grandsires set the trap at the entrance of the tunnel! Their plan was for us to go inside, and then pull down the supports, bringing down a rock fall to seal the tunnels."

"If your kin lives, why do they not dig themselves

out?"

She shook her head. "I do not know."

"Your Grandmare bid you to run?"

"Nay. My Grandmare felt if we waited, the Scarlur would just go away."

"They will not."

"That is what Crescent said. Aunt Crystal felt we should offer them gold but Grandmare had already tried to have Silver Beard render gold to the Scarlur."

"It did not work."

"Uncle Thorne said each payment we gave them made them hungrier for more."

"You stopped paying ransom?"

"Then they killed Silver Beard."

"So your Uncles wanted warriors to fight them?"

"It was my plan, mine and Crescents. My Aunt Silver Crystal gathered sacks of treasure. Sunny joined us, we three shes were the fastest. On the dark of night, we ran down the mountain trail. The Scarlurs were camped at the caravanserai, we smelled their stink and were afraid. Before the moon rose, we started crossing the plain as our eyes are used to the darkness. We were nearly through their camp when their wolves gave the alarm. In the darkness, they chased after us, but we were faster."

Jace nodded. "The Scarlur may have thought you were all escaping. They would have turned their main force to cut off your mines."

"When we reached the next valley, they were screaming their war chants, galloping to the valley. Jace, because of us running they attacked."

Her despair pained him, and he wanted to console her. "They would have attacked shortly anyway. Their siege was just to weaken you with fear."

"Even running in the next valley, we heard the sound of the rockfall echoing off the mountains. We just ran." Her eyes were tearing up as she pleaded with him. "Because of me, Sunny is dead. Grandmare Pearl. My Uncles. The young fillies and colts. They are all trapped. My kin are smiths and miners. They forge weapons, they know not how to use them!" She looked out over the valley, stamping her cloven front hoof until her control was returned.

He waited and then when she did not speak, said, "It has been nearly two moon cycles. My lady, any survivors have had no food, no water, no air..."

"Inside are ventilation shafts drilled out of the mountain, and there are streams of spring water that run through the caverns. As for food, it depends on how the rocks fell. My kin may have access to the wine cellars and the grotto where Grandmare stores the preserved harvests."

Jace continued quietly. "They can also eat the flesh of their dead." The look on her face hurt him all most as much as he hurt her. "My Lady, you must know the fact that your battle is lost."

She lowered her head. "Never!"

"Star, we will soon be out of provisions ourselves. Then we must fight back to the coast and the bazaar. If we leave now, we might make it."

"Nay! You will break through the rockfall soon. There will be riches! Your warriors demand that!"

"The rockfall could have collapsed the whole mountain."

"Nay—it was build to seal the caves temporarily."

"They engineered a trap to hold your own blood?"

"It was planned to protect our treasure vaults."

"These leaders of yours, your esteemed ancestors, forged the finest weapons but sold them to your enemies.

You're fine all-knowing grand sires crafted tunnels and water diversions, but they had no defendable gates to your valley."

She looked away. "It was different then, centaurs were not so greedy. My elders did not expect these times."

"My lady, I will allow a dig for only one more sun."

"Jace, please! Two, they will get through!"

"Two sun cycles and that will probably kill us going back."

She knew he was right, but she looked for any desperate argument to try and turn him, "But your warriors expect riches, they will not leave until the tunnels are open."

Jace knew far better than she did what booty his warriors would be expecting and what they would do if they did not get it. "My Lady, they have marched, fought and dug for you. They must have pay--if not the riches promised, perhaps something lesser. In the shelters and in your burial caves there are fine weapons, gold neck chains, and jeweled eating platters. Even the jeweled goddess cups. I am sending Garrison to collect them."

Star turned to block him with her flanks. "Nay! The Goddess goblets are sacred!"

Jace tightened his calloused fingers on her arm. "This must be done. Warriors take payment in gold, or they take it in blood!"

At first, she stood on stiffened legs as if she thought she could force him back but then Star lowered her tail. "Aye. You have fought for your hire." She looked up pleadingly into his eyes. "But just two more sunsinks–please! We are almost through!"

By the Gods, she was such a stubborn one, but it would take two suns to prepare for the Scarlur battle to come. He nodded, and she trotted away. He had bullied her into submission on the treasure, but he felt no joy in watching those glossy flanks disappear into the tunnel's darkness. For a time he stood in the opening, watching the activity in the valley. Crescent stirred a massive stew pot in the cooking shed, as Per Ben and Sandi worked on building new carts with tools from the Silver's woodworking shop.

Ross and Skull filled water skins at that massive wooden dam. There the Silvers had fashioned a toggle out of wood so that when it was turned, it released a stream of water into the buckets. The Silvers built a massive dam that must hold a huge amount of water so that even the wild streams would work for them. How had centaurs so clever, so practical, been so oblivious to any kinds of defense? Weary, Jace turned and faced the dark tunnels again.

Out in the valley, Garrison was just stiffly easing himself up from his rest rotation. Seeing Jace, he looked hopeful. "Broken through?"

"Too much rock."

Garrison came closer and spoke lowly. "Does Lady Star know there will not be anyone alive in the tunnels?"

"What are our warriors saying?"

"They only see rooms of golden weapons and jeweled helms when the tunnels open up." Garrison looked long at him. "Jace, when they do not get anything..."

"Have we enough provisions to go back to the bazaar?"

"On half hungry stomachs. But Deadrick is whipping them up saying you promised great treasure. He wants to loot everything here."

"Rape the Silvers, tear the place down...that will not get us anywhere. We might as well try to sign on with the Scarlur."

"It has come up."

"Your counsel?"

"The Scarlurs would not have us. Their foolish over-looting gutted the fattened caravans, and now they attack us in desperation."

Both of them fell silent. Jace looked across the valley until finally, he spoke. "I do not wish to be a looter."

"Neither do I, but..."

"I have given our patroness two more sunsinks of digging. Then we will leave here."

Garrison warned, "Scouts report Scarlur numbers seem to be growing."

Jace looked at him. "Could they be wrong?"

"Doubt it."

"Then I misjudged."

"Aye. I did too," said Garrison with a bitter smile.

Jace nodded towards the burial caves. "We will have thirty-two suns marching, and we need some sort of treasure to appease our warriors. Take those leather rock sacks, and dirt baskets then get Per Ben and two more whose strict obedience you trust. Go through the workshops of the Silvers, their shrines and their burials. Try to disturb as little as possible, but we must have treasure to divide!"

"And the promised bonus? They each expect a chief's ransom?"

"They will have to settle for some lady's jeweled necklace."

Garrison swung his tail, he had a mission he could accomplish. "My Lady Crescent. She seems most worldly, I think she could help us. She will trot along the path of reason, that the dead must bow to the living."

"Speak with her. Do it carefully to see how she reacts."

Garrison nodded and trotted away. Jace galloped up the valley, climbing toward the entrance ravine. He could see no real way they could fortify this death trap in time, but Garrison was doing his best. His Second had half a wooden gate in place and work begun on the other side.

Jace took his rest at sunsink, bending over to pick a stone from his hoof. Star did not come to him, and they did not stand head to tail and groom each other, as she knew soon her precious gold goblets, and jeweled plates would have to be broken up to divide fairly among all his warriors. After he passed out her deads' relics, Star would never lie with him again.

Jace rested fitfully, and before sunrise, he rose and loped about the valley. Anything to avoid those dunging mines.

Garrison joined him saying, "I need water." They passed the cooking area and trotted to the wooden dam, where Per Ben poured out water for his Reet. She could barely walk with her huge belly. Smiling she pointed down to the foal that they could see kicking hard within her.

Jace and Garrison waited their turn for water. Alongside them on the grass was a long, trimmed tree trunk, thicker than a centaur's head, and running four lengths long. Curious, Jace struck it with his hoof, which bounced back. It was strong, dense wood. He looked about the valley seeing olive trees, fruit trees, and some small firs. Some he did not recognize, yet none were anything like this tall, hardwood pole. "There is no tree in this valley that such a pole could have been hacked from."

"Crescent said Silver Beard would trade gems for special woods like cedar, ebony, and teak. He traded for that log, and it was hauled from the coast. She said it was terrible trouble to bring it up the mountain. Her males could barely carry it on those steep, tight turns and they finally raised it using ropes." Garrison looked down the length of the log. "If we could take it with us, it would make a fine battering ram."

"Too hard to haul. Why did they not cut it? Make it easier to carry up here?"

Garrison shook his tail as he moved up to fill his water skin from the dam spigot. "Why do these strange Silvers do anything? They have a perfectly fine valley grass, and yet they sleep in stinking caves. They run as fast as the wind, yet for a defense, they bury themselves in a mountain. There is nay reasoning to understand here, Jace."

As the digging the last two suns continued, Jace ordered weapons inspection and kept Sandi and a crew trying to repair what they had. Crescent actually could do a bit of her kin's fine smithing, but Star refused to meet his eyes as her despair turned to anger. Only Axel seemed to come back alive.

At gloaming, Garrison came out of the shadows and getting close to Jace, he kept his voice as low as possible. "We have gathered five sacks full of treasure. Crescent hides them in the cooking niche."

To Jace's raised eyebrow, he added. "Not a chief's ransom but fine pieces of pure metal and beautiful workmanship. It is a shame the armor chest plates are for centaurs much smaller than us."

"They could be bartered at the bazaar?"

"Aye. For a fine price but split among so many? We will have to break them up for the metal and gems."

"Star has one more sunsink, and then we hold a drum and see what our warriors will accept."

"Deadrick is bringing more to his side."

Jace nodded, then sore in body and heart, he limped over to the bathing cave. His hind leg healed, but it still pained him after a long sun. The warm water helped. He lit but one torch, surprised no one else was here, probably all too tired. Jace washed the dirt off his face and beard. He now had a pretty lady, but she did not groom him. When they broke up her Goddess cups, she would curse him, if his own warriors did not kill him first.

There were running hooves in the tunnel, his battle harness and weapons were laying on the sand. In two leaps Jace hauled out of the water, going for the sword in his scabbard.

A slow of hooves in that zig-zag entrance and then Titus showed. "Jace–they have broken through."

"Where?"

"The second tunnel. The one nearest here."

Hauling his harness on, Jace bounded out, taking the tight tunnel at too fast a pace and scraping his hindquarters before finally coming out in the dig area. Now there were centaurs tail upon tail, and in the bobbing light, Jace could see a hole four hands high in the tunnel wall. Kear and two others worked feverishly to widen it. Dust choked out smells as Jace shoved himself up to the wall.

Kear spoke excitedly, "You were right. The wall here is only six hands thick leading to another tunnel that goes sinister and sword hand. Looks a little shorter than this one, a little rougher cut, but with heads bent we could make it through."

To what? Scarlurs waiting for them? Star's dead kin? "Make it wider!"

His digging crew resumed steady, desperate hammering, smashing away at the rock to make a larger hole to fit his warriors. Jace felt the wings of Star's Vulture Goddess brushing him as this new tunnel was even narrower and lower than the others.

Chapter Twenty Three

Fight within

Fight without

All fights come at the same time

The worst time...

Book of Argent

Within that hole, smell of dust, death stink, but another faint smell. Star's herd smell, but living or dead? Scraping against the narrow tunnel wall, Star pushed herself past his warriors and gathered her legs, she leaped over a pile of rubble. She would have bolted past him, but for Jace blocking her with his flanks, pressing her hard against the wall. "Nay! My Lady, you have paid warriors to protect you!"

The crew had dropped their digging poles and were reaching for weapons on their harnesses, as Jace examined the entrance and twisted to Kear. "We need a bigger hole, taller. Kear, work with Skull and Jerrick to enlarge it. Ross hauls rocks away. Keep digging after we go through, we may have to retreat back this way." Jace twisted farther to look behind. "Snake, Wake the resting, bring them up! Orson, warn Garrison and the valley sentries we may be engaging in the tunnels!"

Both immediately did an awkward twisting turn in the tight tunnel and raced off, that put Axel had the head of the line. Jace lowered his voice to the gathered centaurs, "Count off. Every first warrior, shield and sword, every second, takes sword with lamp in his other hand." There were murmurings as this was passed on. "Star, fetch more lamps and oil!"

She looked mutinous but finally turned tail. As this was done, Jace braced himself for an even smaller tunnel with sharp rocks that would tear at his flanks. He should let another lead, Axel? Too big. Clay? Nay, Jace forced himself to wait as he unsheathed his short sword.

"Over here." Kear directed the frantic diggers to strike high. Only pebbles cascaded down. Kear pointed to a spot for Skull to hit and then another near it. "Jerrick, strike there!" Jerrick swung a smashing blow, then Kear followed up between those same points as their clanging hits reverberated through out both tunnels, painfully ringing in Jace's ears. A large shelf of rock cracked and fell. Whoever was inside those tunnels would know they were coming!

More blows, a single rock chunk fell then a lot more. Soon they would be inside. To face what? Scarlurs trapped within? Was there another entrance they found by torturing Star's kin? Would a whole enemy force await them? The damnable mountain pressed down and darkness obscured his vision. Dunging dust dulled his sense of smell, but the excitement of the coming fighting was building. The closeness of battle triggered a blood rush more intoxicating than any flagon of honey mead.

Jerrick's next blow knocked down only three tiny chunks, but Kear's next slam brought a cascade of rocks, leaving a hole just big enough for Jace.

"Out of the way!" Jace ordered.

"We can make larger!" Kear protested.

But Jace was lowering his head and thrusting his torso forward, forcing his forelegs up through the hole. With a bloody scraping of hide and hooves, he was into total darkness.

Could Axel's bigger bulk make it? He did. "Hold your lantern high!" Jace commanded him. The others were scrambling after them as Jace glanced up and down this new tunnel. He was in a centaur cut tunnel, narrower and rougher cut and lower than the tunnels before but walkable. To the sinister, he might be able to circle and outflank anyone in the dragon cavern, but since they knew he was coming, Jace turned sword-arm, heading for the enemy. He lifted on his helmet and had to bow his head to keep from hitting the ceiling, and still the tight walls scraped his withers and arms. Dunging rocks! Dunging Silvers!

The death stink was stronger, but something else. He slowed, taking deep, tasting breaths. The smell of fresh dung of live centaurs! Enemies or friends? The blackness here was worse than a moonless night, worse than the darkest thunderstorm. How could the Silvers endure this Hades?

As Silver Beard's cube had predicted, the tunnel sank steeply. The light from Axel's lantern behind him just grayed the gloom and Jace figured to come out on the other side of rock fall. The stink of death was increasing, no room to turn tail here but to his relief, the ceiling raised as Jace entered a small cavern. The junction with the main tunnel?

Aye! The rockfall was to his sword-arm sticking from the rocks there were more bodies. Two–no three bodies. Two bigger, half buried ones were probably once males with heavy, elaborate armbands hung off rotting flesh.

The smaller body, a bit farther from the rockfall was a youngster? Nay, a grown female with long silver hair. On her skull she wore a golden circlet, set with flowerlets of pearls and what was left of her skin on her thin-fingered hand was age-spotted, so Jace guessed she was Star's grandmare, Silver Pearl. She had an arrow buried in her upper stomach, probably lived for a while and still held a thick stick in her hand. Died ready to fight.

Her colts or grandcolts were probably in the rubble.

Had the grandmare waited too long to have the trap supports pulled down? Had the Scarlurs broken through first? Were they hiding in this cursed darkness, living on dead flesh and waiting to attack?

Jace moved sinister where the tunnel was wider and taller. He must be headed towards the Dragon's Lair cavern; alongside the tunnel walls were jumbled piles of glinting gold plates, silver amour, jeweled arm bands, iron helms, and inlayed goblets. Scarlurs caching their lootings? Or the Grandmare having everything valuable from the valley hauled into the caves?

Slow walking in this taller tunnel was easier, facing a possible attack from any direction harder. Ahead was the sound of pebbles stirring. Enemy? Or some rat scrambling in the darkness? Again the wings of death brushed and the hairs on his back rose.

Behind him, Jace heard the sound of metal scraping metal, and he looked back to see one of his hardies was using the end hook of his battle-ax to pry Silver Pearl's circlet off her skull. "No looting until I say so!" Not that treasure would be a problem, he had passed endless piles of circlets, gold breast plates, and water-metal swords. He stepped a hoof painfully down on what turned out to be a blood-jeweled ring.

This tunnel had been squared by the Silvers' digging and--if he were right--would lead to the Dragon Lair cavern that should be opening up ahead. Some side black holes branched off, but Jace kept on what he thought was the main track. If Star's kin were alive in the tunnels, why had they not covered their own with dirt? Why had they not dug themselves out of this stinking, cold tomb?

From the stick cubes, he knew this trail should soon open out into a huge, natural cavern. It did as soon his hooves settled on deep sand. Their quiet clopping distantly echoed off the walls. This Dragon's Lair must be gigantic, he looked around, "Clay, hold your lamp up!" When Clay did as high as he could, Jace could not see the top of the cave, just stone icicles hanging down. "Axel, rear!" Axel reared his full height with his lantern but the light still did reach the top. Jace hand signaled his warriors to halt as he stepped deeper into the open arena.

The air smelled better in here. Was that due to the Silvers' ventilation shafts? Jace stopped, and half reared as he inhaled deeply. Scent of living creatures, smell of fear and faint scraping sounds at a distance. Nervous breathing? Whoever hides, they were staying beyond the reach of the lamps and not attacking, unless they were building up courage?

Scarlur? Or Star's kin? Were they just afraid of him? His big breed breaking into their safe little cocoon? Jace called lowly to the nearest warrior. "Bring Lady Star up, our friends may respond to her." Then he waited, hearing no more soft movements in the darkness ahead.

It seemed an age, but Star came hurrying up with Crescent, both of them carried larger lanterns, and in that light, he could see tears streaking the dust on their cheeks.

"The skeletons at the rock fall–your grandmare?" He asked.

Star just nodded.

It was Crescent who added in a pained, throaty voice. "The armbands were of Uncle Silver Thorne and Uncle Black Hoof."

Star pushed past Jace, peering into the darkness beyond the dancing lantern light, as she called out. "Stormy? Flame? Aunt Crystal?" Her voice echoed in the emptiness. Legs stiff and head high she stood listening.

Jace loped about, trying to scope the size of this

cavern. He ordered, "Axel, there are ceremonial torches on the walls, light them. Mayhaps these hidden ones will come out."

"Nay." Star said, "They are here, but they are frightened." With a raise of her tail, she dashed off into the smothering darkness of one of the side tunnels.

"Star!" Jace jumped forward but then froze. All the dark, stifling mountain was pressing on his chest, all the pits of the Salt Plains' horror, but his love was in danger. "Axel, take charge!" Jace galloped after her.

At first in the side tunnel, he saw her lantern light ahead and the pale marks on her hindquarters. But he had to slow as the tunnel turned. He had no lantern of his own, and he lost even that faint light from hers. Jace used his sword to sound his way down the tunnel, soon he could only hear her fading hoof falls. The rock tunnel beneath his hooves no longer had any muffling sand, and the ceiling was lowering. Then the tunnel split. "Star?"

He smelled Star, other centaurs and fear but from which black hole did it come from? There were sounds ahead. Had she run into a Scarlur trap? Were they cutting her throat now? If Jace chose the wrong tunnel, he would have to double back, and he might never find her or his own way out! He would die alone in this dung-hole rat's burrow!

Standing helplessly was worse than useless. Jace charged to the sword side. Behind he could hear his warriors stumbling after him. "Swordside!" He yelled.

The ceiling seemed to be lowing further, and bright sparks spit off his sword as he held it up before him to keep from hitting his helmet on the lowering roof. Was the tunnel ending? Did he pick the wrong way? Ahead was a solid wall–nay, an abrupt angle turn with a faint spill of gray light beyond it. Jace plunged on, and suddenly there were centaurs surrounding him. He raised his sword as a male backed away from him. This male was armed with his own sword but holding it at an impossible angle to strike, and behind him, there were other movements of tall, gray shapes in the darkness.

"Nay!" It was Star, placing her body between Jace and the other he. "This is Stormy. My brother, Silver Stormson.

She was standing before a gray male, one not much larger than herself. Looking at his fear wide eyes, Jace realized he was a youngster, almost full grown but not yet and now Jace could smell hes and shes, their scents very close to Star and her sisters.

Behind Jace, there was a rushing of hooves. He would have a hindquarters full of swords in the space of a lope. "Halt!" Jace yelled, half-reared as Axel and Able rounded the bend, "Hold! They are on our side!"

Star put a staying hand on Jace's withers, her voice full of joy. "Aunt Crystal is here. My younger brothers Silver Frost and Rain. Silver Flame. The foals..."

"How many?"

"Twenty or more...."

"Did any of the Scarlur get into the caves?"

"Nay. My uncles pulled down the rock fall as they were entering the tunnel."

Jace looked to the male ahead of him. "Have you water?"

"From the springs,"

"Food?"

"Much of the last harvest is stored in the caverns below."

"Any other entrances?" With the Scarlur below a back way, out would be great.

"Nay."

Star was pushing against him. "There is much gold and many jewels for your warriors–Garrison must return the Goddess cups to our dead."

Gently pushing her away, Jace nodded, her mounds of gold would be fair payment if he could keep control of his warriors. The gemmed rings and cornets his hardies were trampling on might inflame the strongest of the disciplined. He would have to get the untrustworthy out of the mines and have Garrison secure her treasure. "Star lead us to the Dragon's Lair and tell your kin to follow." In tight corners, he turned about to head out of the tunnels.

They were entering the main cavern with its ring of flaming torches when hooves trampled nearer. "**RALLY! JACE! JACE!**"

Axel relayed. "**OVER HERE!**"

Foam flecked, wide-eyed Arjuna bounded in. "They are overrunning us in the valley!"

Looters instantly became fighters as they struggled to rejoin ranks.

Jace pushed forward yelling. "Star–lead us out!"

Hooves clattered on stone, with cursing as heads and elbows bruised against tunnel walls. Those with him would have battle harnesses. Had the guards gotten warning in time? Was Garrison able to mount a defense at the valley top? If the valley was lost, should they just hole up in the tunnels?

Soon they were through Kear's cut and trotting to the entrance from the valley. Sounds of swords clashing against shields, battle screams of the Scarlurs, smells of blood and fear. As Jace saw the light from the main tunnel entrance, he reached ahead and grabbed at Star's tail. "Gather your kin–hide them back in the tunnels!"

He charged past, well aware now he had only a short sword in his hands. At the cave mouth, Jace skidded to a halt with Axel behind him and the sounds of more warriors piling up behind in the tunnels in back of them.

Outside his warriors were fighting a losing battle against a valley of red painted faces screaming as with slashing swords they advanced...

Jace looked at the valley entrance. If Garrison had mounted a defense, it had been washed away by this sea of angry wasps. More still pouring in. Where did they all come from? Deadrick was pushing past with Snake and Axel.

"Hold!" If they went in, it would be just a war of attrition, and it looked like the Scarlurs had twice--nay thrice--their numbers. Jace looked to the valley sides where most of his outside warriors were isolated and fighting from the perimeter. Aye, his enemy was in a jar, but it was the Regiment that was trapped.

This tide could not be turned. Time to just go down and fight to the end, yet Star was behind him. If he left the cave defenseless...

It would not be over! He would not let it! Deep within his memories, he could hear Jachom yelling at him '*stop running your hooves—get a plan!*'

Desperately Jace's eyes swept back across the valley. His warriors in small clumps on the sides. At the gate, Garrison had nothing to rally. Scarlurs controlled the valley floor. Spears and hanging coup tails obstructed his view of the center and even more yelling duns were pouring through the valley mouth.

The workshops along the side mountain walls offered minimal protection for his warriors' backs but still were a pit-fall with no retreat. Any of his Regiment in the valley were cut off from retreat so for those with Jace, there was nothing but fighting or hiding in the caves. Another trap where they would be picked off one by one or starved out.

"Jace! We fight!" Yelled Deadrick.

"Stay!" Jace still stood still scanning the battle, instead of a solid, wooden front gate, the bloody Silvers built that fool's high waterworks...

Suddenly he saw a chance.

"Deadrick! Form around me, we fight to that ground pole over there!" Jace pointed desperately. "Follow us and stay together as a unit!" They formed a wedge behind Deadrick, fighting to the pole. Jace took the sword-arm flank. He grabbed a spear from a warrior Deadrick had slashed. A Scarlur's cutting spear point grazed his harness, blooding his hindquarters. They would kill the Scarlurs in front of them only to have another line of Scarlurs popped up, like fenga teeth. Screaming mightily, Jace rejoiced slashing into dun flesh as he gained ground.

Orson and Deadrick took the fighting lead to the pole. When they reached it, Jace shouted hoarsely above the melee. "Axel, Randy–drop your swords and shields! Pick up the pole–you will ram the Silvers' dam gates! Arjuna! Snake! Arnfinn! Ghost! Join them! Break the wooden gates!"

Another spear bit close, deeply through his flank harness into his haunch. Jace slashed out, his blow knocking the spear-wielding Scarlur off his legs. He looked up and saw Randy drop his side of the pole, collapsing to the ground as he was speared through the chest.

"Shoulder the pole!" Jace yelled at Axel.

With Randy down, there were only five picking up the pole, but without further orders, Deadrick and the rest were clearing the path for them, one dead dun at a time. As they freed up the side workshops, others of the Regiment were falling in with them and forming a wall of fighters about the pole. Clearing a way toward the high wooden gates.

Without daring to look, Jace knew they were obeying.

Deadrick was slashing through the Scarlur line. As bodies fell before the pole, they all cut a path for Axel's crew.

Others of his troop rallied, not hearing his orders over the battle cries but instinctively flowing the battle line from him. These short duns were tough, battle-hardened fighters; most had Nine-Kill's moon and black star shields. In such close quarters, Jace's swings had not their accustomed strength, but bloody-body by bloody-body, they were fighting toward the Silvers' reservoir. That wood dam was three full centaurs high–but how much water was really behind that wooden barricade?

The Scarlurs in the front of them fought well; the Regiment fought better! When a knot of enemy went down, an opening cleared for Sandi, Reet and Per Ben who had been holding a pocket in front of the weavers' tent. They joined behind Jace, as Axel and four others hefted the pole forward. Weaponless, they should have been cut up –but the Scarlurs were focusing on the fighters with swinging swords. They seemed to have no idea of Jace's plan.

The low inclined hillside opened up. "Axel! Smash it!"

Yelling wildly Axel galloping with the pole as the others charged with him.

Five of them were holding the pole when it slammed against the wooden dam gates. It bounced back in a hail of splinters. Bloodying arms and legs as Snake rolled over. The pole dropped, but picking his end up, Axel cradled it, bellowing, "Again!" The others rallied to him as duns seemed to realize they must attack the pole crew. Jace cut the first dun's arm off who tired. Per Ben had dashed to replace Snake holding the pole.

Jace concentrated on trying to slash down the dun line, keep them away from the pole crew. But now some of the

Scarlurs leaders must have realized what he was trying to do. The full tide of battle turned towards them.

With a Silvers' sword in one hand and Scarlur sword in the other, Jace fought like a moon crazed fool.

Behind him, the pole smashed again. Bouncing back. These Silvers built strong.

Smoke and screams. Jace saw that Star and Storm were at the cave mouth. Throwing flaming oil lanterns down on the attackers below.

Behind him, the pole slammed again and then again. Solid wood yielded not.

Its resounding hits were turning more of the enemy's attention. One of the central duns, a red face painted leader, was rearing. Jace could not hear above the yells, but the dun was pointing to Jace's fighters striking the water gates. Red face was directing his fighters to attack the pole carriers. The full tide of the battle was turning to them. If Jace's few could not hold, they would be overrun.

Behind him, the very mountains seemed to rumble as the pole struck again.

A lance thrust towards Jace's chest. Instinctively he recoiled and braced for the blow. The lance was parried when Deadrick's sword slashed ugly's face off. Deadrick used the force of his blow to push the lance and body aside.

Jace just twisted to sword slash the next. For every Scarlur down, two took his place. It seemed endless.

Again, the steady slam of the pole against solid wood–then the blessed splintering, ripping sounds, as a battering ram of white water shot out into the valley. A centaur sized thickness of water, wood, and rock threw Jace to the side. The lighter Scarlur ahead where bowled over in the spurting, white froth.

Jace struggled to his feet, assessing the damage. The

top of the dam held. Only a portion roughly his size had smashed out–spewing pressured water straight out. The frigid water streaming out like a thick lance, stabbing the enemy. Jace and his others were knocked to the side–but the shorter legged, lighter Scarlurs, facing the brunt of the blasting water were washed off their legs. Rolling hoof over head. Choking in the forceful icy stream.

Jace offered an arm to help Deadrick scramble to higher ground, before the broken dam. More and more water poured into the valley. How much was dammed up? It was hand high on the battlefield, and still shooting straight out, hitting the opposite wall of the valley. Mud slipped under his hooves. Soon the icy, frothing water was fetlock high. Fetlock for his warriors. Chest high for the shorter duns. Those deepest in the valley were washed off their hoofs, rolling against themselves. Choking for air. Drowning. Some, slipping on wet clay, were routed, trying to escape, only to be cut down by Jace's warriors closing in from the valley's sides. The jar trap now worked in the Regiment's favor.

Triumphant Scarlur battle cries turned to desperate screams, as trampled duns were literally drowning. Across the valley, Jace could see some of his warriors regaining the gate. They were trying to hold his jar. Garrison must be there. Jace reached down for a Scarlur's shield. Its owner was down but still alive. Jace put his sword through bone and muscle, then ripped the shield from his hands.

This was fighting he knew well.

The water reached withers high on Jace before it started to slow. More of the enemy drowned before his could stab them.

Most were not running. Fighting on–an enemy to be admired! But the impact of deadening water and his trained warriors, the battle tide now ran in the Regiment's favor!

Mid-sun, Jace led Deadrick and Axel at the valley gate. Sandi and others followed, bloody but triumphant. In the valley, they heard screams as his warriors finished off the wounded. Jace looked about the entrance. Where was Garrison? He should be leading the warriors here. A movement in the pile of dead. Deadrick was on it. Stabbing a Scarlur with his lance.

Jace trod on. He wanted to see out the valley, down the trail. Were more dun reinforcements gathering for another attack?

"Jace, hold!"

Jace turned to see a stricken Deadrick.

"What is it?"

"I...I..." Deadrick stopped and stared at him.

What was the matter with the fool? In the midst of battle, he just stands there? "Report!"

"Garrison–over there..."

With a sinking feeling, on weighted hooves, Jace twisted back, loping towards the pile of Scarlur dead. He had a battle to finish...yet, he had to stop and see...

Ahead a pile of dead. Monument to a fighter, who kept killing even while down. Over it, only Garrison's head could be seen. His eyes closed, face strangely quiet. As if asleep. Spear through his body–he must have kept fighting, the hole ripped as he twisted. Totally outnumbered, Garrison had fought on, holding the gate until his last breath.

Near him, helm still on, was Willow. Dead.

Fighting down gore in his throat Jace turned. They were still in battle. He had to attain the top of the gate. It was with great satisfaction--that for Garrison--he skewered two more duns.

At the entrance to the valley Garrison's tree barricade smoldered. The Scarlur must have set fire to it. A hot wind blew against him. Jace's mouth was dry, as he smelled and tasted ashes. They had won–at a terrible cost. Garrison had been at the Gate. Undermanned. Overwhelmed. But he had managed to get the word out to warn Jace, while he slowed the Scarlur with the sacrifice of his own life.

Garrison gone. Willow. The others in this battle. And all the others that Jace had lead to their deaths in battle after battle? Why did not their spirits all rise and kill him?

Deadrick stomped up beside him. "The rest down at the caravanserai are escaping."

Jace looked down. In the distance, they could see dust from running hooves. The duns would have thrown all of their fighters into this battle. Probably females escaping with the foals.

"Pursue?" Deadrick asked.

"Nay." That came from behind. It was Star joining them. "They are females with younglings. Let them go."

They might rejoin other tribes of their kind, become slaves, or they might suffer a long death in the desert. Mayhaps hunting them down might be mercy.

"Please Jace. I am your patron. I ask it..."

The battle had been too long. Jace had lost his taste for blood, he nodded to Deadrick. "We will not pursue." That was probably a bad idea. Although Jace never had any liking of slaughtering the enemies' females and young, he well knew those duns might grow up to challenge the Silvers again.

Still, his troop was wounded and disorganized. They had marched for Lady Star and had freed the Silvers' mines. Now it was time they must rest, apportion. Regroup. Then what? Jace believed they had wiped out the main Scarlur forces–he devotedly prayed they had. Where was their next mission? He was too tired to think. First, they must bind their wounds, sort out their weapons and get rid of these stinking bodies.

In the center of the valley, water still up to his fetlocks, he found one of the recruits. Jerrick, dead. They started this march with four new recruits. Now only Skull was still fighting. Actually, one out of four survival was a good showing for green recruits. Jerrick died well, with sword still in hand. Jace ordered Garrison, Willow and his other dead, pulled to higher, dry ground, before the entrance to the mountain. The enemy he would have dragged out the main gate and thrown down the canyon for the vultures.

Willow's foals? They had survived. The younglings guardian would get Willow's officers' share. He would have to find a protector for Willow's foals. Reet? No–she would be too busy when her first was born.

His front hoof slipped on the mud. Water still poured out from the dam. Kear and the Silvers were trying to close off the hole, with thick boards. Below Jace, a dead, open-mouthed Scarlur had an especially fine sword. Jace had to hack it from the hand that locked on to it even in death. Fine work. Probably by the Silvers–that water wavy metal. Jace added it the growing loot pile. He would order a careful checking of the Scarlur bodies for plunder before they were hauled out of the valley. And the distribution of booty must begin soon–before his worthies decided all the Silvers' treasure belonged to the victors.

Jace headed down the center of the valley. Here the blood-reddened water still rose above his knee. Bloated bodies already floated. The dead were stinking. He heard splashing. Looked up and saw Sandi, in water up to her under-stomach. He saw her reach down, grab a Scarlur's tail. With a savage swing of her short sword, he heard a loud "snap!" as she chopped it off at the bone. First, she held the tail alooft as if for Lord Thunder to see, she then stuffed it into a sack slung over her withers.

With difficulty, she waded to the next body, going for the tail. Jace felt he had to say something, "There are better pickings then bloody tails."

She looked up to see him, colored slightly, but spoke defiantly, "For Kent. I nail their stinking tails to a shrine for him!"

That was a statement, not a request for permission. He generally preferred not to hack up the enemy's bodies, but Jace nodded in assent. A mare's love was a trail that never ended. Anything that would make Sandi's loss easier to bear, he would allow.

A shadow passed briefly over the water near them. Jace and Sandi looked up. High above wide wings of dark feathers silhouetted against the sky, in long, lazy circles. "Dung!" Jace said through gritted teeth, "How do those buzzards find a battle?"

"They smell blood. They were probably following the Scarlurs."

Jace's hide rose in the revulsion he felt for those cursed birds. "Get your tails fast! I want these bodies dragged out of here!"

"Garrison? Willow?" She protested.

"Nay!" Not Garrison–not to the dammed vultures. "Our dead we are gathering on dry ground. Over there by the entrance gate where he fell. We will build a funeral pyre."

"The wood is wet..."

Jace looked about the sodden valley. "Tear down those sheds over the cooking platforms. Get some of the lamp oil from Silvers. We have the funeral pyre this dark."

Sandi nodded with head and tail.

That gloaming they laid wood over Garrison and others. Willow had been laid in his arms. One of her young foals tried to climb on to the woodpile with her. Sandi gently pulled the little she off. Brandy took Willow colt's hand and pulled him away. "Sweet one, mommy sleeps. You must come with us now."

With the dam finally barricaded off, water drained to large pools in the valley. Most of the enemy had been tied with ropes and dragged off. After the sun sank, Jace brought forward the torches to light the funeral pyres. Star insisted they say words to her Goddess. Then Jace put the torches to the wood. Wetted wood that would not light.

Star and her sisters brought forth jars of lamp oils, and cooking oils that they splashed high on to the briars–it dripped down through the wood and branches and darkened the bodies. Jace's torches finally caught, and the fires began.

Much later Sandi came back to watch the flames. She had Willow's gangly daughter asleep in her arms. Painfully Jace looked to the child. In older times foals without a mare would have been mercifully put to death. He had to find someone to take them. "Perhaps one of Star's kin will take her?" He spoke out loud, not realizing it.

Sandi looked up fiercely. "I will take them! Lotus and Kell. They are mine."

"Three to follow your tail? I thought you declared yourself done with younglings?"

She ignored him. "I will have my officer' share and a half share for Kent!"

"Full share for Kent, he died fighting for the Regiment as a warrior." Jace pronounced.

Sandi looked up at him defiantly. "And I claim Willow's share for her foals."

Jace nodded. "Who is their sire?"

Sandi looked sadly into the fire. "Willow never said."

"It must have been Garrison."

Sandi shook her head sadly. "Nay. Some mounted her, but not Garrison."

"I say differently. The filly has brown eyes like Garrison. The young colt holds his tail off to the side, the way Garrison did. Willow's foals shall have the double officers' shares for Willow and Garrison."

Sandi bowed her head to cover her smile. "Sir, your decisions are ever honored."

The smokey fires burned long into the night. Bright flames slowly consuming the centaur who had been trainer, comrade, brother and at times almost sire to Jace. As the stars peeked beyond the smoke, the others walked slowly away. Only a few stayed. Jace. Star. Abel.

Flame light reflected off Star's face, as she stood alongside Jace. She wisely stayed silent.

Finally as red, popping embers turned to white ashes, it was Per Ben who walked sedately up to Jace. "Garrison died in his battle harness–died fighting. Died victorious. He would have wanted nothing less."

Too tight-throated to speak, Jace just nodded.

Per Ben continued, "Reet went into labor during the battle."

Alarmed, Star turned, "She is too early. The foal?"

"Alive."

"The foal suckles?"

"Aye. Spindly legs too weak to stand. But lifting its head. Sucking strong."

Star relaxed. "That is a good sign."

"All ribs and hoof, but drinking from Reet's breasts. Aye." He radiated pride. "Soon it will be standing to her lower teats in no time." If it were possible, Per Ben seemed to swell with more pride. "A fine colt."

Jace found himself smiling gently. "Garrison said that

the shes always give birth in battle."

Per Ben nodded. "Garrison was a wise one." Sadness could not ebb Per Ben's joy at his first foal. Per Ben's tail rose taller. "We think of calling him Jace, to honor a great fighter."

A great fighter, who leads all his comrades to their deaths? "Nay." Jace turned his head to watch the flames dying. "Call him Garrison. To honor a greater fighter."

Per Ben nodded. "Garrison." He too looked to the flames. "A harness to live up to! Aye, Garrison, it will be."

Star's slender fingers gently touched Jace's withers. He looked to her on the other side. "Do you wish me with you this night?" she asked.

He shook his head.

"Then I go to Reet." She started off, then stopped, looking back at him as if she wanted to talk further. Jace just turned his face to the collapsing white charred logs. There were decisions to be made—but not this dark.

Chapter Twenty four

One last battle,

Last for one at least...

Red Tail of Thunderhoof Regiment

The sun rose over a muddy valley and dying pyres. Three of his teams were still dragging Scarlur bodies and hacked off body parts out from the bloody muck. Jace loped the valley. "Deadrick!"

Deadrick had been earnestly talking with a tight lipped Arnfinn. He looked up resentfully, but they both moved to Jace. "Deadrick,..." He nearly said 'have Garrison assign...' Jace stopped. The smell of burnt flesh still pervaded the valley. The others knew what he was about to say. They waited. He could assign Deadrick the task of picking his own scouting party, but that would appear to put the mantel of Second on his shoulders. Instead, Jace looked about, "Arnfinn, you, Skull, and Ghost will scout, with Deadrick leading, down to the caravanserai and beyond."

Deadrick looked to Arnfinn. Arnfinn turned to face Jace, "Who replaces Garrison?"

Who would? Deadrick who wanted to be First? Two Spot who knew not the direction they marched? Arnfinn? Axel, so green? Ardon? "We prepare for apportioning. As soon as the bounty is fairly divided, I will call a drum to decide."

"The Scarlur loot pile is not chosen."

Another thing Garrison would have assigned by now. "Aye. We will...do the loot lines this sun. Arnfinn tell Axel to organize it. We will wait until you return from scouting."

With a nod of his tail, Arnfinn was loping off.

Deadrick stared at Jace. "You have not chosen your Second?"

"You will scout the plateaus below. See if you think we will still face a Scarlur force."

"And this sun we apportion the Silvers' treasure?"

"Our share of it. If Ardon can measure it all out–this sun or mayhaps the next."

"The Regiment should just idle their hooves, while their leader pursues his high tailed lady? She has recovered her mines–is she still eagerly prancing after you?"

"I suggest you get your battle harness on before you lead the scouting."

"But there will be a drum to chose the Second this sun?"

"This sun or the next..."

"This sun. Mayhaps the warriors will also choose a new leader!" said Deadrick.

Jace just turned on his hindquarters. "Kear!" He trotted to him. "You have been talking with the Silvers?"

"Aye." Kear was drinking a horn of porridge.

"Can any of them still mine?"

"Mayhaps Frost and Storm. The rest of the males are too young."

"See if you can get them to drill some kind of anchors for a defendable gate at the valley entrance."

"Will we have time to do this? When do we march?"

"Must everyone question everything?" Jace regretted the cutting edge in his voice. "Just do it! Get Garr–assign anybody you need to help you!"

"Aye, sir. At least this time we will have better tools to drill with."

The Scarlur loot lines would busy his warriors for a time, but they must apportion immediately. Jace looked for

Ardon. He saw Star working in the cooking area. He loped to her and pulled her off to where they could talk privately.

"My Lady, you have promised the Regiment two silvers, per warrior, for every sun on the trail. With a substantial bounty, if my warriors succeeded. We have done your bidding, it is time we have our hire."

She only focused on one thing. "Are you leaving?"

"The Regiment must march."

"They could go–you could stay. With Silver Beard and my uncles gone, we need a strong male."

"I am not a miner."

"But you could lead. Trade for us. Protect us."

"First we must work on settling a fair apportioning."

"Where will the Regiment march to?"

Where? That was a problem. "The caravaners may need us. Tar-bel mentioned unrest to the Black. We may go back to the Headlands bazaar. Rest for a time. Recruit. Train."

"We need you here."

"My Lady, first the payment due us must be gathered! If you and yours do it, you lose less of what you value."

"The Goddess cups must be returned to our honored dead!"

"Aye. Crescent can do that. I will have Per Ben and Brandy help her put them back. But sun silver and bonus must be gathered! You must lead Ardon to pick out what is to be ours."

"You leave us unprotected?"

"The Regiment can not stay here forever. But ones like Kear might choose to dig with you..."

"Only our blood digs in our mountain!"

"Times change, customs must change. Your uncles are dead. Your kin needs strong backs to mine. You need grown males for protection."

"The Scarlurs will not come back. They are dead."

"Riches and weakness always draws predators."

She sadly nodded her tail. "Silver Beard said this." She looked at him, pleading, "Why can you not stay?"

He looked down her tight, confining valley, with those dark, gaping mine tunnels. Jace shifted his weight to his back legs, faintly feeling old battle wounds. Star was beautiful, but he did not want to live in a tomb. "There is much to be settled before we take on new missions." Jace looked about. "Ardon!" Called over from the loot line, Ardon limped slightly. Jace quickly noted bandaging on his arm and sinister hind leg. There had been no report on the dead and the wounded. Garrison would have handled that. "Axel!" Jace yelled over to him as Axel gathered Scarlur weapons from the mud. "Get a count of our dead and wounded. Also get a count of those fit to march and their weapons!"

Ardon reached him. "Sir?"

"How serious are your wounds?"

Star answered, "His hoof frog is badly bruised, mayhaps a moon for the swelling to fully go down." She placed her hand flat out on Ardon's chest. "No burning heat within the skin. No bleeding on the arm bandages. He does well."

Ardon nodded his tail in assent but continued with concern. "Orson's hand is badly sword slashed."

Jace looked at Star, she lowered her tail. "He will probably lose it. We try herbs, but there is too much damage...Aunt Crystal feels we must cut it off, to save him..."

"Swordarm or sinister?" Jace asked.

Star looked confused. It was Ardon who answered. "Sinister. He will still be able to wield his sword."

"But he says he will die before he allows us to take it," Star said.

"When the time comes, we will deal with it," said Jace firmly.

Injuries and weapon loss would mean more rest time needed for all of them. How long the Regiment needed to recover before the next march was another decision that he used to leave to Garrison. Jace would have Axel give him an estimation; he must learn to do this. "Ardon. Lady Star wishes her Goddess cups returned. Find out what is a sacred, then collect marching coin and a fair bonus portions from the rest. Go with the Lady Star and consult her kin on what they will give us. A sun count and a fitting bonus. Put the treasure in warrior piles in the Dragon's Lair. Let me know whether we can apportion this sun or the next."

Ardon nodded. "Aye, sir."

Star still pushed Jace. "Then you will leave?"

"This must be decided at the drum."

Obviously unsatisfied, she hurried off with Ardon.

Jace too started off. He could not answer what he did not know himself. Jace must give more thought to what he would propose at the drum. He had strategies for some of the warriors. He needed plans for all. Although some would just go their own way back to their ranges or to adventure, Deadrick wanted to lead the Regiment. What if Jace just let him and he stayed behind here? Some might follow Deadrick. Mayhaps all would.

But Deadrick would council looting the Silvers and the bazaars and taking everything of value, until the Regiment became a big hoofed Scarlur. The yellow hided fools' leadership would be disastrous. The others had been his comrades for too long for Jace to allow that. He had to counter Deadrick's plans with strategy of his own.

Jace's stomach was rumbling too. He saw one of the young Silver males walking to the line for porridge. Storm or

Frost? All of Silver Star's kin had almost identical markings. He had enough of questions he could not answer. Those could wait! There were things he could learn more of, say Silver Beard's cubes or the forging of wavy metal. "Frost?"

"Stormy." The young male corrected with a smile.

Soon they were both in Silver Beard's Chartroom, swallowing drinking horns of porridge, while Stormy eagerly showed off Silver Beard's cubes. "You are right, sir. The measuring stick is the size of a hoof. The small gold hoofprint here is the scale of the cubes."

"Was the tunnel we broke into deliberately cut for that purpose?"

"Aye. The Scarlur were stepping into our valley. They claimed our gold. They stole from the burial caves. If we were fully attacked, Silver Beard thought to get the shes and the younglings safe in the tunnels. Then he and the uncles would smash the dam, flooding the valley. He said if they were all drowned, no more would come."

"What went wrong?"

Stormy shrugged his shoulders. "Silver Beard was killed. Grandmare wanted to appease the Scarlur. The uncles fought her. Then Star ran with gold for fighters."

"Causing the Scarlur to attack–which they were going to do shortly anyways."

Stormy looked solemnly about the chamber. "Now I do not know what we will do."

"Your kin will start mining and forging again." Jace walked about. "You will start the cubes and measure that new cut in the tunnel and put it in the cube, as Silver Beard would have done."

"He never finished teaching me."

"You and I can work his system out."

Silver Storm sounded totally overwhelmed. "Frost can

forge, Aunt Crystal fashioned most of the jewelry, but with the uncles gone, Frost and I can not manage it all..."

"Mayhaps if you had some of my warriors, like Kear, Black Ears, or Snake to help dig and protect you at least until the younger Silvers come of age?"

Storm looked less afraid. "Then I can start the marking slates again."

Looking about Jace asked, "What is the secret of forging the water-wavy swords?"

"Jace!" an echoing call from the tunnel outside the Chart Chamber.

"In here."

A scramble of hoofs. It was Ross, Sandi's near grown colt. "There is trouble in the Dragon's Lair. Many are unhappy with the apportioning. Deadrick leads them."

Lately, Ross had been close following Deadrick's tail, why was he helping Jace? Warily, Jace followed Ross out into the tunnels.

Sounds of muffled arguing voices and hoof-falls as they reached the opening for the Dragon's Lair. Ahead, smell of what? Star. Fear. Jace stepped into the large grotto, as quietly as his four large hooves allowed. Torches were mounted in holes drilled into the walls about the entire cave. Now light flickered over the huge cavern, as Jace entered to see a strange tableau before of him.

On the sand, woven baskets overflowed with jeweled treasures of helmets, goblets, crowns, and swords. Ardon with his measuring scales and marking parchments stood beside the mounds. He had not yet broken them into piles for the warriors to choose. So why had Ross said there was trouble with the apportioning? Around the chamber stood most of his warriors. Per Ben. Two Spot. Skull. Black Ears. Wheat. Able. Titus, almost the entire Regiment. Standing and waiting. In the center of the cavern were Deadrick, Star and her brother, Silver Frost.

Deadrick faced away from Jace. He was hefting the ornamental sword that had been ceremonially scabbarded into one the niches set in the six directional points along the cavern walls. He loudly proclaimed to all. "A fine piece. It shall be part of my portion!"

Silver Frost glared in helpless anger–but the young he was wise enough to know he was no match for Deadrick.

Star refused to be helpless. She planted her four hoofs widely apart, solidly confronting the yellowed hided Deadrick. "That is not to be given!"

Deadrick just smiled wickedly at her, as he started to slide the sword into his battle harness. "You will stop me?"

She was too angry to think. Her brother reached out to put a restraining hand on her croup, but Star just slid away. Her tail raising ever higher, she angrily pranced to Deadrick.

Jace trod heavily, his hoofs deadened on the white sand. He called out for the benefit of the rest. "Lady Star is our patroness! She has said that sword is not to be apportioned!"

To the side, Ross eagerly stared at Jace, a nasty smile on his face. He was willing his hero, Deadrick, success no doubt. Deadrick turned. No surprise in his icy blue eyes. He was expecting Jace. He wanted this confrontation. Deadrick cared not for the sword. He cared not even for Star. He only wanted the leader's position, that they both knew he could only have if Jace were dead.

Silver Storm joined Jace. "Let him have the sword. Let them have all of it!"

"And your sister Star, can I have her too?" That slow, triumphant smile was spreading over Deadrick's face–he had won. He knew Jace would fight him. Just as Deadrick knew he would win.

Warriors and Star's kin moved closer to the walls to give them room. Jace quietly turned to Silver Frost. "Take your sister from here–out of harm's way."

Frost obeyed. If only all the Silver centaurs would!

Star, of course, did not. She resisted her brother's pull on her arm. She tried to step between Deadrick and Jace. "He can have the sword. Do not fight him!"

But with her brother firmly pulling at her, Star was being forced to move away, she reached out to touch Jace. He stepped forward, gently touching her soft skin. "Later, my lady."

Deadrick had sheathed the Silvers' deadly sword and pulled out his own long sword. He now played with it at but an arm's thrust from putting it through Star. He seemed to be considering it.

Staring straight at Deadrick, Jace pushed Star's hand from his arm. "You have your fight."

Stricken, Star looked to Jace. "Nay..."

Her brother pulled harder at her arm. "You hamper him!" Defeated, she lowered her tail and gave ground. Deadrick had already forgotten she existed. In his excitement, he bucked and pranced across the white sand before Jace. His bright yellow hide and white hair stood out in the flickering torchlight. Jace knew he had the advantage with his darker hide and tanned skin, if he could keep the duel to the shadowed edges.

Deadrick loped eagerly past Two Spot. Two Spot should have thrown him the fancy shield he had looted from the Scarlur. He did not. Two Spot might grumble, but he preferred Jace's leadership. Still, Two Spot--like the others-- must accept leadership from the winner of this battle or challenge themselves. Snake handed Deadrick a shield.

"I challenge for leadership!" Deadrick half reared. His close comrades reared with him.

Abel trotted to Jace, carrying a silver and onyx trimmed circlet shield of metal. He slipped it on to Jace's arm. Star's brother Silver Storm loped back to them. He carried a long, water-wavy blade that he slipped into Jace's sinister hand. "Not as wide or fancy as his. But it will strike harder. Sharper. It will bend, but never break."

Tightening the shield strap on Jace's arm, Abel muttered, "He is younger, faster, maybe stronger."

Jace smiled tightly. "It is so good to have comrades."

But Abel continued. "You have fought many battles, learned many tricks. As Garrison would have said, treachery will overcome inexperience and foolishness confidence in any contest!"

Jace gave a quick smile, as Silver Frost and Abel moved aside. An anxious Axel had entered, and he was moving alongside the wall to where the Silvers stood. Jace looked directly at Axel. Axel returned a steady stare and nodded slightly, as he moved towards Star. He could not stop this, but if Jace died, he would try to protect Star.

Jace moved slowly to the center of the cavern. He expected they would do the formal bows of two honorable warriors about to do ritual battle.

His opponent was too excited. Deadrick closed and struck. Jace parried with the unfamiliar shield and felt his opponent's blade glance off his harness. Bad start.

Jace pulled back–twisting his body on hind legs and half rearing.

Deadrick was wise enough not to follow.

Jace lowered his forefeet. They both circled each other. Looking for an opening, a weakness that was not there.

Move in. Both reared as if performing an elegant

dance that would leave one dead, not just crippled. If Deadrick was to have his leadership of the Regiment, he must fight to Jace's death.

A double clash of swords. Deadrick's strength was unbelievable. His speed. All the tricks Jace had relentlessly drilled into Deadrick were now turned against the master.

They leaped apart in different directions, then returned to circling. Nay sounds other than their heavy breathing, and their hollow hoof falls on the sand. From the outer ring came a taunt, "Get to it!"

Probably Snake, but neither fighter spared a look. Again the combatant's movements mirrored. Their circles grew smaller. Tighter. Swords sparked brightly against shields in the dim torchlight. Jace's sword sliced his wither. Just a slight flesh wound, but it dripped a wine-dark rivulet down his yellow coat. Deadrick seemed not to notice.

He was loping faster. Trying to up the speed. Wear down, Jace.

Jace zig-zagged, cutting across the center. Changing the pattern.

In surprise, Deadrick swung wide. Both reared. Sounds of their swords on shields echoed in the cavern. Each endlessly testing the other. Jace was holding his own, as he parried a thrust, but he realized he could not win a long battle. The endless circling, then closing was tiring him. Rearing brought slight pain into Jace's back leg. With the leg injury, he had not been drilling and running properly. Deadrick had been training continuously on this quest. Far more than usual. He had planned this confrontation for a long time.

Deadrick suddenly closed and swung. His blade grazed Jace's arm above the elbow.

Jace had never faced such a deadly opponent. One who seemed to mirror all his own tricks. Tricks Jace had so carefully taught him. Jace's hindquarter weakness left his best attacks just a bit off. He was tiring. Slowing. Goaded by success Deadrick was not.

But Jace had never before fought for something that meant so much to him. He dared not look at Star, but he knew she was there. He was fighting for her, and that renewed his strength. Deadrick whipped his body ahead of Jace and almost around. A flashy maneuver for show, not kill. A stupid move. Garrison had warned him of that a hundred times!

Deadrick tore back in and planted four legs down, his sword lashing out, cutting through Jace's thick tail, just below the bone. Jace was caught off guard. Still moving, when he should not have been. A mistake. Not fatal, but it showed he was tiring. Thinking woodenly. He whipped his body back, presenting only forelegs to his enemy. An echo of pain in that back leg. He had landed too hard on his back hoof, a slight stumble...

Weakening. Deadrick saw it. Eyes widened in joy. Lips curled cruelly. Deadrick was coming in for the kill.

Jace shifted his weight to flee. His eyes widened in fear. Confident, Deadrick half reared, blocked with his shield and thrusting with his sword. Meeting Jace's sword—that slender, magical sword of the Silvers' forging bent, bent more--it must break—nay! It snapped back! Deadrick's sword was slashing air, throwing him off, as Jace pulled his sword slightly back, then thrust forward, tearing deeply into Deadrick's upper stomach. Lower ribs resisted Jace's blade; he twisted it; then slid it deeper, breaking it out of Deadrick's trunk. Their sweaty faces were almost touching.

Deadrick's eyes widened in shock. No pain. Surprise. Then face of a struck child—why? Deadrick sank to his foreknees. With supreme effort Jace pulled his sword free of the stricken centaur. Rearing, he swung the sword high, slashing it down with a killing blow through the neck that nearly beheaded Deadrick. A merciful, fast death for a worthy opponent.

There was gurgling, thrashing. Then silence. Yellow hide mounded on the cavern floor.

Jace could barely stand, his strength seemed to be rapidly draining from his body to the bloody sand. His weakened knees barely held his own weight. Yet warrior code demanded he must challenge. He raised himself his full height and looked in each warriors' eyes in turn. "The portion the Lady has allotted us is fair. This I, Jace of Thunderhoof Regiment, have accepted. Is there another who dares questions this?"

Jace looked from warrior's face to warrior's face. Two Spot looked at the fallen Deadrick as a brother bereft, but he made no move to step into the ring of challenge. Ross looked like he wanted to challenge, but did not dare. The others either met Jace's eyes directly in acceptance or looked down in submission. No one else stepped a foreleg into the death ring. Jace dropped his shield to the sand.

Abel had bolted to Jace's side and was wrapping a stiff cloth around his bleeding arm.

Only now could Jace spare a look for his beloved.

Star stood still with her head proudly raised in queenly defiance. Only the tears glistening in the torch lights betrayed her. Finally, she moved in a stately fashion to his side reaching up to touch his blood-stained wrappings. "This must be properly dressed. Come to the bathing pool. Crescent, bring me the herb sack." Storm handed her a lantern as they passed him.

On weakening knees, Jace slowly followed her. He limped a little, but that was acceptable after such vicious combat. They left the Dragon's Lair into the blessed darkness of the tunnels. Out of sight of the others, she stopped, wrapping her arms around his chest. Painfully pressing his wounded arm, but kissing him, wetting his chest with her tears.

He passionately kissed the top of her soft-haired head and hoped she did not feel his tears. He well knew of what would have awaited her if Deadrick had triumphed.

Holding each other, they stepped down the tunnel. Hoofbeats. Jace straightened and tightened his hand on the sword he still held. But it was only Crescent handing a sack to Star, who had moved to his flanks as if to protect Jace. Crescent smiled and bounded away. They spoke not at all until they reached the carved stone door of the baths. Star reached up and turned to the wooden moon sculpture to a face that Jace had not seen before: a wise moon, with eyes closed. In sleep?

Star proceeded Jace inside. As ever he enjoyed watching her taut, glossy, white dabbled hindquarters. She lit two more lamps on the walls, while he set the Silver's sword down on the sand and waded deeply into the warming pool, glad to have his weight buoyed by the water.

"Do you want it warmer?"

"Nay. It is good."

Star busied herself mixing some sort of herb potion, with the pouches from the sack Crescent had given her. "Come out. I must work on your wound."

Jace looked down. The rough wrappings on his arm were black stained with blood.

She stood, silhouetted against the soft lamplight. It gave her long wavy hair a halo and highlighted her cascading tail. Those long slender legs stood out so strongly.

"Jace, come out."

He felt coltish. "Nay. You come in."

"First I wish to clean that hole in your arm."

He chuckled. "First I wish to fill a cavity of yours."

She must have blushed. He could see that betraying tail raise in expectation. "Jace..."

"Come in, my honey..."

"You are hurt."

"I feel especially fine."

She hesitated, then said, "My lord, I do so wish to join you. I will, if only you come on shore and let me fix your arm...the sooner you come, the sooner we go back in the water together."

He decided the anticipation would be the best. Jace climbed up to her. Rivets of water ran off his underbelly and Jace swung what was left of his tail, shaking off beading water droplets.

He stood beside her, letting her study his wounds. He saw pride and love in her eyes. Then, as she tried to unwrap his arm, he reached around her and hugged. He kissed her neck. She sighed, raised her head and kissed his lips.

Then said, "Your arm, sir, please."

He allowed her to unwrap it. It was a long, but shallow wound. Jace studied it in a detached manner until she poured some evil smelling, burning potion it. "Oww." It burnt like fire, but he stood still.

"You chose to fight, sir."

"I chose? Who challenged him over a sword? A sword?! When your kin have enough weapons to outfit the Yellow Hided Empire?"

She started to protest, "It was the sword of Silver Black Star..." then Star lowered her eyes in shame. "It was not worth your life."

Even with the pain in his arm, her quick touches excited him. He pressed his lips to the soft hair on top of her head. "Nay. He was looking for an excuse to fight. He would have found another."

"That will clean your cut. This sticky herb will close it and I must tie it tightly. It should heal well."

"It will. Just another scar."

Star looked regretfully at the water. "If we go back into the pool, you will wet the wrappings, and then I will have to rewrap it."

He swept her hair aside and kissed the back of her neck in answer.

She did not retreat, but she kept talking. Most annoying. "Stay here with me. I can guide my brother and Aunt Crystal. You can arrange for fortifications to be built. Then later you can make the buying trips and sell our armor?"

It was a tempting offer, but, "The closeness of these walls." Jace slowly shook his head.

"But you enjoy these baths–perhaps if you gave it time?" Her she aroma filled the air. Star smiled, then continued. "You are just beginning to unravel the secrets of the charting cubes. My brother, Storm, can help you. Show you our metal forging... "

He ran his big hand down her withers and back. "What if you came with me?"

"With you?"

"As a warrior's lady."

"Trot with the Regiment?" She bends her head, considering it. "My Aunt Crystal is strong but unknowing of the outsider's ways."

"Crescent knows much and could learn more."

Slowly she answered, "Aye. Crescent would even be better to guide to the Silvers. Aunt Crystal does not want to lead. Aye, it should be Crescent. She could do it."

Jace lowered his head and gently nibbled at her

shoulder. Star moaned softly, as she breathed deeply.

Both their scents filled the air. Lamp light reflected off the water's ripples. Star stepped nearer the luminous pool. Jace followed.

She reached out, her slender fingers imprisoned his, as she pulled him to the warming waters. "Silver Crescent can guide my Aunt as well as I could. But if I leave with you, perhaps we do not have to find a war at first. We could join the caravans and see the lands to the Yellow. Silk comes from there and wondrous jade. We could trade for my kin?"

Did Jace hear hoof falls outside the bathing cavern? "My lady–perhaps we should find a more private place?"

"Nay." She kissed his arm. "That moon face carving at the entrance. The one I turned to was the sleeping moon, who closes her eyes to all. When that face of the carving shows, none will disturb us."

Jace lowly chuckled.

Star turned to him. "My lord, I will do whatever you wish–as long as we are together." She shifted, brushing her glossy flanks against his furry lower chest. Then, moving ahead of him, she trod into the water, bracing her legs, and lifting her tail to the side confidently.

A warrior knew there was time to make decisions. And time to act. Now Jace would act.

The End

If you enjoyed this book, please put a comment on your favorite social media, so that I can write more Centaur adventures. Lynn

OTHER BOOKS BY LYNN MARRON
COMING SOON
CHECK www.lynnmarron.com
FOR PUBLICATION DATES

MORE CENTAUR ADVENTURES:
CENTAURESSES OF THE JEWELED SPEAR

GRACE FARRINGTON'S OYSTER RIVER
GENETICS RESEARCH MYSTERIES:
ORR: NOBEL PRIZE MURDER
Turned down for this year's Nobel Prize, forty-two-year-old
genetics pioneer Grace Farrington finds out the new Head
of Research of Oyster River is the man who stole her work!
When Dr. Marshall is murdered on ORR's houseboat,
Grace finds herself, chief suspect. She is further implicated
when following an1800's witch's *Curse of Three*, two more
people die in Oyster River Harbor. While finding herself
romantically involved with a billionaire patron and a red-
necked colleague, Grace must use her scientific reasoning
and her eclectic group of friends (cops, séance buddies,
fishermen and some other slightly eccentric New
Englanders) to solve the murders before she's arrested.
ORR: FATAL DNA
ORR: MURDER GENETICALLY ENGINEERED